Also by Sarah Grazebrook

NOT WAVING

THE CIRCLE DANCE

A CAMEO ROLE

PAGE TWO

FOREIGN PARTS

MOUNTAIN PIQUE

MOUNTAIN PIQUE

Sarah Grazebrook

Hodder & Stoughton

Copyright © 2000 by Sarah Grazebrook

First published in Great Britain in 2000 by Hodder and Stoughton
A division of Hodder Headline

The right of Sarah Grazebrook to be identified as the Author
of the Work has been asserted by her in accordance with the
Copyright, Designs and Patents Act 1988.

10 9 8 7 6 5 4 3 2 1

A CIP catologue record for this title is available
from the British Library.

ISBN 0 340 70806 9

Typeset by Palimpsest Book Production Limited,
Polmont, Stirlingshire

Printed and bound in Great Britain by
Clays Ltd, St Ives, plc

Hodder and Stoughton
A division of Hodder Headline
338 Euston Road
London NW1 3BH

For Crystal Holidays,
from whom Ski Dreams Tours could learn a lot . . .

Chapter One

Like most other people, Janet Gale judged the success of a party on whether or not she had a good time. Her criteria were not excessive. Throughout her life she had gone home happy if she had managed to survive the event without spilling squash on her dress, being snogged by the youth with weeping acne and, latterly, being cornered by the most boring couple in the room and lectured on the importance of checking her guttering for tennis balls.

It had been many years since she had entered a room with a view to meeting Prince Charming. Indeed, it had been something of a relief when she had come across her future husband, not at a party, but in the print room of a large office block where he was in the process of force-feeding a mile of continuous stationery into the photocopying machine.

She had often reflected with amazement on Hugh Gale's subsequent success with computers, given his barbarous treatment of the Xerox that day. She also wondered why she had taken the blame for the ensuing fire in the hope of saving the bewildered young man from the sack.

The sacrifice had been in vain and the two of them had found themselves on the street by half past three, each clasping a small buff envelope containing their Monday and Tuesday's pay. Undeterred, they had headed for the nearest pub and then taken themselves off to an employment bureau where Janet had been offered work as a filing clerk, and Hugh as a communications officer with a brand new company just starting up round the corner.

They had been married now for close on twenty years, throughout which time Hugh had worked for the company, ComMend, specialists in lancing the myriad boils that every computer comes armed with.

Time had seen the firm advance from a three-man show, working from a broom cupboard in Stepney, to a major international corporation, but while the intellectual vision that had brought this about was never in doubt, it had not been transferred to the firm's social calendar.

This particular Christmas, looking around the hotel banqueting suite, complete with buffet, band, and disco next door for the youngsters, Janet found it hard to connect the structured festivities with those early days when the entire staff and their families had piled into the local Indian on Christmas Eve. She had been sick in the back of the taxi going home, and Stephen Braintree, now managing director and bald as a coot, had held her head between her knees and sung 'God Rest You Merry Gentlemen' to cover the sound of her retches.

ComMend's success changed all that. To start with it had been exciting to celebrate the company's growing prosperity in increasingly lavish style, but somewhere, not very far along the way, a formula seemed to have evolved. Enthusiasm had given way to expectation. Caterers were brought in, a PR firm engaged. The number of canapés and chicken legs were apportioned by computer, ditto the alcohol. Thus were parties created. The accountants gave their blessing.

Janet stifled a yawn. Was this the same hotel as last year? She couldn't remember. It certainly looked the same. Same decorations, same wizened balloons, same artificial tree twinkling spasmodically at the whim of its fairy lights, and at the far end, same velvet drapes, the podium set with microphone ready for those ghastly little speeches at which every department congratulated itself on its output, adding, in parenthesis, how impossible it would have been without the valuable work of the other sections – how they all fitted together like cogs in a wheel, followed by sycophantic laughter because Stephen Braintree's partner was called Dennis Wheel. The third founding member had been head-hunted by an American firm some ten years before and was never mentioned.

Even the raffle prizes were the same. First prize: a week in a catered villa on some ski slope in Italy. The travel company, Ski Dreams, had been one of ComMend's first customers and this lavish prize was much sought after by the thrusting young executives and their aerobically sculpted wives.

Janet shuddered at the very thought of it. Cold, snow, exercise. It was anathema to her. She wouldn't even have allowed Hugh to buy tickets were it not for the fact that their best friend, Harriet Barton, head of Human Resources and godmother to their children, organised the whole caboodle. And it was for charity, after all. Janet wasn't sure which.

The most sinister part of the prize, as far as Janet was concerned, was the fact that the villa could accommodate eight people, so unless it was won by practising Catholics, Braintree's wife, Verity, would go on pulling names out of the box until every last place was filled.

This had provoked more divorces than was good for a company but never so many as last year when, according to office legend, a husband and wife and an engaged couple had severed all connection with each other after being confined to the chalet with the family of one Bob McDermot, an accountant for the firm, who had so antagonised his fellow skiers that all those involved had subsequently handed in their notice. Harriet had nearly done the same, persuaded to carry on only on the promise that lightning never struck twice.

Janet looked at her watch. It was nearly half past eleven and things were starting to wind down. The musicians were packing away their instruments, the buffet was looking tatty and the bar staff were ostentatiously rounding up empty glasses. She felt the customary relief that swept over her as the first taxis were announced.

Over for another year. And it had not been a complete disaster as far as she was concerned. In fact, in ComMend party terms it was pretty close to a triumph. She had found herself a job. Not with the company. God forbid. One parent almost permanently absent was more than enough with two teenagers at the peak of pubescent beastliness. But this was the ideal solution.

For many years Janet had supplemented the family income by typing out authors' manuscripts. It had begun in a small way with a friend asking her to do a report for him, and mushroomed into regular work via a small advertisement in the Society of Authors' newsletter.

Over the years it had slowly dawned on her that it was not only the presentation of some of the offerings that was wanting. The contents were equally dire. This had led her to experiment with a few short stories herself, several of which had been accepted for publication.

She had pursued her writing in a haphazard way till the demands of Hugh's job had started to take him away more and more and she had been forced to concentrate her energies on running the home. So tonight it was almost without thinking that she had confided in the large cheerful man chucking whisky down his throat that she had once written an article about an Office Do which had netted her three hundred and fifty pounds from a women's magazine.

'You might be just what I'm looking for,' he had responded, reaching out for more whisky. 'Can't promise you anything like that. Fifty a column, max. Interested?'

It transpired that the large man was Bill Oswald, the editor of the local newspaper, and one of ComMend's main sources of advertising, a fact reflected in his ration of smoked salmon, Janet noted as they queued together at the buffet.

He had apparently been thinking about advertising for a feature writer on an ad hoc basis to supplement his 'Out and About' page from time to time. Janet had striven to sound casual as she inquired what it would entail.

'Just send me half a dozen pieces to have a butcher's at. Thousand words max. No libel. No neighbours' tiffs. Light, jokey. Touch of the *Hello*s if you can manage it. Jolly. People like that. Nothing to do with the council. And no bloody tourist guff. Or Women's Problems,' he had added darkly. 'Know what I mean?'

Janet assured him that she did, wondering at the same time what was left to write about, short of the end of the world which did not lend itself much to jollity.

Nevertheless it was with buoyant step that she rejoined Hugh, deep in discussion with friend Harriet as to whether it would be right for Stephen Braintree's wife to draw the raffle again, there having been murmurings about her recurring knack of winning so many of the prizes.

'What about Bernard?' Janet suggested. Bernard was the long-term partner of Dennis Wheel. Harriet's face twitched slightly. 'I know I should ask him . . .'

Hugh shook his head emphatically. 'That's a ridiculous idea, Jan.'

'Why?' demanded Janet indignantly. 'You wouldn't say that if he was a woman.'

'The situation wouldn't arise, would it?'

'Why don't you do it, Jan?' Harriet suggested suddenly.

'Me?'

'Well, Hugh's the next in command after Stephen and Dennis. I'm sure no one would object. After all, you never win anything, do you?'

'Yes, why not?' agreed Hugh, aware that his reaction to the suggestion of Bernard had been less than p.c.

'Because I'd rather die.'

Harriet sighed. 'Looks like it's Verity again, then. But if she wins this time I'll never sell another ticket. I know I won't.'

The two of them gazed dejectedly at Janet, willing her conscience to get the better of her. She struggled to think of a way out. The very thought of standing on stage with people hanging on her every move was enough to turn her giddy. 'I know,' she burbled in a flash of inspiration. 'Why don't you ask last year's winners to draw the raffle? That would make perfect sense.'

'It would,' said Hugh grimly, 'except they've all left.'

'All of them?'

'All except the reason they left. If you think I'm letting Bob McDermot loose in front of a microphone . . . Come on, Harriet. We'd better go for Verity. The natives are getting restless.'

'What about Bob's wife, then?'

'Cheryl?' Hugh and Harriet exchanged glances.

'I suppose we could . . .' said Harriet, her face registering a dozen reasons why not. Janet, who had hardly ever spoken to the woman, could see no devastating objection to her pulling a few names out of a cardboard box. She knew of Bob McDermot by reputation. Hugh had often spoken of the man's ability to bore for Britain. She could see it would be no joke to be holed up in a chalet with him for a week, but Cheryl McDermot, from the little she knew of her, seemed an innocuous creature. Quiet and amiable, drifting in the shadow of her super-egoed husband, making no waves.

Harriet bit the bullet. 'Yes, why not? Good idea, Jan. I'll go and see to it. God, this thing gets more nightmarish every year. This is the last time I'm organising it. You are my witnesses. Never again.'

'You say that every year,' Hugh grinned.

'How do you know?'

'Because we're always the witnesses.'

6

Harriet laughed and hurried away before the idea went cold on her.

'You're looking very cheerful,' Hugh remarked, grabbing two glasses from a passing tray.

'I may have got myself a job.'

He frowned. 'What sort of job?'

'Oh, don't panic. You won't have to stay home and do the ironing.' Hugh looked awkward. It was a running sore between them, how little he did about the house. 'You see that big man over there?' She indicated.

'Bill Oswald?'

'He's the editor of the *Kent Leader*.'

'I know.'

'I didn't. Anyway, we were chatting and he's asked me to write a few pieces for him for the "Out and About" page. Fifty pounds a shot.'

'That's marvellous. Has he seen some of your stuff, then?'

'Well, no, not exactly. Obviously it's not definite. But he said to send him half a dozen short articles and if he likes them he'll use them. That sounds fairly positive, don't you think?'

'Of course it does. What are you going to write about? The Joys of Jam-making? My Way with Root Vegetables?' Janet thumped him. He laughed then nudged her. 'Harriet's made her arrest.' She turned just in time to see Harriet, followed by a distraught-looking Cheryl McDermot, threading her way towards the podium. Bringing up the rear was Bob McDermot, looking very self-important as he elbowed his way through the crowd.

Seeing Cheryl's expression, Janet immediately regretted her suggestion. She's going to hate it even more than I would, she surmised. At least Hugh wouldn't be huffing and puffing in the background like that.

Slowly they mounted the steps. An expectant hush descended as Cheryl was led blinking towards the centre stage. 'They might have given her a blindfold,' Hugh whispered.

'Don't be so cruel,' Janet giggled, but it was hard not to compare her demeanour with someone about to be parted from their head by rusty guillotine.

Stephen Braintree, looking more than a little relieved that he would not have to endure his wife's penchant for picking her own tickets again, stepped forward. 'Ladies and gentlemen, if I could have your attention for a moment ... We have come to what many of you, I suspect, consider the most exciting part of the evening ...' Rumbling laughter, the odd heckle. 'Yes, we did enjoy the champagne. At least if we win it again this year, no one can say it's fixed.' Awkward laughter. 'This year, in a slight change of format, we have decided to ask the winner of last year's first prize to draw the raffle for us, so may I ask you all to put your hands together and welcome Mrs Cheryl McDermot, wife of Bob McDermot from Accounts. Mrs McDermot, kindly step up to the podium and pick the lucky winners of this year's Grand Draw in aid of ...' Harriet mouthed some unpronounceable acronym to do with drainage and tsetse flies, '... another worthy cause.' Loud applause.

Cheryl McDermot edged forward, prodded from behind by her husband who was whispering to her out of the corner of his mouth. What he said was unheard but her own response, edged with tears, was caught by the microphone and wafted into the further reaches of the hall. 'I AM smiling.' This caused huge amusement and a surge of sympathy for the dumpy little woman in whose quivering fingers lay everyone's hopes of a free holiday.

Braintree beamed encouragingly as he guided her to the box. There were copious prizes, ranging from makeover vouchers, through food hampers to portable CD players. Gradually Cheryl began to relax, sounding more and more like a headmaster's wife on speech day, so that the recipients started to wonder if they should curtsey or merely return to their desks, determined to do better next year.

At last they came to the first prize. A nervous quiet

descended as Cheryl, eyes instinctively closed, forced her hand once more into the box and drew out a folded slip. She handed it to the chairman. Gingerly he opened it out, no doubt praying that it would not be his own name that greeted him.

There was a pause as he stared at it. The audience rustled expectantly. 'He's bloody done it again,' came a rather audible whisper from the front.

Braintree raised his eyes, shook his head slightly, and said in a dazed voice, 'Not me, I'm afraid. But this is a little unusual, certainly.' He turned to Harriet who was standing just behind him and whispered something. Her face registered first disbelief then horror. She glanced quickly across at Cheryl who, relieved of her duties, was staring dreamily towards the bar at the back of the room.

'Why are we waiting?' came the drone from a group from Sales who had had more than their share of the free alcohol on offer.

Braintree held up his hand. 'OK. Sorry about the delay. Simple enough. The fact of the matter is that Mrs McDermot, albeit innocently, has in fact pulled her own husband's name out of the box. Now, obviously, since they were the winners last year, it had not entered our minds that it was in the realms of possibility for such a thing to happen again. Harder than winning the Lottery, I'd've said. Or being struck by lightning.' Harriet flinched. 'What I'm going to suggest, therefore, is that we put that ticket aside and Mrs McDermot continues with the draw until we have our party of eight, as per usual. Naturally, we wouldn't wish to see the McDermot family go home empty-handed so I'm going to arrange for some of the Directors' Special Port and a bottle of vintage champagne to be delivered to their home in time for Christmas, by way of compensation and as a sincere token of our thanks for Mrs McDermot's valiant work here this evening.'

Riotous applause followed this announcement, accompanied by a rousing chorus of 'For she's a jolly good fellow' from the

Sales contingent. Cheryl remained where she was, looking like the victim of a blow to the head as the noise buffeted around her. Harriet gestured that she should pick again, but as she stepped forward to do so she was intercepted by her husband, his face a peculiar mixture of pink and purple. 'Excuse me,' he said in a strangulated voice, 'but am I to understand that we are to be deprived of our prize?' Cheryl blanched and stepped back, her eyes flicking panic-stricken between her husband and the chairman.

Braintree's eyes widened. He gave a choky laugh. 'Naturally, Bob, if you want to hang on to the prize there's nothing we can do to stop you. It's just I would have thought one week stuck up a mountain was enough for anyone. Go with the port, old boy. Believe me, it's damned good stuff.'

There was a silence broken by a few uncomfortable titters. Bob's complexion continued its battle with the blues and reds. 'We bought our tickets in good faith.'

'Yes, but surely—'

'I don't remember your wife refusing those bottles of champagne.'

Harriet's eyes were closed. Braintree was silent for a moment then, with an almost imperceptible twitch, he took hold of the microphone. 'First prize, a week's skiing holiday in a catered chalet in the Dolomites, won by Mr and Mrs Bob McDermot and their two children,' he announced in a voice that would not have disgraced a hanging judge. 'If Mrs McDermot would like to draw another ticket, we shall know who is to be lucky enough to accompany them.'

Janet cupped her hand over her mouth. 'I'd laugh if it's him and Verity,' she whispered.

Hugh chuckled. 'I just hope it's not anyone the firm can't afford to lose,' he whispered back.

Cheryl McDermot drew another ticket. Janet prayed the remaining places would go to the lads from Sales. That would teach Bob McDermot.

Braintree almost snatched it from her. 'I see we have another family of four as joint winners,' he said without a tremor in his voice. 'Step forward, please, Mr and Mrs Hugh Gale, and claim your prize.'

Chapter Two

'We can't possibly go.'

It was half past two in the morning and Janet was still pleading with Hugh to find a way out of the skiing holiday.

'Of course we must go. How can we not?'

'We could say it wasn't fair, two families who could both afford to pay for the holiday winning it.'

'There's no point saying that now. They'll've thrown all the other tickets away. Anyway, it's rubbish. We pay our staff quite enough to go skiing if they want to. It was a raffle. We won it. End of story.'

'But think of the ill feeling it will create. Bad enough the chap who won it last year winning again, without one of the bosses getting the other half. No wonder people think it's a fix. What about poor Harriet? She puts a lot of work into that raffle. Do you want her to be left with half the tickets next year?'

Hugh turned on his side and pulled the pillow over his ears. 'Jan, it's nearly three o'clock. At this moment I don't care if she's left with every single bloody ticket and the entire McDermot family on her doorstep. I just want to get some sleep. We'll talk about it in the morning, OK?'

'Yes, we certainly will, so don't go charging off out somewhere. It's got to be settled.'

'I don't see what your objection is. A free luxury holiday. What's so awful about that?'

'It's a skiing holiday for a start. I can't ski.'

'You could learn.'

'I don't want to learn. I've got this far without tying planks of wood to my feet and throwing myself off a mountain. I'd like to continue that way.'

'It's not like that any more. Skis aren't made of wood.'

'And snow isn't made of freezing water, I suppose.'

'Go to sleep.'

'And what about my job?'

'What job?'

'My newspaper job.'

'For Christ's sake, Jan. It's only a few paltry lines for the local rag. He hasn't even said he'll print them, has he?'

'They may be paltry lines to you. How would you like it if I'd said "it's only a paltry little millennium bug" every time you went jetting off to Tokyo?'

'Go to sleep, Jan.'

'I can't. I'm all wound up.'

'Unwind then. Look, next year we won't buy any raffle tickets. We won't even go to the bloody party, if you don't want to, but just for what remains of tonight, can we please go to sleep?'

Janet said no more and soon Hugh was snoring peacefully beside her. She lay on her back trying to think of ways out of the nightmare that, with every passing minute, was acquiring new and more heinous possibilities. Which would be worse — the cold, the skiing, the McDermots? Why, out of a staff of five hundred people, did she and her family have to win? The important thing was to scotch the whole business before Owen and Belinda got wind of it.

Way back in the early days of their marriage Hugh and Janet

had pledged never to allow the children to play the two of them off against each other. No amount of 'but Daddy says' or 'Mummy lets us' would alter a decision once made regarding meals, television, homework or any of the thousand other daily areas of conflict that family life involved. On the whole it had worked.

Janet, tottering downstairs next morning with a hangover, knew from the first sight of her radiant thirteen-year-old daughter that Hugh had broken the pledge.

'Mummy ... Daddy, Mummy's up,' Belinda yelled into the hall where Hugh was suddenly occupied with tidying his computer manuals. There was a grunt. Belinda bounced around her mother as she struggled to reach the kettle. 'Isn't it brill? Daddy told us. He was going to make us wait for you but you were so long. I said he should wake you up but he wouldn't so in the end he had to tell us. Because first of all he said it was nothing, but he kept smiling and looking all pleased, so Owen asked him if we'd won the Lottery, and he said, no, not quite, so we knew it must be something nice so we kept guessing and he had to say cold or warm, and I said, "We've won a prize?" and he said, "Warm," and Owen said, "A big prize?" and Daddy said, "Very warm." Then I said, "Give us a clue," and he said, "Well, even though you're very warm, it's actually very cold." Then Owen said, "Have we won the skiing holiday?" and Daddy said, "Yes." Isn't it the most marvellous thing that ever happened to anyone?' The phone rang. Belinda shot to answer it and could soon be heard telling the friend on the other end all about the most marvellous thing that had ever happened to anyone.

'That's about the tenth one,' Owen murmured. Nearly seventeen, he considered any outward show of excitement the height of nerdism. Nonetheless it was possible to divine a hint of enthusiasm as he casually inquired how much snowboards cost.

Janet knew when she was beat. There was no way now that this holiday was not going to take place. Though privately planning to cash in her life insurance to pay for a contract on Hugh, she accepted that the rest of her family was in favour of going. She was not.

She would have to rethink things.

Hugh, when he finally appeared, was overly solicitous about her hangover, making fresh coffee and even raking out a jar of honey for her toast. Janet accepted his offerings graciously. She knew his game. By playing Mr Nice Guy and getting the children on his side (was there ever any question?), he was making sure that the explosion, if and when it came, would leave no one in any doubt as to who was the villain of the piece.

She would be labelled 'spoilsport', 'meany', 'the worst mum on earth', merely for hinting that there might be better ways of spending a half-term week in February. And in the end they would go, so what was the point? No, she would have to play this very carefully. Let the three of them go. Why not? But one thing she was determined – she would not.

The situation required some serious thinking. It must be handled with the utmost delicacy or she would be doomed to a week of unmitigated terror and misery when she could be safe at home, writing riveting articles for the *Kent Leader*. She might even do a piece on the joys of having the house to herself after seventeen years of joint occupation. That would be very jolly.

'Are you feeling OK, Jan? Shall I get you a couple of aspirin?' Hugh was bending towards her, coffee pot in hand.

Two can play at this game, she resolved. 'I'm fine, thanks. I think I'll go and have a shower.' She moved to the door. 'Oh, and could you remind me to ring Auntie Kay this afternoon?'

'Of course. Any special reason?'

Janet shook her head enigmatically. 'Just a feeling. She's getting on. I can't help worrying about her, alone in that great cold house at this time of year. Maybe I should pop up there for a few days in the New Year? Just to check on things.'

Hugh raised a perplexed eyebrow. Auntie Kay was more resilient than the average mountain goat and a great deal less hospitable. Still, he had better humour Janet for a few days till she got used to the idea of the skiing holiday. He knew her well enough. By Monday she would have simmered down and by Friday she would be as excited as any of them. He breathed a sigh of relief. Things had gone better than he had dared to hope. He made a mental note to buy his wife a ski jacket for Christmas. Something bright. That would help her mood.

Having laid the foundations of an escape route, Janet sought to buttress it. She spent much of Christmas, when she was not shuddering with revulsion at Hugh's gift of a crimson ski jacket, staring anxiously at the weather forecast for Snowdonia where Auntie Kay lived, and murmuring about cold weather payments. Given the unseasonably mild weather, Hugh began to wonder if she was hoping for a bequest from the indomitable old crone.

She had also dotted the new calendar with urgent appointments, leaving only the week of their holiday clear. At first Hugh took this to be a positive sign, but when he found his wife frowning over a timetable for trains to Wales, his heart began to sink.

Serendipity, however, was on Hugh's side for shortly after New Year a postcard arrived from Auntie Kay in Gibraltar, the first stop of a six-week cruise she had treated herself to, 'to get away from all those whinging relatives of mine'.

Reluctantly Janet laid aside her timetables, but being too realistic and too desperate to pin all her hopes on one mere mortal, she had devised a contingency plan.

Plan B, though less compelling than an ailing aunt, had the advantage of better odds. It centred on Janet's fellow volunteers at the local charity shop. Always short-handed, the loss of any two of them would render her indispensable. She set about effecting this.

Some ten years younger than the rest, she had long since wearied of the catalogue of ailments that seemed to descend like the Furies on anyone over fifty who gave up their mornings to charitable work. Now it was payback time.

Instead of sorting jumpers silently while they discussed which part of them would be next to drop off, she urged them to ignore their doctors' advice on how to keep warm in winter. Would they not be better (she had heard it on the *Jimmy Young Show*), to try swimming twice a week or, failing that, walking for long periods along the seafront? Here was the very garment to protect them from the wind. She had marked it down to a pound.

The women listened to her wonderingly – after all, she was hardly ever ill – and resolved to give it a try.

They dropped like ninepins. Mrs Reid was confined to bed with flu, despite her annual jab. Mrs Harlow couldn't remember when her hip had ached so much. Janet took over the Thursday slot when Miss Gambrill called to say she hadn't stopped coughing all night. For a few days she began to wonder if she had overdone things, and whether Dread of Skiing was legitimate defence for serial manslaughter.

Guiltily she dragged herself down to the shop where there were now more germs breeding than in an Iraqi war zone and offered to sort the new arrivals by way of penance. It was while doing this that she came across a pair of navy salopettes in Belinda's size. She asked if she might buy them.

'Of course you can, dear. We've got a whole sackload come in this morning,' the supervisor informed her. 'See if there's anything in that you like. Daughter going skiing, is she?'

'Yes ...' Janet halted, uncertain whether to come clean in case there was anything that would do for Owen.

'With the school?'

'No. Actually, we're all meant to be going ... We won it at Hugh's firm's Christmas do. A week somewhere in Italy. I wish we hadn't, to tell the truth. We've none of us got the right clothes or anything.'

With wartime zeal the volunteers set to, kitting out the Gale family: lemon salopettes for Janet, some quite presentable black ones which Owen might just squeeze into, gloves, socks and, the crowning triumph, a hand-knitted rainbow woollen pixie hat tipped with two red bobbles. 'No losing you in the snow in that one,' they chortled, making her wonder if perhaps they had seen through her heartless stratagem and were setting about their revenge.

Hugh had expressed the intention of hiring his outfit. He was six foot three and had trouble buying clothes. There had been a sinister few moments when Bob McDermot had rung and offered to kit the entire family out with last year's McDermot cast-offs.

'My lot say they won't be seen dead in them again. Apparently blue's the big thing this year, but that wouldn't bother your bunch, would it? They're all beginners, I take it?'

Hugh confirmed through gritted teeth that they were.

'You done any of this sort of thing?'

'I grew up in Scotland. We skied to school.'

This caused McDermot great amusement. 'Must have put the wind up the old kilt.' Hugh thanked him for his offer but said they were sorted. Janet noted his clenched fist with a certain satisfaction.

This was not the first call they had received from Bob McDermot. Far from it. From the moment he had found out with whom he would be sharing the chalet, he had taken it upon himself to ring almost nightly with fresh instructions – how else to describe them? – on what the Gales would require for a trouble-free holiday. These ranged from basics such as decent tea bags through to Cash's nametapes for the family socks – 'No joke in the morning, I can tell you' – and the decidedly sinister injunction that Janet make a note of her children's blood group – 'Never know with these foreign hospitals.'

Hugh was amazed that she had borne the interference so calmly. He couldn't think of many women who would listen quietly to a stranger lecturing them on how to deal with their own children, for McDermot had now gone beyond mere advice and had even informed her what time he expected Owen and Belinda to be in at night.

True, Janet had gone rather pale as she listened to him, but beyond a savage attack on a farmhouse loaf, there was little to reveal what was going on inside her head.

Owen and Belinda's evenings were spent poring over brochures and maps of the area, highlighting squiggly lines that Owen informed his mother were black, red and blue runs, whatever they might be, and discussing how much pocket money the two of them could reasonably be expected to survive on. Hugh, too, seemed indecently interested in the whole process, even suggesting a family trip to a dry ski slope centre, in preparation for the real event.

Janet got out of that by offering to cover three extra shifts at the charity shop, and promising to brush up on her Italian so that she could act as interpreter should the need arise. Her knowledge of the language was confined to three terms at an evening class. As far as she could remember, she had never got beyond the present tense, most of that confined to naming items of furniture. Hugh, however, was much encouraged since he saw this as the first genuine evidence that she was coming round, and promptly suggested they all visit the local Italian restaurant to 'get them in the mood'.

He returned home the following evening subdued, having made the mistake of mentioning the plan to Bob McDermot who had taken it as an invitation and now planned to bring his whole family along 'to break the ice'.

'Why on earth did you tell him?' grumbled Janet. Pre-ski rendezvous had no part in her plan.

'It was a bit awkward, really. He wanted us to go round and see his snaps from last year. It was the only way I could think of to get out of it.'

'I should have thought you could have come up with something better than inviting them out for a meal.'

'I didn't invite them. They invited themselves. He did,

anyway. I just said, "Sorry, we can't make it that night, we're going out for an Italian meal," and the next I knew they were all coming too.'

'Well, next time say we've all got measles or something.'

'I'm hoping there won't be a next time. I'm never buying another raffle ticket.'

Janet shivered. Why, oh why did there have to be a 'this time'?

Chapter Three

As someone who had studied Classics, Janet should have known that the gods do not like to be mocked. They particularly do not like Fate, in the form of costly raffle prizes, to be toyed with.

With an inevitability as inexorable as the dawn, the volunteers began to get better. Miss Gambrill was the first to recover, helped, no doubt, by the lack of a husband to care for her. Mrs Reid was next, still croaky, but determined to pull her weight. Janet begged her to do no such thing but, truth was, it was a lot warmer in the charity shop than in Mrs Reid's cottage, and she was beginning to tire of a diet of fried eggs and beans which was all her husband could cook.

Two days later Mrs Harlow was back, extolling the virtues of a copper bracelet which had banished all but the meagrest twinge from her hip.

There were still two weeks to go till the holiday. For the first time since the night their ticket had glued itself to Cheryl McDermot's fingers, Janet felt the chill wind of defeat sweeping towards her.

Short of a full-scale outbreak of mad cow disease she could see no way the shop would not manage without her. Blast Auntie Kay! She ransacked her memory for other aged relatives who might require sudden visits at short notice. None were forthcoming. The battle, it seemed, was lost.

Hugh discovered her slumped sightlessly in front of her Italian primer. 'How's it going?'

'All right. I'm on to cutlery.'

'Want me to test you?'

She shook her head. There were only two phrases of which she was perfectly certain. *Che sera, sera,* and *Mea culpa.*

As part of their determination to win their mother over, Belinda and Owen continued to badger her on the importance of a visit, if not several, to the dry slope. Hugh, sensing that they had her on the run, now added his voice to the suggestion. 'After all, darling, you've never been before and you'll be using muscles you didn't know you had. You don't want to stiffen up like a corpse on the first day.'

Janet doubted it would take a whole day. Wretchedly she consulted the *Kent Leader*, still woefully short of pithy articles, and found that on Thursdays the centre held a genteel-sounding affair called Ladies' Morning, where she could obtain two hours' tuition for six pounds, to include hire of boots and skis. Perhaps she could write her first column about it. Better still, perhaps she could break her neck and avoid the holiday that way. *And* dinner with the McDermots, which was scheduled for the following evening, come to that. Warily she consented to go.

'Tell you what,' suggested Hugh, relieved to have made his point, 'why don't you give Cheryl McDermot a ring and see if she wants to join you?'

'Are you mad?' asked Janet, aghast. Pity was one thing. 'Anyway, surely she can ski already if they went last year?'

Hugh made a face. 'According to Bob, she's not all that hot. Actually it was his idea about you going together. He thought it might be a chance to get to know each other.'

'It's a chance I'd rather not take.'

'Oh, come on, Jan. I know Bob's a bit of a pain—'

'Only a bit?'

'But that's no reason to assume his entire family's the same. They're probably very nice.'

'Stuart's not,' came a growl from Owen who knew him from school. 'He doesn't just eat his snot, he rolls in it first.'

'Owen, please.' Janet's gorge rose.

'Shut up, Owen,' snapped his father. 'You're a great help. Harriet says Cheryl McDermot's one of the most obliging people she's ever met.'

'That's because she agreed to draw the raffle,' Janet interjected. 'Not that she'd have had much choice with old Taras Bulba behind her. I wouldn't be surprised if he'd stuck a metal pin in his ticket and magnetised her wedding ring.'

'How do you account for us winning as well, then?'

'I don't know. Perhaps you slept with Harriet.'

'If I'd known how you'd react I'd've slept with her to make sure we didn't.'

'Well, do next time, will you?'

Ladies' Morning did not look to be in the least genteel to Janet as she drove into the dry slope car park. It looked more like a hen party for newly discharged lemmings. The slope was covered with gaudily dressed women, all squawking hysterically as they plummeted down the sisal matting towards a heap of rubber tyres, some swooping skilfully past, the vast majority crashing with varying force in the middle.

They were retrieved from these by a collection of bronzed young men who plainly saw it as part of their job to encourage the women to kill themselves, at least as far as Janet could see, because they immediately clipped themselves on to a kind of uphill Lazy Susan and set off back to the top to do the very same thing again.

Her prevailing instinct was to get straight back in the car and drive home, but how would she explain to her family? And worse than that, suppose Hugh carried out his alternative threat, which was to come with her and give her a few 'basic instructions'? She shuddered, remembering the screaming match that had accompanied her first driving lesson.

No, better to get it over with. By the look of it, the very least she would break would be her arm. That way she could avoid, if not the whole holiday, at least the mountain. She could sit in the chalet by a roaring log fire, catching up on all the books she never found time to read and exchanging the odd word in Italian with the homely soul slaving away over the three-course dinner. It was almost tempting.

She made her way to Reception.

'Have you been before?' inquired the young woman behind the counter.

'No. My daughter has. So's my son,' added Janet, as though this might let her off the first half-dozen bruises.

The receptionist smiled. 'You'll be with Neville.'

Neville turned out to be neither young nor bronzed, but snowy haired, with kind blue eyes and a touching enthusiasm, which was presumably why he had been put in charge of the beginners. If anyone could coax them out of their frozen terror, he would.

'Come along, dear,' he purred. Janet, now squeezed into size eight boots over a pair of Owen's football socks, and feeling much as someone whose feet have been set in quick-drying cement must do, followed him out into the sunlight and behind the rubber tyres to the nursery slope. In her right hand she carried skis, in her left two metal poles, and in her mouth her heart which was pumping fit to choke her.

She started violently as a woman swished by, collapsing on top of the person in front.

'Coming on nicely, Rosemary,' beamed Neville as the woman sought to extricate herself. 'Just remember, you're squeezing a walnut.' Janet glanced at the woman Rosemary had landed on and wondered if it was a reference to her expression.

Two other women were waiting on the nursery slope. She was glad to see that they looked as frightened as she felt, until

Neville confided that they had been coming for six weeks and still had not mastered the snow-plough.

With a sickening heart Janet wondered what else was yet to be revealed about this so-called sport. Surely it was enough that she had to manoeuvre herself around on these six foot slide rules, without having to negotiate the slopes in a snow-plough. She had failed her driving test twice on the hill start. How could she possibly be expected to steer a tractor up a mountain? What was Hugh trying to do to her? She made a mental note to look up her life insurance when she got back. Any hint that he had increased it lately and she was moving out.

She was relieved to learn that the snow-plough in question concerned a method – the only method, it seemed – of preventing a person from plummeting head first off a mountain when travelling at speed. Since she had no plans to travel at any pace she wondered how much use it would be to her, but a couple of forays down the nursery slope, both of which ended with her feet facing back up the hill, convinced her that it was not a manoeuvre to be sneered at.

The two veterans watched with satisfaction as Neville loosed her skis, spun her round, replanted her feet in them and sent her off down the slope again, all the time assuring her that it was the most normal thing in the world to stand on one's own ski and that he knew of at least three champions who had been killed that way. Janet drew what consolation she could from this, since it now seemed perfectly plain that fewer people survived a skiing holiday than had the Spanish flu.

By the end of the first hour she felt she was getting the hang of it, the hang being that she stood at the top of the slope, Neville said 'three' and she slid four or five yards then fell flat on her face. She was beginning to wish she had brought the crimson anorak. At least by now it would have lost some of its gloss.

Just when she was getting up the nerve to suggest it might be time for her to leave, Neville clapped his hands and declared her ready for the lift. It took Janet a moment or two to realise what he was talking about. 'But . . . no . . . surely?' she whimpered as he guided her to the Lazy Susan. 'You don't understand,' she croaked pitifully. 'I don't know how to do it.'

'Of course you don't, treasure. I'm going to show you,' explained Neville patiently. 'It's easy. You'll love it.' With which he turned round, seized an oncoming pole and swung himself nonchalantly on to the saucepan lid at its base. Away he went up the slope. 'Stay there,' drifted back to her as he bounced along, as if she had planned to do anything else.

'Are you going?' came an aggressive voice behind her. Janet turned to see it was Rosemary, the walnut crusher.

'No,' she said. 'Neville said I was to wait.'

'Well, not there, surely?'

'Sorry.' She took a step sideways and stood on someone's ski. There was further muttering, suggesting to her that not everyone found skiing a source of fun.

'Were you watching that, petal?' Neville was back at her side.

'I . . .'

'Right, now I want you to follow me. Remember, sticks in left hand, pole in right, legs each side and we're away. You're only going up to the red so it's nothing to worry about. When you get there, it's sticks, leg, pole, other leg.' He demonstrated. 'See? Easy. Just plant your leg, let go of the pole and swing your other one free. Have a go on the flat first. Sticks, leg, pole, other leg.' Janet waved her legs and arms about. 'Perfect. Just follow me. You can't go wrong.'

Later Janet wondered if anyone had ever used those words and not been proved a liar. She was black and blue, first from being clunked by the pole which she had failed to grab hold of properly. This had resulted in her being dragged halfway up the slope, skis threshing like duellists till, exhausted, she had let go, only to be struck from behind by the next metal seat. She had lost her balance, fallen sideways and slithered back to the bottom, every fibre in her body being scratched, bumped and battered.

Even Neville had conceded that she had perhaps had enough for one day, but only with the proviso that she promise to return the following week when he would 'go over it with her again'.

Janet, who would willingly have signed away her firstborn to get out of the place, assured him that she would as she limped painfully back to Reception to be relieved of her boots and skis.

'Remember,' she heard him encouraging someone as she trudged away, 'you've got a walnut between your knees. Just crush it as hard as you can.'

Skiing For Beginners

For those of us not lucky enough to afford the luxury of a week on the ski slopes, what better way to experience some of the thrill than to visit the dry ski slope?

There you will be greeted by friendly instructors, introduced gently to the delights of downhill skiing, and also have the opportunity to mingle with like-minded people, only too happy to encourage you in your first trembling efforts.

Hello!, eat your heart out.

'You coming to bed, Jan?'

'Yes, in a minute.'

'What are you doing?' Hugh appeared in the doorway.

'Nothing. Just making a few notes for my column.'

'Oh, that.'

Chapter Four

———◆———

The family, though sympathetic to Janet's wounds, tended to brush them off as an inevitable part of the enterprise. Far more serious, in Belinda's eyes at least, was the discovery that her jacket had no clip for a ski pass. This apparently rendered it all but useless. 'How am I going to get on the lift if I haven't got a thing for my pass?' she whinged all through supper. Finally Hugh snapped.

'You can keep the damn thing in your pocket and if I hear one more word about it you're staying behind.'

Belinda opened her mouth, then changed her mind and spent the rest of the meal exuding silent resentment. Owen didn't help by describing in some depth the advantages of his own jacket which had everything from a hand-warmer to a whistle for attracting attention. To avoid another row, Hugh suggested they all look at the map again, but since Janet considered she was now in a position to be tested by the Ordnance Survey on it, she refused politely and took herself off for a convalescent soak in the bath.

As she lay stirring the foam around her stiffened limbs she reviewed the situation. They were ten days away from the holiday from hell and the signs were that she would have to go on it. That, or obtain a quickie divorce, granting Hugh custody, and fleeing the house forever. It was a toss-up which she would prefer.

If only there were someone she could talk to about it. But who? Everyone she had mentioned the holiday to had cooed with delight and envy. Maybe the fault really did lie with her. After all, she had never been skiing. Maybe it wasn't as bad as she supposed. Maybe a week of being jostled, frozen and steam-rollered into the snow was just what her inner being craved. If so, she wished it would communicate some of its enthusiasm to her outer being, which still clung to the conviction that she would be happier in a leper colony.

Bloody Harriet!

In a moment Janet was out of the bath. Why hadn't she thought of it before? She would ring Harriet. Harriet had got her into this mess in the first place. She could damn well listen to her moans, she owed her that much at least. And Janet knew that she would. Not only listen, but rationalise, sympathise and, with any luck, make her laugh.

She had known Harriet almost as long as she had known Hugh. In fact Harriet had been part of the baggage that Hugh had brought with him, the girlfriend of his roommate from university, later the wife and, not much later, the deceived and divorced wife. While the men had drifted apart, Janet and Harriet had remained as close as ever. More like sisters than friends, they had bolstered each other through the various dips and crises in their respective lives. Harriet had supported her through post-natal depression, Janet had lived through the affairs and career moves that had finally seen Harriet installed in Com-Mend as head of Human Resources. She had been there five years now and had made a considerable success of it, raffles aside.

There was no reply. Disappointed, Janet was on her way to bed when the phone rang. She picked it up. It was Harriet. 'Hugh?'

'No. It's me. Janet.'

'Janet, how are you?'

'I'm fine. It's funny you rang. I tried you earlier but there was no reply.'

'I've just come in. I dialled one four seven one. That's why I called. Thought it might be something to do with work.'

'Only in a roundabout way. I just wanted to ask your advice.'

'What about?'

'This bloody holiday. What did you think?'

There was a pause. 'Hugh said you weren't too keen on the idea.'

'That's one way of putting it. Frankly, I'd rather swim with crocodiles. I've spent the whole month trying to think of ways to get out of it.'

'Oh, Jan, don't say that. You make me feel so awful. I never expected you to win. Did you?'

'No. Any more than I expected to be spending a week with the freak who won it last year.'

'He hasn't been on to you, has he? Telephoning and things?'

'He's hardly been off the line. It's a wonder I got through to you at all. He's probably in the process of having us cut off at this very moment.'

Harriet sighed. 'Yes, I'm afraid it was much the same last year. I think that's what finally got to the others. They could probably have survived the week. They just couldn't put up with him ringing them all the time before they went. I think they found him slightly overbearing.'

'Enough to make them quit when they got back, from what I've heard. I'd better tell Hugh to start reading the Situations Vacant.'

There was a sound, half whimper, half laugh, from Harriet. 'I'm never organising another thing for that firm. It's just not worth it. It all comes back on my head every time.'

Janet felt a twinge of guilt. 'Oh well, it's done now. It certainly wasn't your fault. You couldn't have guessed the McDermots would win twice in a row.'

'*And* take the prize.'

'Exactly. No, really I just rang to ask if you had any advice on how to survive the whole thing. I mean, did last year's victims leave any suicide notes or anything? Any clues?'

Harriet giggled. 'No, but my own advice would be take plenty of duty free and some decent paperbacks. You won't see much of them during the day, will you? It's really only the evenings you need to worry about. And there's loads going on in those resorts. They shouldn't be hard to lose. Well, not very … And the wife's quite sweet in a dopey sort of way. I don't know about the kids, but they'll be off out, anyway, won't they, probably?'

'Not if Herr McDermot has his way. He told me he thought Owen and Blin should be in by eleven "if they are to benefit from their tuition". He'll probably have his in bed by eight. Oh, God, Harriet, it's going to be awful. I know it is.'

Hugh put his head round the door. 'What is? As if I didn't know.'

'I'm just moaning to Harriet.'

'Does she want to talk to me?'

'Not as far as I know. Do you want to talk to Hugh, Harriet?'

Harriet said she would have a quick word if he was there. She wanted to check about some time sheets. Janet said goodnight and went upstairs. She felt better for having aired her grievances. If she had to go, and really it was looking pretty obvious that she did, perhaps she should try and think of some positive aspects to the holiday. The food might be nice. She would not have to wash up. Here she stuck. There had to be more than that to a week away. The sun will shine, she told herself. Italian men are very sexy – unfortunately so are the women. She could hardly see herself setting passions on fire, tottering around the resort like an inverted trifle.

I shall have time to myself, she thought. Time to write. Maybe it wasn't such a bad thing after all. Six perfect submissions: informed, entertaining, original and, of course, jolly. Bill

Oswald would be panting to retain her services. Who knew? This time next year she might be travel correspondent for the paper. Meanwhile she had dinner with the McDermots to look forward to.

Fun Eating Out
What better way to spend an evening than to visit a favourite restaurant with new friends?

This is just what my family and I did last Friday when we shared a table with the McDermot family — Bob and Cheryl, and their charming children, Stuart, who is fourteen, and Tricia, just sixteen. Such a delightful age. Oh, and let us not forget Bob's adorable Aunt Morag who, though eighty-one, was more than happy to share in our little celebration.

'Never again.' It was hard to tell which of the Gales said this first as they piled into the taxi, or which of them said it the most often.

Il Piccolino was a family-run establishment and Hugh and Janet, who ate there about once a month, were greeted as long lost friends when they arrived. Owen was declared a foot taller than last time and Belinda reduced to blushing giggles by the owner's declaration that she was prettier than Cameron Diaz. Fortunately all this took place before the McDermot clan arrived, because he would have been hard put to keep the banter going.

They were late, apparently due to Cheryl's having missed a turning on the way and ending up in a cul-de-sac from which she had had trouble extricating them. Stuart showed all the signs of living up to Owen's description of him. He arrived chewing gum, in a grubby black tracksuit, plainly not on speaking terms with his father. Add to this Tricia, sinewy and silent, Cheryl, shaking from her ordeal in the cul-de-sac, and Aunt Morag who, for an 81-year-old, seemed to know a lot about AA road routes, and the scene was set for a night of unremitting ghastliness.

Janet wondered if Aunt Morag was coming with them. It transpired that she was not but would be looking after the McDermots' home while they were away. 'We have such a lot of burglaries in our area,' Cheryl informed them apologetically. Whether leaving an 81-year-old alone in the house to fend them off was entirely sporting was not something that seemed to worry her husband.

Any lingering sympathy for Aunt Morag had been eradicated by the sweet course, by which time she had sent back two spaghetti carbonaras and suggested to the wine waiter that he didn't know how to pour. She had also taken it upon herself to voice an opinion on every subject raised, including what Belinda should or should not have for dessert. 'Give you spots,' she snorted as Belinda scowled into her ice cream.

They were no sooner seated than Bob produced a large-scale map of the Dolomites and proceeded to tell them exactly what to expect in terms of ski instruction, night life and currency exchange.

'Personally I always use Visa,' he sniffed, plonking the map on top of Janet's menu. 'The lira's a very tricky unit if you're not experienced in conversion tables.'

'I thought you just thought of a number and added six noughts,' Janet responded lightly, trying to extricate her glass.

Bob arched one eyebrow quizzically. 'I think you'll find a few problems if you try anything like that. Leave it to the fellows, that's my advice. We're used to it.' Janet narrowly avoided biting the edge off her glass.

The waiter took their orders.

'How are we doing this?' asked Bob cautiously, seeing that Owen had ordered steak and Belinda wanted a starter.

'Whichever,' said Hugh. 'Do you want to go Dutch or shall we each pay for our own?'

'Just family, I think. And you can forget about that,' as Stuart announced he would like steak too. 'You can have the bolognese, like your sister.' Tricia raised her eyes to heaven and helped herself to wine.

Cheryl said she only ever ate bolognese because she knew she liked it and cast a pleading glance at the aunt who immediately ordered fritto misto. 'You can't have that,' her nephew hissed. 'It's fried. It'll give you wind.' He turned to Hugh. 'By the way, the missus here and Auntie don't drink very much, so we'd better do the same for the wine, if that's all right with you?' Hugh said it was, perfectly, and proceeded to see the best part of his bottle of Barolo disappearing down Aunt Morag's throat, while the rest of the McDermots hovered round a carafe of house red.

'Is your husband a good skier?' Cheryl whispered to Janet while they were waiting for their food.

'I really don't know,' Janet admitted. 'He used to go quite a lot when the children were small. He always came back in one piece.'

'Didn't you go with him?'

'Certainly not. I never fancied it, to tell the truth.'

Cheryl looked at her, wide-eyed. 'But you didn't mind him going away without you? You didn't, well ... worry he might ...'

'Might what?'

'Might ... Well, you hear so many things ... Men on their own ...'

Janet held out her glass for more wine. 'It never crossed my mind,' she said.

'Take a look at this.' Seeing a gap on the table, Bob was in with a flurry of leaflets indicating the cheapest petrol stations en route for Gatwick. 'I suggest we set off an hour early. That way we'll qualify for the Early Risers' Breakfast Bonanza at Little Chefs. Looks pretty good value to me.'

Here Janet put her foot down. To her certain knowledge they would have to leave at five as it was. She was blowed if she was going to make it four in order to watch Bob McDermot spooning fried eggs down his face. 'I'm really not interested in food at that time of the morning,' she explained. 'None of us are.'

'Still,' murmured Cheryl shyly, 'you need to line your stomach, don't you? In case you don't get anything else.'

'Don't they have food in Italy then?' piped up Belinda.

'There's no need for cheek,' snapped the aunt. Belinda went very pink and glared at her mother.

Bob continued to peruse his pamphlet. 'I hope you're not going to be a party pooper,' he murmured, emptying the last of the wine into his glass.

The waiter brought coffee.

'Aren't we having those things?' Tricia demanded suddenly.

'What things?' asked Bob.

'You know.' Tricia flapped jingling fingers. 'Those things you set fire to the paper.'

'Ah, you mean *amaretta*.'

'*Tti*,' Janet corrected.

'Hmmm?' said Bob.

'*Tti*,' she repeated. 'The plural of "o" is "i" in Italian. *Amaretto, amaretti*.'

Bob smiled condescendingly. 'Oh, of course, I forgot. Hugh told me you were our Italian expert.'

'I didn't say that exactly,' Hugh butted in.

'I can remember that much,' said Janet, blushing despite herself.

'Let's hope it's not all or I can see I shall have to take over,' smiled Bob.

'Bob's done a lot of business in Italy,' Cheryl whispered, looking as though she wanted the floor to open.

'Is that because of his Italian or in spite of it?' responded Janet. Everyone looked at her. Hugh's faced twitched with embarrassment.

'Janet's had a lousy day, haven't you, darling? And she's still black and blue from yesterday at the dry slope.'

'Oh, did you fall over?' gasped Cheryl, as though it was a new phenomenon.

'Once or twice.'

'Oh, poor you. That can be so nasty. Our dentist's wife broke her finger the very first time she went. It never mended properly. She can hardly bend it now, he says. I wouldn't go near the place. If you're going to fall over you might as well have a soft landing, that's what I think.'

There was another silence while the company digested what was arguably the longest speech of Cheryl McDermot's life.

'I think you must be a little bit tiddly, Chicken,' said her husband at last in a voice coated in saccharin. 'Of course you've been. I booked you in last week for a couple of sessions, didn't I?'

Cheryl's face registered several emotions, the prevailing one being alarm. 'Yes, of course,' she murmured rapidly. 'I meant apart from them.'

'Time to get the bill, I think,' said Hugh.

Chapter Five

'That was Bob,' Hugh muttered tentatively the day before they were due to leave. Janet was standing over their bed which was entirely covered in socks, jumpers, thermal underwear, goggles and more socks. She was trying to remember if she had packed Owen's moon boots at the bottom of the holdall in the hall or if he had said he would put them in his own bag. Either way, they were nowhere to be seen.

'He says he's just seen an ad on Teletext about airport parking. He thinks he can get it cheaper for us.'

She threw up her hands in despair. 'For heaven's sake, Hugh. It's all arranged. Can't he leave anything alone? He's already tried to get me up an hour earlier for his blasted cut-price breakfast. I can't get anything done for the phone ringing to see if I've remembered to pack a mosquito net . . .'

'That's not quite fair, Jan.'

Janet flung down a purple and red ski sock she was trying to find the pair for. 'It is, actually. It's more than fair. It's bloody generous.'

Hugh spread his hands soothingly. 'Bob's all right. You just shouldn't take him too seriously.'

'Perhaps you could say the same to him?'

Hugh's face clouded. 'Look, Jan, I know this isn't the holiday you've been dreaming of all your life. You've made that pretty damn clear from the start. But it's done now. It's too late to back out, and I think the least you could do is stop carping about the McDermots the whole time. I know they're not the most exciting people we've ever come across—'

'I'm beginning to think they might be in your eyes. I can't turn round without you delivering the latest pearls of wisdom from the world's number one ski expert. "Don't forget to put Vaseline in your armpits." "Have you been doing those thigh exercises I told you about?" "Don't be surprised if you can't move at all by the third day." I mean, what is this? A holiday or some sort of training for the SAS?'

Owen appeared in the door. 'Mum, have you packed my moon boots?'

'I don't know,' bellowed Janet. 'As far as I'm concerned you can call Pickford's and ask them to clear the house, then we'll be sure to have everything we need.' She sank down on the bed and buried her head in her hands.

Owen took a step back. 'I was only asking,' he mumbled. Hugh motioned him out of the room. He sat on the bed beside her and put his arm round her.

'You're just a bit het up. I'm going to get us both a drink then I'll give you a hand with this packing. It won't take long if we do it together. Oh, by the way, Harriet phoned.'

'What about?'

'Just to wish us *bon voyage*. Why are you laughing?'

Janet shook her head. 'I really don't know.'

'Well, where are they?' Hugh, starving and stubbly, glared around at the anonymous faces queueing to deposit luggage.

It was half past six in the morning and the journey to the airport had not been helped by the torrential rain which had started about ten minutes into the journey and continued the whole way.

'Why don't we just check in then we can go and get some breakfast?' suggested Janet, stifling a yawn.

'Because they won't know where we are.'

'Well, does it matter? We'll meet up on the plane, surely?' The longer she could put off the inevitable, the better she would like it.

'Yes, but you know Bob. He likes to know where everyone is.'

'Well, then he should damn well be here when he says he will.' She squeezed his arm. 'Sorry. I'm not very good at these early mornings.'

Hugh grinned ruefully. 'Me neither.'

As she had lain in bed in the wee small hours, waiting hollow-eyed for the alarm to go off, Janet had thought about other holidays she had had with Hugh. Had there always been this amount of disagreement? She knew he had loved the villa, hated the camping, enjoyed the *gite*. They were feelings she had shared in the main. They had so much in common. As a couple she knew they were sometimes envied by their friends – she, the homemaker, Hugh the provider. The ideal set-up. But you had to go away to provide, and you had to stay at home to homemake. And these things took their toll.

Sometimes she wondered if the strands that held them together were beginning to unwind, with him away so often, and the children struggling towards independence. Was she really all that essential to any of them any more? Did it matter? Surely she should have enough life left in her to stand as an individual?

Wasn't that just what she had been trying to do? To let them go and her stay behind? And where was she now? Lying in bed waiting for the alarm clock – the knell to summon her to join them.

Perhaps it would have been simpler if she'd been honest with them from the start. Explained she didn't want to come, that they would have a far better time without her and let them sort it out. Too late now.

A Lesson Learnt.

She would write the rest later.

'I suppose we could check in.' Hugh's stomach was getting the better of him. 'I could leave a message to say where we'll be.'

'Yes, all right. If I don't get a cup of coffee soon I'll collapse.'

They loaded their luggage on to the carousel and were making for the nearest café when a cry not unworthy of the Quorn stopped them in their tracks.

'I say, Hugh, Jan, we're over here.' Bob McDermot, trailed by Cheryl and, some way behind, Stuart and Tricia, was waving at them like a survivor from a shipwreck. 'I thought we were going to meet at the check-in desk,' he observed as they drew near.

'At six o'clock,' said Janet crisply. 'It's a quarter to seven now.'

'Masses of time. Did you stop for breakfast, by the way? It's a tremendous bargain. They don't normally do poached eggs but I explained that Cheryl's on a low-fat diet and they were quite decent about it. That's why we're a bit late. Now, what I suggest is, once we've checked in we all nip into the DF and stock up. Spirits cost an arm and a leg out there. We always take our own, don't we, Chicken?'

Cheryl nodded wearily.

Bob was now consulting a list. 'I thought you and Jan might like to get the brandy and whisky and we can pick up a couple of bottles of gin. Pity the kids aren't old enough. Still, that should do us, I think. Enough for a pre-prandial and a nightcap.' He turned to the children. 'You kids can have a look round the shops if you like while us oldies are in the DF.'

'What about breakfast?' objected Owen. 'We haven't had any yet.'

Bob looked at him dismissively. 'You can get all that on board. Heavens, a lad of your size moaning about food. When I was in the TA we used to march for hours without so much as a sip of water. Tell you what, there's a W.H. Smiths over there. Nip in and get me a *Telegraph*, would you?' Owen flung an accusing look at his father and headed off towards Burger King. Belinda, in a rare moment of solidarity, followed suit. 'It's over there,' yelled Bob in bewilderment as the two of them marched straight past the newsagent's. He turned to Hugh. 'Going to have a bit of trouble with those two, I can see. Leave it to me. I know how to handle kids.'

The blood rushed to Janet's head. 'Not mine, though. Hugh and I will handle our own.'

Bob gave her a surprised stare then shrugged. 'Duty free, I think, next, or they'll be calling our flight. Stuart, you'd better get me a newspaper.'

'Give me the money, then,' said Stuart.

Bob sighed and handed him a pound. 'And I want some change.'

They were frogmarched to the duty free shop where Bob recommended expensive brandy and bought cheap gin.

Belinda and Owen were waiting for them when they came out, hugely revived by their burgers. Stuart had spent his father's change on a Mars Bar and was arguing the justice of it, chocolate spilling unappetisingly from his mouth. Tricia had disappeared into the Body Shop and came back with a bag bulging with cosmetics.

'I hope you haven't spent all that money you got for your birthday,' murmured Cheryl.

Tricia's pout spread. 'It's my money.'

'Yes, but even so . . .'

Her father came to her defence. 'It's her money, Chicken. She can spend it how she likes.'

Cheryl subsided.

Hugh had just managed to secure a couple of cups of coffee when the first call for their flight went out. 'I'm afraid it looks like you'll have to leave it,' said Bob cheerfully. 'That's if you don't want seats by the kazi.'

Janet clung defiantly to the polystyrene beaker. 'It's only the first call.' She took a deep swig, scalding her tongue.

'Yes, but you have to get to the front of the queue, otherwise you don't get seats by the window.'

'Look, Bob,' said Hugh, who could see him ending up covered in boiling coffee, 'you go on ahead. We'll just have this then join you.'

Bob snorted very slightly, not liking to see his party split, but set off at a gallop and could soon be seen elbowing people out of the way as he fed his family into the front of the line.

Hugh and Janet gulped in silence. 'What are you thinking?' Hugh asked as he set down his empty cup.

'I was just wondering if it was too late to make a beeline for the car park.'

He laughed. 'I wouldn't put it past old Bob to hijack the plane and come looking for us.' He tucked his arm round her waist. 'Look on the bright side. They have to live with him. We don't.'

'Very bright,' – but she smiled.

The flight to Verona was relatively peaceful, Bob having failed to save seats for them despite an almost standing battle with an elderly Italian and his family.

Janet and Hugh sat at the front, Hugh folded like a deck chair. Belinda and Owen were behind, next to a pair of excitable Americans who kept leaning over them to peer out of the window and remark ecstatically on the various cloud formations obliterating the view. 'Oh, look, Mel. Wow! Hey, did you ever . . . ?' till Belinda could bear it no more and asked rather pointedly if they would like to change seats.

This brought forth fresh Wows and praise for her thoughtfulness and generosity. It did not, however, solve the problem, because the Americans felt it would be unfair to take advantage of her offer, so continued to lean across till the clouds finally parted, revealing a dazzling vista of snow-capped mountains pinpricked with pine trees which grew into forests as the plane flew lower. At this point the Americans began a panic-stricken search for their visas and so missed the entire spectacle.

'Did you see that, Mum? Those mountains?' asked Belinda for the fifth time as they waited in the arrivals hall at Verona for their baggage. Janet nodded. She was also waiting for her ears to pop, till which time conversation seemed to be taking place underwater. She swallowed again and pressed her hand against her ear.

'You know what to do for that?' Bob McDermot, who had already had words with a baggage handler – probably the reason theirs had not yet appeared – came marching over, flourishing a map. 'You want to hold the bridge of your nose and blow.' He demonstrated.

There was a rumble as the carousel started up again. Bob went to the opening so that he could shout loudly every time he recognised something belonging to the McDermots. This proved very handy for him and less so for the Gales, as Hugh and Owen were so busy grappling for the bags he identified that they forgot to look for their own, and it was a further ten minutes before they were finally sure that they had everything.

Hugh went outside to see if the courier had arrived and came hurrying back waving his arms. 'She's here. The coach is waiting for us down at the end. We're the last ones,' he added darkly.

'I told you to put coloured labels on your luggage,' Bob reminded him. 'It took me no time at all to spot ours.'

Hugh said nothing, but Janet noted his fists were clenching again.

The coach journey took two hours, mainly because the road was so steep. They had to keep pulling in to allow the traffic coming down, which did not look as though it could stop if it wanted to, to zip past.

It had been hot in Verona, so much so that the party, tired from their early start and stiff from the aeroplane, had begun to wilt. Janet caught sight of a woman looking at her and immediately became conscious of her crimson jacket, which she had all but forgotten in the face of the McDermots' electric blue. Belinda looked a hymn to restraint in her navy.

Once on board the bus, things improved. The seats were wide and spacious, the air-conditioning worked and the windows were made of tinted glass which kept the heat of the sun from stifling them.

Their courier, who introduced herself as Annie, told them a bit about the village they would be staying in, the après-ski activities, producing the first flicker of interest from Tricia McDermot, and the arrangements for the rest of the day.

They would be delivered to their chalet where a picnic lunch awaited them, given a couple of hours to settle in, then taken to the Hotel Meraviglioso, where Annie's assistant, Clive Harley, would give them further information about ski hire, lessons, etcetera, in fact everything they would need to make sure their holiday was a memorable one.

Janet leant back and closed her eyes. Whatever else, she thought, I have no doubt this holiday is going to be memorable.

She was woken from a deep sleep by Belinda who had clearly developed a taste for snowscapes. 'Look, look, look. Did you ever see anything so neat?' Janet looked. It was fair to say that she had not.

They were driving into a little hamlet plucked straight out of Hans Christian Andersen. Snow glistened on the roofs, the sun sparkled on icicles dangling with architectural precision from the guttering. Brightly painted shutters framed the windows of the wooden chalets, and rising behind them lay the frosted spectacle of the pine trees, ranged like frozen warriors awaiting the order to advance. Set back from the main road lay the church, a gold cross glittering in the sunlight on top of the steeple. It was a truly perfect scene.

'Oh, look, look, look.' Belinda had given up all pretence at teenage sophistication. 'Look at that statue. It's made of ice. Daddy, look. Oh, wake up. Do look.'

Hugh rubbed his eyes and gazed blearily out of the window. 'Mmm,' he said. Even Owen thought it worthy of a 'Cool'.

'It's only ice, for God's sake,' came a blasé voice from behind. Belinda blushed scarlet as Tricia McDermot returned to the magazine she had been glued to since Gatwick.

'I think it's beautiful,' she muttered defiantly, frowning out of the window.

'It is beautiful,' said Annie, the courier, firmly. 'You'll see some more on the way up.'

Belinda recovered slightly. 'How come they don't melt?'

'They're on a wooden frame. The water comes down from the mountain. It's pretty cold already, obviously, and when the temperature drops at night it just freezes on to the wood. It's too thick to melt much in the daytime and then at night it freezes up again. Simple really.'

'I think it's the most brilliant thing I've ever seen,' Belinda asserted.

'Simple things please simple minds,' muttered Tricia from behind her magazine.

'Well, I'm simple too, then,' responded Annie. 'I think they're fantastic.'

Tricia suddenly became even more interested in what she was reading.

Bob, who had spent the entire journey folding and refolding his maps, to the profound irritation of the people sitting opposite, now decided a debriefing was in order. He made his way down the coach to where Hugh and Owen were snoring again and shook them both roughly by the shoulder. They leapt with genetic precision and each opened one eye.

'This is what I think,' said Bob without preamble. 'Once we've dumped the bags and had a bite to eat, you and I, Hugh, will take a shufti around. I can show you where to have lunch etcetera, and the best place to go for a snifter. You can waste ages finding these things out for yourself. That's the great advantage of being with us. We know all about the place.'

'I think half the fun of a holiday is finding things out,' said Janet without opening her eyes.

Bob found this funny. 'You wait, my girl. You wait till you've spent half the morning queueing to get your ski pass stamped and you find out you should have gone straight to the tourist office. Cheryl learned the hard way, didn't you, Chicken?'

Cheryl, who had also been dozing, opened her eyes very wide and gazed at Bob uncertainly.

'Just telling Jan about your little disaster with the ski passes.'

She gave a stuttery laugh. 'Oh, yes. That was awful. Our first year. Bob was livid, weren't you, dear? Although, of course, he can laugh about it now,' she added nervously.

'Won't make that mistake again,' said Bob.

The coach lurched and turned off the main road on to a narrow avenue with huge banks of snow lining the pavements, along which various groups of people were stamping purposefully in their brightly coloured ski clothes. Janet felt a thrill of anxiety. They all looked horribly capable, skis stretched jauntily across their shoulders, faces glowing with enthusiasm.

The coach drove on till they came to a wooden chalet, outside which two toffee-brown blondes sat chatting in the sun.

'The Redmonds?' called Annie. A party of five put their hands up and were duly delivered to the chalet girls, who giggled hysterically as they struggled to help the family with their luggage.

More and more people were dropped off as the coach circled the village. Each time Annie consulted her clipboard, Janet felt her stomach tense, till they were the only ones left on board. 'The McDermots,' Annie called finally, a degree of tension in her own voice.

'Here we are, everyone. Up, up, up.' Bob scooped his hands at them like someone cooping chickens. Janet wondered briefly whether that was how Cheryl had got her nickname.

Annie led the way up the path. There were no toffee blondes to greet them. At the door she hesitated, fumbling with her keys. 'Erm, I'm afraid I've got a bit of an apology to make.'

They gazed at her expectantly.

'I'm afraid we've had a bit of a crisis. Nothing to worry about, but one of our chalet girls had a fall on the slopes yesterday. Sprained her ankle quite badly ...' She paused to see if this would elicit understanding. They continued to gaze, their stomachs having long forgotten their breakfast.

'The thing is, Lisa, that's her name, was allocated to Chalet Nevosa.' She gestured helplessly at the name above the porch. 'So I'm having to move people about a bit to keep everything covered. We've got a new girl coming out tomorrow, but in the meantime I'm going to have to ask you to bear with me.'

'What about our lunch?' asked Bob menacingly. The others, though embarrassed by his tone, were thinking the very same thing.

Annie baulked slightly. 'I got the boys to deliver some groceries this morning. There should be plenty here. It's just I'm going to have to ask you to serve yourselves, just this once. I promise I'll have sorted something out by this evening. It's never happened before,' she added hopefully, fiddling mightily with her keys.

'I need a leak,' came Stuart's uncompromising voice. Annie hastily unlocked the front door.

'It's upstairs on the left,' she called feebly as he barged past her.

'I know,' came echoing back. 'We've been here before.'

A look of curiosity, followed by blind panic rippled across the courier's face. 'You're not ... Are you the family who were here last year?' she dithered, struggling to retain her composure.

'That's us, young lady. Can't say I remember you.' Bob strode into the lounge and stared around as though checking for signs of burglary.

'No,' came Annie's dejected voice. 'This is my first season. I've heard all about you, though.'

Chapter Six

Chalet Nevosa was surprisingly spacious. There was a little hall where coats and ski gear could be stacked, opening on to a large living room with a huge fireplace in which a fire had been laid but not lit. At the far end was a long table, sadly bereft of the promised picnic but clearly capable of supporting a decent meal.

Bob, who had been out to supervise the luggage, came bustling in carrying a small holdall, followed by Owen, Belinda and Hugh all laden like Sherpas.

Cheryl emerged from the kitchen at the far end carrying a knobbly loaf and platter of cheese. 'Good, good,' said Bob, dropping his bag in everyone's way and rubbing his hands in anticipatory pleasure. 'Don't know about you lot, but I'm famished.' Cheryl retreated and returned with a salami and some apples. She made another journey for plates and knives and was sent back again by Bob to find wine. Janet went with her and collected glasses and orange juice.

They were about to sit down when Bob made his hissing sound. Cheryl looked up anxiously. 'Haven't you forgotten something, Chicken?' he murmured, jerking his head towards the unlit fire. Noiselessly Cheryl went in search of matches.

By the time the fire was lit, the others had nearly finished. Janet had begged Cheryl loudly to leave it, at least till after lunch, but Cheryl insisted she didn't mind, that it would only take a minute and that she herself was feeling the cold and would be happier once they had a blaze.

'Can I finish this, Dad?' asked Stuart, his hand already on the salami.

'I should think so. Growing lad ...' Bob glanced at Hugh for confirmation.

'What about your mother?' Janet interjected. 'She hasn't had any yet.'

'There's cheese,' said Stuart indifferently and crammed the salami into his mouth. Hugh reached down and crunched Janet's fingers between his own.

After lunch they inspected the upper floors.

The girls were allocated a light airy room with a dangerously slanting ceiling. Although they had yet to exchange a word, Janet was hopeful that at least they would not row. She was less sanguine about Owen and Stuart. Stuart seemed an aggressive boy, stocky and loutish, and though there was nothing remarkable about that in a fourteen-year-old, it was impossible not to detect vestiges of Bob's arrogance in him. Their room was smaller than Belinda and Tricia's but had a balcony overlooking the back, from which Janet duly prayed she would not find Stuart suspended before the week was out.

Between the two was a bathroom and, further along the corridor on a sort of mezzanine level, a large double room which Bob declared would be ideal for herself and Hugh. This immediately gave rise to the suspicion that somewhere else was a better one and, sure enough, following them up the stairs they were confronted by an even larger double, complete with *en suite* bathroom.

Janet felt a gush of pride as Hugh remorselessly decreed that everyone must be sure to knock before going through the bedroom.

The only other room was little more than a cupboard, with a bunk bed, locker and tiny washbasin, presumably intended for the chalet girl if and when she arrived. Janet was a little curious that there were no signs of present occupation. After all, if this Lisa had only sprained her ankle yesterday, how come all her possessions had been spirited away so rapidly? And where had they, and she, gone? She shuddered slightly and made a mental note to include ghosts in one of her articles.

All in all she was pleasantly impressed by Chalet Nevosa, though still uncertain why anyone would choose to call their house 'Nervous'. Perhaps they had renamed it in the wake of the McDermots' previous visit.

At about half past two there was a tap on the door. It was Annie, still looking harassed. 'Was everything all right?' she murmured. 'With the lunch, I mean?'

'Yes, thank you,' Janet assured her. 'Cheryl sorted it all out. Even lit the fire for us.'

'Oh . . .' Annie looked anything but relieved. 'Did she? That was . . . I've got Carla coming to prepare dinner for you. She'll be along just as soon as she's finished at the Redmonds'. I wondered if you were ready to come down and meet Clive? He's got lots of lovely things planned.'

They set off, Bob and Cheryl in matching sweaters of the kind seen on Dateline posters, and Tricia and Belinda, who for reasons best known to herself had decided to model herself on the older girl, in flimsy skinny-ribs and blue with cold. Stuart obviously lived in his tracksuit which had acquired a fresh coating of chocolate since lunchtime. Owen stalked ahead of them all, pretending he was on his own.

As they walked, Janet began to see why people raved about mountain air. It had a clarity unlike anything she had ever known. She felt almost dizzy with exhilaration, though that could have been due to the early start and the wine she had had with her lunch.

She felt an enormous sense of wellbeing. The scenery was fairytale, the village inviting, its shops packed with wildly expensive souvenirs and designer ski wear. Everyone looked healthy and fit and alive. And if they did, stomping around in their outrageous outfits, so surely must she? In a week's time she, too, would be bronzed and confident, uninhibited by the bobbles on her hat and her lemon salopettes. People arriving would look at her and think she must be a regular visitor, someone who knew her way around the slopes. Only then did the familiar zing of panic whip through her. Before any of that could happen she must learn to ski.

Clive Harley was sitting in the lobby of a fairly grand hotel in the centre of town, a cup of black coffee in front of him. Janet recognised several of the other families from the coach. They were chatting cheerfully and examining the clusters of brochures which had been handed to them on arrival. Bob duly collected theirs, hailing Clive like a long lost brother and inquiring in a loud voice if he knew which black runs were open locally. Clive raised distinctly bloodshot eyes to him and said he thought they all were. Bob's eyebrows knitted a fraction but he nodded sagely and went off to demand coffee for all eight of them, although Stuart and Tricia never drank it and Belinda had asked for a milkshake.

Clive introduced himself. He was responsible for guided skiing trips and excursions and would be on hand to help with any queries regarding the local amenities. He could also name some very good restaurants in the area, none of which, he added firmly, had offered him back-handers. This delighted Bob who informed the room at large that he had voiced just that suspicion last year after being overcharged in a pizzeria.

The company regarded him with distaste.

Clive went on to tell them about proposed activities. These included night skiing, toboggan races, the vaunted all-day ski round the Sella Ronda, adding, to Janet's eternal relief, that it was for experienced skiers only, and finally coming back to a trivia quiz which was to take place that evening in an

English-owned inn close to the chalets. There would be mulled wine and prizes and it would give everyone a chance to get to know each other.

He then moved on to the matter of ski school. Hugh booked himself into Intermediate and Belinda, Owen and Janet into Beginners. This brought forth protests from both children who swore they were more than equal to an Olympic run. Hugh was adamant. 'If you're too good for Beginners, they'll move you up. You've neither of you ever skied on snow before. You go into Beginners and that is my final word. Besides, who's going to look after your mother?'

Belinda, who had severe doubts about her mother's hat, grimaced and stalked off to look for another ice sculpture.

Janet was interested to see that the McDermots, with the exception of Bob, who considered himself Advanced, had all gone for Intermediate. She supposed if they had been here before they must know what they were doing. Perhaps it was malicious to think that Cheryl, looking like a beach ball in her brilliant blue, did not quite fit the image.

The next stop was the hire shop to pick up their skis and boots. Janet nursed a dreadful fear all the way that she would have to translate feet sizes into Italian and they would all end up maimed or floating around inside boots the size of the *Titanic*. In the event she was saved by the owner of the shop who spoke excellent English and seemed more than used to dealing with the eccentricities of foreign shoe sizes.

The McDermots had their own boots but this did not prevent Bob accompanying them into the shop and commenting noisily on what they should or shouldn't be hiring. The woman, whom Janet suspected had come across him before, managed to maintain a gracious manner while ignoring everything he said. It occurred to her that this might be the way to deal with Bob, rather than let him drive her to a seething mass of resentment as he had been doing so far. She would try it. Surely here, in the crystal air of the Dolomites, she should be able to practise a little stoicism?

Her good intentions were rapidly put to the test when they arrived back at the chalet to find that Bob had got in ahead and eaten three slices of a chocolate cake Annie had brought them for tea.

'Oh, come on,' he chided, when charged with piggery by his daughter. 'You ladies have got to watch your figures. Can't go eating chocolate cake. Here, there's loads of biscuits and things. Don't know what you're going on about.' Janet was appalled to see his bottom lip protruding. He's like an overgrown boy scout, she concluded. Not even a scout, a cub. She could imagine him in a sleeveless pullover and long flannel shorts, currying favour with Akela and loathed by his contemporaries.

'I don't want any,' she said to save the peace. 'Belinda and Owen can share mine.'

'Why can't we have our own?' demanded Belinda rebelliously. 'There was enough for everyone if some people weren't so greedy.'

'That's enough,' said Hugh sharply. 'Owen can have mine. Come on, Jan. Let's go and unpack.' Janet was glad of the excuse to get away. So, it seemed, was Hugh. The two of them slumped on the bed in silence. Down below they could hear the rumble of voices, none of them particularly cheerful.

Hugh roused himself. 'Sorry.'

'What for?'

'What for?' He stood up and rubbed his eyes. 'God, I'm tired. Must be all this mountain air.'

'And getting up at two in the morning.'

'Oh yes. I'd forgotten about that. Seems like a week ago we were packing the car.'

Janet wished it had been. 'It's very beautiful here,' she reflected. 'And the chalet's nice. Nicer than I'd expected. And Annie and Clive seem nice.' She was drivelling, she knew, but she felt she must try and cheer him up.

He nodded. 'I'm going to have a shower. Do you want it after me?'

'Good idea. I'll hang some of this stuff up while you're in there.' Hugh thudded off up the stairs.

She was just pushing an empty case under the bed when there was a rap on the door. 'Come in,' she called. The door opened and there stood Bob, his face strangely pink. 'Ah,' he said. 'It's you.'

'Yes,' she agreed, wondering whom he had expected to find in her bedroom at four o'clock in the afternoon.

'Only someone's in our bathroom.'

'It's Hugh,' said Janet calmly. 'He wanted a shower. I'm going to have one when he's finished.'

Bob looked at her as though she were mentally challenged. 'But he's in our bathroom.'

She smiled. 'Well, it isn't exactly *your* bathroom, is it, Bob? We all won the holiday, so obviously everything has to be shared equally.' Bob's mouth worked in several directions. 'Including the afternoon tea,' she added sweetly. 'Now, if you'll excuse me . . .' She closed the door, her heart beating at a ridiculous rate. So there! She poked her tongue out. It was several seconds before she heard him retreating.

By half past six there was still no sign of the promised Carla. Janet was ensconced in front of the fire, notepad on knee, but she was plainly not cut out to be the 'starving in a garret' type of writer and, try as she might, her thoughts kept returning to food.

Hugh came out of the kitchen carrying a bowl of olives. 'Cocktail time. I'm going to open that whisky.'

'Shouldn't we wait for Cheryl and Bob?'

'Why? It's our whisky.'

'Yes, but we bought it to share, didn't we? I hope I'm going to get some of their gin.'

'You're right. Still a small one won't do any harm, will it? I don't think I can face them without it.'

Janet smiled. 'Me neither.'

Belinda came downstairs, went into the kitchen and retreated silently again, carrying a large bag of peanuts. 'Don't spoil your supper,' Janet called after her.

'What supper?' came the doleful reply.

Owen appeared on the landing, fresh from the shower. 'What time's dinner, Mum?'

'When Carla gets here, I suppose.'

'When's that?'

'How should I know?'

'I'm starving.'

'We all are. You'd better get yourself some bread and cheese or something.'

'Is that all we're going to get here?'

Janet set aside her notebook. 'Look, it isn't my fault, Owen. Annie said this girl Carla would be along as soon as possible. She's got someone else's dinner to cook first, poor thing.'

'Some holiday. No lunch. No dinner. Can we go to Butlin's next year?' He slammed off into his room.

Hugh trotted downstairs carrying the whisky. 'What's up with Owen?'

'He's hungry.'

'Aren't we all? I could hear Bob giving Cheryl hell when I was in the shower.'

'Oh, surely not? The poor woman got the lunch ready, lit the fire and cleared up afterwards. What more does he want?'

'A harem, I should think. He doesn't strike me as very self-sufficient. Are you having water in this or just ice?'

'Ice, please. And not too much.'

'Ah!' The Gales were to become familiar with this prelude to the arrival of Bob, usually with a complaint on his lips, as the week progressed. 'I see you've opened the whisky.'

'We have indeed,' Hugh confirmed. 'Are you and Cheryl going to join us?'

'Cheryl doesn't drink,' said Bob before she could open her mouth. 'Anyway she's going to sort out the meal.'

'What do you mean, sort it out?' Janet asked.

'Well, it's nearly seven o'clock. We can't hang about all night waiting to be fed, can we? Cheryl's had a look-see and it seems there's some meat of some kind in the fridge. I've told her to get on with it. Perhaps Janet would like to peel a few veg?'

Janet waited for her pulse to steady. 'And what do you plan to do, Bob,' she asked sweetly, 'while Cheryl is cooking and I am peeling a few veg?'

Bob looked surprised. 'I'm going to chat to Hugh here about the proposed relocation of the Accounts Department.'

'Anywhere nice?'

'The western building,' said Bob without a trace of irony. 'We need more work space. I daresay he's told you about it?'

'It's barely off our minds.'

Hugh winced. 'Let me get you a glass, Bob. This is damn good stuff.' He retreated to the kitchen, followed by Cheryl, rolling up her sleeves. Janet and Bob regarded each other.

'Looking forward to getting out there on the slopes in the morning?' he asked.

'Not much.'

'Oh, come now. Chance to use your Italian. How do they say "help", by the way?'

'I've no idea. I've never had to use it.'

Bob roared with laughter. 'You will after tomorrow, take my word for it. Skiing's not as easy as it looks, by any means.'

Nor's being such a complete prat, ran through Janet's mind. Bob must have been practising for years, despite an innate advantage.

They were saved from the need for further discussion by the arrival not of Carla but Annie, now looking gravely in need of a whisky herself. 'I'm so sorry. There's been a slight hitch ...'

Carla, it seemed, had sensibly prepared a double quantity of the casserole she had been making for the Redmond family and had been on her way to Chalet Nevosa when the inevitable had happened and she had slipped.

'Is she hurt?' asked Janet, wondering what chance she herself stood if the residents had such trouble staying upright.

'Just a few bruises, but I'm afraid your dinner ended up in the snow. Don't worry, though,' she added quickly, seeing Bob's face going through its litmus test. 'Brian's on his way up now with a couple of chickens.'

'Alive or dead?' asked Hugh.

'Dead,' said Annie in alarm. 'That is, the chickens are. Brian's alive.'

'He's plainly doing better than the rest of your staff,' Hugh observed. 'What, do you suppose, is his secret?'

Annie's face contorted. This man was madder than the McDermots.

Janet touched her arm. 'Take no notice. He's teasing you. Why don't you have a drink with us? You must have had the most dreadful day.'

Annie almost collapsed with relief. 'It's not usually this bad,' she confided while Hugh poured her a glass. 'It's just when one thing goes wrong, things sort of snowball, if you see what I mean.'

'What do you expect in a ski resort?' Bob chortled, anxiously clocking the size of Annie's drink.

'But I will get it sorted out tomorrow, I promise. Even if I have to cook your meals myself,' Annie confirmed. Janet suspected she was only half joking but her attention was claimed by the arrival of the girls. Not so much Tricia as Belinda who was done up like a slave girl at auction.

'Christ, Blin, what do you look like?' gasped her father.

'Tricia did my eyes for me,' said Belinda, half defiant, half embarrassed.

'So I see. Well, don't go out like that.'

'Will if I want.'

'Will not,' said Hugh firmly. 'You look like a French tart.'

Belinda made a face and went into the kitchen in search of food. Cheryl came out to say she was afraid the meal would take a little longer than she'd anticipated, owing to the toughness of the meat. She stopped when she saw Annie and gazed at her nervously. 'I'm sorry, Annie. It's just we weren't sure if anyone would be round. I hope you don't mind. I've only peeled a few potatoes and things.'

Annie shook her head vigorously. 'Thank you very much, Mrs McDermot. I was just explaining to everyone, there's been a little—'

'Hitch. Yes, I thought there might have been.'

There was a rap at the door and Brian, bleached, bronzed and with a horseshoe of studs round his ear, came bouncing into the lounge with an enormous greaseproof bag. 'There we are. Should keep you going. I've stuck some sausages in. They're all cooked. Just shove 'em in the oven for ten minutes. Hot 'em up. OK?' He ran his eyes over Tricia who fiddled casually with her bracelets. 'Right,' he said. 'Enjoy your dinner. See you around.' Whether this was meant for Tricia or as a general greeting, no one was sure.

'Brian works in the delicatessen,' Annie explained. 'He's saved my neck more times than I care to remember.'

Bob's hands were doing their human fly act. 'Right,' he said purposefully. 'Whose turn to lay the table?'

Chapter Seven

Janet was beginning to see what Owen meant about Stuart McDermot. He ate with his mouth open, which was revolting enough, but he also had a habit of thrusting his forefinger inside and wiggling it about to loosen various bits of food which had lodged between his teeth. She was several places down from him but she could see that Belinda, sitting opposite, was in some danger of being sick. She wondered that his mother did not remonstrate.

'You know what you are, Stuart?' It was Tricia who had spoken. She had inveigled herself into the seat next to Owen and Janet noticed that her nails were now a violent shade of purple. 'You're a disgusting pig.'

'Oi, oi,' said Bob, helping himself to more wine. 'Don't you two start.'

'Yes, but look at him, Dad. There's more food coming out of his mouth than going in.'

'Oh, leave him be. He's on holiday.'

'That doesn't mean he can make the rest of us throw up. If you don't stop him I'm going to vomit. I mean it.' She made a retching noise which diminished the newfound respect Janet had been feeling for her.

'Stuart, love, if you don't like it just leave it on the side of your plate,' murmured his mother. Stuart, who throughout this had continued eating, stared at his mother contemptuously, then shoved his plate away.

'Why aren't there chips?' he asked, before lapsing into silence for the rest of the meal.

'Who's going to give poor old Chicken a hand?' asked Bob as Cheryl clanged around in the kitchen after dinner. Janet stared resolutely into the fire.

'She'll be all right,' said Tricia indifferently. 'Anyway, not me. It's always me.'

'That'll be the day,' said Bob, who was writing down his day's spends in the back of a Filofax.

'Shut up, Dad,' said Tricia sharply. 'I'm always helping Mum at home. You know I am.'

'Only because I make you.'

'You can't make me do anything,' retorted Tricia, pouting.

The impasse was broken by the return of Cheryl. 'Shouldn't we be going? We are going to the quiz, aren't we? We don't want to be late.'

Bob clapped shut his notebook. 'Quite right. Better get off or we'll be at the back.' He tweaked Belinda's ponytail which infuriated her. 'Come on, lazybones. Let's see what they teach you at school these days.'

She looked across at Janet. 'Do we have to go, Mum? I'm ever so sleepy.' She gave a pathetic imitation of a yawn.

Janet would have liked to comply. Normally she quite enjoyed quizzes but the thought of partnering the McDermots did not attract her. She glanced at Hugh, hoping he would come up with a suitable excuse. 'Hugh, Blin's a bit tired. I was wondering if it might be better to give the quiz a miss? After all, it's been a very long day.'

Hugh lowered his newspaper. 'Up to you,' he said unhelpfully, completely missing the hint.

'Nonsense. She's on holiday. You're not allowed to get tired on holiday, are you, Chicken?' Bob was halfway into his coat.

Cheryl gave a deprecating shrug. 'It can be a lot of fun,' she said in a voice which convinced no one.

Hugh stood up. 'Who's for this quiz, then?'

Owen said he would go. He'd seen rather a pretty girl on the coach that morning and was hoping this might be an opportunity to chat her up.

Stuart asked if they had satellite TV. Tricia said she hoped so, because she didn't want everyone knowing her brother was a butt-head. Cheryl said that wasn't a very nice thing to say about her own brother even though she knew she didn't mean it. 'Oh, don't I?' was Tricia's response.

Janet offered to stay behind with Belinda, but she had mysteriously revived at the mention of satellite TV and professed herself ready and anxious to take part.

The eight of them set off, Bob leading the way.

Annie was sitting at a table near the door dispensing tickets. Bob asked if there was a reduction for children and was told yes, but they would not be entitled to mulled wine. This brought forth a roar of protest from Tricia and Stuart. 'Oh, come on, kids. You know you prefer Coke,' pleaded their father.

'We do not,' insisted Tricia. Bob handed over his money, holding up the queue while he entered it in his Filofax.

The tables were laid out with pencils and paper, little bowls of nuts, and glasses in metal holders. Clive was ambling around, still looking hungover, filling the glasses from a steaming jug and dosing himself liberally from his own as he went. Janet wondered, setting aside her inability to ski, if she would feel totally confident entrusting her safety to him.

Annie tinkled a little bell and endeavoured to draw the room to silence. 'We're nearly ready to begin. Has everyone got a table?'

'What sort of table?' called Bob. 'A times table or a timetable?' Those who had not heard this before groaned. Clive and Annie tweaked their lips politely.

'More important,' continued Clive, 'has everyone got a

drink?' There was a roar of assent. 'Right. Let battle commence. Annie will read the questions. At the end of each round you are to hand your answers to the table on the left. I stress *left*, in deference to the fact that you're British.' More laughter. 'And any queries must be referred to me, the final arbiter. My decision is final. Unless you care to slip me a million lire under the table.'

'How much is a million lire, Dad?' asked Stuart, dropping a half-eaten nut back into the bowl. Bob brought out his calculator.

The questions were not hard. Janet and Hugh argued over how many islands were in the Balearics and which film theme Clive was playing. Owen and Belinda argued over who was the first Take That to quit, Tricia and Stuart argued over Stuart spitting nutshells into Tricia's wine, and Bob and Cheryl didn't argue at all, because Cheryl did not venture so much as a single suggestion all evening.

Even when asked for the main ingredients in a Yorkshire pudding, she handed the paper over to Bob to check. This annoyed Janet almost to distraction since her own Yorkshire puddings were generally acknowledged to be *par excellence*.

After the sixth round they had a break. Smokers rushed outside, Stuart sloped off to try the effect of peeing in the snow and Bob went round each of the tables, checking on their score and writing it in a notebook.

Hugh had managed to obtain a fresh jug of wine and was busy refilling glasses when Bob came scurrying back. 'We're third at the moment,' he informed him. Hugh grunted. 'We're only three behind that table over there and I see we've got natural history after the break. It's a speciality of mine so we should be able to pull that back. Our main concern is going to be that family at the front. They've got . . .' He checked his figures once again, 'seven on us. Mind you, they've got one more person so it may be possible to ask for the scores to be calculated *pro rata*. I think I might speak to Clive about that.'

Janet, who had been listening to this, felt the muscles in her jaw collapsing. 'Bob,' she said incredulously, 'what are you talking about? They've got eight, the same as us.'

Bob shook his head so hard his glasses nearly fell off. 'No, Janet. You're wrong. I thought that too. You can't see when you're sitting down, but they've got a baby in a carrycot.' He pointed directly at the parents, who caught sight of him and turned anxiously to see if anything had happened to their infant. 'It's down there between them. I think it's asleep.'

Janet gazed at him. She knew she had had a lot to drink. First the whisky, then the wine at dinner and now the lethal brew that Clive was dispensing, but even she could distinguish between nine active participants and eight people and a sleeping baby. As if it mattered.

'As if it matters.'

Bob stared at her in alarm. 'Of course it matters. It's got to be fair. Otherwise what's the point?'

Janet stabbed a beer mat with her pencil. 'Bob, it's a game. It's for fun, for Christ's sake.' Several people at adjacent tables looked across. She realised her voice had risen several decibels.

'I know that. But half the fun of a quiz, I would like to point out, is trying to get more answers right than any-one else.'

'Including a sleeping baby?' Janet retaliated. 'How many questions has that baby answered so far? More to the point, how many has it got right? I never heard anything so ridiculous in my life.'

Bob turned away, his face suffused with annoyance. 'More than some of the people on this table, I wouldn't be surprised,' he muttered.

Janet was not having that. 'And what exactly does that mean?'

Hugh put his hand on her arm. 'Jan, calm down. It doesn't matter. Leave it.'

But Bob wasn't leaving it either. 'I should have thought a

child of eight would have known how many islands there are in the Balearics,' he said snidely.

Janet blushed. 'Geography was never my subject.'

'Nor cookery either, if you put pepper in your Yorkshire puddings,' suggested Bob.

This Janet could not allow to pass. 'Hugh …' Hugh was sitting, shoulders hunched, watching the pair of them in disbelief. 'Hugh, tell him about my Yorkshire puddings.'

'Jan, leave it. They're waiting to get on with the quiz.'

This was not exactly so. Annie and Clive had been holding these quizzes every week since November. They were bored rigid with them. The spectacle of someone having a go at Bob McDermot was too good to be hurried.

'Everyone knows proper Yorkshire puddings need pepper, otherwise you might just as well buy a packet and add water,' declared Janet, wondering how she had ever got on to the subject.

'I always put pepper in,' said a woman on the next table supportively.

'That's why they always make me sneeze,' said her husband. Everyone laughed.

'Right.' Clive stood up reluctantly. 'I think we've sorted out the vexed question of the Yorkshire puddings. My only advice to you all would be don't eat any that they give you in your chalets. We got a job lot back in December and they're still trying to get rid of the them.'

The company settled back for the second leg, although the baby Bob had spotted had now started to cry quite pitifully. The poor parents finally decided to call it a day which tempted Janet to suggest their team's score now be adjusted upwards to account for the absence of three of the contestants, but she held her peace in deference to Hugh's agonised expression.

Belinda was practically asleep in her chair. Stuart had wandered off again, and Tricia was doing her utmost to gain Owen's attention by giggling hysterically at everything he said and tossing her hair about like someone caught in a wind tunnel. He was making eyes at the girl he had spotted on the coach and had to be nudged every time a question came along that he might know the answer to.

Cheryl, who had forgone the mulled wine, now sat fiddling nervily with a glass of orange juice which she plainly did not like. She looked as though she would rather be anywhere than here. Janet felt much the same, though looking around at the other parties, she could see that it might be possible to enjoy yourself on a holiday like this if you were with people you got on with. She sighed.

'Boring you, are we? Sorry about that,' came Bob's voice. Janet wondered how much he had had to drink. He seemed to have given up even trying to be civil. She said nothing.

They came second, a team in the far corner nipping them at the post with a breathtaking display of general knowledge.

Cheryl was sent to collect their prize, a bottle of red wine. That's the last we've seen of that, thought Janet, watching Bob tucking it behind his chair.

They were all dog tired as they laboured up the path to the chalet. Janet had left the porch light on. Bob tutted about the waste of electricity. 'I suppose he'd rather we all broke our necks in the dark?' she muttered to Hugh, who gave her a strained smile.

'Don't take everything Bob says to heart,' he murmured. 'He doesn't mean half of it.' She frowned, sick of his efforts to defend the man. Anyway, it was the half Bob did mean that bothered her.

'Night, Mum.' Belinda tottered past her. 'Sleep well.'

'You, too, darling. You must be ready for it. Has Tricia gone up already?' she asked cautiously.

Belinda shook her head. 'She's gone clubbing.'

'Oh.' Janet felt oddly shocked. 'Do her parents know?'

Belinda shrugged. 'Don't know. Probably. I heard her saying they wouldn't mind.'

Janet was torn between a desire to leave well alone and a sense that she ought to inform the McDermots that their daughter had gone into the town on her own. Duty won out. She went in search of Cheryl whom she had seen heading for the kitchen. Probably decided to defrost the fridge, she thought.

She opened the door. Cheryl, who was bending down at one of the cupboards, whirled round and leapt up, closing it behind her. Janet smiled awkwardly. 'Sorry. I didn't mean to give you a start. It's just Belinda was saying Tricia's decided to go to a club or something. I just thought I'd better check you knew all about it?'

Cheryl continued to stare as though trying to remember where she had seen Janet before, then, with a little shrug, she smiled back. 'Oh ... Yes. I think she did mention it. Tricia's always been a night bird. Mind you, she'll be in a terrible mood tomorrow. Be warned.' She gave a nervous giggle.

'Well, I thought I'd just better check. I hope you don't think I was interfering?'

Cheryl shook her head. 'No, certainly not. Thank you. Yes, a night bird. Not like me, I'm afraid. I need my eight hours. Yes.' She hurried past Janet and out of the room. 'See you in the morning. Sleep well.'

'You too.'

Upstairs Hugh was already in bed. Janet undressed quickly and slid in beside him. 'What's it like?'

'What's what like?' asked Hugh sleepily.

'The bed.'

'It's OK.'

There was a mighty thud from up above, followed by the creaking of springs. 'Sounds like Bob's found his Viagra,' murmured Hugh and rolled over on his side. He was asleep before Janet got to the light switch.

She was just drifting off when there was another thump from up above followed by the sound of muttered voices and footsteps heading downstairs. What's he up to now? she wondered, waiting for the steps to go past. They did not. She braced herself for the knock. It came. 'Oh, for God's sake.' She hauled herself out of bed and fumbled for her dressing-gown.

Bob stood outside in a plaid dressing-gown and matching slippers. She would not have been surprised to see a nightcap on his head. 'Just wondered what time you're getting up in the morning?' he asked with unnatural brightness.

She stared at him. 'I've no idea, Bob. When we wake up, I imagine. Does it matter?'

Bob made a clicking noise with his tongue. 'Don't want to be late for the lifts. We need to be down there by eight fifteen otherwise you might as well forget it till ten.'

Janet nodded. 'Right. Well, in that case, I think we'll forget it till ten,' she said and closed the door. She could sense Bob preparing to knock again. Quickly she whipped open the door. 'Goodnight, Bob,' she said firmly. Bob, whose hand had indeed been poised to rap, stared at her disconcertedly.

'What does Hugh say?'

'Hugh says he may not get up at all tomorrow. He'll see you on Tuesday,' said Janet and closed the door again.

Chapter Eight

Janet was dreaming that she had been tied to a sledge and was being pushed towards a precipice by Stuart McDermot, chocolate dripping from his jowls on to her ski jacket as he leant over her. For some reason this upset her more than her prospective death, and she was remonstrating with him about the difficulty of removing chocolate stains when a fire engine rushed past ringing its bell.

'Now look what you've done,' was all she could think of to say. 'It costs more before twelve o'clock.'

'What does?' Hugh was grinning down at her. 'I've brought you a cup of coffee. They're placing bets down there whether you've taken an overdose.' Janet blinked at him. He was dressed and looking horribly fresh for someone who had only had eight hours' sleep in the past two days.

She struggled to sit up. 'What time is it?'

Hugh glanced at his watch. 'Twenty to eight.'

'*Twenty to eight?* What sort of time is that to be up and dressed on holiday?'

Hugh looked slightly embarrassed. 'Actually Bob gave me a call. Both of us really, but you didn't wake up. Apparently the queues for the lifts are horrendous if you don't get there early.'

'Oh, don't start all that again,' groaned Janet. 'I had it all from Bob last night.'

'Well, you know ... First day ...'

'You'll just have to go without me.'

'Jan, we can't. You know that.'

Janet slurped some of her coffee on to the bedclothes and cursed. 'I know nothing of the kind. If you want to play puppet to Bob, that's your business, but leave me out of it.'

Hugh looked aggrieved. 'I'm nobody's puppet as you very well know. It's just it's the first day and the kids want to be on time for their lesson. How are they going to feel walking into a load of strangers halfway through the morning? They don't even speak the language.'

Janet set her cup down abruptly. 'Don't tell me the lessons are in Italian?'

Hugh shuffled his feet. 'Well, it's mostly demonstration, isn't it? You don't have to understand everything they're saying necessarily.'

She slumped back on the pillows. 'This is brilliant. You bring us all the way here and enrol us in a class for something none of us know how to do, and then tell me we won't understand a word they're saying? Of all your schemes, Hugh, I think this is probably the most ridiculous. And the most dangerous, come to that. Suppose he says turn left and we all turn right?'

'Well, that's why you're here, isn't it?' snapped Hugh exasperatedly. 'You're the one who's supposed to speak the bloody language.'

'Oh, so that's it. That's why you've brought me. So you'll have someone to blame when our children fall sixty thousand feet off a mountain? Well, thank you very much. That's the last raffle prize I want from you.'

'It's the last one you'll bloody get,' roared Hugh and slammed out of the room. Janet turned on her side and tried to go back to sleep.

It was never an option. Fifteen minutes later Belinda came tiptoeing into the room with a tray of rolls and assorted jams. She stood awkwardly at the foot of the bed.

'I've brought you some breakfast.'

'Thank you.'

Encouraged, Belinda advanced. 'Where do you want me to put it?'

Janet relented. Once more she pulled herself up in the bed. 'Give it to me. I'll have it on my lap. Thank you, darling. This looks lovely.'

Belinda hovered. 'Are you really not coming skiing?' she asked unhappily. Janet buttered a roll and spread it with jam. 'Mum?'

She put down the knife. 'Oh, of course I am. I just hate being told what time to get up when I'm on holiday. It's meant to be a rest.'

But Belinda had gone. 'It's all right. She's coming,' she heard as her daughter flew down the stairs.

'Better late than never,' said Bob, looking at his watch as Janet thudded ungraciously into the lounge. Cheryl, clearly alarmed that this might send Janet scurrying back to bed, stepped forward.

'It's a lovely morning,' she said brightly. 'Don't you look cosy in that hat?'

Janet glared defiantly round at them. 'It was a present from some friends,' she said before they could beg her to dispose of it. Tricia, who was looking paler than a banshee, sniggered into her mitt. Stuart came trailing out of the kitchen, eating a piece of cheese.

'Oh, Stuart, haven't you had enough?' asked his mother in despair.

'I'm hungry,' said Stuart through the cheese.

'Well, don't forget to clean your teeth,' said Cheryl in a hopeless voice. Stuart rolled his eyes.

Bob was now in the hall dispensing skis and ski boots like the host at a children's party. It was gone half past eight and, true to his prediction, the buses were fuller than the Central Line in rush hour, mostly with German tourists, it seemed. He said nothing but even through a ski jacket it was possible to read his body language.

They finally got on a bus by forming a sort of phalanx with Cheryl at the tip, prodding her mercilessly forward with the points of their skis till she had opened up a gap wide enough for the next two in line to compress themselves into.

It was an uncomfortable journey, not helped by the torrent of German abuse being aimed at them by the loved ones of those they had displaced in the queue. Bob seemed to relish this, shouting *'Jawohl, mein Herr'* at anyone who caught his eye, till the bus driver screeched to an emergency stop outside a gaunt concrete building and discharged them all on to the pavement.

Now began another scrabble for the tramway lifts slithering lethargically round a semi-circular platform, and stopping just long enough for a couple of dozen skiers to fight their way on to them.

Janet, already feeling more bruised than from her dry slope experience, found herself jammed up against one of the Germans who had looked most ready to kill Bob. She wondered if her thirty-year-old 'O' level would stretch to 'How may I assist you in your objective?'

Hugh was over the other side hanging on to Belinda, and Owen was pegged into a corner with two obviously gay men who were gazing dreamily at his chestnut curls. Bob and his family had gone on ahead.

The lift lurched and Janet let out an involuntary squeak as it trundled forward then was pitched into the void, at that point a mere six feet off the ground but rapidly progressing to ten, then twenty ... she closed her eyes. When she opened them again it was to see with sickening clarity that they were several hundred feet up the mountain. The village had retreated to jigsaw proportions, the spire of the church just visible in the morning sunlight. Directly below lay the jagged tips of the pine trees, increasingly frosty as they rose higher, increasingly unwelcoming to Janet's eyes.

Her ears clicked and clunked inside her clown's hat till she felt as detached as someone emerging from anaesthetic. Suddenly there was a crunch. Oh my God, she panicked, we've hit the one in front, forgetting that it contained Bob McDermot and she should have been applauding the fact.

They had not and, if more evidence were needed, the unmistakable face of her tormentor was rapidly visible as he thrust his way through the disembarking passengers.

'Quick,' he said as soon as they were safe on the platform. 'I need someone's ski pass.'

They all stared at him in bewilderment. Bob's face creased with irritation. 'I've left my Superski in the chalet. I can't get any higher without it. I'll need one of yours. In fact, it will have to be Janet's because the kids' ones are Juniors'. Quick as you can. They're waiting for me now.'

Janet glanced at Hugh. 'Wouldn't it be better if you took Hugh's?' she asked. 'I mean, they've got photos on. You look more like a man than a woman.' This was the closest she would get to a compliment.

Bob flapped his arms frustratedly. 'He needs it for Intermediate. So do Cheryl and the kids. Oh, come on, Janet. Do you have to make a fuss about everything?'

Janet gave it to him. Not because she wanted him to catch up with his group, nor because she wanted to avoid another scene. She just hoped it would mean the end of her skiing for the day.

It was not to be. No sooner had Bob sprinted away than Clive Harley stepped smartly off an incoming lift and made his way towards them.

'Morning. Sleep well?'

Everyone said they had. He consulted a list. 'I see we have Mr Gale, Mrs McDermot, Tricia and Stu for the Intermediates, and Mrs Gale, Owen and Belinda for Beginners.'

'I've had to give my ski pass to Mr McDermot,' said Janet hopefully. 'He left his back at the chalet. I suppose that means I can't do the class?'

Clive shook his head. 'No, nothing of the kind. Beginners takes place on this level, just over there behind the café.' He gestured to where a mass of tiny infants were zigzagging deliriously down a slope the size of a football pitch. 'Intermediates up one stage and the Advanced you need your Super for.'

'It had my photo on it,' pleaded Janet, still praying the whole thing might be called off on a technicality.

Clive shook his head again. 'Don't you worry about it. If anyone looks, they'll just think Mr McD's a tranny.' Cheryl made a strange whinnying sound at the back of her throat. Owen sniggered and nudged Belinda, who giggled dutifully without having the faintest idea why.

'Right,' said Clive, 'if everyone's ready? Mr Gale, would you and Mrs McDermot like to take Tricia and Stu over to that group by the postcards, while I introduce our beginners to Clemenza?'

'What's a tranny?' Janet heard Belinda whispering to Owen as they made their way towards the bottom of the slope.

A tanned young woman with billowing black hair, dressed entirely in scarlet, was coaxing the youngest of the tots, who looked no more than two, on to the drag lift. Janet was amazed to see the ease with which the child took to it, cocking a padded blue leg over the saucer and bouncing away to the top where a man was waiting to catch her.

Around the base of the slope proud Italian mothers chatted and cheered as the infants came careering down. They seemed remarkably unperturbed by the regular collisions occurring on the way. Janet wondered wistfully if there were some truth in Cheryl's observation about snow not hurting, or perhaps it only didn't hurt if you were made of rubber like small children.

Clive had hailed Clemenza and was talking to her rapidly in Italian. Janet tried to follow what they were saying but the only bits she recognised were hers and her children's names. Her spirits plummeted still further.

'Mum,' Belinda tugged her arm. 'We're not having lessons with all those kids, are we?'

'Well ... I don't know, really. I suppose if we're the only beginners ...'

Belinda's face was a picture. 'I'm not having lessons with a bunch of babies. Half of them have got nappies on.'

'That won't affect the way you ski, will it?' said Janet crossly, glancing round to see if Hugh was still within range. She really didn't think she could handle a full-scale rebellion as well as being outshone by two-year-olds. Owen came mooching over, looking equally morose.

'Forget it, Mum. I'm not having lessons with that lot.'

'Well, what will you do? You can't just go off on your own.'

'Watch me.'

'Owen,' she called desperately. 'Hang on.' Owen halted. 'Look, speak to Clive. He'll sort it out.'

'What's the problem?' Clive had finished talking to Clemenza.

Janet shrugged helplessly. 'They don't awfully fancy having lessons with all these small children,' she said, adding feebly, 'in case anyone gets hurt.'

Clive grinned. 'They'll get out of the way fast enough if they have to. Anyway, not to worry. Clemenza's going to take the three of you aside and see what stage you're at, then she'll know how best to help you. OK?' Owen and Belinda looked marginally reassured.

Clemenza came bouncing over. Janet wondered if it was the boots that made everyone walk like John Travolta or if they genuinely felt that chirpy.

'*Buon giorno, tutti.*' She pumped their hands vigorously.

'*Buon giorno,*' stammered Janet, feeling her credibility was at stake. '*Mi chiama Janet, ecco mio figlio, Owen ...*'

'Owennn,' beamed Clemenza, pumping again.

'*E mia figlia, Belinda.*'

'*Bene, Belinda. Come stai?*'

Belinda blinked. Clemenza roared with laughter and gabbled something long and incomprehensible to Janet, who laughed too, hoping she had not just volunteered Belinda for a ski jump.

'Come.' Clemenza beckoned them to follow.

Clive grinned. 'Happy now?' Owen and Belinda confirmed they were. The three of them followed Clemenza to a secluded part of the slope. It was not much higher than the one Janet had practised on in England but it was a lot harder to climb, owing to the skis' propensity to slide away from her as she moved.

'*Bene,*' said Clemenza again as they lined up opposite her. 'Good. Now …' She swung her legs into the familiar snowplough V. They followed suit. '*Bene …*' She turned and glided gently down to the bottom, signalling for them to follow.

Owen went first, rather too fast, and almost ended up in the Italian mothers. They dusted the flying snow off themselves and continued nattering unperturbed.

Belinda followed, more slowly, and with considerably more style. Clemenza was clearly impressed. '*Bellissima,*' she cooed, clapping her hands together. '*Allora, Mama.*'

Janet, not sure how she felt about being called Mama, edged herself round until she was facing downhill. What had seemed no more than a gentle incline immediately became an escarpment. She stared in horror at their encouraging faces below.

'Come on, Mum. It's easy,' yelled Belinda.

'*Come questo,*' called Clemenza, pointing her skis towards each other. Janet tried to shift her own into the position. Her right leg slithered away from her. She swung her left leg the opposite way and overbalanced completely, crashing down on her bottom and shooting down the hill like a bobsleigher without a sleigh.

'You're meant to lean forward,' said Belinda hotly, aware that the mothers were in fits. Owen was studying the branches of a tree.

Clemenza helped her up, beaming. '*Bene*,' she said. 'We can again.'

After half an hour, Belinda and Owen had transferred to the lift and were being coached on how to turn by the tot-catcher at the top. Clemenza, still beaming, but with the tiniest hint of perspiration, was trying to get Janet to lean over her skis rather than away from them – the reason she was still arriving at the bottom flat on her back.

'Come,' she said at last, ploughing through the children to the foot of the lift. 'You can?'

Janet shook her head. '*Bene*,' said Clemenza in an exhausted voice. 'I make it *prima*.' She grasped hold of the pole and slipped effortlessly on to the lift and away. Halfway up she swung her leg wide and skied down to where Janet was waiting. 'With me. I first,' she said, indicating that she should copy her every move. Again she went up. Two small children whipped in ahead so that by the time the pole came round, Janet had lost track of what she was copying. She was dragged up the hill, half on, half off the seat, finally falling off sideways very close to a group of five-year-olds in mid-descent. This caused a major pile-up, which for the first time that morning had all the mothers simultaneously shrieking and staggering towards their children as though they were digging them out from an avalanche. Savage glances were directed at Janet as she rolled inexorably towards Clemenza who was waiting for her, a look of perplexed bewilderment on her face.

'For today is finish,' she said gravely. 'For tomorrow we make you with the *bambini*. Yes?' She smiled sorrowfully just as Belinda and Owen came swerving towards them, skidding to a halt feet away.

'How're you getting on, Mum?' Belinda asked, her face aglow. 'Paulo says we can go with the Intermediates tomorrow. Wait till I see Dad.'

Owen was grinning all over his face. 'Wait till we tell him you tried to slaughter all those kids,' he chortled.

'That's enough, Owen,' said Janet shortly. 'I did nothing of the kind.' She cast a quick glance at the mothers to see if any of them understood English.

'I'm starving,' said Belinda. 'Look, there's Dad. I'm going to tell him we'll be in his group tomorrow. That means we'll have to go on the chair lift. Weee. Scary.' She unclipped her skis and galloped off to where Hugh was standing talking to Clive. Owen followed suit.

Clemenza was helping the mothers detach their children from their skis. Janet saw her shaking her head and shrugging as the women harangued her. That's me they're talking about, she thought. Well, that's it. I've tried and I can't do it. I don't care what Hugh says, I'm not having a lesson with those children tomorrow. I'll only have to fall over once and half of them will be buried alive. It's not fair.

She undid her skis and wandered over to the others.

'How'd it go?' asked Hugh brightly, clearly only too aware of how it had gone.

'Awful,' said Janet.

Clive laughed. 'Oh, come on, Mrs Gale. It can't have been that bad.'

Janet glowered at him. 'Ask those women over there.'

Clive looked slightly anxious. 'I just need to have a quick word with Clemenza,' he murmured.

Hugh tucked his arm into hers. 'Hungry?'

'I suppose so.'

'Oh, darling, don't look so depressed. It's never easy the first time.'

'How come Blin and Owen are moving up then, after one morning?'

He grimaced. 'Oh well, kids. They're young. It's bound to be different for them, isn't it? I'll tell you something that will amuse you.'

'What?' said Janet, thinking fat chance.

'Cheryl never even set foot on the snow.'

'What?'

'No. She just sat it out all morning. Something about a migraine. She thinks it might be the altitude.'

'But she's been here before. How can you ski if you can't stand the altitude?'

'You tell me. But she sat in the hut all morning. So if you think you're a lousy skier ...'

'I know I'm a lousy skier.'

'At least you had the guts to give it a go.' He bent down and kissed her nose. 'And wearing that hat. That takes even more guts.'

Janet couldn't help laughing.

Chapter Nine

———◆———

'There you are.'

The Gales were seated on the verandah of a giant pizzeria overlooking the slopes. Hugh was planning to take Belinda and Owen for a few practise runs in the afternoon, and Janet was basking in the thought that she could go back to the chalet, have a bath without disturbance and then lie on the bed and read till the others got back.

Bob came striding through the tables towards them. 'Wondered where you'd got to. I meant to tell you, we always get lunch at the Bar Amico.' He pointed to a seedy little shack the other end of the terrace. 'You can get a pizza to share for just under a hundred thou. Very good value. Much better than these places on the front. You're paying for the view, you see.'

'It's worth paying for,' said Janet cheerfully. She had had two glasses of wine and was feeling benign.

'What's this I hear about you knocking all those kiddies over?' asked Bob. 'Clive had us in stitches about it. I understand you're to be put with them tomorrow for your lesson? Is that right?'

Janet stared straight ahead. I must not be goaded, she thought. This man is just a poor pompous fart. I will not let him upset me. She was surprised to hear Hugh saying, as though it were the most obvious thing in the world, 'No, of course she isn't, Bob. We've arranged for Jan to have a few private lessons. Just to give her a push start. I shouldn't be surprised if she's overtaken you by the end of the week.'

Bob positively gaped. '*Private* lessons?' he repeated. 'Crikey, Hugh. That'll cost an arm and a leg, won't it? Round here? And besides, I doubt Janet's Italian is going to be up to it, is it? From what we've heard so far?'

'Rubbish,' said Hugh fiercely. 'She's been chatting away to that woman all morning. Haven't you, darling?'

'Yes,' said Janet. If they were going to lie they might as well go the whole hog.

'Gosh, Mum. Private lessons!' said Belinda with a hint of envy. 'You'll soon be as good as Dad.'

'Better,' said Hugh, so authoritatively that for a moment she almost believed him.

'Where are the others?' she asked, more with a view to avoiding them than anything else.

Bob looked around airily. 'I sent Stuart to buy me some more film for the camera. I've used up two reels since we got here.'

'Whatever on?' asked Janet.

Bob tapped the side of his nose. 'Ahh. That you'll have to wait and see. Actually I've told Stuart to put them in for developing, so we'll be able to have a little showing when I get them back. I can let you have a few prints if there are any that take your fancy.'

'That's very kind,' said Janet politely.

'I daresay you'll let me do the same with yours?'

'Yes,' she agreed, trying to remember if she'd packed a camera.

'I like to make up an album every year.' Bob was warming to his subject. 'Actually I told Cheryl to pack last year's so we could compare. You can have a butcher's at those first, if you like.'

'Thank you,' said Janet, feeling that if Bob were trying to make peace, she should at least endeavour to meet him halfway.

'Over here, Chicken.' He was waving frantically at Cheryl who was standing at the edge of the terrace gazing myopically at the sea of bobble hats. She eventually spotted them and came hurrying over, her face a study in relief.

'I didn't know where you'd gone,' she murmured apologetically, as though it were her fault her husband had abandoned her halfway up a mountain.

'The Gales have opted for the posh part,' declared Bob with artificial jollity. 'I was telling them what good value we get at the Amico.'

A tiny furrow creased Cheryl's unchallenging brow. 'I didn't awfully like the peach pie, actually.'

Bob looked irritated. 'You've always liked it before.'

She sighed. 'Yes, you're right. Perhaps it was the cook's day off?'

'I expect so. Now, what are you going to do this afternoon? Stuart and I are going up to Belvedere so that he can practise his parallels.'

'Oh, Bob, no,' squeaked Cheryl in genuine alarm. 'He's not ready to go up there yet. I was watching him all morning. He kept falling over.'

'All the more reason,' said Bob in a voice that brooked no argument. 'He'll love it.'

'How do you know?'

Everyone turned to Owen, who had been silent up till now.

'What was that?' asked Bob, cocking his hand to his ear.

'I said, how do you know?' repeated Owen, red in the face but determined to stand his ground.

'Because boys do. You're a boy. You should know.'

'I do know,' said Owen stiltedly. 'And you're wrong.'

'I beg your pardon?' said Bob, trying to keep the anger out of his voice.

'If he keeps falling over down here, the last thing he'll want is to be carted off higher up.'

'Aha. Here we have the expert. The young man who, at the tender age of sixteen, is still practising his turns on the nursery slope, takes it on himself to advise an advanced skier on how to help his *fourteen-year-old* INTERMEDIATE son improve his skiing. Well, that is excellent.'

'Oh, fuck off,' said Owen and stalked away.

Silence descended on the group.

'Did Tricia enjoy her lesson?' asked Janet, eventually, in her best hostess voice.

Cheryl turned dazed eyes to her. 'Tricia? Oh yes. I think so. Yes, very much. She's gone ... she's, ummm, arranged to meet that Brian for a coffee somewhere. I didn't think it would matter so long as she's back by teatime.' She looked at Bob nervously.

'No. Why not? She's a big girl now. And Brian seems a nice sort of lad. Polite,' he added pointedly, staring at a spot just past Janet's head.

Janet stood up and picked up her skis. 'Well, if you'll all excuse me I think I'll be on my way.'

'Where are you off to? Quick trip round the Sella Ronda?' asked Bob, chuckling.

'Right first time.'

'Jan's going back down to the village. She wants to have a potter round the shops,' said Hugh in a conciliatory manner.

'Women. Shopping, that's all they think about.'

'And sex,' said Janet, giving him a brazen stare. Bob's mouth fell open like a fish's. Good, she thought. I've embarrassed him. She turned and strolled towards the tramway station. Three whole hours to herself. Bliss. She took a deep breath of the rarefied air. Home, bath, book.

'Janet ... Janet, hang on. I'm coming with you.' Cheryl was stumbling after her, virgin skis dragging behind. 'Bob says he doesn't want me going with them in case I put Stuart off, so I thought you might like some company. It's more fun browsing if you've got someone with you, isn't it?'

Janet struggled to contain her disappointment. 'Actually,

Hugh was joking when he said I wanted to go to the shops, Cheryl. I hate shopping. I was planning to go straight back to the villa and have a nice quiet afternoon by myself.'

'Oh, what a good idea. Well, we'd have to take our skis back anyway, wouldn't we? To tell the truth I'm not all that mad about shops either. I never know what to buy – what's a bargain and what isn't. I leave all that sort of thing to Bob. He enjoys it. I just get in a state and then I end up buying something quite useless and Bob makes me take it back.'

This soliloquy had brought them to the platform. Janet was far more concerned with negotiating the swaying step of the cabin than hearing about Bob's fashion flair.

They began their descent. The lift was a lot less crowded at this time of day, mainly chalet staff reluctantly returning to their duties. Janet recognised the two blonde women they had seen when the coach first stopped, and one or two others who had been at the trivia quiz. Of Annie there was no sign, nor of the legendary Carla. Janet wondered if anyone had turned up yet.

Cheryl was still talking. It was almost as though a plug had been removed and a torrent of bottled-up words was now flowing unrestrainedly out of her, increasing in velocity as gravity dragged them downwards. Janet had very little idea what she was saying because she was fighting her usual battle with the air pressure – something about 'men being men' and 'turning blind eyes', neither of which fitted her impression of Bob.

The ski buses were far fewer in the middle of the day and it was nearly ten minutes before one scrunched into sight. Cheryl had quietened down and seemed deeply concerned in making sure she had enough lire for the fare. 'Bob lets me keep two hundred thousand for emergencies, but it's such a problem, isn't it, with all these noughts on everything?' Set beside a lifetime with Bob McDermot, Janet wondered that anything else could be construed as a problem.

There was no sign of life in the chalet. 'I wonder what Annie's excuse will be today,' she remarked as they surveyed the breakfast dishes still on the table. Cheryl made a little squeaky sound and began piling the plates on top of each other. 'Cheryl, don't you do it. You're on holiday.'

Cheryl tittered feebly. 'I don't mind, really I don't. Anyway, what would the men say if they came back and found it like this?'

Janet took a deep breath. She wanted to shake the woman. She snatched up her jacket. 'I'm going down to the hotel and I'm going to find Annie and tell her this is just not good enough. Fine, we won this holiday in a raffle, but a holiday is what it's meant to be. Not work experience for a life in domestic service.'

Cheryl looked at her with wide eyes. 'Are you going to complain, then?'

'Yes, of course I am. What do you think? If it carries on like this we'll have no one here all week. I don't intend to live off barbecued chicken for the next six days.'

Cheryl gazed at her in awe. 'Do you think it'll be all right? I mean, shouldn't you wait till Hugh gets back or something?'

Janet frowned irritably. 'Whatever for?'

Cheryl looked flummoxed. 'Well . . . I don't know really. Shall I stay here, then? In case anyone turns up?'

'Yes. Good idea. Make yourself a cup of tea and put your feet up for a bit.' At the door she turned. 'And Cheryl . . .'

'Yes?'

'If I come back and it's all done, I shall be seriously annoyed.'

Cheryl baulked. 'I thought I might just light the fire, if that's all right, Janet? I'm a tiny bit chilly.'

Janet relented. 'All right. But don't you touch those dishes.'

Cheryl's face twisted in several directions.

'Promise?'

'Oh dear . . .'

'Promise.'

'Yes, all right. Just the fire.'

✲   ✲   ✲

Annie was not at the hotel, despite a notice saying a representative of the company would be available between two and three thirty every afternoon. Janet left a note at Reception saying she was extremely disappointed to find that no one had been to service their chalet and that if someone had not turned up by five o'clock she intended to get in touch with the London office and lodge an official complaint.

When she got back, the fire was blazing brightly in a gleaming hearth. There was a smell of baking coming from the kitchen, making her regret the fierceness of her note. Probably Carla, or whoever, had arrived the moment she left and had been slaving away ever since. She crossed to the kitchen, only to be met by Cheryl.

'I hope you don't mind,' she stammered. 'I just thought it would be nice to have a few scones ready for when the others got back. I haven't washed up,' she added quickly, pointing virtuously to the breakfast dishes still piled on the table.

Janet felt like a harridan. 'Of course I don't mind, Cheryl. It's a lovely idea. Look, please don't feel you have to take any notice of me. I just don't think it's right that we should be left to fend for ourselves like this. This is the second day. If it goes on like this you'll never get out of the house.'

Cheryl sighed. 'To tell you the truth,' she murmured, 'I wouldn't mind all that much. I'm not awfully keen on skiing. Not that I'd say anything to Bob. It would break his heart when he's tried so hard with me.' She looked up anxiously. 'Promise you won't say a word. I should never have said that. I do like it really, it's just I find it all a bit exhausting. My fault. I should try and keep fit. Bob's always telling me to go to the gym or something. I do mean to, but somehow I never get round to it. I read a lot and that takes up so much time, doesn't it?'

'What do you read?' asked Janet who had never thought of it as a chore.

Cheryl blushed. 'Well, nothing too heavy. Romances, I suppose you'd call them. There's nothing wrong with that, though, is there?' she pleaded, plainly suspecting there was.

'Certainly not,' Janet assured her. 'I love a decent romance.'

Cheryl glowed. 'I've brought lots with me. You're welcome to borrow them, any time you like.'

'Thank you.'

Her face became serious again. 'But when we get back I'm definitely going to take myself in hand. Lose weight. Stop ... I've absolutely made my mind up.'

Janet nodded. 'I'm the same.'

Cheryl smiled. 'Well, I suppose with a man like Hugh you have to keep in trim.'

'Why do you say that?'

'Oh, nothing. Nothing. Just he's a bit of a lad, isn't he? According to Bob.'

Janet relaxed. 'Bob would know. But honestly, Cheryl, I don't care if you never put another foot outside this chalet. In fact, after this morning, I'd be inclined to join you, but that doesn't mean you should act as unpaid skivvy, that's all.' There was a rap on the door. 'I expect that's Annie now.'

It was, dragging behind her – for there was no better way to describe it – a pale young girl bent almost double under the weight of her backpack. 'This is Debbie,' Annie informed them. 'She only arrived this afternoon.'

'Come in.' Janet stood back to let them enter. She wondered if Annie had seen her note. The girl certainly looked as though she might have been snatched off the street and helicoptered in, judging by her expression.

'I'm Janet, and this is Cheryl,' she continued. 'We were just going to make a cup of tea. Would you like some?'

'Yes, please,' whispered Debbie. 'I've been on the coach for sixteen hours.' Not a helicopter, then. Given the choice, Janet thought she would have plumped for a blindfold and parachute.

'I see you've got the fire going,' said Annie, unsure whether to be pleased or apologetic.

'It was no trouble,' said Cheryl, disappearing into the kitchen to make the tea.

Debbie struggled out of her backpack, her eyes falling on the pile of washing-up still on the table. 'Should I make a start on that?'

Janet shook her head. 'Have a cup of tea first. You must be exhausted.'

'I am,' the girl conceded, still hovering by the door.

Annie looked at her watch. 'Well, if it's all right with you, Mrs Gale, I'm going to head back to the hotel. I had to drive over to pick Debbie up and I'm not sure if Clive will have remembered to cover for me.'

'Oh, ummm, yes,' said Janet awkwardly.

'Debbie knows the routine. I've been over it with her on the way. I'll be round in the morning to make sure everything's OK. 'Bye, Debs. Chin up.' She departed. Janet couldn't help thinking she might need the same advice herself when she saw her note, but it was too late now.

Cheryl appeared with tea and a plate of buttered scones. 'Come and sit by the fire, dear,' she enjoined the girl. 'You look frozen over there.'

Debbie did as she was told, eating two scones with about as much relish as an official poison taster.

'Do you want a hand with your bag?' Janet asked, seeing her labouring to get it back on her shoulders.

'No, thank you,' whispered Debbie huskily and began the long trek to her cupboard under the roof.

After half an hour she had not returned. 'Do you think she's all right?' Cheryl asked, clearly itching to start the dinner.

'Oh, I expect so. I daresay she's unpacking,' murmured Janet who was having another go at her column.

Cheryl came and sat opposite her, fingers drumming noiselessly on her knees. Eventually Janet looked up.

Cheryl stopped. 'Am I disturbing you?'

She set aside her scribblings. 'No, of course not.'

Cheryl cleared her throat. 'I'm just a bit worried . . .'

'What about?'

'Ummm, well, Debbie, actually.'

Janet frowned. 'Why, what's the matter with her?'

'Nothing. Oh, nothing at all. I didn't mean that. It's just, you know, she looks rather young. Do you think she's going to be able to manage on her own? I mean, there are rather a lot of us.'

'I imagine so. Otherwise why would she have taken the job?'

'Yes, yes. I'm sure you're right. I just wondered if you thought it would be all right if I offered to help her a little? Just for the first night. Just to show her where things are and that in the kitchen. I wouldn't interfere . . .'

Janet began to feel like a mother confessor. 'I'm sure she'd be delighted, Cheryl, if that's what you want to do.'

'I have been here before, after all. I do know where things are kept.'

'Yes.'

'You think it would be all right, then?'

'Ask her. She can only say no.'

Cheryl looked nervous. 'Do you think she might?'

Janet shook her head wearily. 'I really don't know, Cheryl. Now, if you'll excuse me, I think I'll go and have a bath before the others get back.'

'Oh yes. Good idea. Which one are you going to use?'

'The one next to the girls' room.'

'Oh, right. I think I might take a leaf from your book, then. Only I prefer the one next to us. It's . . .' Imagination failed her.

Yours, Janet thought unkindly. She smiled. 'See you later, then.'

'Yes. Later. Fine. Enjoy your bath.'

'And you.'

First Impressions

Despite an early start we all arrived at our destination determined to get out in the snow as soon as possible. After a delicious buffet lunch we explored the beautiful village and returned to our chalet in time for a superb three-course dinner. After that, down to the local hostelry for a trivia quiz. This proved enormous fun and our team was lucky enough to come second. Celebrations all round!

This morning we were all up early, raring to go. After a hearty breakfast it was off to the slopes for our first skiing lesson. And what fun that proved to be!

Debbie, our friendly chalet girl, has just arrived and is already settling in well.

Chapter Ten

What on earth is that? Janet sat up – she could hardly do anything else considering the shape of the bath – and cocked her ear. It sounded like someone shouting. A woman's voice. Cheryl's, to be more exact. From directly below.

The voice rose and fell, interspersed with silences. Janet strained to hear if anyone was on the receiving end of the tirade, but if they were they had clearly been struck dumb by its intensity.

Curiosity got the better of her. She winched herself out of the bath and dried herself hurriedly. Flinging on her dressing-gown, she padded out on to the landing and down the stairs.

There was no one in the lounge. She went through into the kitchen. Debbie was standing by the fridge, a look of sheer panic on her pale face. Cheryl stood opposite, features tight with fury.

'Is everything all right?' Janet asked, much as she might at the scene of a murder.

Cheryl swung round, clearly unnerved. 'Oh, it's just this silly girl has thrown away a bottle of lemonade I left in the cupboard. Why people can't leave things alone, I'll never understand,' she muttered agitatedly.

'It was flat,' whispered Debbie. 'It was only half full so I

99

shook it and there were no bubbles left, so I poured it away. I can order some more for the morning.'

'Yes, yes,' said Cheryl in an odd voice. 'Oh, it really doesn't matter. It's not important. I think I'll go and have a lie down. All this fresh air exhausts me.' She gave a little laugh and hurried out of the room. Debbie and Janet faced each other.

'I expect Mrs McDermot's a bit tired,' said Janet. 'We all are.' She smiled. Debbie gazed at her red-eyed and Janet reflected that it was probably not a sensitive remark to someone who had just endured a sixteen-hour coach journey.

'Are you a keen skier?' she asked, to change the subject.

Debbie shook her head violently. 'I hate it. I've only been once and I just felt sick all the time.'

'Whatever made you want to be a chalet girl, then?' asked Janet, at a loss. 'I thought that was all they came for. That and the night life.' She didn't add that she suspected Debbie might dread that, too.

She shrugged. 'Mummy said I'd enjoy it. She said I'd have a great time.' She sank down at the table, put her face in her hands and burst into tears.

Janet debated what to do. 'Would you like another cup of tea?' she asked, afraid that too much sympathy would make matters worse.

'Yes please.'

She hunted around for matches and set the great tin kettle on the stove. Debbie found her handkerchief and blew wretchedly into it. 'I wish I'd never come. I really do.'

'You're tired after your journey,' soothed Janet. 'You'll feel better when you've had a good night's rest.'

Debbie sniffed. 'They never said it would be like this.'

'Like what?' she asked, thinking they could compare disillusionment.

Debbie hiccupped. 'Like this.'

Although it did not seem the moment, Janet thought she had better clarify the arrangements. 'Cheryl – Mrs McDermot has stayed here before. She wondered if you might like a little help with the meal this evening? She quite enjoys cooking, you see. It would be no trouble.' The look of horror on Debbie's face persuaded her she should try and occupy Cheryl elsewhere. 'I'll leave you to it then, shall I? Yell if you want anything. The saucepans are under the cooker.'

Debbie nodded and sniffed despairingly. 'I'm very sorry about Mrs McDermot's lemonade. Truly I am.'

'I shouldn't give it another thought,' said Janet, thinking about it all the way upstairs.

'So we have a chalet girl?' Hugh had bumped into Annie in the village.

Janet was drying her hair. 'We have at the moment.'

'What does that mean?'

'Well, she arrived looking like a victim of the white slave trade and then Cheryl reduced her to tears.'

'Cheryl? I find that hard to believe.'

'I was pretty gobsmacked myself. One minute she was asking me if I thought Debbie would let her help with the dinner and the next she was screaming at the girl.'

'What on earth about?'

'That was the stupid thing. Nothing. A bottle of lemonade, for heaven's sake. Debbie had thrown it out because she thought it was flat and Cheryl went completely ape. It was most peculiar. You'd've thought she'd turned off her saline drip.'

Hugh glanced at her but said nothing. 'Fancy a whisky?'

'What I'd actually like,' said Janet, 'would be a giant g and t. I don't suppose you could persuade Bob and Cheryl to part with some gin, could you? Seeing as Bob's had half our whisky already.'

Hugh grimaced. 'Is there no end to your demands?'

✻　　✻　　✻

'Gin all right?' Hugh, having succeeded in his endeavours, was looking for a fitting reward. He was sitting on the edge of the bed.

'It's OK.'

'Only OK? After what I went through to get it?'

'What did you go through?'

'Bob looking aggrieved and pretending he couldn't find it, then Cheryl wittering on about how she'd only wanted to help and she couldn't imagine what had got into the girl. I don't know. They're both bats if you ask me. So, what's wrong with the gin?'

'Nothing. It's just a bit ...'

'Bit what?'

'Weak.'

'It can't be. I put masses in.'

'Oh well, perhaps it's just me. Anyway, I could do with another. And we ought to go down or they'll be wondering what's happened to us.'

'I doubt it. You can hear everything through these floorboards.'

'Oh God, you can't, can you?' asked Janet aghast.

Hugh laughed. 'No, of course not. Well, if you can, Bob and Cheryl must be having a very celibate holiday.'

She shuddered. 'I'd really rather not think about it, if you don't mind.'

Cheryl was not there when they went downstairs. Bob muttered something about 'washing her hair' and not to wait for her. He had plainly taken his own advice because he was halfway through a very large whisky. Janet let Hugh pour her another gin, watching to see if his idea of 'masses' equalled her own. It seemed to.

There was no sign of life from the kitchen. She resisted the temptation to put her head round the door and see if Debbie had put hers in the oven. It was surprisingly quiet for someone preparing a meal for eight. She would give it five more minutes then check.

'How did you and Stuart get on?' Hugh asked Bob. He had already told Janet how impressed he had been by their own children's progress. 'Blin's got a natural bent for it. Owen would be all right if he listened. All he cares about is speed. No finesse. He's OK, though. Good sense of balance.'

She had listened to this with a growing sense of gloom. Was she to be the only member of the Gale family whose acquaintance with snow was purely horizontal?

Bob was talking. 'Lot of talent. We knew that, of course. The instructor spotted it the first year we took him. Val Thorens. What was Stuart then? Ten? Eleven? "Championship material there," he said. The lad's shaping up nicely, I've got to admit. He's the one that could do with some private tuition. If you ask me, it's wasted on beginners.'

Janet swirled the ice round in her glass. 'Still, he's got you, Bob. That must make all the difference.'

Bob nodded seriously. 'I'm not a professional, though, you see, Jan. What he needs is someone trained to pick up on any little problems. Still,' he sighed and looked around for the whisky bottle, 'you need big dollars to pay for something like that.'

They were interrupted by the arrival of Owen and Belinda who had been into the town looking for souvenirs or, in Owen's case, the girl from Chalet Meriel, as he had now discovered.

Belinda had been more successful than he, her arms fairly brimming with carved wooden boxes and keyrings. 'We met Clive,' she informed them, scattering her parcels in amongst the cutlery. 'He says there's tobogganing tomorrow night. We've put our names down for it. It's only a thousand lire.'

'A hundred thousand,' Owen corrected.

'Oh, well, something,' continued Belinda. 'They keep the lights on right up the mountain till eleven o'clock at night. We've got to go.'

'Sounds fun,' agreed Hugh. 'Did you put us down for it too?'

'Sort of.'

'She means she told Clive to ask you for the money,' said Owen.

There was a crash as Stuart attempted to jump from the top of the stairs to the landing, knocking a picture off the wall as he did so. 'I want to go to that, Dad,' he yelled. 'D'you remember last year when that guy hit that stump?'

'I do indeed,' said Bob cheerfully. 'He had to be airlifted to hospital in Verona. End of his holiday.'

Janet felt the familiar nausea sweep over her. 'Where's Tricia?' she asked, to take her mind off death by toboggan.

Belinda shrugged. 'We saw her in one of the coffee bars.'

The question was resolved by the sound of a high-pitched giggle outside the front door then a car driving away. Tricia let herself in, her face immediately resuming its habitual scowl. 'What are you all staring at?' she demanded.

'Is that you, Tricia?' Cheryl came hurrying down the stairs before anyone had time to answer.

'Who else did you think it would be? Father Christmas?'

'Well, you never know with all this snow,' her mother tittered. She looked rosier than usual.

'Who was that in the taxi?' asked Tricia. This time everyone did stare at her. Then they rushed to the kitchen door.

'I'm trying to get Claire for you.' Annie, surrounded by the debris of Chalet Nevosa's second takeaway dinner, backed away as the company closed in on her. She had taken the precaution of leaving the front door on the latch, in deference to her self-defence training on the Duke of Edinburgh's Award scheme. For the first time in fifteen years she suspected it might come in handy. 'I really am terribly sorry. Nothing like this has ever happened before. I knew she was feeling a bit homesick, but a lot of them do. It wears off after a few days. Once they've got into the swing of things.'

'As far as I can see,' said Hugh in a frighteningly calm voice, 'the swing of things round here is slightly less jolly than Ramadan. We have been here nearly two days and we have yet to have a cooked meal. I know the guy who owns this company. I have known him since he started it up. I was a guest at his wedding, but let me tell you, if we do not have a fully qualified, fully competent cordon bleu chalet girl here by first light tomorrow, I am going to take out a full-page advertisement in the *Daily Telegraph*, telling people just what they can expect from a holiday with Ski Dreams.'

Annie nodded silently. 'I'll do my best,' she murmured, feeling behind her for the door.

As if tepid kebabs were not sufficient punishment, they were no sooner digested than Bob announced his intention of showing everyone the photographs of last year's trip.

Hugh and Janet made polite noises, while Belinda rolled her eyes and Owen, who had not spoken a word to Bob since their exchange at the pizzeria, merely stared morosely ahead of him.

'Right,' said Bob when they were settled round the fire with their coffee and the Gales' brandy. 'Who's going to fetch the piccies?' He beamed at Cheryl, who rose quietly and went to get them.

Janet, while accepting that they would be unlikely to get away with less than two albums, was shocked to see Cheryl labouring down the stairs with two carrier bags.

'We've brought a few of some of our other holidays,' she wheezed, setting them down in front of her husband.

'Let's hope they were more successful than this one,' Hugh grumbled under his breath to Janet.

'How do you want to start, dear?' Cheryl asked.

'Oh, I think probably as we mean to continue,' chuckled

Bob. 'Let's show them last year's version, then they'll know what they're up against.' He fumbled about in the bag, selecting folders and thrusting them back till finally he lit upon a particularly bulbous bundle, held together with thick elastic bands. 'This looks like what I'm looking for.' He dragged off the bands. 'Yes, Villa Nevosa, nineteen ninety-nine. These are the ones. Right. I think if I pass them to Hugh, he can start the ball rolling.'

Owen had refused outright to join the circle and was sitting at the table with an SAS novel which Janet hoped wouldn't give him too many hints on how to dispose of Bob. Belinda merely scanned them before flicking them into her mother's lap where they piled up with frightening speed.

The first few were of the outside of the villa, similar to the one in the brochure except that they were mostly out of focus. Next came the hall, piled high with coats and skis, then the sitting room, the kitchen, the stairs . . .

If Janet had been conducting a murder inquiry she would doubtless have found such detail a godsend, but just why anyone on a skiing holiday should expend an entire reel of film on the interior of their accommodation was more than she could fathom.

The second envelope was more interesting in that it showed people – Cheryl unpacking a case. Bob opening the blinds and Stuart eating his breakfast, the last of more use to a fluoride advocate than as a lasting memento of a holiday.

There was one of Bob in the sunshine, then Bob in the shade, Tricia asleep, Stuart asleep (still with his mouth open). Tricia awake, Cheryl halfway between the two, and so on. A more lifeless collection of snapshots it would be hard to envisage.

Janet began to wonder if the minutiae of detail, flipped through at speed, would give the effect of a home video. She wondered if she dared try it. At this pace they would be here all night.

Cheryl asked if anyone would like more coffee. Hugh leapt up. 'Here let me give you a hand with that tray.' He took the heavy wooden tray from her and the two of them disappeared into the kitchen.

'Don't be too long,' Bob called. 'I've got Tripoli here for you next. Some jolly interesting stuff there, I can tell you.'

They had done Skye and were halfway through Malta when the pair finally emerged with the fresh coffee. Janet glanced at her husband enviously, wondering what sort of excuse she could conjure up to avoid the onslaught of Bob and Cheryl on the west coast of Ireland.

Belinda had fallen asleep. Janet would have suggested she put her to bed but for a niggling fear that Bob might produce his camera and record the event for future humiliation.

At a quarter to eleven the last photograph was put back in its folder. Janet's foot had gone to sleep. Tricia was barracking Owen to take her into town. He was resisting fiercely because, although he would have liked to go, he had not the slightest intention of being shackled with Tricia for the rest of the night.

Janet suspected this would not be the case, but she no more wanted her son being called to account for Tricia's nocturnal activities than he did himself. Tricia finally slammed off to the bedroom where she turned up her radio full blast till Belinda came tiptoeing tearfully into her parents' room to say could she sleep on their floor because she was never going to get any rest in her own room. This prompted Hugh to have a few sharp words with Tricia which, surprisingly, seemed to do the trick.

As they lay in bed gazing out at the black night sky, Hugh groaned slightly.

'What's the matter?'

'Nothing. I was just thinking I don't think I've ever been so tired.'

'It's all the fresh air.'

'It's nothing of the kind. It's having to spend two and a half hours looking at the most boring bloody collection of photographs I have ever come across in my life. I mean, for God's sake! Cheryl holding a cup of tea, Cheryl not holding a cup of tea, Cheryl sitting on the bed, Bob standing up. What are these people about?'

'What I found a bit curious was the fact that they say they've been on holiday with all these people, the Greens, the Blakes, the Phillips, and there's never a single picture of any of them. Don't you think that's odd?'

Hugh was silent for a minute. 'You mean, maybe they don't exist at all?' He turned to her in mock alarm. 'I've just thought of something awful. Suppose we're the only people who've actually fallen for it? No one else has ever actually been daft enough to get on the plane?'

Janet giggled. 'It wouldn't surprise me. Anyway, you got off pretty lightly. You missed all of Skye while you were helping Cheryl with the coffee.'

'That was no picnic, I can tell you. Every time I opened a cupboard she jumped. Nervous wreck. Still, is it any wonder?' He leant over and kissed her cheek. 'Goodnight, Mrs Gale. Let's get some sleep before the dawn chorus gets to us.'

'Bob's alarm, more like.'

'That's what I meant.'

Janet lay for a while. 'Hugh, are you asleep?'

'Hmmm?'

'About tomorrow.'

'What about it?'

'I don't have to go for a lesson with all those chil- dren, do I? I don't think I could bear it. Couldn't I just watch you and Blin and Owen? You said that's all Cheryl did today.'

Hugh opened one eye and looked at her. 'I reckon that's all she'll do all week.'

Janet brightened. 'Well then?'

Hugh closed his eye again. 'You could, my darling. Of course you could but for one small thing.'

'What? What small thing?'

'I've arranged for you to have some private lessons.'

Chapter Eleven

The foreboding in Janet's stomach when she woke next morning was even worse than that she had felt the day before. For a moment she wondered whether she was ill as she struggled to cope with the leaden lump, but then it came to her. She was to have private skiing lessons.

Why hadn't she just kept her mouth shut and stuck with the kindergarten? With Belinda and Owen promoted to Intermediates there would have been no one to monitor her progress, and she was pretty certain Clemenza would have been all too happy to leave her to her own devices.

Matters were not helped by the McDermot family's indecent interest in the situation. 'Who're you having?' demanded Tricia, her temper not much improved by a good night's sleep.

Janet shook her head distractedly. 'I've no idea. Hugh arranged it all. It's only for this morning, isn't it? Just to help me try and get my balance.'

Hugh smiled but refused to be drawn on the details.

'I wonder if it's Giuseppe,' mused Belinda who had taken a good look at the instructors during the lunch break. 'He's got the most scrummy brown eyes. He looks like Nicholas Cage.'

'Doesn't,' said Owen. 'Nicholas Cage hasn't got brown eyes, anyway.'

'Who do I mean then?' asked Belinda.

'Al Pacino?'

'Oh, come off it. He's ancient. Giuseppe's much younger than that.'

'How do you know?'

'I just do. Maybe Mum will have Vittorio.' She shuddered dramatically. 'Pity you if you do, Mum. He's creepy.'

'No he's not,' snapped Tricia.

'He is. He keeps trying to put his hand on all the women's bums.'

Tricia snorted contemptuously. 'Oh really, you are so juvenile. Do you know that?'

'Just because you think he fancies you. He does that to all the women. I was watching.'

'Not you, I take it?'

'I wouldn't let him,' said Belinda hotly. 'I'm not that desperate.'

'Could have fooled me, the way you were ogling that dork behind the counter.'

'I was not. And he wasn't a dork, anyway.'

'Actually I'd prefer a female,' said Janet. Both girls looked at her.

'Oh Mum, you wouldn't,' said Belinda despairingly.

'I'm sure whoever it is, they'll be fine,' said Hugh in a voice that said the discussion was closed.

'And whoever it is they'll have their work cut out,' put in Bob who was out in the hall fiddling with his skis. 'Anyone seen Stuart? We don't want to get stuck in that crowd at the bus stop again.'

'Why don't you and the others go on?' suggested Cheryl tentatively. 'I can wait for Stuart and we'll catch up with you up there.'

'He should be here,' said Bob crossly, marching to the foot of the stairs. 'Stuart!' he bellowed. '*Stuart!*'

A few seconds later Stuart appeared at the top of the stairs. He was not dressed.

'What time do you call this?' demanded his father. 'We're ready to go. Get dressed this minute. You'll have to skip breakfast.'

'No way,' mumbled Stuart, his mouth the closest to closed Janet had seen it.

'What was that?'

'I said I'm having breakfast.'

Bob tapped his watch. 'Do you know what the time is?'

'Why don't I just wait?' Cheryl intervened again. 'We'll come on a bit later. He won't miss much.'

'He won't miss anything,' insisted Bob. 'I've paid for those lessons. Two hours a morning. Two hours a morning is what he's going to get. They may not be private,' he added viciously, 'but that's no reason to waste them. Now you get back in that room and I want you down here and dressed in two minutes flat, or there'll be no tobogganing tonight.'

Stuart shot back into his room.

'Only way to treat them,' said Bob like some slave-owning tea trader.

'I hope Bob lives to a very great age,' Janet murmured to Hugh as they watched him ploughing to the front of the bus queue.

Hugh looked surprised. 'I would have thought that was the very last thing you wanted.'

'So that Stuart and Tricia can get their revenge.'

He grinned. 'And I bet you hope you live long enough to see it?'

Janet smiled forlornly. 'If I live through this morning I shall be suitably grateful.'

Hugh squeezed her arm. 'Don't worry about it. I asked for the best they had. I explained you'd never skied before, you were a bit nervous . . .'

'A bit?'

'Very nervous. That you spoke a little Italian . . .'

'Oh God, Hugh. You haven't told them I can speak Italian, have you?'

'If you'd let me finish. But that you were certainly not up to understanding technical skiing terms, and that it didn't matter what it cost, I wanted you to enjoy skiing by the end of the week. OK?'

Janet groaned. Didn't her husband know anything about her after all these years? Did he not remember her driving lessons? He could spend the entire Third World debt and she still wouldn't be able to ski at the end of it. She was not that way inclined. She liked music and books and going to the theatre. She did not like pain and humiliation and being frozen to the marrow. And nothing Hugh could say or do was going to change that, even in the hands of velvet-eyed Italians with impossibly romantic names.

A bus came along. Hugh took Janet's elbow and steered her purposefully towards it. 'Trust me,' he said.

'You never told me about this. If you'd told me about this I wouldn't have come.' Janet, nearly in tears, was confronting Hugh who had just let her know that, in order to avail herself of her exorbitant lessons, she would have to travel a further five hundred feet in a chair lift.

'It's all right,' he repeated, not unlike a psychiatrist who is trying to talk someone down from the roof. 'There are four seats to each of them. We'll all go together. It's easy. Trust me.'

'You keep saying that. Give me one reason.'

'Blin and Owen had no trouble with it yesterday.'

'Blin and Owen never have any trouble with anything,' Janet burst out accusingly, immediately feeling guilty for taking her cowardice out on her children.

'All you do,' continued Hugh, still sounding like someone who has a suicidal psychotic on his hands, 'is go through the gate when it opens and sit in the chair, then the guy pulls the bar down. Hey presto! It couldn't be simpler.'

I will never forgive Hugh for this, Janet swore to herself as she sat, left arm pinned above her head by her ski poles, thirty feet above the ground, in solitary splendour, as her two children and the apostate who had sworn before a man of God to love and cherish her as long as they both should live, swung cheerfully ahead of her, the three of them linked in their united glee.

It had been like a scene from a nightmare, the mass of chattering skiers surging inexorably towards the turnstile which admitted them, four at a time, to the revolving bank of seats. Once through, they would shuffle forward till the seats caught up with them from behind and scooped them into the air, at which point a spindly man with a drooping cigarette would slam the bar down across their laps and they would be swept away up the mountain to the next station.

Just how Janet had got separated from her family she still did not understand. The last she remembered was that Belinda had hold of one arm and Hugh the other. It was when they had shouted, 'Now!' and she had, quite naturally, responded 'Now?' that the turnstile had clicked shut again and she had found herself on one side and them on the other. 'Wait for me,' she had pleaded pitifully, but the spindly man had other ideas and Hugh, for all his hand-waving, had not been able to prevent the three of them being sucked into the chair and dispatched.

Janet's natural instinct was to turn and flee, but this is not easily accomplished in a heavy throng and wearing six-foot metal planks on your feet. With a clang as ominous as the guillotine, the turnstile swung open again and she was projected through it.

Her sole hope was that she would be in the company of experienced skiers who would see her safely up the hideous mountain and off the other end. Her shock was therefore doubled when she turned to throw herself on the kindness of strangers, only to find that the massed ranks were clinging fiercely to their chosen companions, and no one had followed her through. Clearly the prospect of being linked in the air to an hysterical foreigner was no more appealing to them than it would have been to her.

She would just have to wait on one side till Hugh came back to rescue her, hopefully in several hours' time.

Spindly had other ideas. Though unprepossessing in appearance, he had a tidy mind. He did not want a quivering female clogging up his system. Shouting did not seem to work, so he did the logical thing and dragged her into the line of fire, waited for the chair to hit the back of her legs and slammed the bar closed before she had a chance to retreat. Unfortunate that she had not had time to free her poles and would arrive at the next staging post with a dead forearm, but that was a small price to pay for efficiency.

Now Janet was travelling, whiter than the snow beneath her, alone up the mountain. The poles were firmly wedged in the top of the shaft, and she, by dint of the loops round her wrist, was likewise suspended. The only way she could see to free herself would be to try and raise the bar a little with her other hand, but since this would inevitably result in her plummeting thirty feet to the ground or, worse still, arriving at the next stage dangling by one wrist from the overhead cable, it was an option she had decided not to pursue.

The rest of her family, while initially alarmed by what had happened, were now in some danger of falling out of their own conveyance, so hysterically were they laughing. Even Hugh seemed convulsed by the prospect of his wife arriving at the top like a slab of frozen lamb.

Janet stared grimly back at their grinning faces, planning just how much she would demand in maintenance payments. She dared not look down. Soft though the snow appeared, who knew what jagged rocks might lie below its surface? People hiked across these mountains in the summer. Pictures of chortling men in lederhosen, one leg perched jauntily on a razor-sharp crag, floated before her eyes.

They were coming to the crest of a mound. As the lift soared over it, she realised with a gasp that she was yards from her destination. Already the contraption was emitting clunks and rattles of a disgorging nature. Failure to disembark would mean only one thing. Transportation even further up the mountain, to a point so remote it was all but hidden in cloud.

Hugh, Owen and Belinda's pew was now lurching downwards. Janet tried to see how they would manage their escape, but just as they slowed down a flurry of snow swept into her eyes, momentarily blinding her, so that when she looked again they were standing some distance from the lift, beaming up at her.

Slowly, with the inevitability of a kamikaze plane, Janet's row of seats slithered towards the ground. 'How do I get out?' she screeched to Hugh who made double-handed pumping gestures, quickening in intensity as he realised she had no idea what he meant.

'Lift the bar up. Lift it. LIFT IT, FOR GOD'S SAKE!'

But she was not strong enough to manoeuvre it with one hand. Slowly the lift began to climb again. She closed her eyes. This is it, she thought. I'm going to the top of the mountain where I shall die of altitude sickness and cold. The next time my body comes round it will be lifeless.

This little rumination was cut short by an enormous clang as the bar shot up and she was dragged, more or less by her neck, into the snow where she lay face down for several seconds as the great iron chair swung over her head and away. This was no time to relax, however, because hard on its heels came the next one, packed with gabbling Italians who seemed hardly to have noticed the body on the ground in front of them.

'Via! E pazza?'

Janet didn't remember much Italian, but she did know the

scowling goblin now hauling her away from the oncoming lift had just asked her if she was mad.

'It's not my fault,' was all she could manage, wiping the snow from her eyes and mouth. She pointed to the lift. *'Orribile! Tutto orribile!'*

The man shrugged and continued to scowl at her. 'You should lift the bar.'

'I couldn't. How could I? I only had one hand.'

Hugh came swishing up. 'I'm sorry, darling. I never thought about you not knowing how to get off.'

Janet turned on him in fury. 'Well, naturally I knew how to get off. Why wouldn't I? I've been travelling on the bloody things all my life.'

Hugh looked suitably chastened. He, too, had had a bit of a fright, although common sense told him they could have phoned the next stopping point and got someone to extricate her there.

'Sorry. Anyway, you're here now. This is Mauro, by the way.'

'Is it?' said Janet savagely, glaring at him. Mauro glared back.

'This is my wife, Jan,' Hugh said to him.

'Is it?' Mauro responded in perfect imitation.

Belinda came swooshing up to them. 'Come on, Dad. We'll be late. Owen's gone on. You all right, Mum?' she added as an afterthought.

'Yes, thank you. Nice of you to ask,' snapped Janet peevishly.

'You did look funny with your arm up like that.' Belinda began to giggle again.

Janet was about to say something but changed her mind. 'Well, don't let me keep you. You've dumped me up here. I suppose I have to go and find someone to teach me to ski next, do I?'

'Not at all,' said Hugh. 'I thought you understood. Mauro

is going to look after you. By the time we get back I shall expect to see you doing parallel turns.' He grinned, nodded to Mauro, and zipped away after Belinda.

Chapter Twelve

Mauro continued to stare at Janet critically. This is marvellous, she thought. Not only has Hugh deserted me but he has left me in the hands of a man who patently loathes me. And he's not even handsome.

Mauro gave a deep sigh. 'This is your first time to ski?'

'How did you guess?'

He frowned. 'I have to ask this. It is the regulation.'

Janet coloured. 'I'm sorry. I didn't mean to be rude. I just wish my husband hadn't done this. No offence to you, but to be perfectly honest I really have no interest in learning to ski at all.'

'Then why have you come on a ski holiday? These things are very expensive.'

Janet closed her eyes. 'It's a long story.'

Mauro rubbed his hands together. 'Well, now you are here, will you take a lesson or shall I put you back on the lift? It is no matter to me. Your husband has already paid.'

Janet was incensed by such pragmatism. 'In that case I'll have a lesson, if it's all the same to you.'

'*Va bene.* Come. We can go further from this lift. There are too many people.' He preceded her down the softly undulating slope to a flatter area. Janet fell over twice. Mauro didn't turn round but she sensed that he knew what was happening.

'Now,' he said when they were safely out of everyone's way, 'your husband has said you can speak Italian? Shall you want your lesson in Italian?'

'*No*,' she squawked. 'Not at all. I only did three terms. I specifically told him not to ... I said I couldn't possibly ...'

'This is OK, then. I cannot speak it either.'

She stared at him. 'What do you mean? I thought you were Italian.'

Mauro shook his head dismissively. 'I am Ladino. Do you know what this is?'

'Latin?' she suggested, thinking he looked less like a gigolo than anyone she had ever seen. He was short, five foot nine at best, his mouse-brown hair was thinning and his grey-green eyes glittered more with scorn than seductiveness.

'Ladin is for this part of the mountains only. Once this has been its own country. We have our own king, our own laws, our own language. Now is only the language is left. So, now you have learnt one thing.' He gave a short laugh. 'Your husband's money is not wasted.'

Janet bristled inside her jacket. She must not rise to him. If she had handled two days of Bob McDermot she could sure as hell handle two hours of a chippy ski instructor. 'Your English is excellent,' she informed him graciously.

'I know.'

'Where did you learn it?'

'Where will I learn it? In London, of course. I was a waiter. Three, four years. Till I was married.'

'Is your wife English?' asked Janet, wondering what English woman would put up with his arrogance.

'No, no. She is from my village. This is enough. Now I will teach you how to ski. Where are your legs?'

'I'm sorry?'

'This is simple enough. Where are your legs?'

'The usual place,' said Janet. 'Below my hips. Is that a problem?'

'Ah, you are clever. So, yes, it is wrong. When you ski it is wrong. When you ski you must make your legs wider like this.' He demonstrated. Janet spread hers accordingly. 'So. Now bend your knees.' He bounced yo-yo-like up and down, reminding her more than ever of a leprechaun. 'You can do this?' Janet tried one or two cautious bends. 'Yes, but more. Do what I am doing. You see.' He continued to bounce. Janet tried again. 'Yes, this is good. More. Keep going.'

'It hurts.'

'How can it hurt? It is only your legs.'

'They feel as though they're going to snap.'

'This is because you have not done this before. Every day before you ski you must do this for ten minutes. It is your housework.'

'Homework.'

Mauro scowled. 'Shall I correct your Italian?'

Janet straightened up. 'I'm sorry. I was only trying to help.'

'Here I am paid to help you. If I pay you, you can help me.'

'I doubt you could afford me,' she retorted, stung.

'No, probably not. Or I would not have to teach for my living, huh?'

So that's it, Janet reflected. A champion *manqué*. He must be nearer fifty than forty. The grapes are well on the turn.

'OK. So now I will teach you to snow-plough.'

'I know how to do that. At least . . .' She could have bitten her tongue off. 'It's just I had a session on the dry slope before we came. I know it's not the same as snow . . .'

'No, but of course, I must not waste your time. You will please show me your snow-plough which you have learnt on an old rope mat. Perhaps this will help me to ski on the roads? Yes?'

Janet snow-ploughed into the side of a bush.

'Yes I see. But I would say the purpose of the snow-plough is to prevent this happening, not to make it happen quicker.'

Janet, half-choked with the frozen foliage, pulled herself out. 'I said I'd only been once.'

'Perhaps this is a good thing or you might go even faster into the bushes?'

Shivering, she tried again, avoiding the bush but losing her balance as a result. Mauro watched as she struggled to get up. 'First you must uncatch the ski.'

'I'm trying to. It won't come.'

'Try some more or you may freeze to death in the snow.'

'I daresay that's what you'd prefer,' snapped Janet, horribly close to tears. 'Or don't you get paid if I die halfway through the lesson?'

Mauro grunted and swooped down and unfastened her ski. 'What will you do if you are alone and this happens? That is why I say you must do it. Not because I want you to die. Anyway I am paid already, I have told you.'

'That's all right then,' she muttered.

'See. See how I do it.' He popped open his ski and stepped out of it.

'Yes, but you're standing up.'

Mauro duly lay in the snow with his skis over his head and still managed the manoeuvre. 'Now try again. You need not have your feet so high.'

'Jolly good.' Janet sat in the snow and eventually managed to extricate herself.

'That is good. Now put it on again and you can ski some more.'

The ski would not go on. Try as she might her boot refused to trigger the catch. After three or four tries she turned to him. 'It won't stay on.'

'This I can see.'

'I don't know what to do.'

'If you are alone on a mountain you must know what to do.'

'Well, would you mind telling me?' she almost shouted,

tempted to add that the odds of her being alone on the mountain were about as likely as her winning the lottery.

Mauro pointed to the ski. 'It is full of snow. Of course your boot will not stay in. It cannot ...' he flapped his hand around, 'what is the word? Attach?'

'Grip?' suggested Janet.

'Grip. Yes, that will do. First you must clear the snow away from inside the ski.'

'What with?'

'With a Hoover, naturally.' Janet stared at him. Mauro made a noise like a rattlesnake and dived once more at her foot. 'With your hands, with your glove, with a stick – whatever you can.' He clawed at the clogged up snow. 'Now try, please.'

Janet slipped her boot into the ski. It clicked smoothly into place. 'Thank you,' she said, chastened. 'I should have realised.'

'On the contrary, I am paid to show you these things.' He gave a stiff little bow.

Let's hope the money doesn't run out while I'm in mid-air, she reflected grimly.

Mauro handed her her poles. 'What is the first thing you must do when you are skiing?'

'I don't know.'

'What do you think? Close your eyes. Picture yourself. You are on top of the mountain. You are going to ski all the way down to the bottom. What do you tell yourself?'

'That I am mad?'

'Other people can tell you that. No, you say "I am here. I am high up. I want to be low. So, I must bend down. I must be low to the ground. I must bend my knees."' He placed both hands on Janet's shoulders and exerted so much pressure that she was practically genuflecting by the time he let go. 'Now. Lean forward. Forward.' He gave her a tiny shove. She keeled over and was once more nose down in the snow.

'You have a problem with balance,' he told her when he'd dug her out.

Janet glared up at him from the rapidly forming puddle she was sitting in. 'I have a problem with everything, Mauro. Why don't you just say it? I am never going to be able to ski. Never in a million years. I am the worst person you have ever had to teach, aren't I? Just say it, and we can stop pretending.'

'You are not the worst. Not the worst at all. My wife, she was the worst. She fell over so many times I had to marry her.'

Janet smiled despite herself. 'I don't quite follow. Is it a tradition round here?'

Mauro stooped and picked up her ski poles which were in danger of rolling away. 'She had so many bruises her family thought I must be beating her, so they said if that was what I wanted to do I must marry her first. Then it would be OK.'

Janet fairly gawped. 'That's not true?'

Mauro shrugged. 'No, but for a moment you believed me. That is interesting.'

'I didn't. Honestly I didn't,' she fibbed. 'You just caught me off guard. Of course I didn't think that ... that ...'

'That I could be so cruel? But why not? You think I have been cruel to you? Yes?'

She said nothing.

'You are right. And I will be cruel to you all the time, till you do what you have come here to learn to do. Come. We will try again.'

Janet struggled up, Mauro making no attempt to help her.

'Now, listen to what I am telling you. Remember, when you are skiing you want to get to the bottom, so you lean forward. If you lean back you are going back up the mountain. This you do not want.'

'You can say that again.'

'So why do you do it?'

'Because ... If I lean forward I'll fall over.'

'How do you know? You have not done it yet. Beside

anyway, you fall over when you lean back so what is the difference?'

'I'll fall over more,' muttered Janet rebelliously. Mauro looked at her angrily but said nothing. He executed one or two very fast figures of eight which she suspected was his way of counting to ten, then swished to a stop in front of her.

'Now, please, I must ask you to trust me. Do you believe I know what I am doing?'

'Of course I do. It's not that ...'

'It is what then? Do you think your husband has asked me to kill you on this mountain? It is a very expensive way, when you can do it so easily yourself.'

Janet shivered. I hate this man, was running through her mind. I hate him more than Bob McDermot, if that's possible. At least I have the consolation of knowing Bob's an idiot. With this one I can't tell.

Mauro was watching her. 'You are thinking I do not like this man or his teaching?'

She was shaken to think her thoughts were so transparent. 'I just wish you wouldn't act as though I'm not trying. I am. You don't know what it's like for me. You've probably been skiing all your life. It's natural for you. The most snow I've ever seen is a couple of inches on the pavement and that's usually gone by lunchtime.'

Mauro scowled then suddenly his face broke into a smile. 'Gone by lunchtime? You are right. When I was in London, if it snowed it was gone by lunchtime. Always.' He sighed and seemed momentarily lost in his thoughts, then just as quickly he snapped back to the present. 'Here,' he waved his arm, 'I don't think the snow will be gone by lunchtime, so we must learn to live with it. Not live with it, conquer it. You understand?'

'I understand for you. But for me it's not necessary.'

'Why? You are a woman. You are a human being. How can you let nature beat you? It is nothing. It is human beings who control the world. Yes?'

'Up to a point.'

'Up to a point! You believe me, here, in the mountains, if you do not rule them they will rule you. It is a fact.'

Janet would have preferred to discuss philosophy in warmer surroundings. 'Well, I just think you should try and be a bit more understanding,' she repeated feebly.

Mauro nodded. 'I understand. But perhaps you should understand me a little too. I am trying to teach you to ski and you are trying not to learn. This is unpleasant for us both.'

'I'm *not* trying not to learn. That's just what I mean. Just because someone can't, it doesn't mean they don't want to.'

'I know that.'

'Well then.'

'Well then what? Do you think I don't know when I look at a person if they can learn to ski or not? You are right. I have grown up in the mountains. I know what is possible and what is not. And I know with you it is possible for you to learn, but for some reason, I do not know why, you do not want to.'

Janet stared at him. 'That's ridiculous. Why on earth would I be here if I didn't want to learn? Do you think I would let Hugh purposely waste his money, *our* money, on lessons and then not try to make some use of them? That is the most stupid thing I've ever heard.' Mauro looked at her silently. Janet stared at her feet. 'Anyway, if that's what you think, why do you suppose I don't want to learn? Answer me that.'

He turned away. 'How can I know the reason? I don't know you. I don't know your husband. Maybe it is revenge?'

'*Revenge?* Revenge for what, for heaven's sake?'

'Who knows? Maybe because he has brought you on a holiday you do not like. Maybe he has done something before you do not like. Maybe this is how you say "I do not like what you have done".'

Janet swallowed. She felt as though something she had never known about herself had suddenly had a spotlight shone on it. 'You're quite wrong,' she said shortly, gripping her poles purposefully. 'You couldn't be more wrong if you tried. I want to learn to ski. I want it more than anything in the world.'

Mauro gave an imperceptible nod. 'OK. That is fine. Now we will do some more snow-ploughs, then perhaps I will buy you some coffee. If they are good ones.'

Janet, not daring to ask what he would do if they were not, concentrated till her head swam. He skied backwards in front of her, no longer sneering but encouraging her. 'This is good. OK, push out with your heels. Out. *Out*. Yes, good, this is OK. Bend your knees. Lean forward. More. *More*. Good. OK.'

She slithered to a halt inches from him. 'There,' he pointed behind her. 'Now you have skied.' Janet turned. Impossible to believe but she had travelled at least thirty feet without falling over.

'Gosh!' was all she could think of to say.

'Gosh!' Mauro mimicked. 'Now we go back up.'

They practised for over an hour till Janet felt her knees would split open if she had to bend them again.

Her arms ached from prodding her way up the slope, her fingers ached from fighting the catch on her skis, and her head ached from trying to take in everything he was telling her, but little by little she was getting there.

'What is this you are doing?' he demanded as she endeavoured to introduce a refinement. She picked herself out of the snow.

'Nothing. I was just . . .'

'Just what?'

'Crushing a walnut.'

There was a silence so total they might have stepped off the edge of the world.

'You were what?'

Janet blushed. 'Crushing a walnut – between my knees. That's what they said to do at the dry slope.'

Mauro's lip curled. 'Well, perhaps that is why they are still skiing on a rope mat. If you want to ski on snow perhaps you can listen to what I tell you.'

'Sorry.'

'Yes. All right. Now I will buy you some coffee. Here, take off the skis. It is enough for one day.'

Gratefully Janet snapped open her skis and the two of them tramped across the snow to the café.

'I should have bought these,' she said as Mauro sat down with two steaming glasses.

'Tomorrow you can buy them.'

'Tomorrow?' Her mouth went dry.

'After your lesson. Tomorrow I will teach you to turn.'

'But ... I thought ...'

Mauro looked at her over the top of his glass. 'What did you think?'

'I thought I was only having one lesson. Just to get my balance ... I mean, I thought Hugh said ...'

Mauro shrugged. 'Your husband has said, "My wife cannot ski. Teach her."'

'Oh, but surely ... No one can learn to ski properly in a week, can they? Least of all me.'

He shrugged again. 'This depends.'

'What on?'

'On the pupil. On the teacher. On how much they want to learn.'

Janet shook her head wretchedly. 'I haven't set my sights on the Olympics, Mauro. I'm very grateful for what you've taught me this morning but, honestly, it's enough. We're only here for a few days. I don't want to spend it doing knee bends and things. I just want—'

'Aha!' Bob McDermot had spotted them. 'There you are. How did it go? Bloody disaster, I suspect, eh? The kids were telling us about you getting stuck on the chair lift. Hilarious.

Wish I'd had my camera. Could've sold it to *You've Been Framed*.'
He turned to Mauro. 'How'd the old lady do, then? Bet you
wish you'd never taken her on?'

Mauro looked at Bob unemotionally. 'On the contrary. Mrs
Gale will make a very fine skier. I have said to her she must go
on the night skiing at the end of the week.'

Janet watched as Bob's eyebrows shot towards his hairline.
'Oh, come on. You're kidding. She can hardly stand up without
falling over. Must have been a pretty dramatic improvement.
Hear that, Hugh?' he yelled at Hugh who had just arrived with
the others. 'The guy here says your missus is ready for night-time
skiing. Pull the other one, eh? It's got bells on.'

Hugh, looking bemused, came over to them. 'Go all right,
did it?' he asked cautiously.

Mauro nodded. 'Fine. I was telling your friend how good
your wife will be. She is a natural skier. Once she has her
confidence – pouf! She will ski like the wind.'

Hugh's face broke into a beam. 'Well, that is excellent news.'
He turned to the others. 'Hear that, you lot? Mummy's going
to beat the lot of us, according to Mauro.'

The others registered a mixture of surprise, disbelief and,
in Belinda's case, delight. 'I knew you'd love it, Mum. Can we
come again next year?'

Janet smiled nervously. 'I think Mauro's exaggerating. I'm
not quite ready to turn professional yet.'

Mauro stood up. 'But by Friday you will be,' he said
solemnly. 'Now, if you excuse me, I have another lesson.'

'That guy must be raking it in,' said Bob loudly as he walked
away. 'Mind you, that's the way to make money, isn't it? Fool
people into thinking they've got what it takes, so they keep
coming back for more. Wish I'd thought of that.'

Janet knew from a tiny movement of Mauro's head that
he had heard what Bob said. She felt unaccountably furious.
'Actually, Bob,' she said as clearly as she could manage, 'you
did think of it. No one else would stoop so low.'

Chapter Thirteen

The chalet had been cleaned when Janet got back but there was still no sign of any resident staff. She had stopped in the village on the way back to escape Cheryl, who had expressed a desire to go home and lie down, citing the continuing threat of migraine.

Gazing in the chic shop fronts Janet was forced to conclude that fashion-conscious skiers plainly preferred to hurtle to their doom unspotted in cream or silver rather than risk rescue in electric blue and crimson.

Armed with a selection of postcards, she bought herself a cappuccino and settled on a little terrace overlooking the main square to write them.

> *Editor,* Kent Leader
> *Dear Bill Oswald,*
>   *Haven't forgotten our conversation at the ComMend party. Think you'll like what I've done so far.*
>   *Will be in touch when I get back.*
>   *Janet Gale*

> *Tuesday Volunteers*
> *Dear All,*
>   *Hope everyone's recovered now. Having a wonderful time. The clothes look fantastic.*
>   *Janet*

A splosh of coffee landed on her salopettes. She rubbed it in.

> *Dear Harriet,*
>> *What did I ever do to you! Wish you were here.*
> *Love,*
>> *Jan*

Across the road two men were pasting up posters. She squinted to see what they were for. One was a disco, another for some sort of display, the details too small for her to decipher, and the third, a giant picture of a midnight sky, full moon shining on to a gaudy mish-mash of skiers cascading down the mountainside. *VENITE, TUTTI*, it screamed. *LO SKI DALLA LUNA. TUTTI BENVENUTI.* Skiing by moonlight. 'Lunatic' took on a whole new meaning.

She crept into the chalet and stealthily deposited her skis. She had no wish to disturb Cheryl if she was trying to sleep, or anyway, if the truth were known.

It was only four o'clock. She reckoned she had a good hour before the others got back. She would make herself a cup of tea and get on with her column. The postcard to Bill Oswald had energised her. She really must have something good to show him by the end of the holiday.

There was a note on the dining table. 'I have been in touch with Head Office and they are flying out someone straightaway. She will be here tomorrow morning. Meanwhile I will arrange for someone to be with you by five to cook dinner. I am hoping to get Claire. Thank you for your patience. Annie Venn. Supervisor Ski Dream Tours.'

Ex-supervisor, if Hugh gets back before this Claire does, Janet thought dispassionately. She opened the kitchen door. 'Oh ... Cheryl. I thought you were lying down. I was trying to be quiet.'

Cheryl turned a florid face to her, twitching slightly. She

was kneeling in front of the ancient cooker, swathed in a frilly apron, presumably the property of the chalet, and scrubbing at its baked-on grime with missionary zeal.

'Just giving it a little wipe,' she panted, preparing to tackle the grill.

'Headache gone?' Janet asked lamely.

'Yes, thank you. Quite gone. Nothing like a lie down in a darkened room. It's the only thing that shifts it.'

Presumably lying under a gas cooker had the same effect.

'Did you see the note from Annie?'

'Yes,' came Cheryl's muffled voice. 'That's what decided me. We wouldn't want the new girl thinking things, would we?'

Janet reflected that the McDermots certainly got by without. She sat down at the kitchen table which had been scrubbed. 'It's you, isn't it?' she said. Cheryl turned inquiring eyes to her. 'I thought when I came in someone had been round to clean, but they haven't at all, have they? It was you. You've cleaned the whole place.'

Cheryl returned to her task. 'I just had a bit of a tidy up.'

Janet got up. What was the point? 'I'll leave you to it, then, shall I?'

Unfortunately, Debbie was unable to stay with us after all, due to a misunderstanding on the part of the tour company. Not to worry, we all enjoy mucking in with the household chores and Annie, our bubbly courier, has promised us a cordon bleu dinner this evening, so we are eagerly awaiting the arrival of Claire to prepare it.

I had my first private skiing lesson today. An extravagance, but worth every penny. Mauro is very patient with me. I feel sure we shall get on like a house on fire. Italian men are so romantic!

There was a rumble of voices outside, followed by the clash of skis. Janet closed her pad and made for the stairs. She didn't want to be the one to tell Hugh about Annie's note. Cheryl was obviously of the same mind because she came scurrying after her.

'Janet,' she whispered breathlessly as they tore up the stairs. 'Yes?'

'Ummm . . . You won't mention it to Bob, will you? Me tidying up? Please, Janet. He'll get so . . . He doesn't really like me to . . .'

Janet smiled weakly. 'Of course I won't.' They retreated to their rooms.

Although unable to hear the exact words of the conversation going on below, she gathered that neither Bob nor Hugh were very pleased with Annie's latest proposal, particularly since there was no evidence that she had managed to pull it off.

After a while Janet heard Hugh's step on the stairs. He opened the door, face like thunder. 'Did you know about this?' He waved Annie's note at her.

'I saw it, if that's what you mean.'

'Well, where is she? It's gone five o'clock. I can see the same bloody thing happening all over again. If that woman thinks I'm eating another plate of cold chips . . .'

There was a knock on the front door. Hugh swivelled on his heel and marched out. Janet wondered if she had time to shut herself in the shower before he started again.

She did not, because he came back up almost immediately, looking infinitely more cheerful and carrying two large glasses of whisky.

'She's here,' he confirmed.

'Oh good. What's her name?'

Hugh looked perplexed. 'Haven't a clue. Does it matter, so long as she can cook?'

'Spoken like a socialist.' She lay back on the bed. 'Now all we have to do is keep Cheryl away from her till she's had time to prepare a meal. You know, I really think she'd prefer it if no one turned up at all.'

Hugh swirled his drink cheerfully. 'I think that's exactly what she'd prefer.'

✻　　✻　　✻

The latest arrival was called Hayley. She went silently about her work with a sort of stoicism that made Janet wonder if Chalet Nevosa was the tour company's equivalent of Withdrawal of Privileges. Where were all those dippy, night-clubbing Sloanes that she had seen on the soap/docs on television? The answer was obvious. They were with dippy night-clubbing families like the Redmonds, who didn't care whether they won the trivia quiz or got an extra nought on their lire.

Dinner was plentiful if unspectacular. Hayley had prepared a starter based mainly, as far as any of them could tell, on cornflour. Upon inquiry she informed them that they should now be savouring the delicacy of *crema di piselli*, which led Stuart to declare that he was not eating creamed piss for anyone and Bob to laugh till everyone feared (hoped) he would have a heart attack.

It was followed by a casserole. When Hugh quizzed her on the kind of meat in it, Hayley went a deepish shade of pink and admitted her Italian was not up to differentiating between 'dead pig' and 'dead rat', the general consensus of what she might have been sold.

'Do we have to wear skis tonight?' asked Belinda as the plates were being cleared.

'What are you talking about?' asked Janet, her blood running cold.

'For the tobogganing. Do we have to wear skis?'

A hyena-like screech from Tricia signalled the fact that they did not.

'They wouldn't fit in the sledge,' Stuart explained ponderously.

'I know that, thank you,' snapped Belinda, humiliated. 'I just wondered if we needed them to get up there.'

Bob wiped imaginary tears from his eyes. 'Skis in a toboggan!' he chortled.

✳   ✳   ✳

'So how did it go this morning?' Hugh asked while they were getting ready. 'Mauro seemed pretty impressed.'

Janet gave him a dry smile. 'That was for Bob's benefit, as if you didn't realise.'

He shrugged. 'Well, I had an inkling he was probably exaggerating a mite, but from what Clive was saying, he doesn't give praise lightly.'

Janet nodded. 'I should say that's probably true.' She looked at her watch. 'What are those children up to? I hope Tricia isn't painting Blin like a geisha again.'

'It'll keep the wind out,' Hugh observed. He had already given her a rough idea of what the evening entailed. They would be divided into teams, two people to each toboggan, and at the sound of the starting pistol would race the opposing pair down a pre-arranged course, marked out by slalom poles in black and red. Anyone veering from the route would be automatically disqualified.

And killed, thought Janet weakly, seeing that the slope which had looked so meandering on Hugh's programme was in fact a zigzagging plunge of several hundred feet. Unconsciously she gripped his arm.

'What's up? Cold feet?'

'Cold everything. Oh Hugh, I can't possibly toboggan down there. I'd be terrified.'

'Oh, come on, Mum,' said Owen encouragingly. 'You said you liked sledging. You said you did it all the time when you were small.'

'Yes, but it wasn't like this. It was down a hill, not a mountain. And I mean, look at those toboggans. You'd need an HGV licence to drive one of those.'

'You'll be all right,' murmured Hugh a touch wearily.

'*Mum.*' Belinda was glaring at her with ill-concealed ferocity. 'You have to do it. You can't *keep* saying you're scared of *everything*. It's just stupid.'

'Watch it,' Hugh warned. 'Don't you speak to your mother like that.'

Belinda turned on him. 'Why not? It's true. You know it is. Everyone else's mums can do it. Even Cheryl.' Fortunately the McDermot clan were arguing amongst themselves about who had eaten the last of Tricia's chocolate, so heard none of this. 'It's so embarrassing,' Belinda continued, fighting back tears of frustration. 'It's bad enough having Bob making jokes about Mum's skiing all the time, and Tricia being all sneery about her clothes, but if she chickens out of this as well, it'll just be too awful. I wish she'd never come. I wish Auntie Harriet had come instead.'

There was a silence. Hugh glared at Belinda. 'You will apologise to your mother this moment or you get straight back on that lift and home to bed.'

Belinda bit her lip.

'I said apologise.'

Janet took a breath. 'It's all right. Blin's right. I'm making a fuss over nothing. After all, if other people can do it, so can I. I expect I'll love it once I get going.'

Hugh was still frowning. 'Blin had no business speaking to you like that.'

Belinda kicked some snow around. 'Sorry, Mum.'

'That's OK. I didn't know how much it mattered to everyone.' She tried to smile but Belinda's words had cut deep. She's ashamed of me, she thought. And so, presumably, is Owen, although he would never say so. She glanced at Hugh who was sorting out money to pay for their tickets. He looked so stern and distant as he strode ahead of them to the cash desk. What about him? she thought. Is he ashamed of me too?

Chapter Fourteen

Janet had assumed that she would share a toboggan with either Owen or Hugh. This seemed the most rational arrangement.

Bob, however, had other ideas. 'Now, as we've all done this before and you lot haven't, I've drawn up a list of who's going with who.' There was an instant protest from his children, which he ignored.

'Hugh will go with Tricia.'

'I'm going with Brian. It's all arranged,' said Tricia.

'Right. That calls for a re-think.' He frowned as though faced with the choice of D-Day landing spots. 'Not to worry. What I'm going to do, I'm going to put Cheryl with Owen.' He turned to Owen. 'She'll be able to give you the gist of it. The rest you'll have to work out for yourself.'

'I like a challenge,' Owen snarled and Janet braced herself for another scene. None was forthcoming, however, because Bob was having too much trouble adjusting his plan to take in what anyone else was saying.

'I'll take Janet with me, as she's the one most likely to get into trouble. And I don't mean *that* kind of trouble,' he added, his shoulders shaking with amusement.

'That's a relief,' muttered Janet which made Belinda giggle.

'Stuart, you're going to have to have Belinda with you.' This effectively quelled the giggles.

'No way,' Stuart snorted ungallantly.

'I'm not going with *him*,' Belinda averred, equally disenchanted.

'You'll do as you're told, young lady,' snapped Bob, peering at her fiercely.

'Mum?'

Janet shook her head. 'Just let Bob finish. We'll sort it out in a minute.'

'Well, I'm not going with him. I'd rather go with *you*,' Belinda declared with a hint of desperation.

Again Janet felt the sting of rejection. 'Just wait.'

'And that leaves, let me see, Hugh and ... Ah, looks like you'll have to go solo, old chap. How does that sound? Oh, hang on, though. Have you done this sort of thing before?'

'Once or twice.'

'Will you be OK, then, without one of us?'

'I'll give it my best shot.'

'Yes, well, you should be OK. Just remember not to try and brake on the corners. Slow down before you get there. That's the secret.'

'I'll bear that in mind.'

'Now, Owen, you'll have to go in front of my lady wife, but do whatever she tells you. She knows what she's about.'

A glance at Cheryl would have informed even the most novice sledger that she knew nothing of the kind. Her mouth was opening and closing like a landed fish.

Bob continued his briefing. 'Brian, I gather you've done this before?'

'All my life.'

'Right. Well, don't do anything rash. Remember, you get more points for completing the course than for speed.'

Janet shuddered, thinking Tricia's safety might also have crossed his mind.

'And Stuart, that goes for you too. We don't want another mess like last year, do we?'

Stuart scowled and rolled a piece of chewing gum round his tongue. 'I'm not having her with me.'

'You most certainly are.'

'I'm not, Dad. She'll fall off or scream or something. Put me off my stride.'

'I will not,' said Belinda indignantly. 'Not that I'm going with you anyway. Why can't I go with Dad?'

'You're with Stuart,' said Hugh firmly. 'End of story.'

'She's not,' muttered Stuart darkly.

'I'm not,' Belinda confirmed.

'Oh, shut up, you two,' Hugh snapped.

One of the holiday reps was marshalling people into teams. The Gales and McDermots found themselves behind the family whose daughter Owen fancied. This improved his humour at least, and they were soon making 'Aren't parents the pits?' faces at each other as the group was hustled towards the start point.

Several teams had already completed the course and, despite blood-curdling screams from participants and spectators alike, no air ambulance was hovering overhead as yet, and the worst reported wound was a bruised ankle by someone who had stuck their foot out when passing the finishing post.

Janet watched with morbid fascination as the couples were strapped tandem into their seats, shrieking and giggling, before being hurled by the joint efforts of the rest of their team over a little hummock and down the winding course to a distant point where more shrieking people waited to greet them.

Bob had his stopwatch out and was making Cheryl write down the times on the back of her programme. She was having some difficulty as Bob was now wearing a balaclava which made it almost impossible to hear what he was saying. A fine drizzle was beginning to fall.

Brian and Tricia went first. Janet watched them plummeting downwards, the toboggan careering recklessly between the slalom poles, whooping as they went. They actually seemed to be enjoying themselves. She closed her eyes and tried to recapture

the joy she had felt as a child, out on the hills behind her home
– the tangy smell of wet snow, the blast of freezing air in her
face, the thrill of zipping downwards to capsize in a giggling
pile at the bottom. Yes, she had loved it, and no, she didn't love
it any more.

She opened her eyes and felt a dreadful pang of panic as she
saw that Owen and Cheryl were in the process of being strapped
into their sledge. 'Now, remember, brake before the curve,' Bob
was inciting Owen, who stared stoically ahead, ignoring him
totally. Cheryl was having trouble with her strap. The starter
was urging them to hurry as she fiddled fretfully with the buckle.
She looked wretched, squashed like a bag of potatoes into the
minuscule seat behind Owen, himself with his knees under his
chin. The starter fired his pistol. The launching party lunged
forward and the two of them were away.

Owen, who had been having secret driving lessons from
Hugh in the run-up to his seventeenth birthday, handled the
toboggan with considerable skill and the two of them came in
way ahead of their rivals.

Bob clicked approvingly as he checked his watch. 'Good
old Cheryl. Knew she could handle it OK.' Janet felt a spark of
fury, but she had no time to retaliate because Hugh was already
in harness, waiting to set off.

It occurred to her as she straightened up, aching with
the strain, that Bob had not arranged the order of transit
very sensibly. For every couple that went down the slope,
there were two less people left at the top. With Hugh,
Brian and Owen gone, that only left Bob and her to push
Stuart who, possibly due to his diet of chocolate, was a
little on the weighty side, and Belinda who had gone off
somewhere to sulk.

Janet looked around for her. She was standing a little way
away, arms folded, scowling into the middle distance. Janet
beckoned to her. Belinda continued to stare morosely at nothing
in particular.

'Where's that girl of yours?' Bob demanded. 'She's holding us all up.'

'She's over there,' said Janet. Bob followed her gaze and began a series of semaphoric arm movements. Belinda ignored him.

The starter indicated that they were ready for the next pair. 'What's the matter with her?' asked Bob in a voice tinged with hysteria. 'We're going to lose our place.'

'I don't think she and Stuart want to go together.'

'She'll have to. I've sorted it all out.'

'I think it might have been an idea to ask people before you did, Bob,' said Janet, struggling to keep her good humour. 'Teenagers don't like to be ordered about. You must know that from your two.' She was wasting her time. Bob merely stared at her as though she was quite mad.

'Is your team taking part in this round?' prompted the starter. 'We have a lot of people waiting.'

This galvanized Bob into action. 'Yes, yes, of course. They'll just have to come last.'

For some reason, presumably the attribution of human feelings where none existed, Janet took this to mean that Bob was prepared to retire from the race. It was therefore several moments before she realised that he was hauling her like a captured pickpocket towards the waiting toboggan.

'Bob, wait. What are you doing? We can't leave them up here by themselves ...'

'They'll be all right,' growled Bob, eyes popping with messianic fervour. 'Quick. Get in. Just buckle that belt round you. They'll follow us down. No choice.'

'I really don't think ...'

'You are competing?' asked the starter. 'You have thirty seconds, otherwise I'm afraid it's disqualification.'

Bob yelped and all but threw Janet into the back seat. She turned frantically to see if Belinda and Stuart had realised what was going on. Stuart was grinning friendlishly, so she could only assume he had. Bob was right. They had no alternative but to follow them down. That or come down in the lift, and she couldn't see either Stuart or Belinda settling for that.

The crack of the starter's pistol rang out. The other team shot off. Bob and Janet stayed firmly grounded in the snow. They had forgotten in the rush that with Stuart and Belinda sulking, they had no one to give them a push. 'Get out. Get out,' screeched Bob like a hysterical schoolgirl. 'Push us. Quick.' Janet once more undid the buckle of her belt and started to get out. '*Quick!*' squawked Bob. 'We're losing them.'

In fact they were not, because the opposition, also down to their last team members, had been bravely if feebly started by the family grandparents and had slithered almost immediately into a snowdrift, from which they were now trying to extricate themselves.

Janet had one foot out of the sledge when she felt a firm hand on her back. 'Get back in. I'll give you a shove.' It was Clive Harley, too experienced in catering for the McDermots to encourage another complaint from them.

She whipped her foot inside just in time to avoid the starting post and was flung from side to side like a metronome as Bob, fiendish in frosted balaclava, knotted the ropes tighter round his wrists and catapulted them down the slope, skimming the marker posts till Janet could see where they needed painting. She was too frightened to scream. The unfastened seat belt slapped remorselessly at her, catching her in the stomach when she went forward, and the wooden seat cracking across her shoulder blades as she fell back.

Briefly she wondered what Bob's driving was like. In his goggles and balaclava he was a dead ringer for Toad of Toad Hall. 'Get out of the way. *Avanti.* MOVE!' There was a whoosh of snow, the scream of excited children, a thwack, and the sledge spun round at a forty-five-degree angle and came to a halt.

Janet lay slumped in a heap, blinking up at the overhead lights. Were they there? Was she dead? Better still, was Bob dead? She had no time to relish this thought, because Bob was standing over her, shouting something. Unfortunately he seemed to have a large proportion of his balaclava in his mouth so it was some seconds before she realised that he wanted her to get out again.

With joyous relief she saw that they were a mere twenty yards from the finishing point. 'QUICK!' Bob was bellowing. She clambered out, aching in every bone. 'QUICK!' He was pointing up the slope.

Their opponents, who had never really recovered from the slowness of their start, were slithering slowly down the mountainside, still some way behind them.

'PUSH! We've got to get over the line before them. The damn thing's wedged.' Bob hauled at the sledge which was firmly stuck in a mound of snow. Janet just had time to realise it was some child's snowman they had decapitated, when he managed to drag it free. 'GET IN!' he yelled, clearly incapable of communicating in anything but bellows.

Janet shook her head. 'It's all right. I'll walk from here.'

'GET IN!' screamed Bob. 'We've both got to be in it when it goes over the line. *Quick!* They're catching up.'

Janet closed her eyes.

'Go on, Mum. *Get in!*' It was Owen. She glanced down the mountain and saw them all gazing at her with agonised expressions. 'GET IN. THEY'RE COMING.' The whole mountain seemed to be screaming at her.

Wearily she scrambled back in just as the sedate couple in the other team came abreast of them. Janet caught sight of their cheerful uncompetitive faces just as Bob jump-started them down the remaining few yards to the finish.

Once there he leapt out of the toboggan and pulled out his stopwatch as the other couple arrived to cheers from their supporters.

Hugh helped Janet out. 'Bit of a bumpy ride, by the look of it.'

Janet patted herself to see how many limbs she had lost on the way. 'I'm going to apply to be canonised when we get home. *If* we get home. I cannot believe the tour company agreed to allow him back. He must be worse than an outbreak of cholera.'

Owen came over and gave his mother a congratulatory hug. Normally she would have been pleased, but it merely emphasised the pain in her shoulders. 'You were great. I never thought you'd make it after Bob tried to kill that kid.'

'He *what?*' gasped Janet, the decapitated snowman rising up to greet her.

'Well, not exactly. Didn't you see? There was this kid of about eight who was throwing snowballs at the poles and Bob must have lost his concentration or something. When you landed up in the snowman.'

'Looks like it's all up to Stu.' Bob confronted them, legs akimbo. He had a curious habit when trying to make a point of splaying his legs like someone on board a heaving deck. Janet had noticed it several times and was beginning to wonder if it was a sign of late potty training.

'Oh yes?' said Hugh.

'Yup. Want to take a look at the timings?'

Hugh said he did, not having any obvious alternative. Bob handed him the programme, peering over his shoulder as he read them. 'As you can see, the Granvilles were down a smidgeon on the foe, but we started off pretty well with Trish and what's-his-name. Gained seven seconds. Cheryl and your lad did OK. Maintained the lead. We lost five through Janet here's inexperience.' Janet opened her mouth, but she had neither the energy nor the spittle to silence him. 'So now it's all down to my lad.'

'And my sister,' Owen chipped in.

Considering how they bickered at home, Janet was touched by her son's loyalty.

'Yes, if he can get her into it,' said Bob with a fatalism that chilled her bones.

'What do you mean, if?' she demanded. 'He surely won't leave her up there on her own?'

Bob shrugged. 'It's her choice, isn't it? One thing you can be sure of. Stuart won't let the side down. He knows me too well for that.'

With sickening predictability there was a whoop, a cheer and a flurry of wet snow as the last two toboggans of the team came looping down the course.

It was only when Stuart, dribbling slightly with excitement, swung his legs over the side of the sledge that Janet realised Belinda was not with him.

Chapter Fifteen

'Where is she? Where's Belinda? How *could* you leave her?' Janet could hear the hysteria in her voice. 'Hugh, you'll have to go up there. Go now. She's by herself. Owen, go with him. Oh my God, she's only thirteen. She'll be terrified.'

Hugh put his hand on her shoulder. 'Calm down. There's nothing to worry about. Clive's up there, and Annie. They won't leave her to come down on her own.'

This made sense. 'Well, what are we going to do? We can't stay down here if she's up there. She might not come down till the end. She's got no money. This thing could go on all night.'

Already fresh teams were forming at the top. Hugh acknowledged that it could be some while before the event ended. 'I'll get the tramcar up. If there's a space on a team I'll come down with her, if not we'll have to come back in the lift. How's that?'

'Yes, all right. Only hurry. Suppose she gets in one of those toboggans on her own?'

'She won't.'

'Stuart did. The little swine. Honestly I wish we'd never come on this holiday. I really do.'

'Yes, well, all right. It's too late for that. You wait here. Why don't you get yourself a coffee or something? It'll be a while before we're back. The lifts are only running every fifteen minutes.'

'How will I know if you've found her?'

'I'll bring her down.'

'Yes, but I won't know till you do, will I?'

'Oh, for God's sake, Jan. What do you want me to do? Fire off a rocket? Start an avalanche? Just calm down. Owen, buy your mother a brandy. She's getting in a state.'

'I don't want a brandy. I just want my daughter back, not stuck halfway up a mountain on her own in the middle of the night.'

'Don't be so melodramatic,' said Hugh tersely and strode off towards the lift entrance.

'She'll be all right, Mum,' Owen reassured her. 'The worst that can happen is she has to come back in the lift and sulks for two days.'

Janet relaxed slightly. 'Oh, I know you're right. It just makes me so angry that her whole evening – and ours – has to be ruined because that damned man wants to be in charge of everything. What business has he got organising us all the time? Why can't he just keep an eye on his own ghastly children? The way she's going Tricia'll be pregnant by the time she gets home.' She stopped, aware that her voice was rising again.

Owen looked away, embarrassed. 'Do you want me to buy you a brandy? Dad gave me some money.'

She shook her head. 'No, you go off and enjoy yourself.'

'Well, if you're sure you don't want me to hang around?'

'No, of course not. I'll get myself a coffee and wait for them.'

'I'll be in the disco bar if you need me.'

'That's fine.'

Owen went off in pursuit of his new girlfriend and Janet bought a large cappuccino and sat down to wait. She had no idea where Bob and his brood had got to. Keeping out of her way, if they had any sense, she thought savagely. Really, that Stuart was the end. Mind you, Belinda had been equally implacable. Maybe it wasn't entirely his fault. It was a little unfair to put all the blame on a fourteen-year-old boy. God knew Blin could be a pest when she put her mind to it. Well, she'd come well and truly unstuck with this one.

The likelihood of Hugh finding them a place on another toboggan team seemed pretty remote to Janet. There were hundreds of people waiting for a turn. They were hardly likely to give way to someone who'd already had a go and someone else who'd passed up the opportunity.

'There you are. Where's Hugh? I need to speak to him.' Bob, balaclava now coiled round his neck like a woolly concertina, had once more materialised.

'He's gone to look for Belinda, of course,' said Janet with commendable calm.

'Oh, she'll be down. Her own fault, if you ask me. What was Stu to do? He made the right choice, no doubt in my mind.'

Or what passes for it, thought Janet. I will not lose my temper. He's not worth it. She took a sip of her coffee.

'Will he be long? There's a chance, just a slim one, that we may make it to the final.'

'The what?' She nearly choked.

'The final. What they do is, you see, they add up all the points for course completed, then deduct any speed penalties etcetera, then the two top teams pick their best pair for the final run off. There's only one bunch ahead of us so far, so who knows? Fingers crossed.'

'My fingers are crossed,' said Janet coldly. 'They're crossed that Hugh can find Belinda and bring her down as soon as possible so that we can all go home.'

Bob raised his eyebrows quizzically. 'Having one of those days, are we? By the way, I thought you did pretty well considering it was your first attempt. I was quite impressed. Cheryl said she would never have guessed you had it in you.'

'Where is Cheryl?' asked Janet, thinking that some of the

things she had in her, Cheryl would be better not knowing about.

Bob cast his eyes around. 'Oh, she's here somewhere. Actually, if you do see her could you tell her I need her back at the finish point, ASAP. I've left Stuart with the stopwatch but he's not always a hundred per cent accurate. Right, I'd better be making my way back. Don't suppose you've seen Trish anywhere, have you?'

'No,' said Janet.

'Kids! Ah, well, not to worry. She'll turn up.'

If that's meant for me ... Janet glowered at his receding figure. The difference between her and Bob Bigwig McDermot was that she cared what happened to her daughter.

She finished her coffee and looked at her watch. Hugh had been gone nearly half an hour. It would be worth meeting the next lift. She prised herself out of her chair, painfully aware of erupting bruises. Curse Bob. She'd hardly be able to move in the morning which would doubtless give Mauro even more cause to rail at her.

Hugh was coming out of the turnstile as she got there. She hurried towards him. 'Oh, there you are. Thank goodness. Bob's been wittering on about some final. He seems to think our team's in with a chance ...' Her voice died away as she gazed into Hugh's sombre face. 'Where is she? Where's Belinda?'

He took her arm and guided her away from the exit. 'There's no need to panic,' he said steadily. 'I've spoken to Clive. He's—'

'What?' Janet interrupted. 'What's happened? Has something happened to Belinda? Where is she? Oh my God. What's happened? Is she hurt?'

Hugh took hold of both her arms and turned her to face him. 'She's not up there. They put out a call. She's not in the café or the bar. I looked everywhere. That's when I got hold of Clive. He and Annie are phoning through to the *carabinieri* to put out a search for her down here. I've got to go and talk to them now, give them her description. You'd better come. Apparently their English isn't too good.'

'But how can she be down here? How could she get down? Unless she came in the lift, and then you'd have seen her. Someone would have seen her. Surely they haven't let her come down in a toboggan by herself?' A million hideous possibilities were vying for space inside her brain.

Hugh shook his head. 'Clive assured me she wouldn't have been allowed down by herself. Boys are one thing. Girls, never, he said.'

'Well then, she must have caught the lift. Maybe she *is* still up there? Maybe you just missed her. Maybe she was hiding. Maybe . . .'

The look in Hugh's eyes darkened. 'You might as well hear it all,' he said, so quietly she could hardly make out what he was saying.

'All?'

'Clive asked around. Apparently several people remembered seeing her after Stuart went. They said the two of them were having a humdinger of a row because Belinda wanted to go in the front and Stuart wouldn't let her. Anyway, in the end he went on his own. It seems she hung around for a bit and then wandered off towards the lift station.'

'Well, there you are. The two of you must have crossed over.'

'It's possible. The trouble is, what also seems fairly certain is that the last anyone saw of her, she was talking to some Italian guy.'

'But she can't speak Italian.'

'He was speaking English.'

Janet swallowed. 'Belinda's far too sensible to go off with a stranger. She just wouldn't.'

'Not even to spite us?'

A wave of panic engulfed her. 'Oh, surely not. Surely she wouldn't be that . . .'

Hugh took a breath. 'No, I'm sure you're right. It's just that the woman who was telling Clive said she assumed the man must be a relative or something.'

'Why?'

He looked at her blankly. 'Oh, for God's sake, Jan, don't you see? He was old enough to be her father.'

Janet put her hands up to her face. I'm going to be sick, she thought.

Hugh took hold of her arm. 'Come on. Let's go and talk to the police. The sooner they know what they're looking for, the sooner we'll have her back.'

The *carabinieri* were very nice. Janet, in faltering Italian, tried to describe Belinda, every garment and colour she had ever learned fleeing from her mind as soon as she opened her mouth. Their handsome faces flickered with polite confusion as she variously informed them her daughter was black, fat and dressed entirely in sailors. Had this been the case, they would later reflect, she would have been a lot easier to locate.

Hugh managed to give them a far more accurate portrait, indicating her height, hair colour and clothing by pointing at similar figures passing the little cabin which served as their office.

They talked on walkie-talkies to their colleagues up the mountain. Janet, convinced that she had heard the word 'ambulance', was now weeping unrestrainedly – something which the policemen found wholly acceptable but Hugh was at a loss to deal with. He stood silently by the window, gazing out into the sea of happy faces thronging the snowy terrace, every now and again craning forward as someone resembling his daughter passed by.

With the inevitability of the Grim Reaper, into this tableau strolled Bob McDermot, a frown of ferocious pomposity on his face. '*Buona sera, signori,*' he greeted the *carabinieri*. They gazed at him suspiciously, wondering whether he was their suspect, come to give himself up. One thing was sure, he was not a genuine Italian.

'We've found the young lady. *Lei e* ... found. What's "found" in Italian, Janet?'

Janet was on her feet. 'You've found her? Where is she? Is she all right? Is she hurt? What happened? Where is she?'

The *carabinieri* were fairly well able to guess from her reaction what 'found' meant. There was a crackle on their radios. Rapid Italian ensued. The young men smiled and shook everyone's hand. 'Is good,' they confirmed, slapping each other's backs. There was another crackle and Clive Harley was put on the line. 'Mrs Gale? ... Yes, she's fine. On her way over now ... Just a bit of confusion. She said she thought you knew where she was. Didn't know what a fright she'd given everyone.'

There was a screech from Janet as Belinda's face appeared outside the cabin window. She dropped the receiver and rushed out, flinging her arms round her daughter and hugging her to her. 'Where were you? Where have you been? Didn't you know what a fright you gave us? I've been nearly out of my mind. Daddy's been up the mountain looking for you. Clive called the police. We've had the police out looking for you. Oh, how could you do that? What on earth made you wander off without telling anyone? And who was this man you were talking to?'

'What man?' asked Belinda, her face crimson with embarrassment.

'Some man. I don't know what man. A woman said she saw you talking to an older man. An Italian?' Relief was turning to fury. 'For God's sake, Belinda, how could you be so stupid? What have we always told you about talking to strangers?'

'He wasn't a stranger.'

'Of course he was. You don't know any Italians. We none of us do. Anything could have happened. He could have been anyone.'

Belinda turned to Hugh. 'If you'd just let me explain ...'

Hugh nodded. 'Yes, OK. The main thing is you're back and you're safe.' His calm deserted him. 'But Mummy's *right*. You should never get into conversation with strange men when you're on your own. *Never.*'

'HE WASN'T STRANGE,' bellowed Belinda so loudly that the two *carabinieri* shot out of their hut to see what was going on now. 'If you'd just let me *speak*.'

Janet started to say something, but Hugh motioned her to be quiet.

'OK. Fair enough. Go on.'

Belinda stared at the ground. 'It was after that prat, Stuart, went off without me. I was going to get the lift down. Didn't see what else I could do. He saw me and asked me where everyone else was, so I told him and how that prat had meant I couldn't have a go at all now, and he said if I wanted I could go down with him, but I'd have to wait till he'd locked his stuff up. So I said, yes please, that would be ace, so that's what we did.'

Janet felt as though she were listening to a foreign language, so little did she understand of Belinda's explanation. 'But who was he? How could you come down without being part of a team? How did you know he knew what he was doing? Suppose you'd had an accident? Anything could have happened.'

Belinda flung up her arms in despair. 'Because he's allowed to. All the instructors are. They just say they want a toboggan and everyone else has to wait. Of course he knew what he was doing. It was absolutely brill. The most brilliant thing of my life, if you want to know. *And* we were faster than Flubber Face. Bob was nearly crying with jealousy.'

Janet felt relief seeping through her like honey. 'Oh well, why didn't you say it was your instructor? I thought it was ... well, I don't know what I thought ... I was just so worried ...'

Belinda gave her a look that said if she could be declared a foundling on the spot, it wouldn't be soon enough for her. 'It wasn't my instructor,' she said bitterly. 'It was yours.'

Somewhere in the distance Janet registered Owen's mortified

face as he and the girlfriend looked on. I have made a complete
and utter idiot of myself, she thought. I have cried in public, I
have shouted, I have embarrassed my entire family and, judging
by Bob McDermot's expression, I have lost our team a place in
the finals of the toboggan race, and tomorrow I must face my
ski instructor who will also by now have heard what a prize fool
I have proved myself. But I have my daughter back. And as far
as I'm concerned, that's all that matters.

At that moment Cheryl came wandering slowly towards
her from the direction of the Bar Amico where she had been
concealing herself from her husband. 'I've really enjoyed this
evening,' she confided in Janet, with just a hint of a slur.
'Have you?'

Janet's relief at Belinda's safe return was not enough to protect
her from a feeling that she was held to be at fault by all those
involved. Maybe she *had* been too quick to assume the worst, but
what was she to do? How many mothers in a similar situation
would have reacted differently?

Belinda plainly thought otherwise. Her euphoria from her
toboggan ride had given way to a series of accusations. Why had
they made such a fuss? Wasn't it obvious what would happen?
How could they humiliate her so? Imagine! Calling the police!
Tricia would never let her live it down. She hoped they were
satisfied.

Hugh had spoken very sharply to her, resulting in one of
Belinda's silences, more telling than a dozen accusations. Owen,
also plainly feeling his mother had gone over the top, had
retreated to the disco bar with Rachel, as he now knew her name
to be, and the McDermot family were arguing amongst themselves about whether the fact that Stuart had dropped his father's
stopwatch in the snow had radically affected its efficiency. It
seemed fairly clear that they had not made it to the final, either
way, so Janet couldn't see the reason for so much fuss.

'Do you know what these things cost?' Bob rounded on her when she ventured to say as much.

'No.'

'Exactly. This particular model cost me a hundred and twenty pounds. And that was with my Barclay card points.'

'Well then it should be waterproof.'

'Oh, please!' snapped Bob furiously. 'Spare me the benefit of your expertise just this once, Janet. Haven't you caused enough trouble for one evening?'

Janet stared at him. He's a moron, she thought. Worse than that, an alien. Sent to infiltrate himself into the human race for God knew what ghastly purpose. Whatever it was, he was making a stinking awful mess of it.

She suddenly felt deathly tired. I just want to go home, she thought. I just want to go to bed and sleep till this hateful holiday is over. Three days down, four to go. It was longer than a life sentence. And tomorrow she had to face Mauro again. Oh, what did it matter?

They had a long wait for the lift. Stuart was moaning about being hungry. Brian and Tricia were openly snogging at the other end of the platform, watched by Belinda with a mixture of disgust and envy. Cheryl inched her way round to where Janet was standing. 'Did Hugh manage to get through?' she asked.

'Through what?'

'Through on the phone? To Harriet Barton? Oh, didn't I say? Annie brought a message up for him. To ring. This afternoon. I gave it to him when he got back. He must have forgotten about it, what with . . .'

Janet nodded wearily. 'I expect so. I don't know, Cheryl. I'll have to ask him.'

Fun on Sledges
There can be few more exciting and enjoyable ways to spend an evening in the mountains than taking part in a toboggan race.

We were divided into teams and then into pairs. The starter fired his pistol (luckily not setting off any avalanches!) and we were away.

I can hardly describe the thrill of hurtling down the mountainside, zigzagging between the brightly painted slalom poles, racing not just against one's opponents but also trying to beat the clock.

Since it is the whole team's efforts that count towards your final score, it is essential for every duo to give it their all. I was lucky enough to be partnered by a very experienced sledger, which was just as well, as this was my first attempt on a real mountain!

Our team came sixth out of a total of more than twenty, so pats on the back all round, and a welcome glass of Schnapps to round off the night's activities.

'Hugh ...'

Hugh grunted and rolled over to face her. 'What?'

'Cheryl said Harriet left a message for you to ring her.'

'Yes, that's right. She called the hotel.'

'What about?'

Hugh yawned. 'Oh, just to see how things were going.'

'I take it you didn't tell her?'

'Only the good bits.'

'Quick call then.'

'Goodnight, Jan.'

'Goodnight.'

Chapter Sixteen

Mauro was waiting for her at the foot of the chair lift the following morning. He nodded to Hugh. 'OK, this morning, your wife can come with me. I will teach her how to get on and off this thing, otherwise she will be dead by the end of the week and I will have to pay back the money.'

Hugh laughed. 'Sounds reasonable to me.' He turned to Janet. 'You happy with that, darling?'

'Ecstatically,' said Janet darkly.

Her family seemed only too relieved to hand over responsibility for her to the surly Italian. Having gabbled a few meaningless reassurances, they were soon bounding towards the turnstile like newly released prisoners.

I am a liability, she brooded dejectedly, fiddling with the strap of her glove.

'You are ready?'

She sighed. 'Yes, I suppose so.'

'You must do more than suppose or the same thing will happen as yesterday. When I say we are going through the gate you must come with me immediately. Otherwise ...' he shrugged pragmatically, 'you are on your own again.'

'Well, please tell me in time,' she pleaded pathetically. 'It's hard to hurry in these things.'

'All right. You have your pass?'

'Yes.'

'You have your poles, your gloves, your hat.' His eyes lingered tellingly on Janet's rainbow head. 'So, now you are ready, we will go.'

She shuffled along beside him, her heart pumping like a generator, convinced that at the last moment he was going to desert her. It would probably be his idea of a joke. Like throwing small children into deep water to teach them to swim. It had always been Janet's philosophy that such people should be shot, preferably by their victims. Well, if he went off without her, she was staying put. She had made up her mind. There was absolutely no way she was going through that trip again on her own.

They came to the turnstile. Her heart fought its way past her tonsils to land in her mouth, her wrists went so floppy she could not fit her pass into the slot. Someone behind her stood on the back of her ski, effectively nailing her to the ground, and all this in the seconds it took before the turnstile swung open and she found herself dragged forward by Mauro, who had a vice-like grip on her arm.

'OK,' he said firmly. 'When I say "sit", you sit. *Sit.*'

Janet flopped down, feeling like a renegade mongrel in a Barbara Woodhouse class. The edge of the chair clipped the back of her knees as she sank on to it, pressing her spine against the unforgiving metal.

'Poles *down*. Bring your poles *down*.'

Janet stabbed herself in the shin. The safety bar clanged shut. She waited, rigid with fear for the next command. If it had been 'Jump', she would probably have obeyed, so inflexible was the man's tone.

They were now climbing rapidly. No one else had attempted to join them. Janet was not sure whether she was pleased or upset about this. It would have been nice to have some human company on the ride, but there again, did she really want Mauro exposing her profound unsuitability to the sport to total strangers?

'You have enjoyed last night?'

'Last night?' Her thoughts had been firmly vested in the present and immediate future, i.e. how was she going to get off this thing if Mauro was not on the ground to grab the nape of her neck?

'The toboggan races.'

She braced herself for the onslaught. 'No, I didn't at all, actually.'

'No. I thought perhaps you would not.'

Janet bit her lip. 'Did you think that before you abducted my daughter, or afterwards?'

There was a deathly silence. They both stared at each other. I didn't just say that, she prayed. Now he will push me out.

Mauro lowered his eyes. 'Yes, I heard about that. I am sincerely sorry.'

'What?'

He shook his head. 'I had no idea . . . You see, the young boy . . . I had spoken to him earlier, while he was waiting. After they had the argument. I said if he will not go with your daughter, I will make sure she gets back all right. I did not realise he had not told you this. I can see this was very frightening for you. I regret it very much.'

Janet sat silent. 'Stuart knew?' she said eventually. 'He knew you were going to bring Belinda down?'

'That is what I said to him. Perhaps he has forgotten.'

She closed her eyes. 'I don't think so,' she said quietly. 'I think he's just his father's son.' She felt the cold slap of wet snow in her face as they crested the ridge.

'When I say "jump", jump. *Jump.*'

Mauro pulled her out of the dip. 'This is better than yesterday,' was all he said.

'Today we will practise how to turn.'

Janet stood meekly, wondering how it was possible to turn any more than she had already. Mauro had made her recap on yesterday's lesson by snow-ploughing past the same bush that had claimed her the day before. She had nearly made it, and might have done, had not a recalcitrant twig chosen to pop its tentacle above the snow line just as she went past and send her spinning in somersaults some ten yards down the hill.

Mauro had not remarked on this feat beyond saying she needed to bend her knees more. Now she was back at the start point.

'To turn with the snow-plough is easy. Easier than to go straight because you do not move so fast. See, watch what I do.'

With the grace of a swan he glided towards the bush, rising just before he came to it and sweeping his feet round till they and, miraculously as far as Janet was concerned, the skis were facing in the opposite direction. This he continued to do till he had reached the bottom, before leaping athletically back up the slope to where she stood.

'OK. Now you.'

'I'm not sure I absolutely understood what you were doing.'

'I was skiing.'

Her shoulders stiffened.

'OK. We will do it together. You give me your hand. When I say "turn", you turn. OK?'

'No. Suppose they don't turn?' Janet panicked. 'My skis don't seem to move as easily as yours. I'm not sure why.' She waited.

Mauro did not let her down. 'So, these skis, they have their own mind, huh? They can decide when they move? Today I will move, tomorrow I will not move, huh? For this man I will turn, for this woman I will stick myself into a branch so she rolls all the way down the hill. Well, this is new to me. This I had not heard about skis.'

Janet blushed crimson. To think she had almost liked him on the way up. 'You know what I mean.'

Mauro dusted some snow off his boot. 'Yes, I know,' he

said offhandedly. 'You mean you are frightened by what will happen to you.'

'Well, yes, since you ask.'

'You are right to be. But what can happen? You can land in the bush. This you have already done. It is not pleasant but it has not killed you. You can crash into me. This will be worse for me than for you, I think, but it will not kill me either. In all probability. Or, if neither of this happen, you will know how to turn your skis. Now watch me once more, what I do. Before I turn I must take the weight off the ski or it will not turn. I am too heavy for it, so I rise up, like this.' He demonstrated on the spot. Janet copied him. 'That is good. Now I am facing the other way, I wish to go right. I am too heavy, so I rise up, then I am light like a York pudding. Why are you laughing?'

Janet giggled hopelessly. 'I'm sorry. It was just the comparison.'

Mauro seemed pleased. 'You have forgotten I was a waiter in London,' he said more cheerfully. 'I remember all the English dishes. Roast lamb, roast beef, York pudding, roly polly.'

Janet blew her nose. 'You'd have trouble finding that in an English restaurant nowadays.'

'Why not? What do people eat then?'

She shrugged. 'Spaghetti bolognese is very popular.'

Mauro snorted contemptuously. 'Oh yes, all this garbage out of a tin. I know it. "Add hot water and mix." This is enough. Now we will try the turns.'

Having successfully rid Mauro of his good humour, Janet set her face to learning to turn. She was slightly unnerved by his suggestion/order that she hold his hand. Not that electric sparks were likely to flow between them, given the four layers of thermal fleece separating their fingers. Or anyway. She certainly didn't fancy him and it was hard to believe that he would fantasise much over a woman in a crimson airbag with a rainbow tea cosy on her head.

'OK. So we go very slowly. First we go right, then left, then right. OK. Throw away the poles. Give me your hand. Now you have me. I am your pole. OK. We go. Bend your knees. Lean forward. *Forward*. OK, so now we start again.'

Janet pulled herself out of the snow. 'I'm sorry. I thought I had to stand up straight.'

'Only when you turn. When you ski you bend down. Remember, you want to go lower, you make yourself lower. This I taught you yesterday.'

'Oh yes, I forgot.'

'Well, it is a pity if every day you will forget what I have said the day before.'

'I'll try not to.'

'OK. So we go. Bend your knees. Snow-plough. This is good. Very good. Now we turn. Slowly you rise. Take your weight off the skis. Now turn your feet to me. Turn them.'

'I can't.'

'You can. Turn them to me. To me. *Turn* them. OK. Again.'

'I'm sorry. They didn't move. I did try.'

'I know. But you see, you do not listen. You cannot turn the skis. I say to you, turn your feet. I do not say, turn your skis. Forget your skis. Turn your feet. This is all I ask. Think like you have no skis on. If I say to you, come to me, I cannot live without you, do you think, how shall I turn my feet round? I think you do not.'

'I think I'd probably leave them facing the way they were,' said Janet primly.

Mauro sniffed. 'Well, in all probability this is true, but you understand my meaning?'

'That was a joke,' she murmured, afraid she had hurt his feelings.

'Yes, that is OK. We try again. Remember, there are no skis. Only your feet. OK, we go ... And *turn* ... and *turn* ... and ... No, that is OK. That was good.'

＊　＊　＊

'How did it go?' Hugh was horribly chirpy, having been promoted to Advanced and informed by their instructor that both his children were exceedingly talented young skiers.

'Oh, fine.'

'What did you do today?'

'Fell over, mostly.'

'Oh, Jan, come on. Stop being so negative. I just saw Mauro and he said you were doing wonderfully well.'

'Liar.'

'Yes, well, he said you'd come on. That's virtually the same thing with Mauro, according to Clive.'

'"According to Clive." I wonder no one's taken him up on these pearls of wisdom. The Gospel According to Clive.'

'Hold on, darling.' Hugh looked bewildered. 'There's no need to take it so seriously.'

I am a cow, thought Janet, but there was something about her husband's relentless enthusiasm that was beginning to grate on her.

Her morning had not been an unmitigated disaster. By half past eleven she had managed to negotiate four complete turns with Mauro holding on to her and one and a half on her own (if you didn't count the bush, which was hell-bent on influencing the outcome).

'I'm sorry,' she murmured. 'I'm still tired from last night, I think.'

Over lunch they discussed their plans for the afternoon. At least Hugh, Belinda and Owen did. Janet sat silent, guiltily aware that she did not want to join them in any of their proposed activities. She wanted to sit in front of a roaring fire with a plate of cakes and a gory crime novel. Nor did she relish the spectre of Cheryl McDermot or the latest chalet girl hovering over her while she did so.

She would dump her skis and go down to the Hotel

Meraviglioso. It had a wonderful lounge, complete with crackling fire and squelchy leather armchairs where she could lose herself till teatime.

'What are you going to do, Jan?' Hugh asked almost as an afterthought. She hesitated. The children would rail at her if she confessed and Hugh would look reproachful. 'I shall probably go for a long walk,' she compromised. 'I've only seen the village from the cable car so far.'

'With your eyes closed,' Belinda jibed. 'Auntie Harriet said when she went skiing they got stuck in a gondola a mile up in the air and they were there for hours with no food or anything.'

'Dad told you not to mention that, you dork,' Owen broke in.

'Why not? She didn't die or anything, did she? So who's the dork now?'

'You are.'

'Am not.'

Janet slipped away. As she stepped warily into the swaying tramcar she reflected that Harriet had a lot to answer for.

Half an hour later she was just settling into a corner of the hotel lounge when she was disturbed by an explosion of giggles from behind the potted plants.

'So the new girl's not coming?'

'Not by the sound of it. There's a baggage handlers' strike or something. I really thought Annie was going to explode. She *promised* them someone for today.'

'Annie can say what she likes,' came a third voice. 'I'm not going anywhere near them. Don't you remember last year? Poor Wendy nearly had a nervous breakdown. He was all over her. Uuuugh!' They all squawked in horror. 'And his wife's completely mad. Well, she'd have to be to marry him, but Wendy said she used to get up in the night and go wandering. She came in about four o'clock one morning and Mrs McD was just *standing* there, like a ghost. Not saying anything. It freaked Wendy out.'

'Is that why Carla wouldn't go?' asked another voice.

'No, Carla really did fall over. But Lisa didn't. When she saw her name on the list for them she just marched straight into Annie and said she wouldn't do it.'

'What happened?'

'Annie tried to brazen it out. Said if she didn't like it she could lump it, virtually.'

'So she did?'

'Yup. You can't blame her though, can you? I mean the guy is seriously creepy. Wendy said he used to come up behind her in the kitchen and breathe all over her.'

'Just breathe?'

'Yes, but there's breathing and breathing, isn't there? Anyway, Annie's in a right panic because the other family's kicking up a stink about not having anyone.'

'You can see their point, though, can't you? I mean, it's not their fault.'

'Well, why'd they go on holiday with them? No one forced them.'

'No, but it's that stupid raffle thing Mr Alberti set up. The winners don't know who else is going to be there.'

'How come the Perv's got it two years running?'

'Ask me. Poor Annie was nearly in tears when she heard. Clive had just finished telling her about last year when the fax came through saying they'd won it again. This is her first job as supervisor.'

'And her last, the way she's going about it.'

There was a pause.

'Oh well,' said the first voice. 'We'd better get going. Looks like Hayley's stuck with it. Fancy that kid only lasting one night.'

'She didn't even last that, so I heard. She just turned straight round and walked out again.'

'No! What, right back on the coach?'

'So I heard.'

The voices drifted away. Janet sat shell-shocked in her chair. So much for a quiet afternoon. She closed her book and slunk self-consciously out past the receptionist. They all know, she thought, not daring to raise her eyes. Everyone in this village knows that I am one of Bob McDermot's party. I am branded. A member of the Underclass. Tainted by association. It's not my skiing that offends them. It's my choice of companions. The unfairness of it all seeped through her. 'Don't blame me,' she wanted to shout. 'I don't like him either. Have pity. Come and cook our dinner.'

Not wanting to go home, she wandered about for half an hour, climbing slowly on the circular path surrounding the village. She was glad in a way because it meant she hadn't actually lied to her family after all, and it *was* beautiful.

It seemed increasingly possible to her that skiing holidays could be quite fun, if only you could avoid the dreadful requirement to ski. The scenery was superb, the air invigorating, the wine plentiful. Granted, the clothes were preposterous, but everyone had them so even that didn't matter. Perhaps she would have liked one evening at the opera, dressed in something soft and silky, but that apart, she thought she could learn to love the mountains. Here you could sense what the simple life was really like, away from people, traffic, telephones. It was as near to perfect as a place could be.

With these lofty thoughts she retraced her steps, ogled once more a jacket in one of the boutiques, and made her way to the terrace café where she bought a large cappuccino and a huge heart-shaped mille-feuille full of cream and raspberry purée. She was in the middle of showering herself with flaky pastry when she sensed someone watching her. She looked up. There, across the terrace from her, sat Mauro, a thimble of black coffee in front of him.

'So, you are not on the mountain practising your skiing?'

'I was going to,' she stuttered guiltily, wishing she had not made quite such a mess.

Mauro came across to her table and motioned the waitress to bring him another coffee. 'Is it all right if I will join you?'

'Yes, of course,' she murmured, wishing sincerely that he would not. He sat down.

'Please, you can eat your cake. Do not stop for me.'

Janet stuck her fork into it, sending another shower of pastry flying. 'Actually, I've had enough. They're rather filling, aren't they?' She pushed the plate away. The waitress brought Mauro's coffee.

'Do you want another?' He gestured to her cup.

'Oh, no, thank you. I was only having it to pass the time till teatime.'

Mauro grinned laconically. 'This is very English. To have coffee to pass the time till tea. Do you have cake to pass the time till dinner?'

Janet smiled. 'I suppose it did sound a bit daft. Quite decadent too, really.'

To her astonishment Mauro burst out laughing. She was amazed how it transformed his face. In place of a jeering gnome was a weather-beaten imp. There was something oddly appealing about the change.

'What's so funny?' she inquired, infected by his splutters.

'You. Because you are so English.'

'Why should that make you laugh?'

'Because I love this in the English. They say, "Oh, I am having a cake before my dinner. This makes me very wicked." This I have always liked.' He shook his head and swallowed his coffee in one. His face became stern. 'But you are wicked because you are not on the mountain practising to turn your snow-ploughs.'

Janet looked abashed. 'I know. I was going to, I really was.'

'So why do you not do it? Tomorrow you will say to me again, "I have forgotten", so we must start again. Am I right?'

'I hope not.'

'I hope not too, otherwise I think your husband will wish he had not paid me five million lire to teach you.'

'*How* much?' Her mind spun with conversion tables.

'Yes. Is a lot. He must love you a lot to pay all this.'

Janet frowned. 'He's got a funny way of showing it.'

Mauro leant back in his chair. 'You would rather have a diamond ring, I suppose? Or a fur coat?'

'I'd rather have a wet weekend in Clacton than skiing lessons,' Janet snapped, not liking to be patronised.

Mauro nodded thoughtfully. 'That would be very good. Still, you are here now. What can you do? Enjoy it, I think.'

'The way you do?'

'Your husband does not pay me to smile all the time,' Mauro responded stiffly.

Janet brushed a piece of pastry off her sleeve. 'Just as well or we'd have to remortgage.'

There was a silence. The waitress brought the bill. She grabbed it. Mauro said something to the woman. She nodded and went away. Janet ferreted through her purse for the right money. She laid it on top of the bill.

'That is all right. It is paid.'

She looked at him in bewilderment. 'It isn't.'

'Yes. I have told her to put it on my ...' He snapped his fingers irritably. '*Conto, conto, conto.* What is it?'

'Account?' Janet suggested.

'Yes, yes. That will do.'

'There was no need,' she said primly.

'I know.'

'I'd really rather pay for myself, as a matter of fact.'

Mauro picked up her glove which was lying on the table and emptied her money into it. 'I have made you angry.'

'You're always making me angry,' she burst out, caught off guard. 'At least, not you. Well, actually, yes, you. You and ... not just you. Oh, what the hell.' She stood up.

'Where are you going?'

'Home.'

'For tea?'

She tried not to smile.

'Do you come to the display tonight?'

'What display?'

'Ah. Your daughter did not tell you. We talked of it last night.'

'My daughter has hardly spoken to me since last night. Apparently it's not good form to worry when you lose your child up a mountain in a foreign country in the middle of the night.'

Mauro looked genuinely chastened. 'For this I blame myself.'

Janet relented. 'No. You can blame yourself for a lot of things, Mauro. Including making me feel like the lowest form of human life. But that was not your fault, and you are to stop worrying about it. It was nothing to do with you. Without you she'd probably still be up there. And me too. Frozen into the side of the mountain. My very own ice sculpture.'

He considered this, not knowing for once whether to laugh or scowl. 'OK,' he said, his voice clipped. 'Tonight there is a display. The instructors will give a show. It is a circus. The people come to see them make idiots of themselves. To jump through the hoops. Like fools.'

'Like lions, you mean.'

'What?'

She roused herself. 'Not like fools. Like lions.'

Mauro gave a little shrug. 'OK. So, anyway, you will come?'

'What time is it?'

'Nine o'clock.'

'I'll try. It depends what the others have planned.'

'Of course.'

She picked up her bag. Mauro was gazing at her. 'What is it? Why are you looking at me like that?'

He shook his head. 'No, nothing. *Non e niente.* I only was thinking, why if you have hair like that, do you cover it with that hat?'

Chapter Seventeen

Hugh was late back. Belinda and Owen reported that he had said he was calling in at the hotel. Janet's heart sank as she imagined him berating Annie, to the delight of some lurking Ski Dreams employee who would then report back to her colleagues that the other occupants of Chalet Nevosa were quite as vile as the McDermots.

She didn't know why she was so sensitive to their good opinion, particularly since it was fairly clear none of them would cross the road to save her life if they knew where she was staying.

Hugh's face said it all. Or rather Annie's did, for she came trailing in behind him, much as Debbie had done prior to absconding. Janet badly hoped this would not end the same way. If Annie fled they really would be at the mercy of Cheryl's catering.

'Annie has something to say to us,' Hugh informed them, tight-lipped. Everyone looked at her expectantly, except Janet.

The courier swallowed and took a breath. 'I'm afraid there's been a slight . . .'

'Hitch,' they all chorused.

'Yes. Not the company's fault, as I was explaining to Mr Gale.' Not very convincingly, Janet noted as Hugh poured himself a double whisky.

'There's a baggage handlers' strike at Gatwick,' Annie faltered. 'It's only for twenty-four hours and then Teresa will be with you. She studied at the Pru Leith School,' she added enticingly. 'Apparently she's a brilliant cook.'

Hugh swivelled his drink menacingly. 'Meanwhile? Are you suggesting we save ourselves up for dinner time tomorrow or is there any plan to feed us before this paragon arrives?'

Annie stared at her feet. 'I've asked Hayley to stay on,' she murmured wretchedly. 'Just for tonight.'

Hayley did not seem any more enamoured of the arrangement than the rest of them. Looking at the potato soup, followed by boiled chicken then vanilla ice cream, Janet wondered if there was some school of cookery that favoured monochrome ingredients, or whether it was just to save having to wash the tablecloth.

The meal was as tasteless as it was colourless, not helped by Bob's announcement that he supposed they all knew it was Valentine's Day, and the production of a grotesque chocolate heart garnished with trails of pink ribbon, which he noisily presented to Cheryl while Hayley was making the coffee.

Cheryl went as pink as the ribbon and appeared to have been robbed of all speech. Stuart immediately tried to break a piece off which brought forth a roar from his father. 'You keep your grubby little hands off that, my boy. It's your mother's. You don't see Janet's kids eating hers.'

'I haven't got one,' Janet admitted with relief. 'Hugh and I are long past all that.' She didn't add that they'd never actually been reduced to such soppiness.

Cheryl's eyes brimmed with sympathy. 'Oh, but it's so nice, isn't it? Just to get a little reminder?'

'Go on, Mum. Give us a piece,' Stuart interrupted, saving Janet the need to reply.

'I don't want to open it,' Cheryl dimpled. 'It's so pretty.

Look at these beautiful ribbons.' She entwined them round her fingers like a cat's cradle. The heart thumped off the edge of the table into her lap. To the acute embarrassment of the Gale family, she broke into a flutey two lines of 'Anyone Who Had a Heart'.

'That reminds me,' Bob's voice cracked across hers. 'Don't forget the karaoke contest. Got to go in for that.'

Is there no end to this man's competitiveness? flashed through Janet's mind. And no end to his lack of talent? She didn't dare look at Hugh.

'Yeah!' rasped Stuart in an appalling imitation of no one in particular.

'Trish nearly won last year, didn't she, Chicken?' Bob informed them. 'She did a stunning Tina Turner.'

'Celine Dion,' Tricia snarled.

'Will I have to sing, Mum?' Belinda asked in the longest conversation she had had with her mother for days.

'Not if you don't want to.'

'Are you going to?' Belinda sounded even more worried.

Janet burst out laughing. 'Wild horses wouldn't make me sing in public.'

'Aha. Everybody's got to have a go. Rules of the house.'

Janet glanced across at him. 'Your house, maybe,' she said.

'But, darling, I'm absolutely whacked.' Hugh had turned down Bob's invitation to look at his scheme for redundancy payments and was skulking in the bedroom. Janet had followed him and suggested the instructors' display.

'You don't have to do anything. Just watch.'

'I'd fall asleep. You forget I've been skiing since nine o'clock this morning, more or less.' He sank back on the bed and closed his eyes. 'Blin's really coming on. She'll make a brilliant skier once she's got her confidence. That's what it's all about. Confidence. I'm sure Mauro's told you that?'

'He never stops,' Janet conceded, thinking if anyone could destroy a person's confidence for life, it would be Mauro.

He was a strange man. She wondered what he was like amongst his friends — if he had any. She imagined it would take a certain kind of person to get on with someone so irascible and discontented. She wondered what his wife was like; if they had any children; what he would be like as a father; what he did during the summer months.

Hugh's voice broke across her reverie. 'Anyway, I should have thought you could do with an early night. You were moaning this morning about being tired.'

'Was I? I feel all right now.'

'That's probably because you've been skiving all afternoon. Spare a thought for us poor workers.'

Janet sniffed. 'I wasn't skiving. I ...' But she was still in denial about the chalet girls' revelations. 'I went for a walk. Quite a long one, up past the church. It's so peaceful there. You get the most marvellous view of the valley.'

Hugh grunted. 'And?'

'And nothing. Then I walked back down and had a cup of coffee and an enormous pastry in the café on the corner.'

'Is that why you turned down Hayley's ginger cake?'

'That, amongst other reasons.'

Hugh grinned. 'I don't know who taught that girl to cook but they should get ten years, minimum.'

'She does her best.'

He opened his eyes. 'I hope that's not true.'

Janet was silent for a moment.

'What are you thinking about?'

'Nothing. I was just wondering if all Ski Dreams holidays are this chaotic, even without the McDermots, and Harriet didn't dare tell us.'

Hugh flopped back against the pillows. 'Harriet's not like that. She's much too upfront to try to hide the truth — from us of all people.'

Janet sighed. 'I suppose you're right.'

Hugh frowned very slightly. 'Of course I'm right. We've known her long enough, for Christ's sake.'

'Yes, all right. There's no need to get cross.'

'I'm not. Just a bit surprised at you, that's all. She's our oldest friend.'

'Hugh, I'm not accusing her of anything. If she did know and didn't want to tell us, I'm sure it was from the best of motives. There's no point in setting off on a holiday expecting it to be awful, is there?'

Hugh sat up. 'That's rich. Coming from you who've done nothing else from the moment our name came out of that box.'

'Don't start all that again. You're just picking on me because you're annoyed about having no one to cook your bloody dinners. It wouldn't surprise me if you'd prefer me to be like Cheryl and spend half the day cleaning the damn place. That's your idea of a perfect holiday, isn't it?'

'No it is not.'

'Next time I won't tell you what I'm thinking if it causes such offence.'

Hugh reached out his hand to her. 'Jan . . .'

'What?'

There was a perfunctory rap on the door. Bob opened it. 'Sorry to disturb, but have you got our gin by any chance?'

The two of them gazed at him silently. 'Sorry?' said Hugh eventually.

Bob cast an inspector's eye round the room. 'Well, as you know, we bought two at the DF, and one of them seems to have gone missing. Just wondered if you might have nabbed it on the way back from our bath? No problem, you understand, but the old lady was saying she'd like to break all her own rules and have a nip. When I came to look for it, no could find.'

Hugh rose and took a step towards Bob. Janet, moving quicker than she knew herself capable of, grabbed hold of his hand. 'We haven't, Bob. No. I expect it's got stuffed under a pile of dirty socks or something. There's not that much room, is there, once you've unpacked?'

Bob, possibly relieved that he would not have to pursue the matter, took a step back. 'No, fine. Just thought I'd ask. I expect she's found it by now. If not, I'll have a word with the girlie. All very well, these young kids looking after you, but we all know they're no angels.' He retreated, shutting the door behind him.

Hugh turned to Janet. 'Thank you for that.'

'For what?'

'For stopping me killing him.'

'I think that's my priority.'

'You know where that gin is, don't you?'

'No. Why should I?'

'Well, technically speaking, it's probably poisoning the local fish. Cheryl's had it.'

She gaped at him. 'She doesn't drink. Well, hardly at all.'

Hugh's face twisted in disbelief. 'Jan, she's virtually an alcoholic.'

Janet felt vaguely numb. 'What on earth are you talking about?'

He collapsed on the bed. 'Darling, she's at it from eight in the morning. She's got the stuff stashed all over the place. In the kitchen, in the boot store, down the pan, for all I know. Why do you think she had a go at that kid the other evening?'

'Well, I . . .'

'You're not saying you haven't noticed?'

'I did think my drink was a bit weak that first evening,' she havered.

'God, I thought you'd realised. I thought you were having a dig.'

'Oh crumbs, Hugh, what do you take me for?'

'No, I'm sorry. I should have guessed. You're so bloody unsuspecting.'

Janet frowned indignantly. 'What's that supposed to mean?'

Hugh sighed. 'Nothing. I'm sorry.'

'It sounded like another criticism.'

'Well, it wasn't. It's just . . .'

'Just what?'

'Just it would be nice to have someone who was on the same wavelength as me, just once in a while.'

Janet felt as if she'd been punched. She picked up her bag and stalked to the door. 'I should give Harriet another ring,' she said and left him to it.

Belinda did not want to go to the display. Tricia had promised to bead her hair for her. As anticipated, Owen was taking Rachel to a disco. Janet braced herself for the moment when Bob announced that he and Cheryl would accompany her, and had to struggle to contain her delight when Cheryl confided, almost apologetically, that they were going to the bowling alley. Apparently there was some sort of competition. 'You could all have entered too,' she murmured. 'I asked Bob if we should get you a form, but he . . . he . . . I think he forgot.'

Janet warmed to him. 'That's all right. Hugh's too tired to move a limb and Blin and Owen have made their own plans, so it wouldn't have worked out. It's a kind thought, though,' she added, buzzing with relief and goodwill.

'You're welcome to come and watch us, if you like,' suggested Cheryl. 'Cheer us on and that. To tell the truth I'm not frightfully good at bowling. I hope I'm not going to let Bob and Stuart down.' She looked so genuinely fearful that Janet felt a wave of pity. She wondered what had happened about the gin. No more had been said.

The night was clearer than the previous evening. She could actually see the Milky Way as she trudged through the snow, a twinkling shawl enfolding the mountain peaks. The air seeped into her lungs like a tonic. She felt fresh, invigorated, free. She was on an adventure. Going alone, at the specific invitation of her own private instructor, to watch him perform feats of derring-do in front of an audience of hundreds, for her and her alone.

She caught sight of her reflection in a shop window and was brought swiftly back to reality. I am a 45-year-old woman in a crimson puffa jacket with a silly hat, who has just had a row with her husband, she thought dejectedly. I am on my way to watch a middle-aged gnome leaping around in the snow, performing tricks he will taunt me with all tomorrow morning.

She almost turned back. But why? Hugh's accusations had hurt her. Just because she didn't know the signs of a secret drinker didn't mean she went around in rose-tinted spectacles. There were a few things Hugh hadn't spotted over the years, even in his own children. And what about condemning them all to a week with Bob McDermot? Someone he had known or known of for ages? He and Harriet. Perhaps it was some dark conspiracy on their part to drive her mad. Like the woman in *Gaslight*. That had been the husband. She couldn't remember why.

The lift station was crowded with people making their way up. Decision time. Did she really want to be crushed between all these strangers, just for the privilege of half an hour's freezing on a metal bench? Wouldn't she rather go home and curl up in front of the fire with her book? Hugh would have gone to bed by the time she got back if he stuck to his intentions, unless Bob had been kind enough to let him look at his latest bunch of thumb prints. She had seen the package lying ominously on the sideboard before supper.

'So, you come?'

She leapt. Mauro was standing a couple of places behind her in the queue. 'Well, I ... Yes.'

'Where is your family? Have they left you behind again?'

She smiled. 'Not exactly. Belinda and Owen had made other plans.'

'And your husband?'

'He's ... He wasn't feeling too good. He's gone to bed.'

'And you do not stay to nurse him?'

Her smile faded. 'I think he'll survive.'

They were now being ushered on to the platform as the giant lift swung to a halt. Mauro stepped neatly round the people between them and guided her into the cabin. 'What about your friends? The other family?'

She shook her head. 'They couldn't come either. They've entered a competition at the bowling alley.'

Mauro nodded. 'Let's hope they are happy with the result.' Their eyes met.

'That's not very kind,' Janet said reprovingly.

He shrugged. 'True, though, I think.'

'Shouldn't you be up there already?'

'Why? It has not begun, I think.'

'No, but don't you need to get ready, or anything? Get into costume?'

Mauro gave a bark of laughter. 'You think because I say it is a circus I must come on with a clown's face? Well, that I have, but no, I do not need to wear a red nose and a funny hat. It is not that sort of circus.'

'I'm sorry,' said Janet. 'I just thought ...'

'What did you think?'

'Oh, nothing. When Belinda's in a school play she gets there hours in advance. She says she has to get in the mood.'

Mauro cast a scathing glance around the occupants of the lift. 'Perhaps she does not do the school play *ogni mercoledì* for seven months. Yes, every Tuesday — no, Wednesday, the clowns come out to play. The performing ... what are those fish things?'

'Dolphins?'

'No. Oh, come on, what is it?' He glared at her irritably. 'Performing ... black, all slidy?'

'Seals?' Janet shot at him nervously.

'Seals, yes. That will do. I hate to forget my English. I really hate that.'

'Your English is superb,' she pandered.

Mauro grunted. 'For a Ladino.'

This was too much. 'Are all Ladinos bad-tempered?'

He gazed at her in amazement. Now I'm in trouble, she thought, but she was getting rather sick of men in general. How much flattering did they need in order merely to function?

'You think I have a bad temper?'

They were coming into the station. The lift started its customary jolting. Janet lurched forward. Mauro caught her in mid-stumble. Embarrassed, she seized the hand rail and steadied herself. 'Thank you. I lost my balance.'

'This is not new.'

'No.'

'You do not answer my question.'

'Which question?'

'Do you think I have a bad temper?'

Janet thought for a moment. Was honesty what he was looking for? Probably not. 'Well, since you press me, yes, I do.'

Mauro continued to gaze at her, his eyes strangely troubled.

'I'm sorry if I've upset you,' she told him, not feeling remotely sorry, 'but you did ask.'

He nodded, and pushed his black wool hat further back off his forehead. 'You are right to say what you think,' he conceded, plainly still perturbed. 'But with you I have been so patient.' He turned and strode away in the direction of the instructors' cabin.

Janet watched in stunned admiration as the instructors flew over burning barrels, swivelling in mid-air to fling lighted torches to each other.

They skied backwards, sideways, up the mountain again, performed somersaults, back flips – even formed a human pyramid on their skis.

Several times she hid her eyes, fearful that she had chosen the one night of the year to witness a human disaster, but when she looked again, generally prompted by the enthusiastic whooping of the crowd, there they all were, still alive. Still upright, too, which seemed even more of a miracle.

It was late when the show ended, and she was tired. Doubtless Bob would be rapping on their door at seven, regaling them with details of his triumph at the bowling alley.

She found, without realising it, she was searching the crowd for Mauro. There was no sign of him. Just as well, she told herself. I'd hate to have to tell him how brilliant I thought he was. By tomorrow he'll have forgotten all about it.

It saddened her to think that someone who could perform such acrobatic feats should be confined to teaching holidaymakers to snow-plough. Particularly ones with as little aptitude as she had revealed.

The crowd surged forward at the sound of an approaching lift. Janet, yet again, felt herself being edged out of the way by a wall of hardened queue-jumpers.

'So, why do you let these people push you out of the way?'

She looked round. Mauro was forcing his way towards her. For once he was not wearing his hat. She noticed that what hair he had was strangely bent.

'Because they're bigger than me.'

Mauro snorted. 'Well, they are bigger than me, also, but that does not mean they will walk all over me. Come.' He grabbed her arm and frogmarched her between the mighty Germans. Janet said nothing. She would greatly have preferred to catch the next lift.

'So. How have you enjoyed the circus?'

She roused herself. 'I loved it. I thought it was absolutely brilliant. I was nearly sick when you all started throwing those flaming torches to each other.'

Mauro sniffed. 'Me also.'

Janet warmed to her subject. 'Is it actually as dangerous as it looks?'

'Let us hope not or I should not be doing it.'

'Well, I thought it was wonderful. When you all climbed on each other's shoulders I couldn't believe nobody fell off.'

'You would prefer it if they do?'

'No,' said Janet. 'Of course not. Why do you have to turn everything I say against me?'

Mauro made a face. 'Do I do that? Maybe I suppose I do. It is all so stupid. Performing . . .' His face began to twitch again.

'Seals,' said Janet quickly. 'Anyway, how do you know they don't enjoy it? What's wrong with entertaining people?'

'Nothing, if that is what you want to do.'

'You don't, obviously.'

Mauro yawned. It made him look vulnerable. She had not imagined him ever feeling tired. 'I want, I don't want . . .' he said wearily. 'Who knows what they want? Do you?'

The lift lurched unexpectedly. Janet caught her breath. 'Mostly I do. But then I'm not a particularly ambitious person.'

Mauro grunted. 'That is the best. Ambition is for young people, I think. Only young people.'

They were coming into the base station. Janet made sure her feet were anchored this time. 'That's rubbish,' she countered. 'What's the cut-off point?'

'For being young?'

'For being ambitious. For being alive, for heaven's sake. It's the same thing. Surely you can see that? You've got to want something, otherwise what's the point of anything?'

The Italian looked at her curiously. If Janet had not known better she would have thought he was in danger of smiling. They walked out into the frosty air. 'So you must walk home by yourself?'

'It's not far.'

'No. So — I am going the other way. I will see you in the morning. Then I will teach you the human pyramid.'

Janet laughed. 'I'm not sure I'm quite ready for that.'

This time Mauro did smile. 'No, but if this is your ambition?'

She shook her head. 'It isn't. Believe me, it isn't.'

He nodded. 'So, what is your ambition?'

She looked at him. How peculiar, she thought, to be having this conversation at this time of night with this virtual stranger. 'I couldn't begin to tell you,' she said softly.

Chapter Eighteen

The chalet was in darkness when she got back. She stumbled over a bag of rubbish as she was slithering up the path, now frozen to plate-glass smoothness. It tinkled ominously in the crystal air. She froze, like a schoolgirl out of bed after lights out. No one stirred.

She let herself in, her key in the lock as loud as a hammer to her ears. I don't know why I'm tiptoeing about like this, she remonstrated with herself. Tricia made an awful noise being sick the night before last. I'm not sure that Brian's a very good influence.

Guided by the dying embers of the fire, she felt her way into the lounge and switched on a lamp. Signs were she was the last one home. Coats were strewn across the settee and on the table lay a score sheet from the bowling alley. Heartlessly she studied it. Two were reasonable, the third not. Poor Cheryl, she thought. I bet she got hell for that.

'Did you have a nice evening?'

Janet screeched. Cheryl was sitting quite still in the far corner of the room. 'Goodness, Cheryl, you frightened me,' she said shakily. 'I didn't see you there.'

'Would you like me to put the light on?' Cheryl's voice had a strange monotone to it. Memories of the chalet girls' conversation came flooding back.

'It's all right.' Janet groped for the overhead light switch, half expecting the woman to produce a meat cleaver and take a run at her.

Cheryl was in her dressing-gown, a fluffy affair blotched with large blue flowers. In her lap lay the chocolate heart, still untasted, but beginning to show the scars of too much fondling. The paper was torn and the ribbons muddied with escaping chocolate.

'How did you get on at the bowling?' Janet asked with unnatural brightness.

Cheryl stared at her.

'The instructors' display was marvellous. You should have come,' she chattered on, unnerved.

Still Cheryl gazed at her.

'Well,' Janet backed towards the stairs. 'I think I'll get to bed. Are you ... Can I ... Shall I leave the light?'

Cheryl nodded vaguely, then suddenly shook herself. Like someone emerging from hypnosis, her normal voice returned. 'Yes, thank you. I'll be up in a minute. Just make sure the kitchen's tidy.' She clambered to her feet, still clasping the heart like a hot water bottle. Janet started up the stairs.

'I thought it was awfully sweet, didn't you? To remember it was Valentine's Day?' Cheryl called after her.

She turned. 'Oh ... Yes. Very nice. Very kind of Bob.'

Cheryl shook her head quite vigorously. 'I didn't mean Bob. I bought this heart myself. He doesn't even remember my birthday.' She sighed. 'No, I meant Hugh. Stuart heard him ordering the flowers.'

Poor Cheryl, Janet thought as she made gratefully for her bed. Even her children wind her up, but it did seem very cruel of Stuart to tease her like that.

Hugh was lying on his side facing inwards. It was something Janet found strangely endearing, the fact that he liked to sleep with his arms round her. Often she would wake in the night, almost suffocated by the combination of Hugh and duvet.

In her efforts to free herself she would occasionally dislodge his protecting arm and he would rumble and grunt before re-establishing his triffid-like hold on her, always without regaining consciousness.

She undressed and crept in beside him. Hugh stirred. 'Who's that?'

'The lady you bought flowers for,' she murmured under her breath. Hugh grunted and turned over to face the wall.

She heard him get up. It was still dark outside. He stumbled around, trying to find his clothes, and made such a noise that in the end she reached across and turned the bedside lamp on. Hugh jumped as though he'd been caught in the middle of a burglary.

He blinked at her guiltily. She noticed he had hold of her salopettes. 'Are you planning to wear those today?'

He glanced down, clicking with irritation as he swapped them over. 'I didn't wake you, did I? I was trying to be quiet.'

At least we're speaking again, she thought. 'No, that's all right. I was only dozing.' She caught sight of the clock. It was a quarter to seven. 'Why on earth are you getting up at this hour? It's not even light.'

'We've got to be at the lift by half past.'

'What?' she groaned, trying to remember what awful treat Bob had lined up for them today.

'We're doing the Sella Ronda. Right the way round. Twenty-six miles. Got to make an early start.'

'Who is?' She sat up in bed, her head fairly popping with panic.

'Bob and me. It's all right. You go back to sleep for a bit, why don't you?'

'You didn't tell me about this.'

Hugh looked slightly abashed. 'No, well, I planned to last night but things got ... well ... and then you went out. I was going to leave you a note if you didn't wake up. Cheryl knows all about it.'

'She knows about a lot of things.'

Hugh glanced at her, puzzled. Not now, Janet decided. She would tell him about last night's encounter later. 'I take it she's not going?'

He laughed and rolled his eyes. 'Isn't one of them enough?'

'So you'll be away all day?'

'Till teatime, providing the weather holds. Clive was saying there're some storms on the way but they shouldn't arrive before the weekend.'

'What's everyone else doing?'

Hugh shrugged. 'Same as usual, I would imagine. Blin and Owen are going skating after their lesson. Don't know about the others. Mauro'll take care of you, won't he, for the morning? What are you grinning about?'

Janet composed her face. 'Nothing. Just from what he was saying last night, I wouldn't be surprised if we met you halfway round this Sella Ronda. He was threatening me with all sorts of party tricks.'

A flicker of a frown crossed Hugh's face. 'You saw him last night?'

'Yes, of course I did. I went to watch the display.'

His face cleared. 'Oh yes, of course. How was it?'

'Brilliant. You should have come. You would have enjoyed it.'

Hugh was hunting for his watch. 'Maybe. Anyway, I needed an early night. I was shattered. Look, I'm sorry about last night. Having a go at you and that. You were right. I was just so angry with that silly cow, Annie. I mean, how many cock-ups can one person make? I shouldn't have taken it out on you.'

Janet nodded sleepily. 'So long as you don't buy me a chocolate heart to atone.'

'Spoilsport.' He bent over and kissed her forehead. 'I'd better go or he'll be sounding the reveille outside the window.'

'Have fun,' she muttered and pulled the covers back over her. A whole day without Bob McDermot. How good could things get?

Tricia did not appear at breakfast at all. Cheryl seemed unperturbed. Belinda confided to her mother that her roommate had been violently sick when she got home and had sworn she had no intention of going anywhere near a mountain or a bar ever again. The first seemed more likely than the second.

Stuart, who had assumed his father's mantle *in absentia*, nagged Cheryl mercilessly about the bowling match. Why had she not taken his advice and worn a pair of gloves? How had she managed to miss on the final strike? Why had she let them all down so miserably? Poor Cheryl was beginning to look every bit as browbeaten as when her husband was around.

Owen appeared and asked/demanded that Stuart go and remove his socks from the shower immediately if he didn't want them fed down his throat one by one. Stuart was clearly in some fear of Owen, whether because of his size or for some other reason. He rose without demur and returned some minutes later to inform his mother that they were on her bed and needed drying. Cheryl scurried off.

Janet got up. 'I suppose we'd better be making a move.' Owen and Belinda stared at her in amazement. 'What is it? What have I done now?'

'Is this our mother?' Owen asked Belinda solemnly. 'Is this the same person that arrived with us on Sunday? Actually telling *us* it's time to get going? A revolution has taken place. Mum is now a ski addict like the rest of us.'

'I wouldn't go that far,' said Janet cautiously. 'I just don't want Mauro to leave me to go on that chair lift by myself, and if there's one thing I know, he won't wait if I'm not there.'

'Do you think we should give the others a yell?' suggested Belinda. 'At least let them know we're going?'

'Yes,' Janet agreed, shamed into action. 'Of course. I was just going to. Give them a shout, will you, Owen?'

Owen called up the stairs. After a few minutes Cheryl came to the landing. 'I'm so sorry, I'm afraid I'm going to have stay back at the chalet this morning. Poor Tricia's not feeling at all well. Must be something she ate,' she added sharply just as Hayley appeared to clear the table.

'Or drank,' muttered Owen under his breath.

'Oh dear,' said Janet. 'Do you want me to ask Clive to send for a doctor?'

Cheryl shook her head, obviously flustered. 'No, no. I'm sure there's no need for that. She just needs to rest, but I'd rather stay with her. You know how it is, us mothers.' She gave a trilling little laugh. 'Stuart's coming, though. Stuart,' she called. 'The others are waiting. Do get a move on, pet.'

Stuart emerged from the lavatory eating a bar of chocolate. 'All right. Keep you hair on.'

'And don't forget that little bit of shopping I asked you to do for me,' added Cheryl nervily.

'Half a litre of cherry brandy,' recited Stuart.

Cheryl's eyes widened in alarm. 'It's just a little gift,' she explained rapidly. 'For Bob's aunt. I think you met her. She's looking after the house while we're away.'

Janet nodded. 'Yes, of course. We had dinner together.'

'Mmmm,' said Cheryl unhappily. 'I think I'll just pop upstairs and see how poor Trish is.'

'Are you sure there's nothing I can get her? Some aspirin or anything?'

'No, really. Thank you. She just needs to rest.'

They separated at first base, Janet having made Owen promise not to eject Stuart on their way up. 'Why not, for — Frank's sake?' growled Owen.

'You'll pollute the snow,' said Belinda, which Janet thought was pretty good for thirteen.

'Anyway, think of the fuss Bob would make,' she added. 'And poor Cheryl would be frightfully upset.'

'When she sobered up,' said Owen.

Janet glanced at him, shocked. Am I the only person not to know what's going on around me? she wondered. Am I really so blinkered? The answer was not entirely to her liking.

Mauro was waiting for her, dressed as always for a funeral. His black clothes suited his personality, she thought. Like Masha in *The Three Sisters*, in mourning for her life. Was that what Mauro was doing? Mourning for his life? And what would that life have been? Head chef at the Savoy? His own restaurant, serving York puddings and roly Polly? He had about as much of the 'mine host' about him as Basil Fawlty with a migraine.

He stepped forward. 'You are late.'

'Am I?' she stammered. 'I'm so sorry. There was a bit of a problem at the chalet. Tricia, that's Mrs McDermot's daughter, wasn't feeling too well.'

'So? You do not stay to nurse your husband but you will stay for someone else's child?'

'She isn't a child,' said Janet irritably. 'If you ask me, it's a hangover. I didn't feel I could just walk out. Anyway,' she added with more confidence than she felt, 'the lift was full. We would have been late anyway.'

'This is, in all probability, true.' He turned abruptly and strode off. Janet bustled after him, catching several people with her skis as she went. They exclaimed bitterly but she was not going to be left. 'Please wait,' she panted as they got to the turnstile.

'I have no choice. The gate does not open.'

'I know, but the other side. Please don't rush off. I'll never get on it by myself.'

'Of course you will get on it. The question is, will you get off?'

'Probably not. I'd rather go with you,' she pleaded.

Mauro made a clicking noise and shooed her through. 'When I say "sit" sit. *Sit.*'

They sailed off into the white wilderness. 'Where is your husband this morning?' asked Mauro after a while. 'He is still ill?'

'No, not at all. He got up hours ago to go on some trip all round the Sella Ronda. Bob's gone too. It was only for advanced skiers,' she added in case he had any ideas.

'In which case your friend Bob will be in trouble.'

'Will he?' asked Janet. 'He's been here before, you know. They came last year.'

'So I have heard. Also I have heard that he had to be rescued on a black run by the police helicopter. This was an expensive ride for him, I think.'

'Really?' Janet's eyebrows rose. 'He never said.'

Mauro glanced at her ironically. 'Would you say?'

'I doubt I'd have much choice in the matter. My family would never let me forget.' She started to laugh.

'Why are you laughing?'

'I was just thinking about all those photos he forced us to sit through the other evening. Of last year's holiday. Pity no one took any shots of him being hoisted into a helicopter.'

Mauro grunted. 'Perhaps it is better you do not say I have told you this. There are some things it is better not to remember, I think. You are ready? Try to lean forward when you leave the chair. Then perhaps you will not fall over.'

'Can I ask you something?' she asked as Mauro pulled up.

'Ask me. Bend your knees. Remember what I have told you.'

'Sorry. Do you think Clive should have let Bob go on this excursion if he's not up to it? I mean, surely it's his responsibility to make sure everyone's capable of getting round?'

Mauro shrugged. 'They are all adult, I think. They must make up their own mind. With a child – your daughter, for example – he can say, no, she is too young, I will not answer for her. But for a grown man, what can he do? If the man says, I can do this. I have done it before ...' His shoulders rose expressively.

In truth, Janet was not thinking about Bob McDermot who, she felt sure, could be ducked three times and boiled in oil without any noticeable effect on his health. She was thinking about Hugh. How well could he ski? On his own admission, he had hardly done any since his twenties. Still, his instructor seemed to think he was ready for the Advanced class, and he had gone on the trip with Clive the other afternoon. Also Hugh was approachable, which Bob was not. If Clive said to him that he didn't think he was ready for it, Hugh would take his advice. Yes, he was bound to be OK.

'*Bend* your knees, I said. Now we will turn, so what must you do?'

'Point my skis – feet, I mean – the other way.'

'And?'

'And ... turn?'

A rattling sound came from Mauro. 'Where is your weight when you turn?'

'Oh. Stand up. Point my feet, and stand up.'

'So. Do it.'

Janet started to wobble.

'OK. Too late. You must turn clean. Like so.' He swooped in a perfect semi-circle. 'Now you.'

Janet swivelled towards him.

'OK, and left ... and right ... and left. This is good. Now stop. I said *stop*. You have forgotten how to stop? This I cannot believe.'

'I have stopped,' she grumbled, hoisting herself back on her feet.

'So I see. Still, this is not bad. Now I will teach you to ski parallel. Then this afternoon you must practise and tomorrow I will take you on the Sella Ronda myself.'

'*No!*' shrieked Janet.

'Ah, but this is a joke. Now come. This time instead of the snow-plough you must point both your feet the same way.'

'Which way?'

'It does not matter, so long as they are both the same. Only not down or you will … OK, I should have said this first. I did not think you would do this like Tomba la Bomba.' He skied down to where Janet sat, having torpedoed into a handy snowdrift.

'Here is some advice for you. Always on a mountain, face the left or the right. Never the up or the down. OK? *Never.* You understand?'

'I think so.'

'OK. We try again. You are a funny woman.' He chuckled to himself.

'I'm glad I amuse you.'

'Yes. Very much. OK. Do you make your husband laugh?'

'I would if he could see me now.'

'Yes, still he must love you a lot to give you so many lessons.'

Janet stopped searching for something to clean her goggles with. 'Maybe,' she said. 'Maybe.'

Chapter Nineteen

Parallel skiing was not like snow-ploughing. In fact, it was so manifestly different that Janet several times wondered why Mauro had bothered to teach her the latter in the first place. Except that if he had not, she would undoubtedly be dead.

It seemed to her that every step she had mastered in the art of turning, stopping and staying upright now had to be unlearnt. Her balance was all wrong. Instead of keeping low she had to pop up and down like a jack-in-the-box, remembering at the same time to turn her feet, sink back down, widen her arms, straighten her body and not fall over. SAS training could hardly be more complex. She made a mental note to apply for a commission when she got back.

Mauro was merciless, haranguing, criticising, rebuking, all the time pounding out the relentless rhythm. 'Up . . . down . . . up, right, *right* . . . down, left . . . up, right and stop. OK. Again. Lean, up, down, left. That's left? OK, I am a monkey. Right . . .'

Janet consoled herself with the thought that, if nothing else, she must at least have lost a stone in weight. By the end of the morning she seemed to be getting the hang of it. That, or Mauro had got sick of shouting at her. Finally he called a halt.

'OK. So that will do for now. This afternoon you must practise this till you are blue in the face.'

'I am blue in the face,' she wheezed. 'I'm exhausted.'

'To ski well you must work hard.'

'I have worked hard. And I still can't ski well.'

Mauro was silent for a moment. 'Well, perhaps you are not too bad,' he said shortly. 'Now come on and I will buy you some lunch.'

'What?' she asked, not quite trusting her ears.

'I will buy you some lunch. If you like. Perhaps you are meeting your friends?'

'No. That is . . . No. Thank you. That would be very nice. If you're sure you don't mind?'

'Why shall I mind?'

'I don't know. I thought perhaps you were getting a bit sick of me.'

Mauro surveyed her critically. 'With you I can practise my English.'

Janet looked around her. Mauro had eschewed the main terrace for a tiny dark trattoria set to one side of the main lift station. For a moment she had feared he was leading her to the Bar Amico, beloved of the McDermots, for pizza out of a packet, but the Osteria Nevosa was tucked away just behind the *carabinieri* office. It seated around thirty people, all of whom were Italian, and served the most delicious soup she had ever tasted.

She blew once more on the *osso buco*. 'Can I ask you something?'

'Of course.'

'Why are so many things called *nevoso* here?'

'Are they?'

'Well, our chalet is and so's this restaurant.'

'Two is many?'

'It is for such a funny name.'

Mauro looked confused. 'How is this so funny?'

'Well, why should you call your chalet nervous? Or your

restaurant, for that matter? It's a bit odd, don't you think? What's so funny now?'

He had exploded into laughter. The waitress came over and demanded to be let in on the joke. Soon the whole restaurant seemed to be in corporate stitches at Janet's expense.

Mauro wiped his eyes. 'I like that.'

'What?'

'You are one funny woman.'

'Obviously.'

'*Nevoso* is not nervous. That is *nervoso*. *Nevoso* is snowy. Lots of snow. You see, it is not such a stupid name, perhaps? Not a very good one, either,' he added. 'Not ambitious, huh?'

'Ha ha.'

His face became serious. 'You are offended?'

She shook her head. 'No, of course not. I asked for that, didn't I? Promise me one thing, though?'

'Is what?'

'Not to tell Bob McDermot. I'd never hear the last of it.'

Mauro's eyes narrowed in distaste. 'I don't tell that man anything,' he said, tearing at a piece of bread.

'Do you teach many Brits?' Janet asked, seeing she was the only one in the restaurant.

'No. You are the first.'

'You're joking. But surely Ski Dreams have been bringing people here for ages?'

Mauro grimaced. 'Yes, of course. But they want to ski in a big bunch. I do not teach the big classes.'

Janet was taken aback. 'Do you only teach privately then?'

'Yes, of course.'

Suddenly it all became clear. 'You don't normally teach beginners, do you?'

Mauro shrugged. 'I will teach anyone if they pay me to.'

'So Hugh has paid for an advanced instructor to teach me how to snow-plough?'

'Yes, he has.'

'And you didn't bother to tell him that? That he was paying for the services of someone who usually coaches Plomba la Bomba?'

'Is Tomba. Alberto Tomba. Italy's greatest skier. He brings his own coach. I do not teach him.'

'No, and you don't teach people like me who've never skied before either, do you?' Janet felt the anger rising in her. 'You've taken my husband for a right ride, haven't you, Mauro? You've charged him enough to pay our mortgage for the next two years, just to stop me falling over in the snow. Well, actually, I don't much care whether I fall over or not, because we don't have *any* snow at the seaside. That's something you didn't know, did you? For all you say you love England.'

Mauro sat back in his chair. 'All right. You are angry. You are right. I tell you something. This man, Clive, comes to me. He says, "I have a customer. He wants his wife to learn to ski. She is English. Her lessons must be in English. Can you teach her?" What do I say? "No, I can't teach her"? "No, I can't speak English"? "No, I don't need the money"? I tell you something. In the summer this place is full of people walking. They come to walk. What do I do? Do I teach them to walk? I think they can do that. So, I am a guide. I show them the flowers, the view, the birds, all about. What do I care about the fucking birds? I am a cook. I cook the fucking birds if I can, but no, I have to say "*Veniamo.* Come this way. Here are beautiful birds. Let us look at their ..."'

'Plumage?'

'What? Anyway, all I want really is to cook these things and make soup from them but I must say how lovely they are. This is my life. Saying how lovely the birds are.' He stuck a fork silently into his food and tasted it. 'Too much salt.'

Janet tasted hers. It was wonderful. 'I'm sorry,' she said eventually. 'I had no right to have a go at you like that.'

Mauro looked up from his dish. 'Do you think I have not tried hard with you?'

The question threw her. 'No one could have tried harder. I just wish I hadn't let you down.'

'Why do you say that?'

'Because you're right. What you said in the café yesterday, I should have been out practising. I should have progressed a bit more.'

Mauro shook his head. 'It's nothing. You do your best. You are on holiday. Why should you work all the time? For me it is different. It is my job.'

They ate in silence. Several of the other diners obviously knew Mauro because they spoke to him in the rough Ladin dialect which seemed to contain more grunts than syllables. Janet tried to follow what they said, but the longer she was in Italy the less she remembered of her Italian.

Suddenly the door opened and the two young *carabinieri* came in. She sank down in her chair in the hope that they would not see her but, to her dismay, they made straight for the table where they were sitting. Catching sight of her they nodded briefly and launched into a rapid-fire conversation with Mauro. He answered them in monosyllables, the expression on his face scarcely changing.

When they had gone he looked across at Janet. 'You understood what they were saying?'

'No, not a word.'

He grunted. '*Ben.* It is nothing. There is a small problem they need my help with, so I cannot watch you ski this afternoon after all.'

'I didn't know you were planning to,' said Janet in some alarm.

Mauro chuckled slightly. 'You would never have known. Anyway, now I cannot do it, so you need not worry. You can say to me tomorrow, "Yes, I practised very hard," and I will not know if you have been to the shops instead.'

Janet bridled. 'I said I would practise, so I will. I may be a rotten skier, but I'm not a liar, so far as I know.'

Mauro looked grave. 'I am sorry. I meant this for a joke.'

She relented. 'I'm sorry, too. I shouldn't be so touchy. What did the *carabinieri* want, or can't you tell me?'

Mauro fiddled with his spoon. 'Nothing. Just they need someone to help with some skiers who are ... having a small problem. Do you want another coffee? There is time.' He looked up and saw her staring at him, her face full of dread.

'It's them, isn't it? It's Clive's party. What's happened to them? Is—'

'No, no, no. You don't worry yourself. It is all OK. Why do you think I am sitting here, if it is serious? It is nothing. Only a very small problem. You can believe me.' He reached across and patted her hand in a perfunctory way. 'They are a bit slow, that is all. The *carabinieri* have asked I go and show them the quicker way, that is all. Otherwise the storm may arrive.' He looked behind him and signalled the waitress for the bill. 'Anyway, they are wrong. The storms will not come till Friday, if then.'

'How do you know?' asked Janet in agitation, her mind already full of St Bernards and avalanches.

'Because I know the mountains. I know when a storm is coming. Today it will not come. I make a bet with you. I can bet you if the storm arrive today, tomorrow you need not make the descent.'

'What descent?' she gasped, terror piling on terror.

'Oh, I forgot to tell you. Tomorrow we ski from Il Cordone down to La Pedana, so I advise you to practise your turns very well this afternoon.' He paid the bill. 'OK, so now I must leave you. You are OK?'

Janet made a small squeaky sound. Mauro gave her arm a quick squeeze. 'You will be fine. I see you tomorrow.' With a brief wave to the proprietor he was off.

Janet sat for a moment contemplating her fate. Widowhood, if the storm arrived, and death if it did not. She became aware that the clientèle was observing her cautiously. Clearly women did not sit alone in restaurants in this part of Italy. She rose and made her way quickly out into the chilly afternoon air. The sun had disappeared and a layer of filmy cloud was drifting slowly over the mountains. There was scarcely any wind and patches of blue still dotted the sky although, even as she watched, they became fewer and further between. There was a dampness to the air that made her shiver. I'd better start practising, she thought, just in case this storm doesn't break in time.

An hour and a half later, Mauro's instructions still pounding in her head, she resolved that she had done enough. The light was now very poor, the cloud having thickened to a sort of dense yellowy mass from which an icy sleet was beginning to fall.

She had virtually mastered the turn, provided she went very slowly, and concentrated rigidly on what she was doing. As soon as she allowed her thoughts to stray, even for a moment, some dreaded hillock or snowdrift would rise up to trap her and she would be flat on her back again.

She ached, she throbbed, her palms were crisscrossed with the indentation of her nails through her gloves, her hair was flattened against her forehead with perspiration and her eyes stung behind her steamed-up goggles, but she could turn and she could stop. She wished in a way Mauro had been there to witness her efforts. She wondered what he would have made of them. Probably found something to scold her for.

She had never known anyone so volatile – one moment he was snarling and snapping, the next capsized with giggles, although the balance was firmly weighted towards snapping.

She wondered what he really thought of her, if anything. Why should she be any more to him than a source of income and a grammar check? And yet once or twice she had caught him looking at her with such a strange expression in his eyes. She shook herself. I must be getting light-headed, she rebuked herself. Altitude sickness has set in.

The queues for the lift were as bad as in the morning, reminding her that this was the first time she had spent a full day on the mountain. She felt a stab of pride. I'm a skier, she told herself, and jostled her way to the front of the platform.

Cheryl was sitting by herself at the table with her back to the door. Hayley had left them a jam sponge which looked as though it would bounce off the wall. Ignobly Janet wished she had stopped off for a cake in the village.

'How's Tricia?' she asked cheerfully, still glowing with achievement.

Cheryl jerked her head. 'Tricia? Oh, fine. She went off to the bowling alley at lunchtime. She's friends with one of the lads there. Well, I thought it wouldn't do any harm. She needed some fresh air.' She gave Janet a quirky little smile. Janet wondered if she was waiting for Stuart to return with the cherry brandy.

'I take it the others aren't back yet?'

'What? Oh, no. No, you're the first.' She turned round suddenly. 'Janet, I think there's something you should know.'

Janet looked at her. Confession time, she thought. How do I handle this? 'Oh?'

'Yes. It's not been easy for me. In fact, I've been trying to decide all day what to do for the best.' She lapsed into silence and Janet half hoped she would leave it at that. Did she really want the burden of Cheryl admitting she had a drink problem? It was insensitive of her, she knew, but she was rather hoping that after this holiday she need not see the McDermots again. The last thing she wanted was to be cast in the rôle of confidante. Where might it end?

Cheryl sighed. 'It's about Hugh.'

'What about him?'

'Well, just . . . Bob and I have been married for a long time. Nearly thirty years.'

'Congratulations,' she murmured, fearful that a celebration was being planned.

'So it's not as though we're not experienced.'

Janet felt slightly sick. Not the secrets of their sex life, she prayed.

'And all I wanted to say was, I'm sure it's perfectly innocent and everything, but I just thought it was right that I should let you know – the way you mentioned about Tricia going into town the other evening. I didn't think you were interfering in any way. I mean, we women should stick together, shouldn't we?'

Janet was now hopelessly confused. 'I'm sorry, Cheryl. I seem to have lost the drift. What exactly are you trying to tell me?'

Cheryl looked increasingly nervous. She was clearly not used to so direct an approach. 'Well, nothing. But, you know, these telephone calls. Bob says he's made one nearly every night. And, you know, what with him being a bit of a ... You can't help worrying, can you? I mean men will be men, won't they? I just thought it fair to let you know.'

Janet stared at her. 'Bit of a what?'

'Well, no, I didn't mean it to sound like that.' Cheryl was now very flustered.

Janet's tone hardened. 'It didn't sound like anything, Cheryl. That's why I'm asking you. Unless you're suggesting Hugh is having some kind of clandestine affair with the telephone operator?'

'No, no, not at all. I just thought you might want to know. Because of the flowers. I only wanted to help. Men of that age ... You read about it all the time.'

'*You* may do, Cheryl. I prefer to rely on facts and I think I know my own husband well enough to spot if he's cheating on me.'

'Yes, of course. I didn't mean to interfere ...'

'I'm sure you didn't, but please, Cheryl, *never* make a suggestion like that to me again.'

Cheryl's cheeks flapped in dismay.

'*Never*,' Janet repeated ominously.

There was a rap on the door. She crossed quickly and ripped the door open. There stood an enormous ruddy-faced girl with an equally enormous suitcase and a teddy bear the size of a small child tucked under her arm. 'You'll be Mrs McDermot,' she announced in a strong Irish accent.

'Mrs Gale,' said Janet firmly.

'Right,' said the girl. 'I'm Teresa. You'll be wanting your tea, I daresay,' with which she bundled past Janet and swept into the lounge. 'Hi, there. Would you be Mrs McDermot?' she demanded of Cheryl who was still sitting by Hayley's sponge as though waiting for the order to detonate it.

'I ... Yes. I ...'

'Will I make us all a nice cup of tea?' Without waiting for an answer she barged into the kitchen and began clattering around inside.

Cheryl tiptoed after her. 'Would you ... It's just I've been here before. If you'd like any help?'

'No, dear. No thank you,' came the unequivocal reply. 'You just relax and leave it all to me. Holy angels, will you look at the state of this cooker?'

Several clangs later Teresa re-emerged with a tray of tea and, unbelievably, a plate of home-made biscuits. 'Excuse me if they're stale. I made them last night for if I got caught up in the strike again. Now you tuck into those while I just sort out my pots and pans.'

Cheryl and Janet ate silently, accompanied by a cacophony of crashes and a running commentary, addressed mainly to the holy martyrs, from the kitchen. Teresa's arrival had rather taken the wind out of both their sails, somewhat to Janet's relief because although she was annoyed with Cheryl, she had no desire to pursue the matter. Let Cheryl fantasise all she liked so long as she kept it to herself. Poor woman, it was probably the only pleasure she had, apart from her Mills and Boons. With a surge of literary hauteur, Janet settled herself by the fire.

THE EXCITEMENT BUILDS

Last night I was privileged to witness a spectacle of rare intensity and brilliance.

I was a guest at the private invitation of my personal coach, Signor Mauro ...

She thought. What was his surname? No point in losing the flow.

Signor Mauro Tomba, at the famous Instructors' Display, an event which takes place every Valentine's Day high up in the Dolomite mountains.

It is rumoured that the event originally came about when a poor peasant goatherd, fearing that he would lose his adored sweetheart to a wealthy farmer further down the valley, lured her into the mountains during a horrific snowstorm and, to take her mind off her terror as the lightning crashed about them and huge ice boulders tumbled past their heads, he performed feats on his skis of unimaginable skill and daring, not only distracting the maiden but also securing him her undying love.

I can only say that if the goatherd showed half the skill of the highly talented professionals who had us all on the edge of our seats last night, I'm not surprised the young lady gave him her heart! What more romantic way to spend St Valentine's Day?

Today I have been practising for my grand descent tomorrow. Mauro is convinced that I am ready and I have every faith in what he says.

Teresa, our new chalet girl, has just arrived, and seems like a lot of fun.

There was a crash as the front door flew open. Stuart appeared, carrying his skis and a brown paper carrier bag. 'Got it,' he announced, dumping the bag on a chair and helping himself to a handful of biscuits. 'Saw Trish down the town.'

'Oh. How was she?' asked Cheryl in a staccato voice.

'OK. She was trading tonsils with some guy up the bowling alley.'

'Stuart, honestly,' his mother clucked. 'I don't like to hear you talk like that. Have you seen the others? They should be back by now.'

'On their way. Someone said Dad got stuck on the same run as last year. Had to send some dork out to rescue him, otherwise they'd've been stuck all night. The police refused to go this time. Said he could stay there, for all they cared. That's the fuzz, for you. These biscuits are crap.'

'We'll have less of that sort of language, thank you,' came a voice from the kitchen.

Stuart's mouth fell open, revealing an even larger quantity of crumbs than usual.

Chapter Twenty

Janet heard Hugh come in. At least she heard Teresa telling him who he must be and her shrieks of delighted laughter as he denied it mightily. A few minutes later he opened the bedroom door, a plate of biscuits in his hand.

'She seems like an improvement,' he said cheerfully. 'Home-made biscuits. That's more like it. Kids back yet?'

'I haven't heard them.'

He offered her a biscuit. 'I asked if she'd like a hand with her luggage but she said no, she could manage. I didn't like to argue.' He grinned.

'Very wise. She's already put Stuart in his place.'

Hugh's eyes widened. 'Has she? I like her better by the moment. What did you say her name was?'

'I didn't. It's Teresa.'

'Right. I shall try and remember it.'

'I should. How was the trip?'

'Fantastic, for the most part. You can't believe how stunning the scenery is round the other side. Even better than here, if that's possible. One minute it's all brilliant sunshine and the next you're in forest. That's what it feels like, anyway. Probably only a thicket from up above. You'll be going along through the trees and you think you're miles from anywhere and suddenly there's a tiny cottage or a hut with smoke coming out of the chimney and someone actually living in it. It's like "Hansel and Gretel". I half expected a witch to appear.'

'You had Bob,' she reminded him.

He laughed. 'He did manage to put his usual evil eye on things.' He hesitated. 'No, that's not really fair. It was a pretty scary run. That's the thing about these Italian maps. Their idea of a red is nothing like anyone else's. They're much closer to black, some of them. Poor old Bob got stuck coming down, between a couple of rock faces. He wasn't the only one. Two or three people had trouble, but Bob's problem was he lost his nerve. He got sort of jammed up against a ledge and Clive just couldn't get him to let go. We were there for ages. In the end Clive phoned through to the *carabinieri* to drop him a rope from the helicopter. Fortunately it didn't come to that.'

'What happened?' asked Janet.

Hugh looked slightly aggrieved. 'Well, actually, they were a bit of a pain. Apparently something of the kind had happened last year and the guy's insurance company kicked up stink about paying for the 'copter, so they sent a guide over instead. He sorted him out OK. It was just a matter of persuading him to let go of the ledge.'

'Mauro.'

Hugh frowned. 'How did you know?'

'I had lunch with him. The *carabinieri* came looking for him while we were in the café.'

'So you knew about Bob?'

'I did, yes, but not from him. All he told me was the group was getting behind time and they were worried about the weather breaking, so he was going to show you a quicker way back.'

'How did you find out then?'

'Stuart. Nothing like family loyalty, is there? I wouldn't be surprised if half the village knows.'

Hugh bent down and undid his shoelaces. 'God, I ache. Yes, quite a day. How was yours, by the way? Learnt any new stuff?'

'I think so. I had a practice this afternoon by myself.'

Hugh looked encouraged. 'That's good. Mauro will be pleased. He was telling me how well you'd come on. I think he quite likes you.'

'He keeps it very well hidden,' she murmured, oddly gratified.

Hugh laughed. 'He is rather dour, isn't he? Still, he worked wonders with our Bob.'

'Did he shout at him?'

Hugh shook his head. 'Nooo. Nothing of the kind. It was interesting really, the way he talked to him. Almost as though he was asking his advice. "How do you think we should do it? What would you suggest?" etcetera. Well, you know Bob. Worked a treat. He was so busy trying to impress, he was off the ledge before he knew it. I must say I've got a lot of time for that guy. I didn't know it when I booked him but I doubt I could have found you anyone better.'

Janet shrugged. 'You could have found me someone with rippling muscles and a year-round tan.'

'You've got me.'

'So I have.'

Bob was back when they went downstairs. So were Belinda and Owen, both vying with each other over who could do the best Michael Jackson impression in preparation for the karaoke contest that evening. Teresa was watching them, tears of laughter running down her face. 'Would you look at them? Aren't they the dandiest things you ever saw?'

'My daughter nearly won last year,' Bob informed her.

'I'm not surprised,' chortled Teresa. 'She's a grand little mover and no mistake.'

'She's not back yet,' Cheryl explained.

'Oh goodness, well, I shall look forward to meeting her,' declared Teresa. 'Is she a little joker like this one?'

No one felt able to describe Tricia in those terms. 'She has a very fine singing voice,' Bob said stiffly. 'Now, who's for a game of Scrabble before supper?'

'Yes, yes, you get on and enjoy yourselves,' Teresa instructed. 'I'll just give that old fire a bit of a poke and then I'll get on with the meal.'

'Would you like me to give you a hand?' Cheryl pleaded, trotting hopefully towards the kitchen.

'Great heavens, no. You sit down and unwind a bit. Sure I come from a family of twelve. It's nothing for me to get a bit of dinner on.'

'Come on, Chicken,' Bob intervened. 'We haven't got all night. Let's get this table cleared.' He started to shove things unceremoniously off the coffee table, including Janet's notebook which she dived upon indignantly and tucked behind a cushion for safekeeping.

'Do we have to do this?' she whispered to Hugh while Bob was distributing the letters.

'Hmmm?'

'Play Scrabble? I hate it.'

'Oh, well, if it keeps him happy. He's had a hard day, poor sod.'

'Whose fault's that?'

'Come on, you kids,' ordered Bob. 'Get yourselves sorted. We're ready to start.'

'I can't play, can I, Mum?' Belinda said. 'I haven't had my shower yet.'

'No, OK. You go and get washed,' said Janet quickly. Belinda shot away.

'Come on, you boys. Let's see if it really is sawdust inside those heads of yours.'

'No way,' said Stuart, flicking a piece of chewing gum into the fire. 'Scrabble's crap.'

'Rubbish. It'll improve your vocabulary. Now get sat down.'

Stuart slumped sullenly on to the couch beside his mother,

who looked even less disposed to play than he did. Owen started off up the stairs.

'And where do you think you're going?' Bob demanded peremptorily. Owen stopped. Janet glanced at Hugh. Here we go, she thought. Bob's about to learn a few new words.

'I think it's probably better if I don't play,' said Owen in his best prefect's voice. 'You see, I'm dyslexic. I wouldn't want to hold everyone back.'

It was every bit as ghastly as she had expected. Stuart couldn't spell, Bob cheated, running up a score several times that of everyone else's, Hugh was half asleep and Cheryl clearly had no idea what she was doing. Janet struggled on, making weedy little words that for some reason or other were almost never allowed in the McDermot version of the rules.

'That's triple for me and I get ten for an X,' he droned, slapping down 'Exocet' right across where she had been going to put 'fox'.

'Isn't that the name of something?' ventured Cheryl, who had 'exit' all ready.

Bob ignored her. Hugh came to her rescue. 'I think it is, actually,' he said, stifling a yawn. 'Yes, I'm sure. It's a brand name. Sorry, Bob. No can do.'

Bob bristled with annoyance. 'That's absurd. It's like saying Biro's a brand name. Or Hoover.'

'They are,' said Janet indifferently.

'They *were*, I grant you,' snapped Bob, 'but they've passed into general usage. They are allowable.' He fumbled for the rules.

'Well, Exocet isn't,' Janet persisted. 'It refers to a specific thing.'

'It does not. It refers to any form of heat-seeking missile.' Bob was beginning to look like one himself.

'Oh, Bob, come on,' said Janet, delighted to see him so rattled. 'That's like saying Concorde's the same as "aeroplane".'

'It is. It isn't,' said Bob, thoroughly confused. He flapped the rules at her. 'I think you'll find it's perfectly permissible. Anyway, it's my game. I think I might be allowed to know the rules of my own game.'

'Now, now, no arguing.' Teresa appeared in the doorway, the frilly apron stretched ludicrously across a very small portion of her bosom. 'I'm making a few blini for your starter, with a bit of smoked herring pâté, then I've some lovely veal escalopes that I'll do with *rösti* and a light onion marmalade, and an endive salad to follow. I hope that suits?' She beamed at their salivating faces.

'Is it ready?' asked Stuart hopefully.

'Sure, give me ten minutes. Time for you to wash your hands and brush your hair.' She departed, leaving the entire party uncertain to whom she had referred.

Janet got up. 'I'll give Blin and Owen a call.'

Bob frowned. 'We haven't finished yet.'

'Well, you've won, that's for sure.'

'You don't know that. You might come back with a challenge.'

Janet took a deep swig of her depleted gin and tonic. 'Trust me, Bob. I won't. I've got J, S, M and Q. Now if you can make a word out of that you're a better man than I.'

'Gunga Din,' said Bob.

'She hasn't got a U,' Stuart pointed out, kicking the table so that everyone's letters fell over.

The dinner exceeded their wildest dreams following, as it did, four days of gastronomic famine. Janet would have liked to linger over the cheese board and Bob was reduced to going halves with Owen on the last slice of *tarte tatin*. They ate in grateful silence. Even Tricia, who had turned up halfway through the first course declaring that she couldn't eat a thing, fought her brother very hard for the right to scrape the *rösti* dish.

Bob rubbed his hands. 'What's everyone doing?' he asked as Teresa bustled around with coffee cups.

'Digesting the best meal I've had since I got here,' said Hugh.

'I mean for the karaoke. It's best to decide in advance so you're ready when your turn comes up.'

'Sure, I love the karaoke,' declared Teresa dreamily. 'My da does it down at the Peppercorn and he gets the prize every last time.'

'Who does he do?' asked Belinda.

'The Three Tenors.'

'All of them?' asked Cheryl, plainly struggling with the thought.

'Sure he's got a beautiful voice.'

'Tricia nearly won last year,' Bob broke in.

'I didn't, Dad. I came fourth,' muttered Tricia, looking genuinely embarrassed.

'Only because that girl had had lessons. She should have been disqualified. I said so at the time. Either it's amateur or it's not.'

'She was twelve, Dad.'

'Age has nothing to do with it.'

'Anyway, I'd only have been third if she had been, so what's the point?'

'It's a matter of principle.'

'Who are you going to do, Bob?' Janet intervened, seeing another row in the making.

'Me? No one.'

'No one?'

'No, I just like to watch. I've no intention of making an idiot of myself in front of a load of strangers.'

'Twice in one day, you mean?' As soon as she had spoken Janet regretted it. Not because Bob didn't deserve it, but for the expression on the others' faces. She sought to backtrack. 'Assuming they have heats and you get to the final.'

'It's not like that,' said Bob shortly. He looked at his watch.

'Time to be off, I think. If we don't want to be stuck at the back.'

'Remind me not to confide in you again,' Hugh muttered as they made their way down to the inn.

Janet kicked a bit of ice. 'I'm sorry. It just came out. Anyway, he must have known you'd tell me what happened. Not that you did. It was Stuart. I notice no one's having a go at him.'

'He didn't do it in front of Bob.'

'Oh, for heaven's sake, Hugh. Bob's a grown man. Theoretically. It's all right for him to make jokes at my expense all the time. I'm just not allowed to retaliate.'

'You can take it,' said Hugh gruffly.

Janet stopped dead. 'How do you know? How do you know how I feel being sneered at morning, noon and night? I have Mauro yelling at me all morning, then Cheryl stirring things in the afternoon, and Bob ruining every bloody evening with his bloody awful organising. I'm sick of it. I wish I'd never come.'

'So do we all,' Hugh retaliated angrily. People shuffled past on either side as the two of them confronted each other. He shook his head. 'I'm sorry. You know I didn't mean that. It's just you seem to be making such heavy weather of everything. What's happened to your sense of humour? You always used to laugh when things went wrong. Surely it's fodder for this column of yours?'

Janet stared at the ground, her eyes stinging at the injustice. 'Yes, I suppose so.'

Hugh tucked his arm into hers. 'Come on. Let's catch up with the others. Who knows, perhaps Cheryl's going to surprise us all with her scintillating impression of ...' His imagination failed him.

'Precisely,' said Janet.

* * *

'By the way, what did you mean about her stirring things?' he asked as they settled themselves as far from the microphone as possible.

Janet shrugged. 'I think she's a bit loopy, to tell the truth. She's got this idea you're the office Casanova. Something about you ordering some flowers on Valentine's Day. As if you ever would.'

Hugh looked slightly embarrassed. 'What did she say?'

'I don't know. It was in the middle of the night. I think she must have been at the booze. When I got home after the display, she was sitting in the dark in her nightie. Gave me a terrible fright.'

'I'm not surprised. I've seen her slippers.'

Janet giggled. 'Something about Stuart had seen you ordering some flowers down the town. I didn't believe a word of it. Just as well since they haven't appeared.'

Hugh cleared his throat. 'I did.'

'Did what?'

'Order some flowers.'

Janet stared at him. 'What on earth for?'

He shrugged. 'I don't know really. Because we were here, I suppose.'

She eyed him warily. 'You're not planning to turn into a romantic at this late stage, are you?'

Hugh laughed. 'You wouldn't let me.'

'Not if it involved chocolate hearts with pink ribbons.'

'That's next year's treat.'

Janet nodded. 'Actually, I'll tell you something rather sad. Something she let drop at the same time. Bob didn't buy her that heart. She bought it herself. Apparently he doesn't even remember her birthday. Imagine that. I bet he kicks up stink if she forgets his.'

'Exactly,' said Hugh so forcefully that several people turned to look at him. 'That's why I sent the flowers.'

Janet frowned. 'But what's happened to them? It can't take

much to transport a bunch of flowers from the village to Chalet Nevosa. Unless the locals won't go near it either. The curse of the McDermots.'

There was a burst of applause as four of the chalet girls finished their stab at the All Saints.

Hugh drained his glass. 'The flowers weren't for you.'

'Who were they for?'

'Harriet, of course.'

All Janet's feminist cool deserted her. 'Harriet?'

'Yes.'

'You sent Harriet flowers on Valentine's Day?'

'The fourteenth. Is that Valentine's Day?'

'*Is that Valentine's Day?* Of course it damn well is. Why else would you send someone flowers?'

Those engrossed in the five final Meatloaves shushed them.

'Because it's her birthday, of course. You can't have forgotten that? She comes to dinner with us every year. We've been doing it since I met you. Christ, Jan, what are you on about? Bloody Valentine's Day?'

Janet was mortified. 'I'm sorry,' she said at last. 'I lost track. Being here. It makes you forget. I should have sent a card.'

'The flowers were from all of us.'

'Thanks. I'm going to take her something back. Something really nice.'

'She'll like that.'

'I should have remembered.'

'You had other things on your mind.'

'Anyway, I don't suppose she was that bothered. I mean, we're only friends, aren't we?'

'Yes,' said Hugh. 'Only friends.'

Chapter Twenty-one

There was a distinctly icy atmosphere at the McDermot end of the breakfast table the next morning. This despite the aroma of fresh rolls and coffee, the wafer-thin slices of ham and cheese and a cornucopia of jams, honeys and gudgey-looking spreads to do with hazelnuts.

The reason was simple. Teresa, squealing, pink and doubled up with giggles, had taken second prize at the karaoke contest for her full-throated tribute to Shirley Bassey. She had been pipped at the post by the middle Meatloaf, amidst rumours that he had won three times before and might even be semi-professional.

Tricia had again come fourth, the chalet girls slipping into third, so that Bob's list of grievances had grown by the minute as he frenziedly noted the names of all the judges and cross-matched them with the competitors for signs of nepotism or worse.

Tricia herself seemed impervious to his frustration. Her attention had been caught by a slithery young Elvis and most of her energies had gone into exposing her chest, rather than using it to project the notes of her song.

Cheryl tried to soothe Bob as he rumbled into his coffee, emerging every few moments to complain about its temperature, the hardness of the butter, staleness of the bread, and anything else he could think of. Throughout this Teresa beamed good-humouredly, largely ignoring his demands. 'Sure I think someone got out of bed the wrong side this morning,' she observed cheerfully as she swept up the pile of sugar by his plate.

'What's that supposed to mean?' Bob snapped, his eyebrows like two sparring caterpillars.

'Nothing. Nothing at all,' Teresa soothed. 'Sure that was a lovely dress you were wearing last night, Mrs McDermot. Did you make it yourself by any chance?'

Cheryl went a blotchy pink and said she had got it from a catalogue.

'Sure it was the perfect colour for your skin.'

'When you two have finished discussing my wife's wardrobe, I think I asked for some more milk,' Bob snarled, but even he seemed to sense he was on to a loser.

'Sure you did, and I'll be forgetting my own head next,' Teresa agreed, not stirring an inch. 'Don't a lot of people think you can't wear red if you've auburn hair like yours, Mrs McD? But I always say they're quite wrong about that. Will you look at Fergie, how quaint she looks in some of her things. And she wears a lot of red.'

No one could make out whether Teresa thought this a good or bad thing so they grunted politely, and went to collect their skis.

Teresa came hurtling out of the kitchen as they were about to set off for the bus. 'Now did I remember to tell you about tonight, or did I not?' she asked.

'What about tonight?' asked Bob, stony-faced.

'It's my night off,' Teresa explained. 'Sure Annie would have let you know all about it when you arrived, but I thought I'd just better check.'

Bob did his fish-coming-up-for-air act. 'Night off? My dear girl, you've only just got here. How can it be your night off? What is this? One night on, one night off? If you ask me, you had most of last night off anyway. And I'm not at all sure staff are eligible to enter the karaoke, by the way. I'm going to inquire at the office this morning.'

Teresa bubbled with laughter. 'I know, and isn't it a terrible thing me just arriving, and then off I go for a night on the tiles. My da would shake his head over that, I can tell you. But it's not my fault. Every Friday. It's in the contract. Chalet staff have one night off a week and that's a Friday. Sure there'll be some lovely places to eat in the village. Will I ask about a bit and see what's recommended?'

'No you will not,' bellowed Bob and swivelled on his heel. He marched so quickly down the path that he lost his footing, nearly knocking Cheryl over in his efforts to right himself. 'I'm going to write to the managing director. It's simply not good enough. The next thing we'll hear is she can't make the beds because she's got a skiing lesson. Not that she'll be able to afford that on a chalet girl's pay,' he added, flinging a savage glance in Janet's direction.

'I doubt she'll need to depend on it much longer with a voice like that,' Janet shot back at him. Hugh rolled his eyes.

Mauro was waiting for her.

'I did practise,' she told him as the lift took them away.

'I know.'

'How do you know? I thought you were off rescuing Bob McDermot from some icy ledge?'

Mauro stared straight ahead. 'He told you this?'

'Of course not. Hugh did, though. Wasn't he meant to?'

Mauro shrugged. 'That is for him to decide.'

'Don't you tell your wife things?' asked Janet, stung by the implication that her husband had grassed.

'Only what she wants to hear,' said Mauro quietly, his face suddenly desolate. Janet wondered if she had ever seen anyone look so lonely.

'How do you know I practised?' she asked after a few moments.

Mauro continued to stare ahead. 'Because you said you would.'

Once he had got her back on her feet he seemed more his old self. 'You have done this every morning.'

'I know.'

'Why do you not listen when I tell you how to get off this lift?'

'I do listen. It's just too hard for me.'

'One day I will not be there and then what will you do?'

'Drown, I expect.'

Mauro made his clicking noise. It was a cross between a rasp and a rattlesnake. Not at all comforting. 'OK, if you want to drown you should go to the Mediterranean. Not *i dolomiti. Capisce, signora?*'

'*Si,*' said Janet, unaccountably buoyant. '*D'accordo.*'

'*Va bene.* You remember what I have said?'

'Yes. What about?'

'The storm? You remember I have said the storm will not come?'

'Yeees,' said Janet, her optimism beginning to wane.

'So, today we can make the descent. Down to the tramway station. You are ready for this?'

'No,' she wailed. 'Honestly, I don't think I am. I did practise. Really hard. It was dark when I got back, nearly. I was out for hours.'

'Well, so then you are ready. First we do a little exercise then I will lead you the way down.'

All Janet's confidence in her hard-won skills evaporated. She dithered and floundered and fell over more times than on her first morning. Mauro watched all this without comment. After about fifteen minutes he called a halt.

'OK. I can see you are not ready. This is OK. We will practise some more. Maybe next year you will be ready, huh?'

Janet was unsure whether this was a reprieve or an insult. She felt uniquely relieved either way.

Mauro led her to the top of a little crest. 'There.' He pointed. 'Do you know what that is?'

'It's the tramway station,' said Janet wonderingly. It was miles away. How could he have ever even considered making her ski down to it?

Mauro grunted. 'And you do not want to go there?'

'It's not that I don't want to,' she explained. The valley fanned out below them, putting her in mind of the Temptation of Christ. All this could be hers if only she weren't such a rabid coward.

'OK. We ski down to that rock. You see where I mean?'

Janet nodded.

'First you go right, then left. OK, I am behind you.'

Janet concentrated with all her might. Gradually the rhythm she had acquired came back to her. With the prospect of the first base off the agenda she began to relax.

'That is good. OK, now we go left first. We go as far as the path, see, where the snow-boarders are coming.' Off they went.

At the path Mauro skied round in front of her. 'This is much better but you are forgetting to lean your shoulders. Forward, when you go down. Keep your ...' he slapped his hips. 'What are these?'

'Hips.'

'Yes, OK. Ips. Keep them straight. Don't wiggle them. Is not a dance. OK. To the trees. You are ready?'

'Yes,' said Janet breathlessly. She was actually beginning to enjoy the motion, swinging gently left and right, the sun pouring out of a brilliant sky, the snow sparkling up at her. She glanced around at the distant skiers, like so many spilled Smarties tumbling down the slopes. I'm one of them, she thought proudly. Nonetheless she was glad Mauro had kept her away from them. Although common sense told her that their sole purpose was not to mow her down, it was hard to escape the feeling that she would be a sitting target for any sadist loose on the slopes. Her mind blurred as she pictured Bob McDermot bearing down on her, goggles steaming, teeth bared.

'What are you thinking?' Mauro was watching her in amusement.

She tried to compose herself. 'Nothing. I was just thinking how easy it would be to get knocked over by someone. I mean, it looks so crowded. I don't understand how people manage to avoid each other.'

'When you walk on the pavement do you knock people over?'

'No, of course not, but that's not the same at all, is it?'

'It is completely the same. When you drive a car in the traffic, do you run into the one in front? With skiing it is the same. You can stop, you can turn, you can go a different way. The mountains are big enough, I think, to hold all these people.'

'But they go so fast.'

'In the traffic the cars go fast. They do not all crash into each other. If you understand what you are doing you do not hit them, they do not hit you. OK, you are ready? We go a bit further.'

It was only when she glanced back and saw how far away was the ridge from which they had started that she began to worry. Mauro noticed this. 'You have a problem?'

'No. I was just wondering how we were going to get back up to the top. It's quite a climb, isn't it?'

He considered. 'We have a choice.'

'Yes?'

'Either we can stop here and climb back up to the top which, I think, will take us about one hour.' Janet's heart sank. 'Or we can ski down to that little hut and over the ridge, and then we will be at the first base.'

Her mouth dropped. 'What? You don't mean it? How can

we possibly …? I mean, I can't ski. How could I …?' She looked across the slopes. It was true. The terminal was lost to sight. That could only mean two things. They were the other side of the mountain, or they were below the mound that ran down to it. She gazed at him, her eyes shining. 'I've done it. I've skied all the way down. Well, nearly. All the way. I never thought I could do it. Well, I didn't do it. You did it. You never said. I hadn't the faintest idea. You are wicked. Oh Mauro, you are so wicked. You are the most wonderful teacher alive.' She flung her arms round his neck. Mauro backed away.

'Is OK,' he muttered gruffly, suddenly interested in his watch strap.

'Wait till I tell Hugh. He won't believe it. Just in one week. I can ski. *Wait* till I tell Bob. Maybe I won't. He's bound to spoil it. No, I don't think I will. Oh, Mauro, thank you. You are so clever. Thank you.'

'Yes, OK. I think now we should go. I have another appointment this afternoon.'

Janet sobered up. 'Yes, of course. I'm so sorry. I didn't mean to make you late.'

'Is OK. You don't. Not unless now you break your leg or something.'

'I probably will,' she said cheerfully, confident that she would never fall over again in her life.

They arrived back at the first base before the main influx. 'I ought to buy you lunch today,' chattered Janet, still euphoric. 'Can I do that?'

Mauro shook his head. 'What would your husband say?'

She was amazed by the question. 'He'd be delighted. Why not? Anyone who can teach me to ski. He should be buying you a champagne dinner.'

Mauro smiled slightly. 'Well, perhaps he will do that one day. When you have won the gold medal.'

Janet laughed. 'I've only got two days to do it in.'

'Well, I expect that is enough. Tomorrow I will take you

another way and then you can ski with your family all over the mountain.'

'Is tomorrow my last lesson?' She had not thought about it till that moment.

'Tomorrow is the last.'

A strange sense of disappointment flooded over her. 'I have enjoyed them,' she said feebly. 'I have really.' She felt Mauro's eyes on her.

'Me, too,' he said briskly. 'I will see you tomorrow.'

'Yes. Oh, Mauro ...'

He turned.

'Could you recommend any restaurants for us to eat in tonight? It's the chalet staff's night off. Not that they've had many on, in our case.'

Mauro shrugged. 'There are many places in the village.'

'Yes, I know. But somewhere Italian. Like where you took me. With fish. I really fancy some fish for a change.'

'For fish you should go to Il Pescatore. It is the best.'

'Thank you. See you tomorrow.'

'OK. Will you practise this afternoon?'

'Of course.'

'That is good. *Ciao, Janetta.*

'*Ciao, Mauro.*'

'You're looking jolly pleased with yourself,' Hugh remarked at lunch.

'I can ski.'

'What did you do today? More turns?'

'I skied.'

'Uhuh? That's good. Was Mauro pleased?'

'I think so. We came down to first base.'

'Oh? Why'd he do that? Too crowded up above?'

'For practice.'

'Oh, right.

'Hugh,' Janet put her hand on his arm, 'you haven't been listening to a word I've said, have you?'

Hugh looked unsettled. 'What do you mean?'

'I skied down from second base to here this morning. Mauro brought me all the way down. I can do it. Slowly, I grant you, but I can do it. And this afternoon I want to do it again.'

All three of her family fairly gaped at her. 'Really, Mum?' asked Owen. 'You came all the way?'

'Yes.'

'Did you fall over?' asked Belinda.

'Not once.'

'Bet you do next time.' Belinda had fallen over twice that morning.

'I expect I shall, but it doesn't matter. The thing is I'm not scared any more. I don't mind if I do fall over. I shall just get up and carry on. That's the difference.'

Hugh grinned incredulously. 'That guy's some teacher, even if he is a tetchy bastard.'

'He's nothing of the kind,' said Janet sharply. 'He couldn't be nicer if he tried.'

Hugh raised his eyebrows very slightly. 'If you say so, darling.'

Chapter Twenty-two

MORE SURPRISES!

Last night we went to the karaoke contest down at the inn. It was huge fun. Imagine all our delight when Teresa, our wonderful chalet girl, turned out not only to be the best cook in Italy, but also the best Shirley Bassey. Fellow guest, Bob, could hardly control his enthusiasm as she was voted the silver medal, just two places ahead of his own daughter, Tricia.

A sticky moment for me when I realised I had forgotten our best friend's birthday. Luckily, Hugh had not and had arranged, with his usual thoughtfulness, for a bouquet of flowers to be delivered to her back at home. It must be all this mountain air that is making me so forgetful. That, and the gorgeous Italian men!

Tonight is Teresa's night off so we shall be sampling the culinary delights of one of the local restaurants. Everyone is looking forward to trying something new.

Janet could hear the sound of raised voices as she tottered up the path to the chalet.

It had taken her a lot longer to come down the mountain without Mauro to guide her. The landmarks he had used now seemed impossibly distant and twice she had lost track of them, having to rely on the general direction the other skiers were taking. She fell over several times and once nearly lost her poles as they rolled down the slope away from her. She had nearly panicked when that happened. How would she get down without them? Or up, for that matter? She would be forced to wait for help (shadows of the *carabinieri*), or go the rest of the way on her bottom.

The prospect of either was too dreadful to contemplate, particularly as she would be sure to pass Bob McDermot and his brood en route, either under close arrest or with her lemon salopettes in tatters.

Fate had taken pity on her and the poles had stopped a few yards further on, trapped by a lump of snow, but she was glowing less with elation than perspiration when she finally slithered down to the terrace. She was exhausted, her head ached from the effort to concentrate, every muscle in her body crying out for a hot bath. The last thing she wanted was to walk in on a family row between the McDermots.

And she did not. For it was her own son's voice which greeted her as she opened the front door.

'All I said was, why don't you leave the poor sod alone for five minutes? That's all I said. It's meant to be a holiday, for Christ's sake.'

'Don't you adopt that tone with me, young man.'

'He's not even drunk. He only had a swig.'

'That's not the point. I do not want my fourteen-year-old son being initiated into the evils of alcohol by you or anyone else. When he's older he can choose for himself. He's at an impressionable age. You should be setting him an example, not egging him on.'

'I wasn't egging him on. He was the one with the bottle. I just said it would do him no harm. Christ, he was so scared he needed it. There was no way else you were going to get him down.'

'Stuart is a very competent skier.'

'I know he is.'

'He was perfectly capable of negotiating that run. He

did not need advice from a beginner like you, let alone bad advice.'

'It didn't exactly help, you yelling at him all the time.'

'I think I know what's best for my own son.'

'Humiliating him? Oh yes, that's really the best, isn't it?'

'I was not humiliating him. I was encouraging him. Stuart knows perfectly well what's expected of him. He has no problem with that. None at all.'

'That's all you know.'

'And just what do you mean by that?'

'I mean you're not sharing a room with him. He shouts in his sleep. He has nightmares, every fucking night. You knew that, did you?'

There was a silence then Bob spoke again. 'A few lessons in good manners would do you no harm, young man.'

'So long as they don't come from you.'

'Oh, ho, ho. They certainly wouldn't. If you'd been one of mine you'd have learnt some respect for your elders.'

Janet stood in the hall, transfixed. What do I do? she wondered. Do I let them fight it out, or do I sweep in and tell Owen to apologise immediately, or do I open the front door again and bang it shut? This seemed the best option and she was about to do it when Owen's words stopped her short.

'I respect people who deserve respect. You know what you are, you're a fucking bully.'

'Now hold on one—'

'No, I won't hold on. I've held on all this week. I've seen how you bully your wife and you bully Stuart and you've tried to bully my mother. Well, your family's your business, but you lay off my mother.'

'I don't know what you're talking about, young man.'

'You fucking do. You've been picking at her from the moment she arrived just because she can't ski. Well, I'll tell you something, she can now. She'd fucking ski you off the slopes.'

'Oh ho. Now I think I see what the problem is. A bit of

an Oedipus complex we have here, eh? I thought you were a bit slow off the mark with the young ladies. I think perhaps that explains it.'

Dots began to shoot around before Janet's eyes. 'Here I am back,' she screeched, hurtling into the lounge like the bringer of news from Ghent. 'Has anyone put the kettle on? We have to get our own tea this afternoon, remember.' She was through the lounge and into the kitchen before either of the men could draw breath. 'Where does Teresa keep those biscuits?' She set up a rattling of tins that would have deafened a banshee. Where are the others? she wondered desperately. Why don't they get back and rescue me from all this?

It had gone horribly quiet in the other room. Perhaps they've killed each other, she thought hysterically. I'll go back in and they'll both be lying there, slit from head to navel. She shuddered. Bob McDermot certainly wouldn't go quietly, and Owen, for all his moral courage, made an awful fuss about plasters.

'Hi, Mum.' She looked up from her sedulous search for teaspoons. Owen was standing in the doorway. 'I'm off out. I'm meeting Rachel.'

Janet formed her lips into a silly smile. 'Oh, right. Are you having dinner with us? It's just we haven't quite decided where we're going.'

Owen shook his head. 'No. We'll get something out. See you.'

'Yup,' said Janet, wondering if she sounded as ridiculous as she felt.

When he had gone she realised she should have asked if Bob was still in the lounge. If he was, there was no way she was going back in there on her own. Owen might not have killed him, but there was no guarantee that she would not.

She opened another cupboard and hunted amongst the packets and tins, her desire for a piece of Teresa's shortbread suddenly bordering on the fanatical. She found a large earthenware canister lodged behind the baking trays. It seemed a likely hiding place, given the need to conceal things from Stuart. She pulled the lid off. 'Oh my God!'

The floorboards creaked. She turned. Cheryl was standing in the doorway watching her. 'Bob said you might like a hand with the tea things,' she said in a detached voice.

Janet shot up. 'Oh. Right. Thank you.'

They busied themselves with setting a tea tray, Cheryl moving about the kitchen like an old hand. 'That looks about it,' Janet said cheerily when everything was ready. 'Could you just open the door for me, please, Cheryl? The others must be back in a minute, surely?'

Cheryl nodded. 'By the way,' she murmured, 'I hope you didn't mind Bob speaking to Owen like that. I know he's older and maybe you don't mind about him drinking, but I really don't think he should be encouraging Stuart. It's a little bit irresponsible, don't you think?'

Janet just looked at her. She thought hiding gin behind the baking trays was a bit irresponsible herself.

Tricia, surprisingly, was the first to arrive back. She had split her trousers – no one dared to ask how – and was in a worse mood than normal, complaining noisily to her mother that there were no crisps in the store cupboard. From the speed Cheryl moved to find some for her, Janet suspected there might be something else.

Belinda was full of plans for the night skiing when she came in. 'We've got to go. It'll be our last night. I wish we weren't going home,' she added forlornly.

'Well, perhaps we'll win the raffle again next year,' said Hugh blandly. None of the McDermots batted an eyelash.

'Are we going, Mum?' asked Stuart, grabbing a handful of crisps.

'Well, I . . .'

'Oh certainly,' Bob confirmed, rubbing his hands together. 'Definitely all be going to that. Let's hope the weather holds.'

'Clive thinks there'll be storms at the weekend,' said Hugh.

'He thought there'd be storms yesterday. The guy doesn't know what he's talking about.'

Listening to him, Janet was fascinated by Bob's ability to blot out anything he didn't want to think about or remember. Who would guess that he and Owen had been at daggers drawn half an hour earlier, or that he now knew his own son had nightmares about going skiing with him?

It tied in with her theory that he was an alien. He was probably operating in a completely different time zone from their own. Maybe he and Owen hadn't even had their row yet. No wonder his wife was a secret drinker.

'We thought we'd try the bowling alley for dinner tonight,' he announced, downing the last of the shortbread. 'They do a bolognese with side salad and a carafe of vino for a couple of hundred thou. Then the kids can have a game afterwards.'

'Stuart was saying he's got a bit of a headache,' Cheryl ventured.

'Rubbish. He's just hungry. I'm going to complain to Annie about this, by the way. It's all very well that girl having a night off, but she ought to have laid in a few cakes or something, don't you think? Anyway, back to more important matters. I take it we're all happy with that?'

'With what?' asked Janet suspiciously.

'Oh, didn't you hear? I said we'd pop down to the bowling alley for dinner tonight.'

'You can. I'm having fish.'

'They don't do fish. They've got a pizza if you don't fancy the bolognese.'

'I haven't come all the way to Italy to eat spaghetti bolognese, Bob.'

This amused him greatly. 'No, you'd rather have fish and chips. Pretty jolly adventurous.'

Janet felt her teeth beginning to grind. She glanced across at Hugh. 'Oh, come on, Bob,' he intervened. 'I think we want something a bit more upmarket than a pizza bar. The kids can go bowling afterwards if they want. Besides, I don't want to eat with all that crashing and shrieking going on.'

Bob's bottom lip began its customary advance. 'I've had a look round what's available and that's by far the cheapest. Pretty good bargain if you ask me.'

'Well, you go there then,' said Janet. 'I'm not and that's all there is to it.'

'There must be somewhere we can all get what we like,' said Hugh diplomatically.

'I'm not coming anyway,' Tricia announced. She had changed into a very short skirt and lurex T-shirt. 'I'm meeting Rico at half past six. We don't know what we're doing after that.'

'Oh, Tricia, do please get something to eat tonight, pet. I'm sure you're losing weight again,' pleaded Cheryl.

'Don't fuss,' retorted Tricia and went away again to apply more make-up.

'I suggest we just do our own thing,' said Hugh finally. 'Those who want, go to the bowling alley. Those who don't, try somewhere else. We'll be arguing all night otherwise and frankly I could do without it.'

'I'm sure we all could,' said Bob, giving Janet a savage smile. 'Still, there's always one, isn't there?'

Janet opened her mouth to respond but Hugh took her by the arm. 'Come on. You'd better get in the shower before rigor mortis sets in, all the exercise you've had today.'

'And try and leave us a bit of hot water, can you?' Bob's voice trailed her up the stairs.

Hugh closed the bedroom door. 'Sanctuary.'

'I hate that man.'

'Oh, Jan, come on. I know he's a bit irritating some-times.'

Janet glared at him in disgust. 'Hugh, what are you on?

"A bit irritating sometimes." Flaying alive would be too good for him.'

Hugh hunted around for a clean towel. 'You shouldn't let him get to you. It only makes him worse. If he sees an opening he's in there. It's only teasing. He doesn't mean anything by it. The more you react, the more he likes it.'

'Exactly,' said Janet sulkily. 'Which only goes to prove what a prat he is.'

'He's all right.'

She flopped on the bed and closed her eyes. Hugh came and stood over her. 'What are you thinking about?'

'Fish,' she said without opening her eyes. In fact she was thinking, is Hugh always so wrong about other people?

They met Teresa in the hall on their way out. She was wearing a very tight purple dress which made Janet think perhaps she had been genuine in her praise of Cheryl's.

'Are you all right there?' she asked. 'Decided where you're going?'

'We thought we might try Il Pescatore,' said Janet. 'I fancy some fish.'

Teresa pealed with laughter. 'Sure you're a better Catholic than I am, Mrs Gale. Do you know, I had sausages for my lunch? And here's me, I'll have to go to confession and tell the priest all about it. I only hope he won't understand a word I'm saying.'

Janet smiled. 'I can think of worse sins.'

Teresa's face became serious. 'Still, I shouldn't have done it. I feel awful now I think about it. My da would go mad if he knew.'

Hugh looked at his watch. 'I think we'd better get going if we want to get a table.'

Teresa beamed. 'And here's me making you late. I'll try not to wake you when I come in, but sure I'm hopeless in the dark. Would you be able to leave a light on for me, perhaps, do you think?'

The prospect of Teresa finding her way up the stairs in the dark was not one either of them fancied. 'Of course we will,' Janet promised. 'Have a nice evening.'

'I'll do my best,' Teresa promised and bounced off into the night in an enormous puffa jacket and mock snakeskin boots which Belinda eyed enviously.

'She'll be the next one to break her neck,' said Hugh ominously as she tottered down the path ahead of them.

Chapter Twenty-three

Il Pescatore was full when Hugh, Belinda and Janet arrived. They scanned first the menu and then the window. 'Looks a bit crowded,' said Hugh doubtfully. He was starving and the possibility of having to wait half an hour to be seated did not appeal. Belinda was now regretting not having come down on the side of the bowling alley, although she, too, relished the thought of an evening without the McDermots.

'Well, we're here now. We might as well ask if they've got a table,' said Janet stoutly, unwilling to be defeated at this late stage. She pushed the door and the three of them were sucked into the steamy warmth of the restaurant.

A waiter came over to them. *'Ha fatto reservazione?'* he asked.

'No,' said Hugh, preparing to leave.

'Inglesi?' said the man. *'Scusi.'* He hurried away towards the kitchen.

'I said it was full,' Hugh grumbled. 'Come on. Let's try that place near the fountain. There was plenty of room there.' Janet accepted she could do no more and was about to follow him when the waiter returned.

'Signora Gale?'

'Si,' she answered, flabbergasted.

'For how many?' asked the man in careful English.

'Just three of us. Come back,' she mouthed to Hugh who was waving at her from the street.

'Please, to coming this way.' He gestured to a table on the far side of the restaurant. It was set for four but the waiter swiftly swept away the extra setting and held out a chair for her. Belinda and Hugh came hurrying in.

'That was a stroke of luck. They must have had a cancellation,' Hugh remarked as the waiter took their coats and held out a chair for Belinda, who blushed mightily.

'Well, yes ... except he knew my name,' said Janet, still hopelessly confused. 'You didn't ring up earlier and try to book or anything, did you?'

'Me? How could I?'

'It's very odd,' she said. It became odder when the waiter brought a bottle of *spumante*.

'*E gratuito*,' he confirmed when Hugh expressed surprise.

'Perhaps it's Bob's way of saying sorry,' he suggested. Both Belinda and Janet nearly choked.

'It's probably a mistake. Any minute now the real Gales are going to arrive and we'll be thrown out on the street,' Janet speculated.

'Better drink up then, before they do.'

'I quite like this,' said Belinda.

'Well, don't get a taste for it,' warned her mother.

The waiter brought them the menus. 'What's ...' Belinda ran through the whole menu, testing Janet's long-forgotten vocabulary to the hilt. She came completely unstuck on *puledro sul pane tostato*. The waiter suggested unconvincingly that it was 'young horse on toasted', which they all thought they could do without.

Hugh had wild boar, Belinda pork with sour cherry sauce, and Janet a sizzling fillet of monkfish garnished with pine kernels and spinach.

'Your meal is good, all right?' inquired the waiter at regular intervals. No other Gales having turned up, they were beginning to think perhaps Bob or, more likely, Cheryl had made the booking. Doubtless they had told the proprietor that Hugh was an eccentric millionaire who would be happy to pay up to two thousand pounds for his dinner, Janet reasoned, loath to attribute any more philanthropic motive to a McDermot.

Hugh asked for the bill which, though not cheap, was not in the two thousand pound league.

'You will have *liquori*?' asked the waiter. 'The cooker say is on houses.' There was a small pause while they all debated what that might mean. '*Sono gratuiti*,' he explained, plainly not convinced of his translation either.

'Perhaps they have a deal with Ski Dreams,' Hugh speculated. 'There don't seem to be many other Brits here. Maybe they want to get more in.'

'It's not exactly empty, is it?' Janet pointed out.

'Well, why do you think we're getting this five-star treatment?'

'How would I know? Perhaps they're like that to all their customers.'

'I wouldn't give much for their chances of survival if they are.'

'Oh, well, whatever. I just know it was lovely.'

The waiter brought their coats. Belinda had arranged to meet a friend at the disco and was anxious to be off. They parted at the door, having instructed her to be back by eleven and on no account to go anywhere with Tricia. 'Fat chance,' came her parting words.

The two of them walked in silence past the glistening ice sculpture and on through the square. 'We don't go out much at home, do we?' Hugh ruminated.

'You're always away. And when you are home you're too tired to do anything.'

'I like your cooking.'

'I like other peoples'. I particularly like their clearing up.'

Hugh grimaced. 'I asked for that, didn't I? Do you fancy a drink somewhere?'

'Yes, all right. Where shall we go?'

'Clive was telling me the bar at the hotel's very good.'

'Let's try that then.'

They settled in a quiet corner of the hotel bar, Janet having scanned it for Ski Dreams' reps, and ordered brandies. 'I'll say one thing for this mountain air, it stops you getting hangovers,' said Hugh.

'I hope you're right. I've drunk more tonight than since we arrived. I feel quite whoozy.'

'That's because it was full strength,' Hugh observed.

Janet put her hand to her mouth. 'I knew there was something I meant to tell you. When I got back this afternoon Owen and Bob were having a bit of a row.' She hurried on before he could ask what about. 'Anyway, I didn't want to get involved, so I made a beeline for the kitchen to start on the tea. And while I was looking for the biscuits I opened a jar and there was a bottle of gin, half empty. So it looks like you were right.'

'Of course I was right. Didn't you believe me?'

'Well, yes, I suppose I did. But a drink's one thing. Hiding it all round the house is another. And Cheryl of all people.'

'You shouldn't take people at face value.'

'I don't.'

'You do, actually, Jan. You assume because Bob acts like a pompous prat, that's what he is.'

'Let's leave Bob out of it, shall we?' she retaliated. 'I was talking about real people.'

Hugh looked mildly annoyed. 'All right. Tricia, then. You think she's a little scrubber, don't you?'

'You don't, I take it?'

'No, I don't. I think she's a young kid with a few problems. That doesn't mean she's no good.'

'I never said she was. What is this?'

'And Stuart. All right, his table manners leave a bit to be desired . . .'

'You were the one who said he should be fed to the pigs.'

'Yes, well, he'd used all the shower gel.'

'I see. So when I make an observation it's because I have no understanding of the wealth of human decency buried deep in all these people, but when you make it, it's because you can't find the soap?'

'I don't mean that at all. Why don't you just listen for a change?'

'Oh, so now I don't listen?'

'No, you don't. Not to me, anyway.'

'Chance would be a fine thing.'

'Don't start that again. I'm going to make more of an effort. I'm going to be around more. OK?'

'Do what you like.'

'Jan . . .' Hugh put his hand out to her. 'What is this? Why are we arguing?'

She put her hand up to her head. 'God knows. Too much to drink, I expect. I think I'll walk back by the river. See if your theory works.'

Hugh smiled. 'If it doesn't I've got some paracetamol.' He glanced at his watch. 'I'd better make a detour round by the disco, make sure Belinda gets home all right.'

Janet looked at him in surprise. 'Why shouldn't she? There are plenty of them coming our way.'

Hugh fidgeted. 'Yes, I know, but still . . . After the other night on the toboggan run . . .'

Janet felt a stab of guilt. She hadn't mentioned that Stuart had known all along that Belinda was safe. Was this the right time? 'Do you want me to come with you?' she asked.

'No. You have your stroll. I should keep to the near side of the path though. It's not a night for a dip.'

They separated, Hugh heading into town, Janet retracing her steps. The lights were dimmed in the restaurant, with one or two diners lingering over their liqueurs. Again she was struck by the oddness of it all. She knew Mauro had recommended the place, but only because of the fish, not because the owners rolled out a red carpet for each new customer.

'You enjoyed your dinner tonight?'

She spun round. He was standing by the door of the kitchen, his hands deep in the pockets of a brown leather jacket.

'Mauro?'

'That's me.' He picked up an empty tin and tossed it into a wheely bin.

'But what are you doing here? Round here, I mean? Round the back?'

He shrugged. 'Going home. You?'

She nodded distractedly. 'Me? Oh yes, I'm going home too. I just needed a bit of air. I . . . Do you work here?'

He came down the path towards her. 'On Fridays. It is a busy day for them. All the chalet workers, they are off, so there are a lot of customers. Sometimes I help. It is good for the English. The others do not speak it very much.'

Recalling 'young horse on toasted' Janet could see he would have his uses. 'I didn't see you,' she blustered, feeling oddly exposed without her quilted coat and salopettes. Mauro, too, seemed strangely vulnerable in normal attire. He was no longer the impregnable controller of her destiny, just a small Italian man moonlighting at a restaurant. 'No, I am in the kitchen. I prefer to cook. Besides, I am too bad to be a waiter.'

'I thought you were a waiter in London?'

'Yes, but then I was young. I was more . . .' He glared at her. Janet struggled to find the word.

'Energetic?'

'No, no. I have energy. Enough for two hundred. I was not so . . .'

Where to begin? she thought. 'Old', 'crotchety', 'scathing' all came to mind.

'I was more kind with the customers. I could listen to them

choosing for five, ten minutes. Now I think, eat this, you stupid man. You will not know the difference if I give you fried grass. *Erba fritta.*' He permitted himself a smile.

'Impatient?' she suggested.

'Impatient. *Impaziente.* Is the same. Well then I am very stupid to forget this.'

'It can't be easy, translating things all the time.'

'It is good. It makes my brain work. Otherwise I forget everything. Where are you walking?'

'Oh, just along the path for a bit. I was going to go back by the river.'

'Are you not afraid on your own?'

She shook her head. 'This isn't London, is it?'

'You are afraid to walk in London?'

'I don't know. It's so long since I lived there. I think there are parts I might not like to walk alone in after dark.'

Mauro let out a long slow whistle through his teeth. 'When I was there it was not like that. Ful Ham. That is where I lived. King's Road. Swinging London. Yes? You remember that, or you are too young?'

'I remember reading about it. It sounded wonderful.'

'And did you go there?'

'Sometimes for the day. We lived in Croydon so some of my friends and I used to go up at the weekend. We were never allowed to stay late, though. Very tame, really, but it seemed exciting at the time.'

Mauro grunted. 'Maybe we remember things better than they are. Do you think this is possible?'

'I'm sure it is. That's why old people are always going on about the long hot summers we were supposed to have had. The records show they were nothing of the kind.'

Mauro kicked a lump of frozen snow out of the way. 'Me, I remember the long wet summers.'

'There you are, then.'

'Yes, but I loved them. They are what I miss. Rain. Wet,

wet, wet. Here is always snow or sun. Snow or sun. It is too cold to rain like in England, and in the summer it is too hot.'

They had rounded the corner of the little park that ran alongside the river. Janet could see the lights from the chalets further up the hill. 'Do you ever go back?'

Mauro sucked in the cold night air through his teeth as though debating a choice of answers. 'No, I have not gone back at all.'

'Why not? Wouldn't you like to?'

'I think if I went back I would not like to come home.'

This shocked Janet. She felt she was getting into dangerous territory. 'Perhaps you're right. It's usually a mistake to go back to places where you've been happy, isn't it?'

'You think so?'

'I think things tend not to be as good as you remember. At least that's been my experience. I can't speak for other people.'

Mauro was staring at the ground. Glancing around, Janet wondered how anyone could want to swap the fairytale beauty of the Dolomites for a rain-soaked London. Maybe if she lived here long enough she wouldn't see the icicles shimmering in the moonlight, and the stars, and the snow-covered mountains gleaming majestically above the valley. Maybe she'd be as bored and disillusioned as Mauro.

'Did you reserve that table for us tonight?' she asked suddenly.

He looked startled, his thoughts clearly miles away. 'I said if you came he should try to fit you in. Is all. We cannot make exceptions, you understand?'

'Yes. Yes, of course I do. I was just curious. We were very lucky then. It's obviously a very popular restaurant. Justifiably,' she added, sensing that she was blathering again.

'You are right. One time I thought I might buy it but they want too much money. Besides . . .'

'Besides what?'

Mauro shrugged. 'Is my wife's family own it. I think it is

not so good to be all together too much. Then everyone knows what you are doing always. You understand?'

'I suppose it could get a bit claustrophobic.' She glanced across.

Mauro nodded wearily. 'Yes, yes, this I know. *Claustrophobia.* Is the same, I think. Is the same wherever you go.' He stopped. 'OK, so this is far enough. Now you are home nearly. I will leave you.'

With a jolt she realised he must have come completely out of his way. 'Oh, but wouldn't you like to come in for a drink or something?'

He shook his head.

'Not even coffee?'

'No. Thank you. I must go. I have things to arrange. I will see you tomorrow. Tomorrow we go another way. You did well, by the way, today.'

'I'd never have done it without you.'

'No, I meant in the afternoon. You did well. Tomorrow you will do better.'

Janet watched him go. And then what? she wondered.

Chapter Twenty-four

Teresa woke them up when she came in, mainly by her efforts to be quiet. She was a big girl and the wooden stairs did not lend themselves willingly to stealth. They creaked and crackled as she tiptoed up them and had only just calmed down when she set off again, to the bathroom. Back in her room, and she appeared to have forgotten to turn the lights out. Down she came again, weariness making her clumsy.

'Christ, what is that girl up to?' growled Hugh as the banisters reverberated.

'I think she's putting the lights out,' murmured Janet.

'Why doesn't she just shoot them out? It would be quieter.'

'She comes from a family of twelve,' Janet reminded him. 'I expect she's used to noise.'

'She must be used to it. She makes so bloody much.'

'Let's hope she hasn't woken Bob and Cheryl.'

'Why not? Why should we be the only ones to suffer?'

'Because . . .' The question was answered for her by the rattle of a door opening and Bob's irate voice.

'Do you have to make quite so much racket, young lady? Some of us are trying to sleep,' he bellowed. Not any more, they aren't, thought Janet irritably.

'Sure I'm awful sorry, Mr McDermot. I was trying to be quiet, you have my word for it.'

'Yes, well ... Try a bit harder, can you?' The door slammed.

'Shut up, Dad,' came Tricia's peevish voice.

That's Belinda awake now, Janet reflected. We might just as well all get up and have breakfast.

Bob did not look his normal bumptious self next morning. In fact, he looked decidedly sallow. 'How was your meal?' asked Janet meanly, suspecting it might be the cause of Bob's complexion.

'Fine, very good. Excellent,' he snapped, ferreting for the sugar bowl.

'It was very reasonable,' twittered Cheryl. 'I think Bob said the wine was a little rough. I didn't have any myself.'

'Oh dear,' said Janet sweetly. 'It can play such havoc with your stomach, can't it? A really bad wine?'

'It wasn't bad,' said Bob dyspeptically. 'Just a bit young. Cheryl's right. Excellent value. Jolly good choice. How was yours? We took a look at the menu. That must have dented the old credit cards.'

'That's what they're for,' purred Janet.

Bob snorted and turned to Teresa. 'I don't know what you've put in this coffee this morning. It tastes like vinegar.'

'It's the same as yesterday,' she assured him, beaming from ear to ear.

'Must be the water then. Throw it away and start again. That's the only solution.'

'Mine's all right,' said Belinda innocently.

Bob's eyebrows began their customary tango up and down his forehead. 'Well, mine isn't. And since I believe I've contributed a lot more to the cost of this holiday than you probably have, missy, perhaps you'll allow me to know my own mind.'

'Bob ...' said Cheryl nervously, 'I don't think she meant it like that.'

Bob turned to her, then changed his mind. 'All right. Sorry, kiddo. Feeling a bit crook this morning. Nothing to do with the meal,' he added hastily. 'Anyway, Tessa, get us some fresh, there's a good girl. Make an old man happy.'

'It's Teresa,' Teresa smiled forgivingly. 'Sure, don't you worry about a thing. I'm used to old folk and their funny ways.'

Mauro was not in his usual spot when they got out of the lift. Janet looked around the sea of faces.

'I'll hang on till he turns up,' said Hugh. 'Blin and Owen can manage the chair blindfold now.'

She shook her head. 'No, don't worry. I'm sure he won't be long. You go on. You don't want to miss your last day's teaching.'

'Well, if you're absolutely sure?'

'I am. Mauro is one hundred per cent reliable. He'll be here, I know he will.'

Hugh nodded. 'I'm sure you're right. See you later then. Usual place?'

'I suppose so.'

'What?'

'Usual place, yes. See you later.'

After ten minutes she was beginning to wonder if she had been right to let Hugh go. Supposing Mauro was waiting for her up at the second base? Did life never get any simpler?

She was saved from having to find out by his arrival, looking extremely angry. 'I am late,' he told her accusingly.

'It doesn't matter,' she murmured, not sure how he had managed to make her feel responsible.

'Of course it will matter. I do not like to be late.'

She was silent, sensing whatever she did would be wrong.

'It is a small matter at home. I apologise. I will give you extra time for this so you do not lose your husband's money.'

'Oh, for heaven's sake,' she exclaimed, genuinely hurt. 'How can you possibly think I would care about a thing like that?'

Mauro looked slightly ashamed. 'Well, of course I do not think this, but *I* care. That is all I meant. Now you are angry too. I am angry, my wife is angry, my pupil is angry. This is a good start to the lesson.'

'I'm not angry,' said Janet, horribly tempted to laugh. 'I'm just glad you're here, and you're all right, and I don't have to get on the lift by myself.'

Mauro relaxed slightly. 'Well, by now you should be able to do this.'

'I know, but I can't. I just can't. I've been practising my knee bends,' she added sycophantically. 'I did twenty before I came out.'

Mauro glanced at her suspiciously. 'Well, all right. You would be better to practise getting on and off the lift but *non importa*. Now we go. We have much to do today if you will go to the night skiing.'

Janet's face contracted in alarm. 'I'm not doing that, Mauro. I'm just going to watch. Everyone's going. It's our last night.'

'So, if it is your last night you must ski. Otherwise all this lessons is wasted.' She noticed how he lost control of his grammar when agitated. She said no more but let him lead her to the lift, bending so low when the chair arrived she might have been receiving a knighthood.

'Thank you so much for last night,' she said as they soared away.

'Why do you thank me?'

'For reserving us a table – sort of. And for the wine and everything.'

'It is nothing. This is quite usual for new customers.'

Janet smiled. 'I don't care what you say, it felt pretty special to me.'

Mauro grunted.

'And for walking home with me. Making sure I didn't fall in the river.'

'Do you often fall in rivers?'

This man is such hard work, crossed her mind. 'I'm not sure I've ever fallen in one, but I'd had quite a lot to drink. I wouldn't want to start with one that's frozen.'

'Yes, I can see that. OK, now we are nearly there. This time I do not tell you when to jump. You must decide yourself.'

Janet's body went rigid. 'Oh no, Mauro, please. You must. Otherwise I'll be right up the mountain.'

'No, no. You will be fine. Trust your instincts. When your skis can nearly touch the ground then you jump – just a little, not a big jump or the chair will bang you on the head. OK. You are ready?'

'No ... o ... o ... o.'

'OK. That time you nearly did it. It was a good try.' Mauro dusted her down. 'You know you are much smaller when you do not have this jacket on.'

Janet felt herself blushing. It was merely an observation, but if he had said he'd seen her naked in the bath she could hardly have felt more vulnerable. She searched for a suitable reply, discarding the obvious one that he looked pretty puny out of his.

'It was a Christmas present.'

'And the hat?'

'That was a present too.'

Mauro smiled. 'I thought perhaps you had not chosen it yourself.'

Janet suddenly found herself giggling. 'It's terrible, isn't it? Blin won't come near me when I've got it on. I can't see it so I forget. Anyway, I've got too many other things to worry about.'

'What are these things you worry about?'

'Skiing, I mean. Trying to remember when to bend and when to rise. All of that.'

Mauro grunted. 'Well, if these are all the worries you have you are a very lucky woman.'

This irritated her. 'They aren't all the worries I have, but I can't stand people who moan all the time. It's very boring, don't you think?'

Mauro stopped dead. 'You think I moan, is that it?'

'No,' she retreated. *Do not annoy him halfway up a mountain.* She should have it tattooed on her wrist. 'No, not at all. I think you're very patient, considering what I've put you through. It's just ...'

'Yes?'

'I think, perhaps, you take things a bit seriously sometimes. More than you need to – perhaps.'

'You think so?'

'I do, yes. But it's only my opinion.' She began to picture herself, buried up to her neck in snow and Mauro standing over her with a shovel. To her surprise he gave a deep sigh.

'You are maybe right. Who knows? Maybe I should try to be more like your friend, Mr McDermot. He is always laughing.'

'Is he?' asked Janet, wondering what gave Mauro that impression.

'Not out loud. In his head he is laughing. You can see this from what he says always. *Sarcastico.* How is it in English?'

'The same.'

'The same.'

'And Mauro, promise me right now you will *never* be like Mr McDermot.'

In a week of surprises, the greatest was to see Mauro's face light up with laughter. He laughed, a long deep hiccupping sort of laugh, a bit like a child's. When he had finished he took hold of her arm. 'Come on, Mrs English. Today I will teach you to fly.'

If not to fly, then at least to lift one foot off the ground as she turned. It took her a while to get the rhythm, but once again with Mauro's mantra-like chanting she found she was eventually getting to grips with it.

'There you see. Then that is for parallel turns. When you can do this properly you are ready for the Olympics.'

'Ha ha.' Janet swerved to avoid a snowman and went crashing over. Mauro bent down and hauled her up.

'Sometimes I wonder if you do not prefer to lie down in the snow. You are always there when I look for you.'

'That's not fair.' She picked up a handful of snow and threw it at him. It crumbled all over his jacket.

'You make a big mistake if you throw snow at me, Mrs English.' He scooped up an enormous lump and held it directly over her head.

'Oh, no.' She cowered in anticipation.

'You are sorry?'

'Yes, yes. Terribly sorry.'

'You are sure?'

'Yes. Very sure.'

Mauro flung the snow behind her. 'OK, this time I forgive you. Now for this you must ski very well for the rest of the morning.'

'I will, I promise.'

'OK. I think now is time we go down or you will be late to meet your husband.'

'It doesn't matter.' She glanced up. He was gazing straight at her. For a moment they stared at each other, both unsure of what they were seeing.

'Well, yes, I think it will matter,' he said shortly. 'Come. We are going a different route. Different route, same skiing. First we go left.'

He hardly spoke on the way down, except to issue instructions. Janet was concentrating so hard that it was not until the terrace with its shops and restaurants came into sight that she realised the lesson was nearly over. A hard lump began to form at the back of her throat. This is ridiculous, she told herself. I've only known the man five days and most of those he's been horrid to me. How am I going to say goodbye? A dreadful thought struck her. Was she supposed to tip him? Her insides caved in. Hugh, please be there, she prayed. Please, please be there and save me having to say goodbye to him by myself.

She became aware that Mauro was speaking to her. 'That was not bad. OK. Remember, take the weight off before you lift the foot. You are waiting too long. That is why you cannot balance, you understand?'

Janet nodded and sniffed.

'You have a cold?'

She shook her head.

'So, what is this? You are crying? Because I am unkind?'

'No. *No*. Not at all.'

'Because your lessons are finished?'

Janet sniffed again. 'It seems like it.'

Mauro rattled slightly and produced a large patterned handkerchief. He handed it to her silently. She blew her nose.

'This I had not expected.'

'Nor me.' She tried to smile as a large tear plopped on to the slush at their feet. Mauro rubbed it into the snow with his boot.

'I think there is enough water here without you make some more.'

'I'm sorry. I never could say goodbye to people. Even people I don't like.'

'Like me?'

She looked up and saw that he was grinning. 'No, not like you,' she said quickly and without quite knowing why, reached up and kissed his leathery cheek.

'Well, here is your husband. What will he say when he sees his wife kissing a strange man?'

She turned to see Hugh's grinning face as he bounded down the slope towards them. 'We watched you come down. That was some skiing.' He turned to Mauro. 'Jan said yesterday she could ski. We didn't know she meant she could really ski.' He shook Mauro's hand. 'I can't thank you enough for this, you know. Jan wasn't looking forward to this holiday all that much. I'm right, aren't I, darling?' Janet finished pretending she had something in her eye. She felt better with Hugh there. Mauro was a stranger again.

'Yes, I suppose you are. It's been very nice. Thank you for all your help, Mauro. Perhaps we'll see you again some time. If you do decide to come over to England, you must give us a call. Has Mauro got our address, Hugh?'

Hugh fished around for one of his business cards. Mauro tucked it inside his jacket. 'Yes, thank you. That is fine.' He raised his hand. 'So, good luck with your skiing. I have told your wife she must go with you on the moonlight run. It is fine. She can do it. Just it may take her till daylight.' With a slight incline of his head he turned and tramped away.

'OK, darling? You look a bit fed up.' Hugh put his arm round Janet's shoulders.

'I'm fine. Bit achey.'

'And starving?'

'Starving, yes.'

'Blin and Owen have gone to grab a table. What's that?'

'What's what?' Janet looked down and saw that she was still clutching Mauro's handkerchief. 'Oh, nothing. A hanky.'

'Doesn't look like one of mine.'

'Doesn't it? Oh well, perhaps it's one someone left behind at the chalet.'

'Let's get some lunch.'

Janet followed him over to the restaurant, wondering what exactly had burst inside her head to make her lie about a thing like that.

Chapter Twenty-five

It was with some reluctance that Janet took to the slopes again that afternoon.

Owen and Belinda, having also remarked on her progress, were enthusiastic in their praise, and urged her to practise vigorously in preparation for what they considered would be the highlight of their holiday – the trip by moonlight down the mountain.

Dutifully she took herself back up to the nursery slopes after lunch and skidded around listlessly for three-quarters of an hour, but her heart was not in it. This is so stupid, she told herself repeatedly. In a week's time I won't even remember what he looks like.

There was just something so intangible about the relationship that had built up between them during the week that she found it impossible to believe it was over. Mauro angry (easy to recapture), Mauro quizzical, Mauro clinging to his dreams of a London long gone, Mauro skiing, soaring, swishing and swerving, flinging lighted beacons at his partner, flinging snowballs over her head. I'll never see him again, she thought, and went back to the chalet to start on the packing.

She was surprised to find the place empty. She had got used to Cheryl padding around. She pottered about collecting up dirty washing and thrusting it into a holdall, then sorted out what would not be wanted again and retrieved the suitcase from under the bed. It felt oddly heavy.

She hauled it on to the bed and opened the lid. 'Oh my God!' Inside the case lay an opened bottle of cherry brandy and a litre of duty free gin.

It wasn't the fact that Cheryl was using their suitcase that sickened her most. It was the thought that she was walking freely in and out of their room. The biscuit jar, her suitcase, where else might she be storing it? And what had all that been about between Bob and Owen yesterday? Stuart had obviously got hold of some booze from somewhere. His own room seemed an obvious place.

With a yelp she ran to the girls' room. If that woman has been hiding drink in amongst my daughter's things I am going to have it out with her, was all she could think. Hugh and I are one thing. Owen can handle it, but I am not having Belinda made party to her pathetic subterfuge. All right, she's got a problem, but she's not visiting it on my daughter.

She rummaged through the chaos in the girls' room, flinging open drawers and scrabbling through the cupboard. There was nothing that she could see. She crouched down and looked under the bed. Nothing. Feeling slightly ashamed she made her way back along the corridor.

As she rounded the corner she stopped. Cheryl, still in her outdoor clothes, was standing in the doorway of the bedroom, clasping the two bottles. She looked at Janet and smiled almost beatifically. 'Bob will be so pleased it's turned up,' she murmured, then turned and trotted away in the direction of her own room.

Janet knew before she opened the door that it would be Bob. She had heard him come back, listened to him complaining about the state of the fire, and heard the tramp of his feet on the stairs.

She wondered what story Cheryl had conjured up for the

return of the gin, whether she had mentioned it at all or just hidden it somewhere more accessible till Bob was out of the way.

She had finished packing as much as she could and was trying to concentrate on her column, although still she found her thoughts straying to impossible schemes for Mauro to visit them and for her to take him round all his old haunts.

What a mistake that would be! Never go back. Even this week would soon be confined to memory. She would forget the fears, the panics, the unbearableness of Bob McDermot, and only remember the good bits – sun glinting on the church steeple, Belinda's face when she first saw the ice sculpture, Owen zipping past her laughing like a lunatic, Mauro ... The knock came again. She got up and opened the door.

'Ah, Janet. Wonder if I could have a quick word?'

'Of course, Bob. Excuse the mess. I thought I'd better make a start.'

'Yes, yes, fine. OK.' He stepped into the room. 'All right if I close the door?'

'If you want to.'

'It's not so much me I'm thinking of, but Teresa's downstairs. We wouldn't want her overhearing anything.' He hesitated. 'I'm afraid this is a bit awkward ...'

'What is?' She had no plans to make it easier for him.

Bob harrumphed. 'I'll come straight to the point. Now, basically I realise this is none of my business, but as a colleague of Hugh's ...'

At least he's had the grace not to call himself a friend, Janet reflected.

'And friend, I felt it my duty to have a word.'

'About what?' she demanded, her hackles beginning to rise.

'I think you know what about.'

'If I did, Bob, I would hardly have asked, would I?'

Bob gave her the kind of look she had not received since secondary school. 'Very well. I've been talking to Cheryl.' He paused. Janet raised an inquiring eyebrow. 'And she told me about a rather unfortunate discovery she made this afternoon.' Again he waited. She said nothing. 'I think you know what I'm talking about now.'

Janet considered her options. Although she owed no loyalty to Cheryl, she was loath to make matters worse for her. How best to proceed?

'Just what did Cheryl say she'd discovered, Bob?'

'It was an unopened bottle of gin, Janet. Bought in the Duty Free on the way out.'

'Did she tell you where she'd found it?'

'She did indeed.'

'So what is this all about?'

Bob frowned. Clearly he had a prepared script and Janet was not sticking to the words. 'It's about the fact that Cheryl found the gin in your suitcase. You can deny it if you wish, but I must warn you in advance that Cheryl is not given to lying.'

Janet's jaw dropped like a broken cat flap. 'Why should I wish to deny it?'

Bob looked seriously taken aback. Not only was she deviating from the script, she was in the wrong play. 'Well, I ... So you don't deny Cheryl found a bottle of gin in your case?'

'No.'

'I don't know if you recall, but Cheryl and I bought that gin?'

'Yes, you bought two. We bought the brandy and the whisky.'

'You may also recall I asked if either you or Hugh had any idea where it was the other evening?'

'I remember very well.'

'And yet you had it all the time?'

'*I* had it? What on earth do you mean?'

'I should have thought it was obvious. Look, I didn't want it to come to this, Janet. I really didn't. I have struggled this week to put up with your behaviour because I recognise that you have a problem.'

'I have a problem,' Janet repeated like an automaton.

'I have the greatest respect for your husband and Mrs Barton, too, but I have to say that had I known how it was going to be, I would have thought very seriously before agreeing to share the chalet with you.'

'Bob,' Janet struggled to control herself. 'Can I just say that, had I known how it was going to be, I would have opened my veins before I got within fifty miles of the airport.'

Bob gave her a pitying smile. 'You need help, Janet. For the sake of all your family, you have to come to terms with your illness.'

'My *illness*?'

'Alcoholism is an illness, and like other diseases it can be cured. It just takes time and, of course, a willingness on the part of the victim to accept that they have the problem. Maybe you're not quite ready for that yet, but I think you should give it some very serious thought.'

Janet stared at him silently. The poor bugger, was all she could think.

Bob began to fidget with his shirt cuff. 'Well, there it is. I've said my piece. I hope you'll accept it was meant for the best.'

Still she said nothing. What could she say? 'Your wife's in a lot worse state than I am'? 'Does she drink because you're like you are, or are you like you are because she drinks'? What an awful situation to be in. Cocooned in a web of deceit and self-deception.

Down below, the front door slammed. 'Where is everyone?' came Hugh's voice. 'Can someone come and give me a hand with these logs?'

Bob almost leapt in his eagerness to get away. 'Coming, Hugh,' he yelled and without another word was away down the stairs. Again, the front door slammed.

Janet crossed to the window and looked out. Hugh and Bob,

assisted half-heartedly by Owen, were chopping logs and loading them into a giant wicker basket, surpervised by a gurgling Teresa who looked as though she could fell a tree with one hand. Janet calculated it would take them at least fifteen minutes.

Cheryl opened the door of her bedroom in her dressing-gown. She shrank visibly when she saw Janet. 'I was just going to have a bath,' she quavered, avoiding her eyes.

'This won't take a moment, Cheryl,' said Janet, although she had no idea what she was going to say to the woman.

'Well, if you're very quick . . .'

'Don't talk to me like that, Cheryl.' Cheryl started nervously. Janet braced herself. 'I just want to know why you've told your husband that I stole that gin and hid it in my suitcase.'

Cheryl began to tremble. 'I never said that. I didn't say anything like that. Really, Janet, you must believe me.'

'Why?'

'Why? Because . . . because it's true. I don't know what Bob's been saying to you . . .'

'Don't you? I rather thought you'd primed him to say it?'

'No, no. Surely you don't believe that? I'm so sorry if he's offended you in any way. He can be a bit impetuous sometimes, but he doesn't mean anything by it. He really doesn't.'

It was like talking to a rubber wall. Whatever you threw at her came back at a different angle, the words inverted. It was impossible not to feel sorry for the woman.

Defeated, Janet shook her head. 'Cheryl, it doesn't matter about the gin. What matters is what it's doing to you. Surely you can see that? All these lies, all these fantasies . . .' She had expected Cheryl to break down. She was already trying to calculate how to react if she did. She had not reckoned on what came next. Cheryl drew her dressing-gown very tightly round her and pulled herself up to an unprecedented height.

'I'm sorry for you, Janet. We both are. But that does not

give you the right to come up here accusing me of lying and
... and things. I am absolutely not prepared to put up with it.
Absolutely ...' she hesitated slightly and Janet realised that she
was, in fact, extremely drunk. 'Not,' she finished and turned to
close the door.

'Well, please stop insinuating things about Hugh and other
women. I've put up with it as long as I can and I'm sick of
it. I don't like gossip, particularly gossip that is unfounded
and malicious,' Janet burst out in a last ditch attempt to get
through to her.

Cheryl stopped with her hand on the door. 'Unfounded, you
say? I wouldn't be so sure of that, Janet. I really wouldn't.' She
went to close the door. Janet grabbed it and forced it open.

'Just what exactly do you mean by that, Cheryl?'

'Nothing. It's none of my business, obviously.'

'It bloody isn't,' snapped Janet, her blood dangerously near
boiling. 'But since you've started, you may as well finish. If you
have any evidence that my husband has ever had an affair with
someone, you'd better come up with it now.'

Cheryl's eyes popped with alarm. 'Don't blame me,' she
quavered. 'I only know what Bob tells me. You'd be better
asking him.'

Janet forced herself to be calm. 'I doubt there's any need
for that, Cheryl,' she said quietly. 'Hugh's downstairs. I think
I'll ask him.'

'Oh, but ...' But Janet was already halfway down the
corridor.

'Jan ...' came Hugh's voice from down below. 'Jan, can you
come down here. I've got a surprise for you.'

Chapter Twenty-six

Hugh had bought her a sweater. It was black, embroidered with a clown holding a bunch of silky balloons, and must have cost the earth. She took it as he held it out to her, scarcely seeing the hurt in his eyes as she set it aside. 'Don't you like it? Blin helped me choose.'

'Yes, yes, it's lovely.'

Owen and Belinda, who had also been out souvenir hunting, gazed at her expectantly. 'You can wear it tonight,' Belinda prompted.

'Yes,' Hugh agreed. 'Mind you, I think you'll need your jacket as well. The weather's turning pretty foul up the mountain. Must be those storms Clive was on about.'

'Clive's been on about storms all week. We haven't had any yet,' Owen derided him.

'They'd better not come tonight and spoil our last night,' declared Belinda. 'D'you know, Mummy, they're going to have people with lighted torches skiing down and all sorts.'

'Lovely,' said Janet distractedly.

'Are you all right, darling?' asked Hugh solicitously. 'You haven't gone and overdone it, have you?'

'What? No. Nothing like that. Hugh, can you come upstairs a minute? There's something I need to talk to you about.'

At this moment Teresa emerged with an enormous chocolate

cake. Owen eyed it hungrily. 'Let's get some before the vultures arrive. Want some, Mum?'

'What? Yes, in a minute. I want to talk to Daddy.'

'Can't it wait till I've had a cup of tea? I'm gagging.'

'*No.*'

'Don't forget the snowball fight, Dad,' Belinda reminded him excitedly. 'Mummy can be on Owen's and my side, against you two. We challenged Teresa to a snowball fight after tea and Daddy said he wanted a go too, so he's with her because Owen's the biggest, so you can be with us,' she informed her mother.

'Give us a yell when you're ready,' said Hugh. 'Mummy just wants to discuss something. We won't be long.'

He followed her up the stairs.

Once in their room Janet turned to him. Seeing his cheerful, open face she felt the absurdity – tackiness, really – of what she was about to ask, but it had to be done. Otherwise that tiny flicker of doubt would remain. She had been with Hugh for so long that she should have known without question what his answer would be, but the past few days had shown her that nobody's behaviour was entirely predictable. Not even her own.

'I've been talking to Cheryl.'

'Oh dear.'

'Why do you say that?'

'Because from your face it doesn't look like good news.'

'Well, you're right, of course. We had a stinking row. At least we would have had if I could have got any sense out of her.'

She sighed, sank down on the bed and put her head in her hands. Hugh sat down opposite her on the flimsy wooden chair. He reached across for her hands. 'Are you going to tell me about it?'

She roused herself. 'I came in quite early. No one else was back. I thought I'd make a start on the packing. I went to get that case from under the bed. I could feel something rolling about inside and when I opened it, there was a bottle of cherry brandy and the duty free gin Bob was on about.' She looked at him in exasperation. 'She'd been using our room to store her alcohol.' His face registered suitable distaste.

'Anyway, then I thought, if our room, why not everyone else's? I didn't tell you, but the reason Bob and Owen were arguing yesterday was because Stuart had got hold of some booze from somewhere. Anyway, that's another matter. I just didn't want Belinda coming across a secret store and thinking she might like to try it too. She might have thought a good drink would get her some kudos with Tricia, I don't know. I just know I couldn't bear the thought of it, so I went along to their room and had a search round.'

'Did you find anything?'

'No, thank God. But when I came back Cheryl must just have come in. She's usually the first back, isn't she, so I suppose she thought it was safe to go and help herself. She obviously realised I'd seen it, because the case was on the bed, open. Anyway, when I came back she was just standing there, holding the two bottles. She made no attempt to explain herself, just said something about "Bob will be so pleased the gin's turned up" and swanned off back to their room.

'The next thing I know is Bob's banging on the door telling me I've stolen their bottle of gin and that I have a serious problem because *I'm* an alcoholic.' She paused and looked to see if he was taking it in. 'I didn't know whether to laugh or cry. Then I thought, I'm not having this, so while you and Bob were out getting the logs I went up to talk to Cheryl.'

Hugh's face had become strangely immobile. 'And?'

'And basically she denied knowing anything about any of it. So in the end I just told her I would not put up with any more of her insinuations.'

'What insinuations?'

Janet hesitated. Hugh had let go of her hands. 'I didn't want to tell you this. In fact, if she hadn't been so objectionable I wouldn't now, but I really think, for your own sake, you should know the kind of people you've brought us on holiday with. Cheryl has been hinting from day one that you've got a woman in every filing cabinet.'

She waited. Hugh's face flickered with undisguised relief. 'Me? Come on, Jan. Can you see it? I mean, chance would be a fine thing.'

She smiled. 'Of course I knew it was all rubbish, but it was beginning to get to me, so I thought I'd knock it on the head once and for all. I told her I was going to ask you straight out. You should have seen her face.' Hugh glanced at her unhappily. 'Oh, come on, Hugh. Don't look so disapproving. I know she's got problems but she had no right to say what she did. Better I stop her before she does some real harm to someone.'

'What exactly did she say?'

'It wasn't what she said, really. It was the way she said it. Sort of hinting. She's always doing it. Even in the restaurant before we came away she inferred I was mad to let you out of my sight. I didn't clock it at the time, but it's like water on a stone. Drip, drip, drip. "Don't you worry?" "Don't you ever wonder?" You know the sort of thing.'

'Nothing specific then?'

'No, of course not.' She stopped. It was as though an icy hand had suddenly touched her back. 'Why?'

Hugh shook his head vigorously. 'Nothing. No reason.'

'Why did you ask if she'd said anything specific?'

He got up and went to the window. 'I just thought if she was accusing me of playing the field she might have had someone in mind,' he said, trying to sound flippant. It fooled neither of them.

'Who?' she asked in a voice not her own.

Hugh turned away. 'No one. It doesn't matter. The woman's mad. We both know that. Let's forget about it. The kids are waiting.'

She watched him fiddling with the window catch. A sense of detachment flowed over her. 'Who was it?'

'Jan—'

'Who was Cheryl talking about?'

'I don't know.'

Janet picked up the nearest thing to hand, an alarm clock, and flung it at him as hard as she could. 'Who did you have an affair with?'

'Listen to me—'

'Is it still going on?'

'No. There was no affair. It was ... There was nothing. Not what you think. It was ... Oh Christ, I'm going to throttle that woman for this. For ...' He stared at the floor then slowly sank down beside her and buried his face in her shoulder. 'I do love you. You know that, don't you? It was always you.' Janet felt a thin trickle of panic pumping through her. Carefully she pushed him away.

'Tell me,' she said shakily. 'Tell me everything.'

'Where's Mummy?' Belinda and Owen, already in charge of a sizeable arsenal of snowballs, were lining up opposite Teresa.

'She's not coming,' Hugh informed them. 'She's got a bit of a headache.'

'Oooowwww,' wailed Belinda. 'Now we'll get slaughtered against you two.'

'I'm not playing,' said Hugh abruptly, then softened. 'I'm referee.' He picked up a huge wodge of snow and flung it at Owen's head, then one at Teresa. 'Which means I can throw snowballs at anyone.'

With a whoop of delight all three set on him.

Upstairs, Janet undressed, wrapped herself in a towel and went to have a shower.

ANOTHER SURPRISE

This has been quite a week for surprises.

First I found that I was sharing a chalet with the holiday companion from hell. His name is Bob McDermot and I hate him. He is the most pompous, conceited, bigoted, ignorant idiot I have ever come across. Well, perhaps not quite, because according to my husband, I fall into most of those categories too.

I have not been a good wife to him, having devoted far too much of my energy to bringing up our children single-handed while he jet-setted around the world mending piddling little computers for megabucks. For this I should be grateful. Our mortgage is manageable and I have my own small car.

I have not been driven to drink, like Bob McDermot's wife. Instead I have occupied myself learning to cope with all the things that two-parent families normally share the burden of. This, again, is a fault, since it makes my husband feel excluded on the rare occasions he does come home.

Other surprises this week have included the discovery that I like skiing, loathe toboggans, have developed a pathetic and unrequited crush on my skiing instructor, and that my husband of nineteen and a half years has been making love to my best friend on a regular basis since my daughter was eighteen months old. Thank goodness we're not here for a fortnight.

'Where's Janet?' Bob reached for the bread. 'She'll miss her grub if she doesn't get a move on.'

'Perhaps we should wait,' suggested Cheryl with all the vivacity of a society hostess.

'We can't,' objected Stuart. 'You have to get up there early or you miss all the best bits. There's fireworks, Clive said.'

Hugh shook his head. 'No, don't wait. She was feeling a bit rotten. Overdid it on the slopes today, I'm afraid. She's just not ready for a full day yet.'

'But she's coming on the night ski, isn't she?' Belinda turned her anxious face to him. 'And wearing her new jumper?'

Hugh hunted for his napkin. 'I'm not sure. See how she feels. Now eat up or we'll all be late.'

'But we bought it for her specially. She must come.' Belinda was close to tears.

Hugh patted her arm. 'She probably will. She's just having a little rest. If you lot want to go on when you've finished dinner, I'll follow you up with Mummy when she's ready.'

'She must come,' repeated Belinda, but she seemed satisfied with this solution.

'Looks like Clive was right about those storms,' said Bob, peering through the shutters. 'Conditions could be treacherous on the top.'

'They won't open the whole way up if the weather's iffy,' said Hugh. 'Clive was saying they close the lift down from second base. Of course if it's really bad it won't take place at all.'

There was a horrendous groan from the youngsters. He shook his head. 'It's not that bad. Still, no point in hanging about. It's not going to get any better by the sound of it.'

It was true. The wind had definitely increased, even while they were having dinner.

'Tell Mummy to be quick,' were Belinda's parting words as the rest of the party set off.

Hugh sat for a while at the deserted table. Even Teresa had gone, with the promise that she would get up extra early to clear the dishes.

A pack of photos lay on the sideboard. He thumbed through them. The grinning faces leered up at him. Carefully he selected one of Cheryl. Equally carefully he drove a toothpick through her right eye, then he went upstairs.

'Jan . . .' It's come to this, he thought. I'm knocking on the door of my own bedroom. There was no reply. He opened it. 'Sorry. I thought you might be asleep.' Janet was lying on the bed, still in her dressing-gown. She looked up as he came in.

'Jan . . .' He took a step into the room, closing the door behind him. 'Are you hungry at all?'

She continued to stare at him. 'No, I'm not hungry.'

'You ought to have something. I could bring you something up, if you like. On a tray.'

'No thank you.'

'Jan ...' He sank down on the edge of the bed. She moved her feet away. 'God, Jan, I'd give anything for this not to have happened.'

Still she said nothing.

'The kids, Owen and Belinda, really want you to come on this thing tonight. They really want you to. Belinda made me buy you that sweater this afternoon. She said it was just the thing for you to wear on the last night. Now you can ski.' His voice died away. Janet turned on her side and became very interested in her notebook. In desperation Hugh ripped it out of her hands and flung it against the wall.

'Christ, Jan, you made me tell you. I had to tell you. Don't you see, I wanted you to know. I've wanted to tell you for so long. I wanted a way out. You don't know what it's like. It's like being in a trap. You and Harriet ...'

'*Me* and Harriet?'

'You're so close. I didn't dare say anything. I never wanted it to happen. God knows I didn't. I've hated it – all the deceit. It's not even as if ... I mean, it was an accident – there was nothing to it. Not on my part, anyway. Just comfort, after she split up with Roy. She was so desperate. You didn't want to know.'

'I had post-natal depression.'

'Yes, I know that now. I didn't then. I just thought you'd lost interest in me. Harriet was just sort of there. She made me feel ... I don't know ... wanted, I suppose.'

'How convenient. Look, go away, would you, Hugh, because if you don't I think I'm going to be sick.' She retrieved her notebook. Hugh watched her hopelessly.

'Jan, look at me. I swear to you, it's you I love. With Harriet it's nothing. Just going through the motions. It's the same for her. She never comes near me when she's got a man of her own. I'm just a sort of . . .'

'Backup? How suitable for a man who works with computers.'

Hugh stood up. 'You don't want to understand, do you? You're on about Cheryl saying don't trust a man out of your sight. She's right. I see it every day of my life. Foreign trips, conferences. It's like a bloody Roman orgy on some of them.'

'That must be fun for you.'

'It isn't. I don't take part. You can believe that or not, as you like. All I'm saying is that the occasional, and it is occasional, night with an old girlfriend, someone I've known half my life, seems a lot less damaging to me than bonking my way round the hotels of Europe.'

'It had to be one of the two, did it?'

'Are you saying you've never looked at another man?'

Janet stared at him. 'Since when have looking and screwing been the same thing?'

Hugh shook his head. 'You're right. I'm sorry. I shouldn't have said that. Look, Jan, I swear it's over now. I'll tell Harriet as soon as we get back.'

'Why don't you phone her? You've hardly been off it since we got here, have you? "I'll just see if Blin's all right." "I'm just stopping off at the hotel for a moment." Better still, send her some flowers, why don't you? "Darling Harriet, wife's a pain. Thinking of you always."'

'*Shut up.* Don't talk like that.'

'Why? Because it's true?'

'It's not true.'

'True enough to send her flowers.'

'I told you about that. I explained.'

'You don't send me flowers on my birthday.'

'You wouldn't want me to.'

'How do you know? What's so special about me that I wouldn't like flowers on my birthday?'

Hugh looked bewildered. 'But you scoff about things like that. I just assumed . . .'

'I don't scoff. I laugh. I laugh because I know I'll never get any so I have to pretend I don't care.'

Hugh shook his head angrily. 'Well, it's a bloody good pretence. You had me fooled.'

'Yes, well, it seems there are a few things we didn't know about each other.'

'Jesus, Jan, can we stop this? I wish I'd never set foot in this place. It's brought us nothing but misery.'

'Yes. Still, at least Harriet shifted her raffle tickets.'

Hugh ran his hand through his hair. 'God knows I didn't know it would turn out like this. I thought it was a chance for us to be together. I didn't know they'd be so shit awful. I didn't know you'd hate it all so much.'

Janet dusted an invisible hair off the sleeve of her dressing-gown. 'You're wrong,' she said tonelessly. 'I haven't hated it. It's going back home I'm going to hate.'

Hugh gulped in despair. 'Because of me?'

'Because there's no point. All these years of me being the good little housewife, learning how to cook, how to mend fuses, and fix punctures and change wheels on the car, and make sure your suits are back from the cleaners so that you can fly off and . . . fuck our children's godmother.'

'Oh, come on, Jan. Don't be so melodramatic. I've told you how it was. I slept with Harriet long before I met you. That's why she married Roy, if you must know. On the rebound. I chucked her for you. Did she never tell you that in all your sisterly chats?'

'No.'

'Well, I did.'

Janet was silent.

'Are you coming to this night ski thing or not?'

'Not.'

'You'll ruin it for the kids.'

'The way I ruined the tobogganing?'

Hugh stood up. 'There's no winning with you, is there? Does it ever occur to you, if you'd been a spit less independent and capable and . . . and fucking wonderful, I'd never have gone near Harriet? You bring nothing to this marriage, do you know that? I might just as well be married to a machine. You take no risks. You make no mistakes. Everyone tells me how lucky I am. I tell you something, I would have loved to buy you flowers. You just made me think you'd despise me for them. Mrs fucking Perfect. Well, do what you want. Let Owen and Blinny down. See if I care. I really thought we'd moved on. When I saw you today coming down the slope I thought . . .'

'What did you think?'

'I thought you looked happy. But then, how would I know? I've never seen you like that before.'

Chapter Twenty-seven

After Hugh had gone, slamming out of the house, still hurling accusations at her, Janet went and had another shower. She scrubbed herself with a viciousness that would have rid her of nuclear fallout, till her skin burned and her fingers felt raw. That done, she rubbed herself all over with the expensive moisture balm she had bought as a present for Harriet.

She went down to the kitchen, thinking she should find something to eat, but the sight of the congealing leftovers nearly turned her stomach so she drank a glass of water and went back upstairs.

She had forgotten to close the shutters. Sleet was driving against the panes. She opened the window and felt the damp cold flakes slapping at her face. Not a night to go skiing. They would probably all be back within the hour. What then? She could hardly banish Hugh to the settee. It was something that they had managed to keep their row private from the others. She didn't want to give Cheryl and Bob the satisfaction of knowing what they had achieved between the pair of them.

Her anger began to mount again. How could Hugh have deceived her so cruelly? Wickedly? With her best friend. Harriet. No longer a friend but a rival, and a tenacious one at that.

All those years of holding each other up. Confiding, sharing, trusting. Dead. Dead in the water.

And to find out from Cheryl McDermot of all people! Cheryl, with her hidden booze and her collection of Mills and Boons and a husband who made Bluebeard look cuddly.

She must have got it from him in the first place, which meant it was probably common knowledge at ComMend. She imagined all those colour-coded young wives staring at her, whispering . . . 'Is that the wife of . . .' 'I wonder if she knows about . . .' 'No wonder he . . .'

Well, if they thought that when she was in evening dress, wait till they saw her in her ski jacket. Hugh must have chosen it on purpose. 'I don't want her, but I'm going to make sure no one else does either. Ah, beetroot. That should do the trick.' The voices knitted together in her brain till she could no longer remember who had said what about whom, and over it all rode her own voice, chivvying at Mauro. 'Don't you tell your wife things?'

'Only what she wants to hear.'

She shuddered, the energy seeping out of her. Hugh's excuses began to give way to his accusations in her aching head. 'Mrs fucking Perfect.' What had she been supposed to do? Ring him in New York and say, 'The light bulb's gone. Can you come home and fix it, please?' Run up enormous bills at the garage because she didn't know how to check the oil? Feed the children on ready-made meals because she couldn't roast a chicken? She had had to become adept at all these things. It hadn't been from choice.

Did he really think she wouldn't rather have spent her time jetting round Europe, staying in top hotels, wearing Max Mara suits and going to the theatre? Did he really think she enjoyed being on PTA committees and harrying the local council to put Belisha beacons on the crossings? Was that how he saw her? And if it was, why had he married her in the first place? Because she certainly hadn't been like that at the beginning.

Didn't he remember them making love in the documents library at work? How she had hidden him from her landlady night after night, and had to listen to the entire hideous history of the woman's floating ovaries so that he could escape undetected through the back garden? And that first holiday in Cork when she had mistakenly led him into someone's front parlour and ordered two pints of their best Guinness — and got it?

It had been she and not Hugh who had been the instigator of every major event in their life together. And what was her reward? To be dragged off into the middle of frozen nowhere and told he'd been screwing her best friend for twenty years and it was her fault. 'Mrs fucking Perfect.' 'You make no mistakes.' 'You take no risks.' Oh, don't I? she thought. Don't I just.

The crowds had thinned out at the lift station. She was surprised to see quite a few people getting off. They looked disappointed, so she assumed the higher reaches must have been closed off due to the worsening weather.

The wind positively howled as the lift trundled up the mountainside. It juddered horribly as they crossed the points and for once in her life Janet wished it were full, rather than holding just the handful of surly-looking maintenance men. They muttered amongst themselves, throwing curious glances at the lone skier in the corner. She tried to understand what they were saying but they spoke so quickly she was only able to pick up the odd word. One of these was *turbolenza* and another *pericoloso*, which she had seen attached to signs of falling rocks. It did not sound auspicious.

At the top she was again surprised by the number of people waiting to come down, but there was still a mass of people milling around outside, so obviously the evening's entertainment was not over yet.

Her chest started to tighten as she forced herself towards the turnstile. I can do this, she told herself, her mouth bone dry.

I can do it. I've done it every day this week. I know what I'm doing. I am a skier. I can do it.

The queue was surprisingly short and almost before she knew it she felt the familiar clunk of metal behind her knees. Instantly she swept her poles out of the way as the bar came down. First step accomplished. She fixed her sight on the seat in front. It contained a family, the parents and two fairly young children who were squeaking and squealing excitedly. If they can do it, I'm damned sure I can, she told herself. I am the kind of person who takes risks. Her heart sank sickeningly at the prospect of the next one.

The journey up was unpleasant. The sleet was now falling steadily, interspersed with gusts of wind which seemed to suck the lift upwards then drop it, juddering, back into the void. As if to emphasise the danger, the contraption whined and creaked like something from a Hammer Horror film. Images of ski lifts stranded hundreds of feet in the air, dangling helplessly at forty-five-degree angles, began to invade her mind. This is ridiculous, she told herself, craning to see if any of the skiers whipping past below resembled her family.

One thing was certain, she would never be able to ski down by herself. She would have to wait for the return lift and get straight back on it. She must have been mad to think she could ski in weather like this. On her own. At night. Risks were one thing. Suicide another.

Still, it would take a lot of courage for her to get back on the chair by herself, so that would be another (small) mountain climbed in her quest to re-establish her wild side.

Craning, she could just make out the hump of the final ridge through the dank mist that was slowly shrouding the valley. She closed her eyes and concentrated. Remember, when your skis can nearly touch the ground, up with the bar and jump. Up with the bar and jump. Up with the bar and *jump*.

No one could have foreseen what would happen next. As the family in front prepared to ski off their chair, the mother, reaching back to catch her daughter's arm, overbalanced and fell directly in line with the landing spot. Every drop of adrenaline in Janet's body went into overdrive as she strained to see if she could jump over her. It was impossible. The ground fell away sharply into a dip. If she jumped from there she would break her leg, if not her neck. If she jumped before, she would plough straight into the woman. The husband saw what was happening and shouted to the attendant to stop the lift but it was too late.

With a cry of panic Janet was swept past the landing station and on up the mountain. 'Oh, God help me,' she screeched, catching a brief glimpse of the attendant's shocked face as she flew past.

An eerie silence descended, broken only by the relentless scraping as the lift passed under the power points. Emergency lights glimmered on the giant posts straddling the route but beyond that, nothing. Clearly everything above second base was now off limits. Below, the snow lay serenely unblemished by human tracks.

'What am I going to do? What am I going to do? What am I going to do?' she intoned helplessly as the chair jolted her away into the darkness. She didn't even know what the third base looked like. How would she know when she was there? How would she know where to get off? Perhaps she should stay on and go right to the top, then the lift would just circle round and bring her back down? But it was getting colder all the time. The sleet had turned to hail. Egg-sized lumps of ice were beginning to ping off the overhead cables, sparking like fireworks as they struck. Without the weight of other bodies the lift swung more and more chaotically, buffeted by the wind which now came in low, swirling gusts, catching the chair from below and rattling it like a giant's plaything.

Suddenly ahead of her she saw the outline of a hut. That must be it, she thought. It's just like the one I passed. What am I going to do? They saw what happened. Perhaps there's someone there.

Even from the distance she could see it was in total darkness. But there must be a phone, some means of communicating with the bases below. The clarity of her thought process astonished her. Her mind felt sharp as a knife edge.

I get off. I make contact. They rescue me.

That is what she had to do. She must not risk her life going further up the mountain in this weather. She'd be frozen to death. She was a risk-taker. She would take the risk. Up and *jump*.

'JUMP!' she screamed at the top of her voice, flinging open the bar and launching herself at the small patch of flattened snow. She fell hard and awkwardly and lay for several moments, watching the lift swing by above her, half hypnotised by its monotonous clanking.

I did it, she told herself, euphoria seeping through her. I did it. I got myself off the lift. I did it by myself. No one helped me.

Slowly, painfully, she pulled herself up. She had hurt her elbow in the fall, but it didn't feel serious. She stood for a moment gazing down the mountain. The distance between third and second base was much less than between the first two. This encouraged her. Even if I do have to ski down, she told herself, it can't be more than twenty minutes away.

It was then that she realised why the second base looked so close. It was at an almost perpendicular angle to where she now found herself. She was standing at the top of a black run.

The euphoria vanished. She stared, dry-mouthed, down the mountain. The rhythm of the lift became a mocking rasp. The wind whipped up more snow and flung it contemptuously into her face. The mist that had been fitfully puffing around the edges of the slopes now sank down with its blanketing silence.

Janet turned towards the hut. I shall be all right, she told herself. I will go in the hut and stay there till someone comes to rescue me. There may even be a heater. She grasped the handle of the door and pressed it firmly down. It was locked.

She rattled it desperately, to no effect. She banged on it with her fists, took off her skis and kicked it savagely, twisted the handle up and down. '*Open!*' she screeched. 'Open, damn you.' Her voice was dragged away by the wind. She leant her back against the door and closed her eyes. What do I do now? she wondered.

The common sense answer would be to make her way round to the other side and get herself back on the lift, but it was so dark. She had never got on the lift without help. Suppose she did manage, then couldn't get the bar down? She would drop like a leaf into the void below. How long would it take to freeze to death? An hour? Two hours? She had read somewhere that it took only twenty minutes to die of hypothermia in the English Channel. How much quicker thousands of feet up a mountain?

No, she had to get inside the hut. It was as simple as that. If she couldn't open the door, she would have to break a window and crawl through the hole. She fingered the frosty glass, hoping for a loose catch. It was sealed tight. She scraped at it with her ski pole, trying to see inside. There was no moon, the only light coming from the emergency bulbs on the lift. Why the hell don't they put the lights back on? she wondered. They must know by now that I'm up here. Surely they don't expect me to survive in pitch darkness?

An hysterical thought crossed her mind. Supposing the *carabinieri* were refusing to do anything in case her insurance policy didn't cover the cost? Surely it must run to flicking a switch so that she could at least see how she was going to die – hypothermia or a broken neck?

She realised that she was giggling. Get a hold of yourself, she told herself. Find something to break the glass with.

She picked up one of her poles and swung it behind her head, closing her eyes and cracking it down on the window pane. The glass was reinforced. She barely scratched the ice on it. Again she struck, and again and again. The pole buckled. 'Oh, for God's sake!' She flung it down the valley. 'Now what have I done?' she shouted after it.

She still had one but it was clearly not going to be strong enough to do the job. She needed something more substantial. Pressing her back hard against the hut she edged her way round it, peering for a rock or piece of piping. There was nothing. She cursed the Italians for being so tidy. If this had been England she would have been guaranteed at least an old bicycle pump.

I could kick it in, she thought. If I could hoist myself up to window level, I'm sure I could smash it with my boot. But there was nothing for her to stand on. The only alternative seemed to be a can-can kick of Bluebird velocity. She tried one or two preliminary hops. It was plainly not an option. If she took her boot off, how long before her toes were lying in a blackened heap beside her?

A shutter creaked. Reaching over to it, she realised that the cross-bar was dangling, its catch broken. It occurred to her that if she could detach the bar completely it would make a very handy battering ram.

As she reached to unhook the shutter, the wind caught it and wrenched it out of her grasp, hurling the wooden slats against the glass. There was a gratifying crash, followed by the music of breaking glass. 'Yes!' she whooped, dancing up and down in the snow.

She advanced once more, only to be nearly upended by the shutter careering back again. She leapt aside then lunged for it, hooking it fast before it took another wallop at the window.

The glass was very jagged, most of it having landed inside the hut. Peering in she could see fragments glinting up from a table just below the sill.

With her remaining pole she jabbed determinedly at the fractured glass, trying to direct it outwards. That done, she leant cautiously through the gap and swept what she could see of the rest of it on to the floor. Then she removed a glove and ran it slowly over the rim of the window. Each time it snagged she chivvied away till the ledge was smooth.

Finally satisfied, she hoicked herself up and clambered through the gap, easing herself on to first the table and then sliding her legs down to the floor beneath. There was a disconcerting crackle as her boots further pulverised the glass.

She stood stock still. I'm in, she thought. I am inside the hut. I have done it. I have broken into the hut so that I will not die of cold and I have not amputated my leg on the way. *Who dares wins.*

Cautiously she crunched over to the door and fumbled for the light switch. The hut was illuminated just long enough for her to note where the worst of the glass was before, with a resounding pop, the bulb went. 'Oh well, of course,' she muttered bitterly.

It was colder inside the hut than out, and darker. What next? she wondered hysterically. A dead body? A wolf? An avalanche? I must have more of these adventures.

It was while she was prodding every knob and nodule on the wall, in the hope of exciting some form of light, that the pencil-thin beam of a pocket torch came flickering through the window. It took her a moment to register. Slowly she turned.

'Did I say you were ready for the black runs?' asked Mauro, before letting himself in with a key.

Chapter Twenty-eight

'Mind. There's glass,' seemed slightly less than an adequate response to the man who had come to rescue her from imminent death. Janet comforted herself that, 'Dr Livingstone, I presume?' was now considered a classic.

Mauro flicked the light switch and clicked irritably with his tongue. 'So, already you have broken the window and broken the light. This is a good start.'

'I didn't break the light. It blew as soon as I turned it on. Continental lighting is very unreliable, it seems to me,' she retorted sharply. After what she'd been through, she was in no mood to be criticised.

Mauro muttered something in Italian and shone his torch on a small overhead cupboard. He opened it, extracted a new bulb, removed the old one and replaced it. Once more they had light. The pair of them regarded each other suspiciously. 'So, you are OK?' asked Mauro as though they had met in the street. Janet cleared her throat.

'Yes, thank you. Fine.'

He nodded. She saw that he was carrying a knapsack which he now removed. Dusting down the table he placed it carefully on top and looked around the hut. 'First we close the shutters, I think, or we may as well sit outside in the snow.' He went outside and with a degree of cursing managed to secure the broken slats across the opening. The hut immediately felt warmer and Janet realised that the wind had been howling right through it.

She looked around for something to sweep the glass up with. The best she could contrive was her ski pole to which she attached an old towel hanging from a chair. With this she managed to shovel most of it into a corner and, pleased with her efforts, sat down to wait for Mauro's rescue plan.

He was still outside and she guessed from the flickering of his torch that he was round the other side of the hut. After a few minutes she heard him prodding his way back. The wind howled as he opened the door, sending a flurry of snow on to the floor of the hut.

Slamming the door, he reached behind it and unhooked a phone from the wall. He held it up to his ear, shook it, punched some numbers, listened again, rattled it viciously, then practically flung it back on its rest. Crossing to his knapsack he extracted a mobile phone which he also pummelled like a punch ball, with the same result. He slung it down and looked across at Janet.

'So this is good. I cannot tell them you are found.'

'But how did you know I would be here?' she asked, suddenly conscious of the odds.

Mauro shrugged. 'I didn't. I was on my way home when I met your husband. I asked him if you had come, but he said no, you had a . . .' He touched his head. 'I said this is perhaps a good thing, because it is too bad weather for a beginner. Then this guy tells me Lorenzo has telephoned from second base to say someone was still on the lift because a woman has fallen in the way. Everyone says, "Well, what can they do? They must stay on the lift and come back down. That is sense. Then Lorenzo says it is the English *signora* with the funny hat who cannot get off, so she will definitely stay. He asks to put the lights back on but the guys say it is too dangerous because of the storm. When it is like this the power is very low and if he puts all the lights on we may lose the electricity and she will be stuck up there till it is mended. Maybe all night. So they say, OK, leave it with only

the emergency lights. She will come down. So everyone waits.'
He stopped and Janet saw that he was actually very shaken.

'And?'

He raised his eyes to her. 'The lift comes back. It is empty.
Your husband ...' He was silent for a moment, then shook his
head. 'Poor man. He is very frightened. He wanted to come with
me when I said I will see if she has got off higher up. He said
he must come, but I told him, no, it is better he stays with the
children. He does not know the mountain. I am better on my
own. I can ski down in the dark. He cannot.'

Janet felt her stomach pumping. 'Have we to ski down,
then?' She had thought she couldn't be any more frightened
than she had been, but this was mighty close.

Mauro gave a laconic smile. 'No, we don't do that. Even
I do not want to ski in this weather. I said that to him so he
will not worry. We will take the lift. If you make a pig's ear,
I will leave you.'

Janet could feel her eyes beginning to sting. 'I was going
to try and get on it, honestly I was. But it's so dark, and I
thought, supposing I can't get the bar down and I fall out?
I just felt so sick. Oh God, this has been the worst day of
my life.' She fumbled in her pockets. Mauro fumbled in his.
She pulled out his handkerchief just as he produced the twin.
'Snap,' she said weakly.

'Here.' Mauro handed his to her. 'If you are going to cry
you will need two.'

Janet blew mightily. 'I'm not. It's just ... it's just ...'

'Just, just ... I know. You are thinking I wish I had never
come to this horrible place, with this horrible mountain and
this man who shouts at me all the time. I would like to be
home with my pot of tea and my lovely husband.'

'You're wrong about that.' She gave her nose a savage blow.
'It's because of him I'm here now.'

Mauro gave a deprecating shrug. 'Yes, I know, but he
did it for your sake, because he thought you would like

to learn to ski. How could he tell you would hate it so much?'

'I don't mean that,' said Janet bitterly. She sensed him watching her and looked away.

'Come. We should not wait much more. The weather gets worser all the time.' He picked up his bag and thrust his arms through the straps, then grabbed the torch and forced open the door of the hut. The wind whipped it out of his hands and sent it crashing against the wooden frame. He cursed and turned to Janet. 'OK, we put our skis on in here. When we move we go very slowly. Keep low, all the time. Remember what I have told you. Bend your knees like you are skiing, not walking, OK? The higher you are, the more wind can blow you over. You understand?'

'I think so,' she quavered.

'OK. It is not far. Just round the cabin a little way. When we are there the walls will protect us from the wind, then we can take the lift. Soon you will be home.' He reached out and patted her arm awkwardly. 'You are one crazy woman, Mrs English.'

Janet tried to smile. 'I know. Mauro ...'

'What?'

'Thank you.'

He rattled irritably. 'Why do you thank me? It is my job.' He turned away abruptly and Janet, feeling as though she'd been slapped in the face, bent as low as she could and braced herself against the storm outside.

The wind was far worse than when she'd first arrived. It was impossible to hear anything above it, so that even if Mauro had issued some last-minute instruction she would not have understood him.

They inched their way laboriously round the side of the hut. At one point she slipped and almost lost her footing. She was saved by her remaining pole which she drove into the frozen snow with the force of a pikestaff.

Mauro had been right about the walls protecting them to a

degree. At least they could breathe round the other side. She stood pinned against the rough shelter, her face flayed by the driving snow, watching as the lift continued its relentless circuit, impervious to their dilemma.

Mauro put his mouth to her ear and bellowed, 'OK, you are ready? Still you must keep low, OK, because if you slip I cannot help you.'

Janet nodded, offering up prayers to every deity known to see her safely on to the lift. After that it was up to them how they disposed of her.

A streak of lightning blistered the sky high up in the mountains, followed immediately by the growl of thunder and another forked shaft, then another. Somewhere very close there was an almighty splitting sound, then a sizzle. With a slow lethargic hiss the emergency lights dimmed to nothing and the lift slumped to a halt.

As if to signal the end of their reply, the gods let off another shaft of lightning and the sky returned to darkness.

The two of them crouched in stunned silence as the wind hammered at them with all the savagery of an undetected bully.

'What shall we do?' asked Janet at last, petrified that he was going to suggest they ski.

Mauro said nothing. She could feel him beside her, feel the fury inside him that things had not gone right. Finally he spoke.

'Now we are both stuck, it seems.'

Her eyes widened with fright. She had absolutely counted on him to get her down. She now realised that from the moment of his arrival she had felt totally safe — safe enough even to argue with him. She certainly had not entertained the possibility of Mauro not knowing what to do.

He grunted. 'Well, perhaps we should go back inside, unless you prefer to spend the night here?' She said nothing. She would rather he had sworn at her, shouted at her, than reverted to the icy sarcasm of their first encounter.

Crouching low, they crabbed their way back round the hut, full into the force of the wind again. She could sense him behind her and was almost more afraid of his seeing her slip than of it actually happening. It was with double relief, therefore, that she stepped inside the shack again, reaching for the light switch as she did so. Nothing happened.

'The power is gone,' said Mauro, so close behind her that she jumped.

'Oh yes. I forgot.'

He removed his skis. She followed suit. He thrust the torch at her. 'Here, take this. Shine it where I can see.' Again he went outside and wrestled the door shut. Janet remembered thinking that if she listened carefully she would never be short of an Italian swear word again.

Once more he removed the knapsack and started to rummage around in it. 'Here. Shine the torch, woman. What is the matter with you?'

Janet waved it at the bag, thinking if she just once began to tell him she might never stop. He pulled something metal from the bag.

'What's that?' she asked.

'Is a light. Do you want to spend the whole night in darkness? No, I don't think so. So here is a light.' He set the hurricane lamp squarely on the top of the table and took some matches from his pocket.

The light seemed to cheer him slightly. He dived back into the bag, producing a bottle of water, two bars of chocolate and a polythene bag from which he emptied a selection of plastic sachets. 'What are those?' asked Janet, beginning to sound like a Blue Peter reporter.

Mauro picked up a couple. 'These? They are very good. They are for warming the hands. The hands, the feet, the ... anything. Here. Try.' He unwrapped one and handed it to her. 'You squeeze it with your fingers. It makes them warm.' Janet did as instructed. She wasn't sure it was working. Mauro watched her wearily. 'I think you will find it is better if you first take off your glove,' he suggested eventually.

'Oh yes, of course,' she mumbled, wondering if her brain had completely frozen over. He was right. She could feel the heat from the sachet positively glowing in her palm. 'They're very good,' she enthused, hoping to regain favour.

Mauro nodded. 'Not so good as this, I think.' He pulled a small leather flask from the bag, unscrewed the lid and held it out to her.

She took it.

'Go on. Drink. It will do you good.'

She took a swig. A glorious gush of warmth swamped her. 'What is it?' she gasped, handing it back to him. He held it up to his mouth and drank deep.

'It is life,' he said.

'I could have done with that before we went outside.'

Mauro shook his head disapprovingly. 'No, you must never drink alcohol for the cold. You did not know this?'

Janet frowned, confused. 'What about all those St Bernards with barrels of brandy round their necks?'

He snorted disparagingly. 'They are for the chocolate boxes. If your body is freezing and you give it the alcohol, what do you think will happen?'

'You'll feel better?' she ventured.

'Yes, yes, you *feel* better. You just must die sooner.' He sought to explain. 'When your body is very cold it is saying, OK, I can die of this cold. But I don't want to. So, if I have to die, I will die little by little — one tiny bit at a time.'

Janet shuddered violently.

Mauro shrugged. 'Yes, but it is necessary. First the fingers, then the toes, etcetera. Your body is careful, it will only let the littlest bit die it can manage, OK?'

'OK,' she echoed unhappily.

'So, now comes your St Bernard with the big barrel of brandy. You take the big drink and suddenly your heart is saying to your head, I'm okay. Don't worry for me any more. So, what happens?'

'What?'

'The brain says, fine, she is OK. I can stop worrying. And what happens?'

'What?' croaked Janet, enthralled.

'The heart has no more protection. *Finito il cuore, finita la vita.* The heart is finished, the life is finished.'

'But why did you bring it if we shouldn't be drinking it?' asked Janet, 'Elvira Madigan' floating before her.

'In here is OK. We are here till tomorrow. We need this, I think.'

'Have you got lots?'

'Enough. In a minute you can have some more. First we must arrange the place.'

'Arrange it?'

'Well, of course. If we must sleep here, we must make it the best we can. Otherwise in the morning we will be like two woods, all frozen over.' He opened the locker and ferreted around inside, emerging with a raggedy-looking blanket. This he shook, tutting like an offended housewife at the dust which flew from it. 'Is a disgrace,' he muttered.

'Oh, but it's a miracle,' marvelled Janet. 'Fancy someone leaving a real blanket here.'

Mauro threw her a pitying look. 'It is the regulation. Of course the base must have these things. Medicine, etcetera. Also blankets, lights, matches . . .'

He started an inventory of the base's provisions, snorting derisively at the paltry complement. 'Where is the battery for the phones? Where is the fresh water? Where is the torch? Ah!' He hoicked a torch out of the cupboard and switched it on. The beam illuminated the cabin. 'This is good.' He propped it up on a shelf. 'You want some chocolate?'

'Yes, please.'

'I have some bread too.' He pulled a great slab of rye bread from the Aladdin's cave of his knapsack. 'Here. We have a picnic. We have drink, we have food, we have light and a little bit of warmth. What more can we ask for?'

'Music?' suggested Janet.

Mauro looked uneasy. 'You are right, of course, and if I was Italian, not Ladino, I would sing to you like Pavarotti.'

'I doubt if being Ladino's got much to do with it,' Janet pointed out. 'It's like me saying if I was Australian I could sing like Joan Sutherland.'

'Or Frank Ifield?'

She burst out laughing. 'Is he still around?'

'Of course. What do you think? Here in the mountains. Every time they ask a request, someone says, "Oh, Frank Ifield. He is my favourite," and we get this fucking yodelling.' He coughed. 'I am sorry. I do not mean to swear. Excuse me, please.'

'That's all right.'

'You know this man, Frank Ifield?'

'I know who you mean.'

'You like his singing?'

'I think it's dreadful.'

Mauro was silent for a moment. 'My wife loves him. She says him and Julio Iglesias. These are her two favourites.'

Janet could see why he got depressed. 'What sort of music do you like?'

Mauro picked at his cuffs. 'Oh me, I am a peasant, I think. I like Puccini and Elgar. I mostly like "Greensleeves". That is my favourite. That and "Danny Boy". And The Who. They are very great, I think. Better than the Beatles.'

'Oh, come on,' snorted Janet.

'You don't think so?'

'I certainly don't. I think "Yesterday" is one of the best songs ever written.'

'Oh well, that,' said Mauro, so sadly that she didn't say any more.

Chapter Twenty-nine

'What are you doing?' Janet asked. She was lying by the wall furthest away from the door, her head on Mauro's rolled up knapsack, the blanket, which he had insisted she take, coiled round her like a winding sheet.

She felt very guilty, despite his assertion that he was used to the cold. His face was tired and pinched as he sat by the hurricane lamp, the hand-warmers tucked inside the collar and cuffs of his jacket, two more protruding from his socks. He was fiddling with the big torch.

'Nothing. I don't know. It is an experiment. Go to sleep.'

She closed her eyes, feeling like a child who has been caught out of bed, but it was no good, she was never going to be able to sleep. Even the home-brewed kirsch, as she now knew it to be, could not overcome her insomnia. She felt just as alert now as she had on the ski lift all those hours ago. Or was it hours ago? She had lost all sense of time.

'What time is it?'

Mauro continued with what he was doing. 'About ten minutes after the last time you have asked.'

'Oh. Really? I thought it was later than that. What time did you say it was then?'

He took off his watch and slung it at her. It was ten to two.

'What *are* you doing?' she asked again.

'Nothing. Go to sleep.'

'I can't, Mauro. I really can't. Why don't you have the blanket and get some rest yourself? You must need it far more than I do.'

'Maybe I need it, but I don't do it. I never sleep much. Is a habit.'

Janet unwrapped herself and came and sat near him.

'Now you are in my light.'

She moved. 'Can I help?'

'What with?'

'That. Whatever it is you're doing. I could pass you things or something. Do you want some more chocolate?'

Mauro set aside the torch from which he had unscrewed the front. 'What is the matter with you? Are you going to talk like this all night long?'

She subsided. 'I'm sorry. I just feel sort of jumpy.'

He softened slightly. 'Yes, well, it is reaction. OK, I tell you what I am doing. I am trying to see if I can make a signal with this torch that they can see at second base. Now it is only the workmen there but maybe they can pick up the light. Then they can tell your husband you are found. It is a long night for him, I think, in any case.'

'But would they be able to see it from right up here?'

'I don't know. Maybe, maybe not. But yellow is no good. It is lost in the fog. I must find another colour.'

'Like red, or blue, or something?'

'Red is best, I think, if we can find some red in here.' He threw a disparaging glance around the hut. 'Otherwise perhaps it must be blood.'

'*Really?*' choked Janet, thinking his compassion for Hugh was possibly being taken a little too far.

'Is a joke.'

'Oh, right. Shall I look for something?'

'If you like.'

She started a frantic search of the hut, resulting only in the discovery of a pair of old leather gloves and a pin-up calendar from 1997. She sat down again, then leapt up. 'I know. My coat. It's red. We could cut a piece out and fit it inside.'

Mauro looked doubtful. 'Yes but then your coat is spoilt.'

'It's better than blood. Anyway, I won't be needing it again after today.' She stopped. Mauro was staring steadfastly at the dismantled torch. For one brief second she had seen the hurt in his eyes and hated herself accordingly. 'Not this year, anyway,' she muttered unconvincingly.

He nodded. 'Well, OK. You can take it off then. I have a knife.' She undid her coat and laid it on the table. He inspected it like a seasoned tailor, finally opting for a piece of the quilted lining which he slit with the precision of a surgeon.

'There,' he said when he had slotted the material in and reassembled the torch. He flashed it once or twice. A beautiful coral glow lit up the cabin.

'It's lovely,' declared Janet. 'Can I have a go?'

'Have a go?' snapped Mauro furiously. 'This is not a children's party. Do you want to use all the battery?'

'No,' she muttered contritely.

'No. So you put on your jacket again before you freeze and you stay over there because I must open the door again.'

'I'm coming with you.'

'No. You stay here. I insist.'

'I must come. Suppose anything happens to you?'

'Nothing will happen. It is more like to happen to you, don't you think? Then I will freeze to death trying to rescue you.'

Janet saw that she was on to a loser. 'Well, all right. But you must promise to have the blanket when you come back.'

Mauro made a hissing sound.

'If you don't promise I shall follow you right out.'

'OK, OK, I promise. You are a great trouble to me, Mrs English. You know that?'

Janet smiled demurely. 'I suppose I am.'

'You are ready?'

She nodded.

'OK. Here goes.' He unfastened the door, but this time managed to keep hold of it. Janet grabbed the handle from him and dragged it shut as soon as he was through. 'Lock it,' she heard his muffled yell. 'Or it comes open again.' She did as she was told, listening for his footsteps as he made his way round the hut. She heard nothing apart from one or two thumps as his boots scuffed against the wooden walls.

Rushing to the other end she peered to see if there were a crack in the wood through which she could watch, but the hut, for all its barrenness, was strongly constructed and admitted no light from outside.

She waited for what seemed an age, wondering if he were having any success. How would he know if they had seen him? Would they flash back and, if so, would he see it? Suppose they only had yellow? Suppose he had missed his footing and rolled away down the valley where he now lay freezing/frozen to death? Her heart began to pound hysterically in her chest. I shall have to go and look, she thought, dragging herself unwillingly towards the door.

She was saved the need to by the decidedly animate sound of Mauro kicking it. She stood back. After a further few thuds Mauro called in a less than friendly voice, 'Is it possible, perhaps, you can unlock this door before I die out here of the cold?'

She flew across the room. 'I'm so sorry,' she burbled as he plunged into the hut, slamming the door behind him. 'I had a bit of trouble with the key.' Mauro turned it effortlessly and fixed her with a glare.

'I think if you were in the desert you could not build a sandcastle,' he remarked.

'I'm actually quite practical at home,' Janet assured him. 'I can change tyres, and I once had to drain the whole central heating system when the boiler started playing up.' She became conscious of the sound of her own voice. 'Sorry.'

Mauro grunted and shook some of the snow off his jacket.

'Did you have any luck with the torch?'

He shrugged. 'Who can tell? Once I thought I saw a light, but maybe it was just electrics. They have to mend the cables at night. It could be that.' He slumped down in the chair. 'Who knows?'

Silently Janet went and fetched the blanket. She stood for a moment watching him. He looked so tired sitting there, his pointed features thrown into relief by the lamp. So tired and solitary. Gently she laid the blanket round his shoulders. Instinctively he reached up and caught hold of her hand, then realising what he had done, immediately let go. '*Scusi,*' he said in an exhausted voice. 'I forgot . . .'

Even through his jacket Janet had sensed the tautness of his muscles, like a caged tiger waiting to spring. She tucked the blanket round him.

'What did you forget?'

'Uhh?'

'You said you forgot. What did you forget?'

Mauro frowned and rubbed his head. 'Nothing. I am tired. I thought for a moment you were . . . someone else.'

A strange kind of giddiness began to creep over her. She no longer felt like a part of the world she belonged to. The mother, the wife, the changer of car tyres. 'Who did you think I was?' she persisted softly. 'Your wife?'

Mauro gave a snort of laughter. 'No, not Angelina. Never her.'

'That's a beautiful name,' said Janet. 'Angelina.'

Mauro rested his head in his hand. 'You like it?'

'Oh yes. I always dreamt of having a name like that, instead of Janet. Could there be a more boring name? I haven't even got a middle name. When I was small I would only answer to Selena for ages and ages.'

'Selena?'

Janet blushed. 'Well, it was Princess Selena, really, but I only told my parents about that.'

Mauro chuckled. 'Why them only?'

She smiled. 'Well, can you imagine what a bunch of seven-year-olds would make of that? I'd've been a laughing stock.'

'What is that?'

'Someone everyone laughs at.'

He nodded. 'Not so good, uhh?'

'Not when you're seven, anyway.'

'Princess Selena. Is beautiful. *Principessa Selena. Va bene.*'

'Now you're laughing at me.'

Mauro looked at her. She had never seen his eyes so free from strain. They looked bigger, darker, kinder. 'No. Everyone must have their dreams.' He kicked a fragment of glass into the corner. 'Just as everyone else must break them in bits.'

Janet was shocked. 'Is that what you believe?'

'Is what I know.'

She shook her head. 'No, Mauro, you're wrong. I'm sure you are. You're right to say people should dream. You can't really believe other people would want to spoil their dreams?'

'Well, of course. Why should they not? Why should one person be allowed to rule the world? He must be stopped. Why? Because the next person wants it also.'

'Yes, but it's only fantasy. Everyone knows that.'

'Do they? Do they, Principessa Selena? Then why do the children laugh if you want to be a princess? Because they want to be one too. And because you cannot have so many princesses they have to make you know you are not one. That is how it goes.'

Janet fell silent, considering this bleak perspective. 'Oh well, it was all a long time ago.'

'Did you have no dreams since then?'

'Of course.'

'What happened with them?'

She smiled. 'I learned to keep quiet about them. What about

you? Tell me about your dreams. Apart from being the most famous skier in the world.'

Mauro sniffed derisively. 'Actually, I don't care much for skiing.'

Janet was unimpressed. 'Oh, go on. You must do. You're brilliant at it. I saw you the other night at the display, remember.'

'Yes, and remember what I said to you before. Circus animals, that is all. I have been skiing since before I could walk. If I say to you, your great dream is to speak English, what do you say? This man is mad. Because you have always done it. You ask me what my dream is. It is to have my own restaurant, in England. I love England. I love it so much. Kew.' He rolled the name erotically round his tongue. 'Kew is so beautiful. The gardens, the houses, the rain, the mist.'

'It's doesn't always rain in Kew,' she warned him.

Mauro dismissed the suggestion. 'In three years, every time I go it is wet. That is enough for me.'

'You'd be safer in the Lake District,' she suggested.

'Well, it is my dream. I want Kew. And since it does not happen, I can choose, I think?'

'Fair enough. Is there no chance it could happen, then?'

'No. I do not think so. My wife will not leave the village. My son will not speak to me if I go.'

'You have a son?' She didn't know quite why it surprised her so much.

'Yes. Pietro. After Peter Townsend. My wife thinks it is after Santo Pietro, but who names his son after a fishmonger?'

Janet giggled. 'How old is he?'

Mauro grimaced. 'Older than the mountain. He is twenty-four. Already he has arranged for his retirement. He is a builder. He has built a house for him and the girl he will marry, a house for her parents, a house for her brother and his wife, and another house for him and this girl when they are too old to climb the stairs.' He sat back, a look of bewildered desperation on his face.

'Hasn't he built you one yet?'

'Pah! I don't let him. I say if you want to build me a house you build it like a restaurant and you put it on wheels so I can drive it away.'

'What does he say to that?'

'Nothing. It makes him angry. He thinks I should not say such things because it upsets his mother.'

'She must know you're only joking.'

Mauro was silent. He pressed the palms of his hands against each other and stared at them as though it was the first time he had seen them. 'It's not a joke,' he said finally. 'That's what she knows.'

Janet said nothing, sensing that she had uncovered quite a wound. Mauro glanced at her. 'So, I should not say these things to you, Janetta, Princess Selena, Mrs English. My wife is a good woman. A very kind woman. She works hard, the home is clean, the food is OK. I have no complaints for her. Only she plays Frank Ifield – that is her only sin. And for this she goes to confession twice a week. So, what can I say? I am a lucky man.' He reached behind her and picked up the last slab of chocolate, breaking it in two.

'Here. Your husband is a lucky man too, I think?'

Janet took the chocolate and put it in her mouth. 'By your lights I suppose he is,' she said at last.

'I don't follow.'

'You were talking about Angelina. You could have been talking about me.'

'No!'

'Oh yes. I cook, I clean, I do all the right things that men say they want their wives to do. And what's the result? You bore them to death. Angelina bores you, doesn't she, Mauro? And you feel guilty. You've probably trained her up to be this puppet and now you don't like the creature you've created.'

'That is not true. I always let her do what she wants. Always.'

'Was she like that when you married her?'

Mauro waved his hands about. 'I don't know. Of course she was. How would I know? She was young, she was beautiful, she was the worst skier in the world even though she lived here all her life. How could I not fall in love with her?'

'Well, perhaps that's the reason. You were looking for someone to dominate, and now you've done it you don't want to know any more.'

Mauro looked genuinely pained. 'Why do you take her part? You don't even know her. You never met her. Anyone will think she is your sister.'

Janet sighed. 'You're right. I don't. Anyway, I'm not talking about her. I'm talking about me.'

Mauro shook his head emphatically. 'What do you mean? You are so different – you don't know. When I see you trying to ski, fighting – all the time you are fighting me. You don't say, "I can never do this."'

'I think I did. You probably weren't listening.'

He looked at her, his eyes strangely tender. Janet felt her insides give a huge lurch. Slowly he reached across and took her hand. 'You said it with your mouth. You never said it with your heart. You never let me beat you. Not once.' Gently he rubbed her thumb with his. 'You were right. You did remind me of someone. A girl I knew when I was a waiter in London. She worked in the same restaurant. She was waitress, but she wanted to be an artist. She used to draw everywhere – on the menus, on the tablecloths, on the pavement outside sometimes. She would just crouch down on the ground with a piece of . . . that white stuff, and draw. The proprietor is *furioso* but the customers like it. Because she just laughed. She was always laughing. Nothing could make her serious. She was so beautiful. Like sunshine.'

'I thought you didn't like sunshine,' Janet reminded him.

Mauro grinned. 'Well, I like it in people. Just not in the sky. Sunshine in people is different.'

'Was she a good artist?'

He shrugged. 'How do I know? Some things were good, some I didn't like. I would tell her this and then we would argue and she would shout at me that I am a stupid ignorant wop. I would tell her she is a stupid ignorant lime, and she would start to laugh. Always when I call her this she laughs. I don't know why. When she laughed, everyone laughed. They cannot help it. Everyone loved her.' Janet wondered how she could possibly have reminded him of this nonpareil.

'Nothing frightened her. She seemed so free, so . . . For me it was a miracle to meet someone like that. Everyone in my village is so . . . They have no ambition. "Oh, you must get a job. Oh, you must get married. Oh, you must have children to take over your job when you are too old to do it any more." That is why I left. I wanted more than that. Jenny had ambition. She had so much hope, and energy – everything, or so it seemed to me.' He paused, staring at the lamp.

'What happened?'

'Oh well, like in all the stories, you do a bad thing, you are *punito* punished. She wanted to have a show of her work. Just in a hall, you understand, nothing great. Just where people can come and see. She asked all the customers if they will come and they say, "Yes, of course. We will be happy." Then she said, "All right, if you want to come and see my paintings, first can you give me some money to make this exhibition?"

'With some of them it was fine, but then one man's wife heard about it and she complained to the proprietor. He was so angry. Jenny just laughed. She said, "Oh well, too bad. Now he will sack me." But he didn't. He called the police and said she had tried to get money from his customers. They said it is against the law. They wanted to arrest her.' He paused and gave a deep hopeless sigh. 'So I said, "No, it was my idea. I made her do it."' Janet guessed what was coming next.

'So I am arrested, and I go to prison for two months. Then when I come out, because I am foreign they say they do not want to keep me in this country. I must go back to Italy. So you see, it is not all that probable I shall open my restaurant in Kew after all.' He gave a little smile.

'What happened with Jenny?'

'Oh, she was fine. One of the customers paid for her exhibition. She got some work from it. Not much, I think, but it didn't matter because by then she was . . . with this man.

'She came to see me in prison the week before they let me out. After I knew I must come back here. She said how sorry she was, and how grateful, and how she would never forget me – what I had done. I asked her – well, I didn't ask, I begged her to come with me. I said I would find someone to help her to sell her paintings. I told her how in Italy artists are admired. Not like in England. I said she would be happy living there with me. I begged her to come. But she said, no, she could not do that. She belonged in England. She did not want to leave. Then she told me about the man. She explained how she didn't love him or anything, but then she said she didn't love me either. She only loved to paint.' He shook his head. 'To paint and to laugh, she should have said, perhaps.

'So I came back here, married Angelina.' He glanced at her. 'And you are right. I did know what she was like. She was gentle and quiet and she only wanted to do what I told her. She was as different from Jenny as is possible to be. I thought that was what I wanted.'

Janet watched a solitary tear trickling down his face. 'Are you crying, Mauro?'

'Is allowed. Italian men are always crying.'

'What about Ladinos?'

Mauro smiled unhappily. 'Is the only thing the same.'

Janet thought of Harriet and Hugh, and Jenny and the unknown sponsor. Passionless, empty, practical. Love in a cold climate.

Mauro opened his eyes and blinked rapidly. 'So, you are thinking this man is more stupid even than I believed?'

She shook her head. 'I was thinking how easy it is to be

wrong about people. Still, the past is done. It does no good to think about it.'

'I think about it all the time.' He fished for a handkerchief. 'More when I talk to an English person.'

Janet sank back. 'I've made it worse, haven't I? Reminding you of it all. Oh, I wish Hugh had never booked those bloody lessons. I wish I'd never come here, I do really. It's been nothing but disaster from day one.'

Mauro wiped his eyes. 'No,' he said fiercely. 'Not disaster. Life. "It is better to have lived and lost, than never to have lived."'

'Loved,' said Janet.

'Uhh?'

'Loved.'

He watched as she rose and gently took the handkerchief from him. Bending down, she kissed his eyelids, then his cheeks, then his mouth. He gripped her in his arms and pulled her against him, kissing her as though he had been wanting her for twenty years. She was both frightened and electrified that someone should desire her so totally. His hands were tearing at her jacket, then her new beautiful jumper lay on the floor beneath her as he tore systematically through the layers of clothing.

As he finally laid her on the pile of discarded garments, his tongue still feverishly entangled with her own, she remembered thinking, very briefly, I hope no one rescues us just yet.

Chapter Thirty

The two of them lay entwined amidst the chaos of their clothes, Janet thinking that if it took being snowbound on a mountain, in a storm, at night, to achieve what she had just experienced, it was a small price to pay.

Mauro lay beside her, at last asleep. His face, so anguished in waking, was smooth and peaceful in repose. Or perhaps it was the laying of a ghost that made him look so serene? Was she a ghost? She certainly hadn't felt like one as the two of them made love amongst the debris on the floor.

I am a fallen woman, played around in her mind. I have committed adultery with a man I have known for five days. I am a slut, a woman of easy virtue, white trash, no better than I ought to be.

All these thoughts gave her immense pleasure. How could anyone accuse her now of being boring? And certainly not perfect. I have a lover, she reflected ecstatically, an *Italian* lover. And everything they say is true. He is beautiful. He is wonderful. He worships me. I have found myself. We will stay here on the mountain and make love ten times a day. In between he will give me skiing lessons. I shall die within three weeks, of exhaustion.

She snuggled closer to him and put her arm protectively round his waist. Mauro wriggled and placed her hand a little lower. She glanced to see if he was awake, but there was no sign of it. He still looked just as childishly innocent. His top lip stuck out slightly, she observed, wondering why she had never noticed before – but when had she ever been in a position to? Only when she fell over, on which occasions Mauro's facial quirks had been the very last thing on her mind.

She smiled to herself, thinking how impossible it was to believe this man, around whose body she was now wrapped like a creeper, was the same one who had so terrified her at the beginning of the week.

I love him, she thought. I love everything about him. His crossness, his face, the way he speaks, his disillusion. She even loved Angelina and the dreary son, and Jenny and her stupid paintings. I don't love the proprietor or the sugar daddy, she conceded, though perhaps she should have, for taking Jenny off the scene. There was no doubt in Janet's mind that the two of them would have been happy together.

In what was fast becoming a eulogy, she loved him for going to prison and wanting to own a restaurant, and the way he talked about England and Kew, and the rain. She especially loved roly Polly.

With a little shudder of happiness she curled herself tighter and fell asleep.

When she woke up the dream was over.

Mauro was shaking her, not hard, but insistently. 'Janetta, come on, Mrs English. Wake up. Put your clothes on. Quick.'

She lay for a moment staring up at him. He looked different. With a stab of panic she wondered if he was not Mauro at all, but a sterner version who had replaced her passionate, gentle, magical lover during the night. Then she realised it was because he was dressed.

She felt suddenly vulnerable, conscious that underneath the tacky blanket there was nothing but her nakedness. Mauro crouched down. 'Janetta, *tesoro*, come, you must get dressed. They are coming. The power is on again.'

'Who is?' she asked, more concerned with locating her underwear than who might be on their way up the mountain.

'Everyone,' said Mauro with a hint of desperation. 'The *carabinieri*, the doctor, the *giornalista*, your husband . . .'

Janet blinked several times. 'Why's *he* coming?'

Mauro had gathered up her clothes and was flapping them at her like someone trying to ward off seagulls. '*Carissima*, because he loves you. He is so happy you are safe. Of course he will come. What are you saying? *Please* put these clothes on. Please.' He stopped, looked at her and flung the garments down in a heap. 'Oh, *dio mio*, what do I care? He will kill me. Still, this is OK. If he does not, my son will.'

'Your *son*?' repeated Janet.

'*Si.* If I sleep with another woman he will kill me.'

'Surely not?' she gabbled, scrambling into her clothes. They felt colder than a wet swimming costume.

'Well, of course. Your son will do the same, I think, if your husband will sleep with another woman?'

Janet picked up her new jumper. The clown leered up at her, waving his balloons in triumph. 'The English aren't like that,' she said disconsolately.

Mauro put his arms round her neck and looked into her eyes. 'Well, perhaps we are not here any more, but it will be a long winter for me if he finds out.' He smiled and kissed her gently on the mouth. 'And anyway, it is our secret. Our dream. Then we don't hurt no one, and no one can hurt us. *D'accordo?*'

'*D'accordo*,' whispered Janet.

Mauro took her jumper and held it out for her. 'This is very lovely. Did you always wear this under your jacket?'

She shook her head. 'No. Hugh bought it for me today – yesterday, that is. I think it was to make up for the jacket. And the hat.'

'Oh yes, the hat. When I think of you I will always think of you in that hat.'

'Thanks very much.'

His face became serious. 'Of course I will not. I will remember you how you are last night. Little Englishwoman. Crazy woman. *La mia Janetta*. And how will you remember me?'

She looked away. It all sounded so final, which, of course, it was. Tonight she would be on a plane back to England. Back to school uniforms and gas bills and remembering to collect Hugh's suits from the cleaners. 'I'll remember you as you are,' she said.

Where the day began and the night ended, she never knew. There was no brilliant burst of sunlight on the mountain, no sign from the avenging gods that their wrath was quenched, certainly no indication that anything fundamental had changed for the two people about to be rescued. Only a slackening in the wind speed and a diminution in the size of the hailstones till they finally dwindled to slush.

The chair lift, when it arrived, was not full of baying *paparazzi*, but a jaded middle-aged man with a camera that would not work, an equally jaded sergeant from the *carabinieri*, a junior doctor who needed practice in hypothermia treatment, and Hugh Gale, his face grey and shadowed, looking ten years older than Janet remembered him.

The party clattered off the lift and trundled towards the hut. The two of them had watched their ascent in silence, standing a little apart from each other, like diplomats receiving a fact-finding mission.

The sergeant immediately strode over to Mauro and the two of them engaged in a rapid conversation.

The journalist, having failed to get a picture, pulled a pad from his pocket and made desultory notes as the two men talked. Janet looked across at Hugh. He was staring at her, his face expressionless. He looked like a stranger at a party who has no idea why he has been invited. She tried to smile. He did not respond. Slowly she walked towards him till they were close enough to touch. Hugh shrugged his hands in a gesture of complete incomprehension. 'Why?'

She reached out tentatively to him. He made no effort to reciprocate. Gently she put her arms round him and almost dragged him towards her. 'To be alive,' she whispered. 'Just to be alive.' Gradually she felt his rigid body beginning to relax. He was silent for a long moment.

'I thought it was the other.'

She looked up. 'What other?'

Hugh's eyes were full of tears. 'Not to be alive.' He buried his face in her shoulder. The other men nodded approvingly and the journalist fiddled desperately with his flash in the hope of catching the moment.

Mauro took the sergeant into the hut so that he could phone down orders for the lift to be reopened. It was generally agreed that this would be the best way to avoid unfavourable publicity for both the rescue services and the resort. The journalist agreed, on the condition that he be allowed an exclusive interview with the victims on the way down.

Hugh disentangled himself from his wife and went up to Mauro. 'I don't know what to say to you,' he faltered.

Mauro shrugged dismissively. 'Don't say anything. It was nothing. These things happen all the time on the mountain.'

'It *was* something,' said Hugh vigorously. 'You saved Jan's life. And you risked your own. I just want to know what I — we can ever do to thank you enough?'

Mauro looked uncomfortable. 'Is nothing. OK? Please? I don't like all this . . .'

Hugh nodded heavily. 'Just so long as you know . . .'

'Yuh. OK. I know. I think now we should go down. The sergeant wants his breakfast. Me, too, I guess. And your wife.'

Janet caught his eye. He looked away. Yes, she thought.

That's it. I'm Hugh's wife. And Angelina's his. And I have two beautiful children waiting for me. Time to put away the dream.

She turned to Hugh. He was gazing at her with a look of such profound relief and tenderness that she felt a stab of guilt. She tucked her arm into his. 'Better get our skis on, then. And don't leave me behind this time.'

He tried to smile. 'I promise. I do love you, Jan. I always have. Whatever . . .'

She sighed. 'I know. I know you do, Hugh. Come on. We must go.'

Hugh didn't move. 'Do you still love me?'

There was a shout from the sergeant who was getting impatient.

'Come on, or he'll probably arrest us.'

'I don't care. Answer me, Jan. Please. I've been thinking about this all night. What I'd driven you to. I made myself a promise . . .'

'What?'

'That if you were all right . . .'

'You'd never cheat on me again?'

Hugh looked palpably shocked. 'I never meant to. I never thought of it like that. I was trying to be kind.'

Janet looked at him. 'You really believe that, don't you?'

Confusion descended on Hugh. 'Well, maybe sometimes it was quite sort of . . . flattering. To be that important to someone. You always seemed to manage so well without me.'

She squeezed his arm. 'Only because I had to. What will you tell Harriet?'

'I've already told her. I phoned her from the hotel after we'd had our row.'

'And?'

He sighed exhaustedly. 'She sounded quite relieved, actually. Far more worried about you – how you'd taken it.' He drew himself up. 'I suppose she was trying to put a brave face on things. I said we could still be friends.'

Janet smiled in spite of herself.

Hugh put his arm round her. 'But it's up to you. If you say not, we won't. I'll never even see her again.'

'How can you do that?'

'I'll change my job. I'm sick of the bloody place. I'll go freelance. Something. I'll think of something.'

Janet shivered. 'You'll do nothing of the kind. You love your job. Harriet and I will work it out. We've been friends a long time.'

Hugh nodded. 'I never meant to hurt you. I just hated growing older and being so bloody respectable all the time. It seemed like a way out. A last gasp . . .'

She squeezed his hand. 'I do understand, Hugh. Better than you think.'

'It's different for women. You just improve with time.'

Janet shook her head incredulously.

'Why are you doing that?'

She laughed. 'All these years and I've been living with a blind man. To think I never knew.'

'Well, perhaps not all women. But you do. Even now. You've just been through the worst night of your life and you're positively glowing.'

'Oh well,' she said, 'let's hope it lasts.'

'Why has Bob got a black eye?' Janet whispered to Belinda as they sat amongst their cases waiting for the coach to pick them up.

She had received an ecstatic welcome from Owen and Belinda, both of whom had had scarcely more sleep than their father, despite being consoled with the news that a red light had been seen signalling from the third base, which almost definitely meant their mother was safe and well.

Teresa, weeping as though she had known Janet all her life, had erected a crucifix over the fireplace and spent the night on her knees in prayers for the dead, which had not proved terribly comforting to the others who would have preferred silence, or at least some hot chocolate to see them through their vigil.

The McDermots' reaction to her return had been uncharacteristically muted, Cheryl peering at her through a haze of gin, and the offspring hardly aware that she had been away in their determination to spend the last night in the disco. Bob had avoided her but for the briefest of nods, before disappearing into his room to 'finish the packing'. He had not been quick enough for Janet to avoid a glimpse of his eye which sprouted purple, blue and yellow from beneath one bushy eyebrow.

'Didn't Dad tell you? He hit him.'

'He *what?*' she gasped.

'Yes. Dad was terribly worried when he heard you were on your own up the mountain. We all were, and I was crying my head off and Bob said something about pulling myself together and not acting like a baby, and the next thing we knew Dad punched him.' Belinda giggled suddenly. 'He fell right over in the snow on his back and everyone sort of gathered round and the *carabinieri* guy came, but when he saw it was Bob he just turned round and went away. Anyway, he knew Dad was worried about you and everything, and he let him stay in their hut to wait, and gave him brandy and things.' She hesitated and stared at her fingers, garishly adorned with some violet nail varnish Tricia had let her have in a fit of sympathy for the potential loss of her mother. 'Everyone's been ever so kind and things.'

Janet put her arm round Belinda's shoulders. She could feel them trembling. She, too, was close to tears. 'I've been an awful lot of trouble to everyone,' she murmured. 'I should never have gone out on my own. Never.'

To her surprise Belinda shook her head indignantly. 'Yes, you should,' she declared. 'You were fantastic. So brave. Even Mauro said that. *Bravissimo*, he said when the bloke told him it was you that was stuck up there. Over and over again. *Bravissimo.* I like that word, don't you? It's loads better than cool.'

Janet grimaced. 'I doubt he'd say it now.'

'He would. Why not?'

'Because he knows it's not true.'

'He doesn't,' said Belinda truculently. 'He told me when we were waiting for the toboggan, and I said to him what a coward you were and how I wished Auntie Harriet had come instead.'

'You told him that, did you?'

'Well, I was cross,' said Belinda sheepishly. 'Anyway, it didn't matter because he stuck up for you like mad. He said there was nothing brave about doing things you weren't scared of. It was doing things that frightened you that was brave. So I said you must be the bravest person around then, because you were scared of everything.'

'What did he say to that?'

'He just laughed.'

There was a rap on the door. 'That'll be the coach, I expect. It's early.' said Janet, reaching round for her jacket. 'Where are the others?'

'Out the back having a snowball fight. Dad said it was the only way to stop Teresa crying.'

'Why's she crying? I thought she was pleased I was safe.'

'Yes she is, but she says it's a miracle and they always make her cry for hours.'

'Just as well there aren't too many then.'

'She says now you're back she'll have to dedicate her life to the poor. She promised one of the saints she would when she was praying last night.'

'Oh dear,' said Janet, suffused with guilt. 'I do wish she hadn't.'

Belinda yawned. 'I wouldn't worry. I don't think it was a famous one or anything. It was one she'd seen in a film. I think she fancied him. She said he entered her dreams.' She wrapped her arms round herself and made exaggerated kissing noises.

'You daft thing.'

There was another knock on the door.

'Be a pet and go and fetch the others. I'll tell him we're on our way.'

It was not the coach driver.

Janet felt her heart contract. 'Mauro?'

'I came to say goodbye.' He had on the leather jacket he had worn the night he had walked her home. He no longer looked so small in it.

They had said a formal goodbye on the mountain, avoiding each other's eyes and making staccato comments about the impending improvement in the weather. Janet had gripped Hugh's arm so tightly he winced as they walked away, but he had said nothing, sensing that her emotions were not entirely under control.

She cleared her throat. 'That was very kind. The others are out the back. Would you like me to ...' She groped for her handkerchief. 'Oh, why did you? I wish you hadn't ... I was all right. I was perfectly all right ...'

Mauro took a step back in the snow. 'Yes. I see. I am sorry. I see now I should not have come. These things ... It is always best ... I am sorry. I will go now. Good journey. Please give my best wishes to your ...'

'Can I borrow your handkerchief?'

Mauro fumbled in his pocket, producing a pure white cotton one. 'This is my best. You cost me a lot of money in handkerchieves, Mrs English.'

Janet laughed through her tears. 'I'll send them back to you.'

'You don't know my address.'

'I'll send them to the restaurant. No I won't. I'll send them to the Third Base. Mauro, Third Base, Italy. That should reach you OK, shouldn't it?'

'Without doubt.'

'And you're not to lend them to whichever crazy English-woman you're romping around with at the time. Promise?'

Mauro smiled as he took her face in his hands. He kissed her very gently on both cheeks then softly on the mouth. 'One crazy Englishwoman is enough for me,' he murmured. '*Arriverderci, signora.*'

'*Arriverderci.*'

He turned and was gone, away down the path and out of sight between the ice-spangled trees.

There was a crunch of brakes as the coach came grinding up the road and stopped outside Villa Nevosa. Annie appeared at the door. 'Everybody ready?' she called.

Janet nodded. 'I'll just fetch the others.' She tore round the corner before anyone could register she was crying. Owen was just lobbing a snowball at Hugh who ducked. It hit her full in the face. Thank God for that, she thought, as she wiped the ice away. 'You beast, Owen. The coach is here.'

'*Bravissimo,*' Belinda screeched as everyone rushed to fetch their bags.

Teresa, glowing, came to wave them off. 'Be sure and take care of yourselves now,' she called as they boarded the coach.

Janet was just settling herself into the seat when Teresa's face appeared at the window, mouthing something to her. 'What's she saying?' she asked Belinda, who was better at lip-reading.

Belinda screwed up her face in concentration as the coach started up. 'Not sure. Something about posting a book for you. To ... an ... editor? I don't know. She's too far away.'

'Thank God that's over,' said Hugh as he slid into the seat beside her.

Janet stared at her hands. 'Don't say that. It was a lovely holiday – barring the odd hiccup.'

Further up the coach they could hear Bob McDermot asking if he would receive a refund for the curtailing of the night skiing trip.

'That's one way of describing him,' Hugh observed. He

reached for her hand. 'I promise, next year we'll go somewhere hot. We'll lie under palm trees and be served drinks by the pool and you need never move from the sun-lounger except to eat, and you can read till your eyes pop out.'

'Sounds good to me.'

'Unless there's something you'd rather do? A cruise. Would you like that?'

'I might. What I'd really like is to go away in the summer for a change.'

There was a silence. 'Summer's so difficult for me. It's our busiest time.'

'I know. It was just a thought. Perhaps I might go away by myself for a few days. Just a short break. Blin and Owen could stay with your sister.'

'Would you like that, though? To go away on your own?'

'I might. Why not?'

Hugh shook his head. 'I don't know. I just always assumed you preferred having the family around on holiday.'

Janet shrugged. 'I didn't have much choice. But they're growing up now. Owen would rather do his own thing, I'm sure. And Blin gets spoilt rotten when she goes to Meg's. Besides, I think you and I both need a bit of space – time for ourselves – wouldn't you say?'

Hugh glanced at her. 'Maybe.'

'Worth a thought, anyway.'

'Yes, but what would you do? You could hardly lie on a Greek beach by yourself. Anything might happen.'

Janet laughed. 'I doubt it. Not everyone has Shirley Valentine's luck. Anyway I didn't mean a beach holiday. I thought I might do something for a change.'

'You hate "doing" holidays. Look at this one.'

Janet gazed out of the window. Already as they drove down the mountain the icicles were turning to raindrops on the pine branches and the mist on the hills to dull cloud. Fairyland was disappearing fast.

'I've changed my mind,' she said slowly. 'I've vegetated far too long. I want to try something new.'

'I see. Paragliding it is, then.'

She laughed. 'I don't think I'm quite ready for that. Halfway house. I'd like to go walking. Somewhere beautiful and peaceful. Where I can just be me for a while.'

'Where? The Lake District? It'd be bound to rain.'

'Oh no,' said Janet dreamily. 'I think I might come back here before the snow sets in. Just for a few days.'